Maggie Hope was born and raised in County Durham. She worked as a nurse for many years, before giving up her career to raise her family.

Also by Maggie Hope:

MAGGIE HOPE
Eliza's Child

EBURY
PRESS

3

Ebury Press, an imprint of Ebury Publishing
20 Vauxhall Bridge Road,
London SW1V 2SA

Penguin
Random House
UK

Ebury Press is part of the Penguin Random House group of companies whose
addresses can be found at global.penguinrandomhouse.com

First published in 2005 as *Early One Morning* by Piatkus Books Ltd
This edition published in 2015 by Ebury Press

www.eburypublishing.co.uk

A CIP catalogue record for this book
is available from the British Library

ISBN 9781785034268

Typeset in Times LT Std by Palimpsest Book Production Limited,
Falkirk, Stirlingshire

Penguin Random House is committed to a sustainable future for
our business, our readers and our planet. This book is made from
Forest Stewardship Council® certified paper.

MIX
Paper from
responsible sources
FSC® C018179

Printed and bound in Great Britain by Clays Ltd, Elcograf S.p.A.

Acknowledgements

With acknowledgements to the Durham Miners' Association and Durham Mining Museum, and also to the Durham Records Office.

Any mistakes in the historical details are my own.

To my father, a miner all his life, and his father and grandfather too.

PART ONE

Chapter One

1862

Eliza Mitchell-Howe stared down at the necklace she was holding in her hands. The blue-red stones glinted in the candlelight and reflected on the silver-coloured setting. 'It's not silver, it's gold, white gold,' said Jack.

Eliza sighed and put the necklace back in its case and the case on the table. She gazed at the blue leather with the name of a prominent Newcastle jeweller tooled in gold leaf.

'Yes, yes, we can. I can always afford to buy beautiful things for you, hinny,' Jack said softly, tenderly. He put his arms around her and held her unyielding body to him. 'Howay, man, Eliza, don't look like that. I've had a grand day at the races. My luck was in and I doubled up twice and won both times on the nose. I'm telling you, my luck has changed. We're going to be fine; just you wait and see.' He gazed at her face for any sign of her relenting but she showed none. 'Don't spoil it now, hinny,' he coaxed. 'Let's away to bed, I've missed you, pet.'

Eliza sighed. What was the use of talking, of trying to make him see what he was doing to her and the bairn she carried in her belly? Besides, already she could feel herself weakening. The old magic he raised in her when he touched her was dimming every other thought and she gave herself up to it.

When his father found out he had taken money from the business to go to the races they would be thrown out. John Henry Mitchell-Howe hated gambling. Gambling had been the thread running through his family that had ruined them. His great-grandfather had been gentry, a respected man, but with a son who was a gambler, a man who would bet on anything and everything. The family had ended up with nothing except for their name, Mitchell-Howe. John Henry's father had been a gambler too and he had ended up in the gutter, shunned by his fellows. By his own efforts, John Henry had built up his business.

It was a warm June night but Eliza shivered. She put a hand on her belly; what would happen to the babby? It was almost dawn before exhaustion caused her to drop into a disturbed sleep.

*

Eliza woke suddenly and sat up in bed. 'Jack? Jack?' she called, and put out a hand to him but he was gone; his side of the bed was empty. What time was it? She climbed clumsily out of bed and went to the window to draw the curtains. Blinding light flooded in, the sun was high in the sky; it must be well into the day. Hastily she poured water from the china jug on the washstand into the matching bowl and splashed her face and arms, gasping at the coldness of the water. The baby moved inside her as though joining in the protest and she put her hand on the bump caressingly.

There were sounds from downstairs, voices and small thuds, but the house was too solidly built for her to hear much. She paused in her dressing and listened, thinking she had heard a note of anger, but no, it would just be Annie, her mother-in-law, cleaning the stair carpet with tea leaves and berating her little thirteen-year-old maid, Bertha, for something or other. Annie liked to do most of the work herself for she didn't trust anyone else to do it properly but all the same she would be annoyed that Eliza had slept in. She took it as a sign of sloth. Eliza was expected to do her share of the housework even though she didn't do it well enough for Annie either.

'Expecting a babby is not an illness,' she would snap at any sign of weakness on Eliza's part.

Annie was not on the stairs and the hall below was

5

deserted. As Eliza came out of the bedroom she shared with Jack she saw the stairs were already cleaned and not a speck of dust dared to dance in the sunbeam that came through the tall window on the bend of the staircase wall. Lordy, Annie would be mad. She was halfway down the stairs when the door to the study burst open and Jack came out, followed by a roar of anger from his father.

Jack took the stairs two at a time, barely pausing as he passed Eliza to say, 'Come back upstairs, we have to pack.' His face was white and his lips set in a thin, hard line.

Eliza's anxious 'What?' was drowned out by her father-in-law's shouting.

'Get out of my house, you limb of Satan, get out and don't come back! I have given my orders and if you ever try to get into the workshop or my office again I'll have you charged with trespassing. You will not get the chance to rob me again, I swear by all that's sacred you will not! Now, you've got ten minutes to pack your bags and go.'

'John Henry! What are you saying? What about Eliza? The lass is almost ready to drop her bairn!'

'She'll be all right, remember where she came from,' John Henry snapped. 'Her folk live in a hovel up by a pithead down Durham way. Any road, I'll not have your thieving son in this house nor in my workshop, I'm telling you I will not.'

Eliza missed what else was said between her parents-in-law as Jack grabbed her arm and dragged her up the stairs and into the room, banging the door behind them. Eliza stumbled a couple of times, once tripping on her skirt, but he had such a hold on her she couldn't fall. She felt the baby move within her as if in protest and she held a protective hand over it for a moment but the movements subsided.

'You took the money from the office,' she said flatly as she turned to face Jack. 'You promised me, Jack.'

'Stop whining, woman,' he snapped. 'It came out all right, didn't it? You got your bauble, didn't you?' He smiled cruelly, wanting to hurt her as he was hurting. 'It's more than your da could ever buy for your mam, isn't it?'

Eliza shrank inside herself for a minute only before remembering, of course, she had the necklace. She could sell it and it might be enough to pay John Henry back and then maybe he wouldn't throw them out. It was as though Jack had heard her thoughts.

'Give me the necklace,' he demanded.

'Why?'

'Never mind why I want it, just get it.' Jack was impatient; he held out his hand and wriggled the fingers. Eliza gave an involuntary glance at the drawer of her dressing table, where she had put the necklace. Jack saw and strode to the dressing table and took it out and slipped it into his pocket.

'It's mine, you gave it to me!' cried Eliza.

'Don't be stupid,' he snapped. 'I need it, don't I? Now get my stuff packed, we'll go down to the inn for now. I'm going out, I'll be back when I've finished the bit of business I have to do.' He swept out of the room and she heard his footsteps as he ran downstairs and the bang of the front door as he went out. Crossing to the window, she saw him walking jauntily along the road in the direction of Alnwick. She watched until he turned the corner then turned back into the room and started to pack their belongings.

Two o'clock, dinner time and Jack had not come back. Eliza sat by the bed with the luggage on either side of her and waited. Though her stomach rumbled she did not go down to the meal and no one called her to it. It was as though the household had given up all thought of her or Jack.

It was only when she heard the clanging of the front doorbell, followed by a loud hammering on the door and his voice shouting, that she realised he was back and the door was locked against him. Inside her the baby jumped as though in alarm. Eliza stood up hastily and went to the bedroom door and out on to the landing. Jack continued to ring the bell and shout through the keyhole but no one answered him. The noise stopped and he ran from the house, and after a moment she heard him trying the back door but it was locked too and no one let him in.

Eliza's stomach churned; she didn't know what to do. She couldn't even reach the top bolt on the front door so she couldn't let him in. And even if she could, what good would it do? His father would simply send him on his way again. No, she would have to go down with the luggage and get his father to let her out. Perhaps that was the way: John Henry might take pity on them when he saw her so far gone with the babby and let them stay. She picked up the bags and began her descent of the stairs.

The bags were heavy and because of them she couldn't hold on to the balustrade. She leaned over to one side, using the rail as a support. Pain shot through her back and she gritted her teeth and forced herself to put one foot in front of the other. She felt for the edge of the carpeted riser but she was too far to the side and her foot met the newly polished wood at the side and slipped. She was holding on tightly to the handles of the bags and the weight of them went forward and dragged her with them, and her foot lost the stair altogether and she fell heavily, banging her head on the ornate cast-iron post at the bottom. The bags thudded against the floor of the hall, skidded a few inches and stopped. Eliza lay in a crumpled heap at the bottom of the staircase. The cut on her forehead where she had hit the post oozed a little blood. Blood also began to stain the seat of her dress a darker brown against the light brown serge but a startling red against the white maternity smock she wore over it. She was spared the shame and embarrassment of having her father-in-law see what was happening as she had lost consciousness. She wasn't even aware that John Henry and his second son, Henry, had carried her back up the stairs and laid her on the bed she had shared with Jack.

'You see? You see what's happened now?' Annie cried. 'What are you going to do?'

'Aw, see to the lass and shut your mouth, Annie Mitchell-Howe,' snarled John Henry. 'I'll away downstairs and tell that young hellion to hadaway for the midwife. Henry, get back to work, we're behind on the orders any road. This has nowt to do with you.'

Henry looked affronted. 'Aye it has, Da. An' the way I look at Eliza here, she needs a doctor, not just the midwife.'

'Aye well, get the doctor then. But mind, don't you let your brother in, do you hear me? I'm behind you, I'll get the midwife.'

'Yes, Da,' said Henry, and went out.

'By, John Henry, you'll rue the day, you will an' all,' said Annie. She was leaning over the bed, trying to help Eliza. 'The bairn's on its way, tell Bertha to put water on to boil and bring it up. A full kettle, mind. That newfangled doctor is forever washing his hands.'

John Henry paused with his hand on the door. 'As soon as the lass is over this she can be on her way an' all. She's no responsibility of mine.'

'Aye well, let's see if she does get over it, John Henry,' said Annie. She lifted Eliza by the shoulders to take off her dress and the girl's head rolled and she moaned. Annie hastily laid her back on the pillow.

'Mebbe I shouldn't have moved her,' Annie said anxiously.

'She'll be all right,' said John Henry. 'She's off tough stock.'

Annie glared at him, her anxiety making her shout at him. 'Are you still there? Will you get away for the midwife or have I to go myself? Do you want the lass to die here and the babby, our grandbairn, with her?'

'No, no, I'm going now,' said John Henry. 'It's not but a cock's stride to the midwife's place.'

Chapter Two

Eliza opened her eyes and there was her mother-in-law bending over her. 'God be praised,' said Annie. 'She's coming round, John Henry.' Eliza was bewildered; what were they doing in her and Jack's room? John Henry's face appeared at the bottom of the bed. He stared at her, unsmiling.

'Aye, I can see that,' he said gruffly.

'Jack?' Eliza asked and the word came out as little more than a whisper. She tried again. 'Where's Jack?'

'You needn't think he's getting in here again,' said John Henry. 'I'm a Christian man. You can stay until you're up to the moving but as soon as the doctor says you are fit for it you and the babby are out.'

'John Henry!' said Annie.

'Don't you "John Henry" me. She was fool enough to marry a gambler and a thief and she'll have to abide by it. No doubt her and her folk thought she had done

12

well for herself. Our Jack would be a great catch to them.' He laughed grimly. 'Aye well, now they'll know just what sort of a catch.' He turned his back and stalked to the door.

'Eeh well, Eliza, I'll have to abide by his word,' said Annie. 'I know me an' thee haven't been close but I wouldn't have thrown you out, not with the babby an' all. I'll try to keep you for a while longer but you'll have to go soon.'

Eliza was barely aware of what her mother-in-law was saying. Her body ached, her head ached and a fog of weakness enveloped her. But over it all, she longed for Jack.

'Jack? Where's Jack?' she asked again.

'You'll see him soon enough,' said Annie. 'Now howay, you'll have to feed the bairn. Here he is three days old and he's had nowt but cow's milk.'

The bairn? She'd had the babby then? She had thought it was all a terrible nightmare. The pain she had thought was tearing her in two; the pain that had gone on and on, and she had dreamed she was in hell and it was her punishment for her sins. Everlasting hellfire.

But Annie was lifting her shoulders and putting a pillow behind her, and she was handing her a shawl-wrapped bundle. Eliza gazed down at her son. He had a fuzz of dark hair and his blue eyes were unfocused yet still he turned to her and nuzzled at her with his mouth wide open. Not finding what he wanted, his tiny fists waved in the air and a small crease showed on his forehead. He made sucking noises and moved his head around impatiently.

'Why, man!' said Annie in exasperation. 'Let me unbutton your shift or the lad will die of starvation before he finds your titty.'

He was not long in finding the nipple once he felt bare skin; he took no guiding towards it. He found it and hung on, sucking hungrily. And Eliza, gazing down at him, felt the purest bolt of love sweep through her. All her difficulties and miseries were forgotten or at least submerged as she communed with her child.

'He's a grand little lad,' Annie said softly. Eliza glanced at her. Her mother-in-law's face was softened, her normally harsh expression gone. She caught Eliza's eye. 'He's our first grandbairn, isn't he?' she said defensively.

Eliza said nothing. She had no energy to point out that when she had to go then it might be the last Annie saw of the baby.

The following Saturday Eliza found herself standing on the step at the front of the house. She had the baby in her arms and boxes at her feet. She hugged the baby to her breast and gazed down towards the bend in the road. Surely Jack would come any minute. He would hire a horse and trap to take her into Alnwick, wouldn't he? Annie had sent to tell him to come and collect his wife and bairn.

Jack had not yet seen the baby. He had come to the door and made one more attempt to get in, shouting up at her window, 'Eliza! Eliza!'

She had been feeding the baby and by the time she got to the window he was gone. John Henry had been at home and he had sent Jack packing. Eliza lay down on the bed and cried with frustration and the ache she had in her for Jack and the weakness of her body that stopped her running after him.

Now, almost a week later, she was still not herself but stronger than she had been and the doctor had pronounced her fit to move.

'I don't suppose you have far to go in any case,' he had said. 'Your husband has work away, has he? Not too far away?' Inquisitively he looked at John Henry who had just come into the room. He had heard talk of how wild Jack Mitchell-Howe had turned out to be and of a rift in the family.

'Aye,' said John Henry. 'Now, if you'll give me your bill, Doctor, I'll pay you now.' He held open the door and the doctor found himself following him out. Eliza was alone as she stood on the step waiting for Jack. Neither John Henry nor Annie had any intention of seeing their eldest son. It was as if he didn't exist any more,

Eliza thought. By, John Henry was an unforgiving man, oh aye, he was. The clatter of horses' hooves on the stones of the road made her look again towards the bend in the road, but it couldn't be Jack for it was a carriage and two horses pulling it that came along the road. But it was Jack driving she saw, and she didn't know whether to laugh or cry as he halted the horses and jumped down in front of her. Dear God, what had he done now?

Relief and love for him swept all other emotions from her as he took her in his arms and kissed her on the lips extravagantly, and the feel of him holding her brought back the old intoxication.

'Mind the babby, Jack, don't squash the babby,' she cried, but softly, and Jack let her go and looked down at the baby, though all he could see of him was the top of his head, as he was swathed in a shawl against the cold wind that blew at this back end of the summer.

Jack moved the shawl aside and looked down on his son's face. The baby looked him straight in the eye solemnly for a few seconds then away, turning slightly towards his mother and making sucking noises. The tip of his tiny tongue showed between his lips, pink and milky. Jack laughed with delight.

'Howay then, let's have you both into the carriage,' he said. 'The lad wants his dinner.'

'Where are we going?' Eliza asked.

'You'll see.'

As he turned the horses, a curtain at one of the first-floor windows of the house twitched, but neither Jack nor Eliza noticed. They bowled round the bend and through the village and people turned to stare and mutter among themselves that mebbe Jack Mitchell-Howe and his father hadn't fallen out. Mebbe it was all gossip and Jack was doing all right for himself. Anybody at all who could keep a carriage and pair like that must be doing all right.

'An' good luck to him an' all,' said Bill Oxley as he clasped his hands over his apron as he stood in the doorway of his grocer's shop. 'If he stays off the gambling he'll do all right. He has as good a hand as his father when it comes to the carpentry.'

'Aye well, it's a big if,' commented Mrs Wearmouth, who was standing in front of him with a large basket in her hands. 'Now, are you going to let me in to do me shopping or not? I can always go into Alnwick if you're too busy to serve me.'

Eliza sat in the carriage and watched the countryside roll by. There were hundreds of things she wanted to ask Jack but now was not the time. Now was the time to enjoy sitting beside him with the baby on her lap and being happy, for soon enough she would have to ask. He was revelling in driving her to whatever place he had found for them. In *being* in a position to be able to take her away from his father's house in style. The child had been lulled into sleep by the movement of the vehicle but then he woke and was hungry and she suckled him, enjoying the feelings he roused in her and murmuring softly to him.

'Where are we going, Jack?' she asked after they had left Alnwick behind and were rolling south along the Great North Road.

'You'll see, it's not far now,' he replied.

They bowled over the bridge across the Tyne and into County Durham and ate a meal in an inn in Chester-le-Street and went on again until at last they stopped in Durham city, in front of a tidy little house in the shadow of the cathedral.

'Where are we, Jack?' Eliza asked as he handed her down from the carriage, for all the world as though she were any grand lady. 'Whose house is it?'

'It's ours, Eliza,' Jack replied. He made a flourishing gesture with one hand and put his other arm around her shoulders. 'Our luck has turned, hinny, our boat came in. I knew the necklace would be our good luck charm. I couldn't put a foot wrong at York races and since then every card I take is an ace.'

'The necklace?' Eliza felt sick. She pictured the necklace in her mind's eye. It seemed evil to her now, glittering in the light of the candle as it had that night in his father's house. 'It's sold then?'

'It was but don't worry, pet, I have it back. It was the first thing I did, get the necklace back. I'll put it round your pretty little neck and there it will stay.'

Eliza clutched the baby to her and he stirred as though in protest. 'I don't want it!' she cried.

'Don't be daft, pet,' said Jack, smiling. 'Howay in, I have a surprise for you inside. You don't want to catch your death out here in the cold, do you?'

The front door of the little house was opening and he drew her towards it. And there, wiping her hands on her apron, was Eliza's mother, Mary Anne.

'Mam!'

Eliza forgot all about the necklace as she felt her mother's arms around her. All the tension of the last days seemed to dissolve and she found herself weeping onto the snowy bib of her mother's apron.

'Hey, man,' said Mary Anne gently. 'Pull theesel' together, our Liza. You're all right, there's nowt the matter that cannot be put right. You'll squash the life out of me little grandbairn in a minute. Let's have a look at him, any road.'

She drew Eliza into the parlour of the house while Jack stood aside, beaming all over his face at the success of his little scheme.

'Give him here,' Mary Anne commanded, and she took the baby and moved the shawl away from his face so she could look at him properly. 'Aye,' she pronounced after a moment. 'He's a right bonny bairn. But then, why wouldn't he be? He's got his mother's face on him.'

'I think he's like his da,' said Eliza. 'A handsome lad.' She smiled over her mother's head at Jack.

Mary Anne barely looked up at Jack. 'Aye well, handsome is as handsome does,' she commented.

'Oh, Mam,' said Eliza. She hadn't seen her mother since the day of her wedding to Jack. They had left the cluster of houses which could hardly be termed a village and which had grown up round the pithead near Haswell in the county of Durham. The place didn't have a name in the early years when Mary Anne had followed Tommy as he carried his pick and shovel across the coalfield as he looked for better paying work than was to be had in the old worked-out bell pits of Cockfield. No one named it, not even the mine owner, but it had come to be known as Blue House after an ancient tumbledown farmstead that stood nearby.

There was a Wesleyan chapel, though not much of a one, for Wesley had paused nearby in his perambulations about the countryside and worked his magic on the local people. The chapel was tiny and barely accommodated Eliza's family, and no one from Northumberland had turned up to see Jack married.

'They'd think our Eliza wasn't good enough for the lad,' said Mary Anne.

'Nowt of sort,' Tommy had retorted. 'Our Eliza is

good enough for any man an' I'll fell the one that says she isn't!'

Jack had been on his way home from Durham, where he had been delivering a beautifully crafted mahogany sideboard to a friend of the bishop. The friend had been visiting the duke in Alnwick and seen some of John Henry's work. In the event he had got the sideboard for less than half he would have paid a more fashionable furniture maker and was well pleased. Not pleased enough to pay up immediately, though. Jack had the thankless task of going home to his father without the money due. So he had put off the day and driven the cart around the countryside a bit, and when he saw a 'pitch and toss' gambling school in the shadow of a pit heap he went over to it and joined in.

The idea was to gamble on which side a coin would land when pitched in the air, and he was lucky, he won most of the pitmen's pennies. He and Tommy, that is. Afterwards Tommy invited him back to the two-roomed cottage for a bite to eat before he went on his way. A stranger was something of a novelty at Blue House and the miners were hospitable when they were able. Tommy had bought pies at Granny Hadaway's tiny shop on the corner of the row and they'd had a feast in the little kitchen along with Mary Anne and the bairns. Eliza was the oldest, and she was bonny, with a wealth of dark curly hair and deep violet eyes. All the pit lads were after her but once she saw Jack she knew he was the one for her and they were married within three weeks.

She was so happy to leave Blue House with her new husband. It was like living a dream. She was delighted when they crossed the Tyne and saw the wonder of Stephenson's railway bridge and the bustling city beyond. She was delighted with driving through the Northumberland countryside beside her lovely man and she was delighted with the ancient town of Alnwick, still fortressed by great walls 'gainst the Scots.

'Against the Scots?' she had asked fearfully when Jack told her the reason the town was like that, and he had laughed.

'The Scots don't come down now, you goose,' he had said. 'It was centuries ago.'

Eliza felt foolish. She hadn't gone to school, had never had the chance. She couldn't write her name even. But she would learn, she told herself. Someday.

The disillusionment came when they reached Jack's parents' house and she stood with him in the hall facing John Henry and his wife. The air in the hall was icy and the looks John Henry and Annie gave her were icy to match. They stared at her then looked away towards their son.

'Where the hell have you been?' demanded John Henry.

'Hello, Father,' said Jack. 'I got married.' He indicated Eliza. 'This is Eliza.'

'Where's my money?'

'He's sending it to you at the end of the quarter,' said Jack. He was flushed; he looked like a small boy caught out in some naughtiness. Eliza stared at him; he seemed like a different man from the one she had married.

'You've gambled it away! I should have known better than trust you,' said John Henry bitterly.

'No, he did not!'

Eliza couldn't help herself; she jumped in in Jack's defence as she would have done for her little brother James, who was always into scrapes.

'You speak when you're spoken to, lass,' snapped John Henry.

'Sssh, Eliza,' said Jack at the same time.

Almost a year later, in the little house in Durham city, the memory of her introduction to her husband's family flashed through her thoughts as she watched her mother hold her baby with practised ease.

'By, Mam, I'm that glad to see you,' she said, her voice breaking. 'You and Da are worth two of that lot in Northumberland.'

'Now then, you're a bit overwrought,' said Mary Anne, looking keenly at her daughter. 'Howay, sit down by the fire and feed the bairn. You'll feel better come the morn.'

Chapter Three

'I don't want to wear the necklace,' said Eliza.

'Why not?' asked Jack. 'I like to see it on your pretty neck.' His expression was genuinely hurt and puzzled. He felt he would never understand Eliza. Surely every lass liked real jewellery? Anyway, he had to find out where the necklace was.

'It's not really mine, is it? It's your emergency fund for the next time you lose all your money on a horse or the turn of a card or whether a black beetle will beat a cockroach in a race—'

'Eliza! How can you say such a thing? I've told you, it's yours and I'll not take it away from you again, I won't!'

Eliza lifted Thomas out of the tin bath and sat him on the towel on her lap. Thomas smiled at her with eyes wide and innocent-looking as his father's. She wrapped the towel round him and rubbed him dry then dusted him with boracic powder before taking his flannel vest from the brass line under the mantel shelf and putting it on him. Thomas wriggled but was still smiling when his face emerged from the neck of the vest. He was a sunny-natured bairn, she thought. She looked up at Jack, who was lounging against the edge of the table, waiting for her to reply.

By, she thought, Jack was a bonny lad, he was, especially when he raised one eyebrow at her when he saw he had her attention again.

'I have the necklace put away safe,' she said and pulled Thomas's petticoat over his head and pushed the linen buttons through the holes.

'Where?' asked Jack.

Eliza sighed. 'Jack, you're not being dunned for money again, are you?'

Jack flushed. 'No, I'm not. How could you think it? I told you, I don't want to take the necklace away from you, I'm not going to do that. I just want to know where it is. I like to see you wearing it, Eliza.'

'I have it safe,' she said stubbornly.

Jack stood up straight and stomped to the door. 'What you mean is, you don't trust me. Well, I'm warning you, Eliza, I won't have you keeping secrets from me. I'm your husband and it's not right. I'll give you time to think about it.'

As the back door crashed behind him, the brass sneck

dropping onto the bar with a metallic click, Eliza stared out of the window as he strode down the yard and round the corner into the street. Thomas struggled as she held him against her and murmured in protest, and she looked down at him.

'There, there, pet,' she said. 'We'll go to the shop in a minute and buy something nice for dinner. Then we'll walk along by the mill race, you like it there.'

She sat the baby in the fancy carriage Jack had brought home after a day at the races. It was the only baby carriage in the street, for though this part of Durham was a little better than some of the mean little terraces which clustered at the foot of Castle Chare, the folk living here being artisans rather than labourers and pitmen, it was only the really better off who could afford such a thing as a baby carriage.

'Nothing but the best for my lad,' Jack had said when Eliza questioned the wisdom of buying it. So it stood in the tiny hall and they had to squeeze past it to get in and out, which was the reason they used the back door rather than the front.

Thomas crowed and waved to everyone who went by as they made their progress down the street towards the steep path leading to the river. The sun sparkled on the water as she pushed the baby carriage along the towpath. There was a cool wind blowing on the top of the hill but here, sheltered by the high banks of the Wear, it was warm and almost springlike. In spite of her niggling doubts and worries Eliza felt her spirits rise.

Perhaps Jack was not in debt to anyone, perhaps he had made a new start and she just didn't trust him enough, just as he said. He had opened a workshop-cum-shop in Saddler Street and she knew he was a good carpenter just like his father. Why, they had only been in Durham for six months and already he had satisfied customers who came back for repeat orders. His reputation was beginning to grow. She should have more confidence in him. Since Thomas had been born he spent less time at the races and he worked hard at the joinery, she knew he did.

Only, whenever he asked her about the necklace her heart sank. She had it hidden away in a bag of sugar in the back of the kitchen press. He would never look there, she was sure he would not. The necklace was her insurance.

Eliza stood by the mill race so Thomas could watch the water rushing over into the pool below and spreading out in ripples to the wider river. Thomas crowed and clapped his hands, an accomplishment he'd only recently acquired. She smiled at him and he smiled sunnily back and tried to bounce up and down on the pillow, succeeding only in falling back against it. Eliza turned him on his side and pulled the coverlet over his shoulders.

'Time for your nap, my little pet,' she said and began

to push the baby carriage up the steep path to the shops. She would call in to see Jack at the workshop, she thought. She hated there to be bad feeling between them. Pausing at the top of the hill, she allowed the wind to play on her face while she got her breath back. She felt slightly sick and leaned against the ancient wall surrounding the cathedral grounds until the feeling receded. Thomas was asleep, she saw, his thumb firmly in his mouth. Eliza smiled fondly and walked on, the baby carriage jiggling on the cobblestones.

The shop was closed, ornate cast-iron shutters over the windows and door.

Where was Jack? Eliza stared at the shutters as though she had made a mistake and they were open.

'Howay, move out of the road, Missus,' an impatient male voice said. 'That thing you've got there is blocking the way.'

'Sorry.' Hastily, Eliza moved to the alley at the side of the shop and set off down it. Of course, Jack must be in the workroom, he just hadn't opened the shop yet. But the door to the workshop was closed and locked. Maybe he'd gone out to a customer? With some difficulty, for the alley was narrow, she reversed the carriage and went back to the street. She couldn't understand it; Jack would have told her if he was going off somewhere, wouldn't he?

A man was hammering a notice to the front door of

the shop. He had to reach through the bars of the shutters to do it.

'What are you doing?' Eliza demanded. 'That's my husband's shop, you have no right!'

He hammered in the last nail before answering. When he did turn to her he looked her up and down, unsmiling. 'Your man's, is it, Missus? Well, mebbe you can tell me where I can get hold of him?' It was the man who had asked her to move out of the way; a big, broad-shouldered man with a ruddy face and small blue eyes.

'Why do you want to know? It's none of your business.'

'Aye but you're wrong there, Missus. It's my business all right. An' I mean that, I have the deeds here in my pocket.'

Eliza reeled with the shock. 'The deeds! You can't have the deeds, you're a liar!'

The man patted his pocket. 'Oh but I have. An' if you were a man I'd knock you down for that.' He stopped and glanced down at her white face. She looked stricken. His tone softened. 'Listen, I'm a reasonable man. You tell that man of yours to bring me the keys by four o'clock the day and we'll say no more about it. But it's no good him thinking he can run off with the keys and get away wi' it. You just tell him that.' Putting the hammer in his pocket, he strode off towards the market place.

Eliza stared after his broad back until he disappeared

round the bend in the road. It was a nightmare, she told
herself, it couldn't be true. Jack had given no sign that
morning, he had not. She turned to the notice on the
shop door. But she couldn't read it, of course. She looked
about her for someone who might be able to read it to
her.

'Did you not go to school?' asked the man in a clerical
collar and the black garb of a clergyman who happened
to be walking past on his way to the cathedral, she
presumed.

'No, sir,' Eliza muttered. She burned with the shame
of it.

'It is not too late, you know,' he said kindly. 'We are
holding adult classes in the Town Hall. It will cost you
two pounds only for the whole course—'

'Please, sir, just read it to me,' cried Eliza, and Thomas
woke and began to whimper. The clergyman hastily read
the notice, then, lifting his hat, hurried away.

FOR SALE
JOINER'S WORKSHOP AND
RETAIL PREMISES
An opportunity to take over a thriving business.
APPLY:
JOSEPH MENZIES AND SON
19 SILVER STREET
DURHAM CITY

Eliza stood gazing after him for a moment then stared at the notice again, trying to decipher it for herself. But it was just a mass of symbols to her. She began to walk away.

'Is something wrong, Missus?' a concerned voice asked, but she shook her head blindly and stumbled on, for once oblivious to Thomas's cries. Down Silver Street and over the bridge, up the hill a short way then right to the street where she lived. The door was locked; she rarely locked it after her so Jack must be in. She banged on the knocker and called, 'Jack!' There was no answer. But she did have a key, she remembered, and fumbled in her reticule for it. Once inside she left the crying baby in the baby carriage in the entrance and ran through the house. Drawers were open and their contents spilled out. She ran up the stairs, still calling, 'Jack! Jack!' But he wasn't there. Of course he wasn't, one part of her mind told her. She went down the stairs and picked up Thomas. He was soaking wet.

'Whisht, babby, whisht,' she murmured to him. 'I'll have you dry in a minute.' First she had to make sure Jack had not found the necklace. She stood in the doorway of the kitchen and gazed at the trail of sugar that spread from the press to the kitchen table. The bag was on its side on the floor by the table and it was empty.

Eliza was frozen into stillness until Thomas's cries and his scrabbling at the bodice of her dress made her

31

sit down almost automatically and undo the buttons and allow him access to her nipple. The baby sucked, frantically at first then more slowly. She looked down at him and Thomas stared back with wet, reproachful eyes though he was still nursing. Milk dribbled down his chin and wet her dress but she was barely aware of it.

'Oh, Thomas, what is going to happen to us?' she whispered. Thomas blinked and grabbed her finger and held on tightly. Both of them jumped when there was a loud knocking at the front door. Eliza waited, her heart thumping in her chest and her nervousness communicated itself to Thomas, who stopped sucking and began to wail. The knocking came again, louder this time. Eliza covered herself and went to answer it.

'Now then, Missus, we don't want any trouble. We've come to take what owes, though. You've to be out by noon.' The burly men on the doorstep thrust past her.

'Hey! What do you think you're doing?' Eliza shouted and Thomas howled louder. But she knew what they were doing, oh yes, she knew. They were candymen, bum bailiffs.

'Howay, Missus. We're only doing our job, like,' said the one who had spoken before. The other one was clearing the hall table, emptying drawers onto the floor then pulling it away from the wall. 'I have the papers here if you want to see.'

'I'll take this out, will I?' the second candyman asked

his mate. 'It's in the road here.' He had hold of the baby carriage.

'You can't take that, it's the babby's,' cried Eliza.

'Aye, but he can,' said the one who was evidently the boss. He nodded to his mate. 'Gan on then.' He turned to Eliza. 'Look, Missus, if I was you I'd be getting you and the bairn's clothes together. You can take them and something to put them in, a bundle or something.'

Eliza stared at him. The man hadn't a cruel face; in fact if she saw him in the street she would have thought him an ordinary, kindly sort of man, most likely with a family of his own. 'Please, I need it to get the bairn and my things to my da's house,' she said, her voice trembling.

He pursed his lips and for a moment she thought he was going to let her take the baby carriage but in the end he shook his head slowly.

'Nay, lass, you can't get round me, I can't afford to lose this job. Just take your things and go. I'm doing you a favour letting you do that. I could send you off now wi' nowt. Away wi' you now. Your man hasn't paid any rent for weeks.'

Half an hour later Eliza was walking up the street towards the railway station. She had the baby, tucked into her shawl and slung against her breast, supported with one hand and in the other hand she carried the bundle. Thomas was sleeping after his feed so at least that made it easier for her.

'Is something the matter, hinny? Can I give you a hand?' a woman, standing at her open front door, asked. She stood with her arms folded over her skinny chest and in spite of her offer didn't move to help at all. She was avid with curiosity. Eliza noticed for the first time that there were a few women standing about and watching her. They must know exactly what the matter was. They would know the candyman's cart with his name painted on the side.

'No, thank you,' she said as haughtily as she could. 'I'll manage fine. I'm just going to see my parents for a few days.'

She didn't look back and see the women smiling knowingly at each other. She straightened her back and strode on towards the railway station at the top of the hill. When she got there she bought a second-class ticket for Shotton. It wasn't a good idea to ride in the third-class open carriage with Thomas; he might catch his death. But it made a frightening hole in the few shillings she had left in her purse.

At least Eliza had a seat in the compartment. A wooden seat, for it was second class not first, but still a seat, so she alighted at Shotton station fairly rested. Outside, the late afternoon was already darkening and a few drops of rain fell. She tucked the shawl more securely round Thomas and picked up her bundle. It was two or three miles to Blue House and she would like to get there before it was totally dark. The road was barely a track and stony and she couldn't afford to trip and fall, with Thomas in her arms. She set off, the wind blowing wet in her face at times so that she was thankful for the bends in the track.

She was about a mile from her parents' small house in the row by the pithead when she had to stand aside for a horse and gig coming up behind her. As it passed, one wheel dipped into a hole filled with rainwater and splattered her already wet dress with mud. It was the last straw for Eliza.

'Watch where you're going!' she shouted, rather unfairly, for the track was narrow enough and the driver hadn't had the chance to avoid the pothole. He stopped the gig a few yards further on and waited for her to catch up.

'Are you talking to me?' he asked softly.

'Aye, I am,' said Eliza. 'You might have knocked me and the bairn down.' He looked at the woman with the filthy dress and sodden hair and a baby wrapped in her shawl. She was soaked through and so was her bundle. Just at that moment Thomas began to struggle against the wet confines of the shawl. His tiny fist and arm fought free and waved in the air and he let out a furious cry. Eliza's tone changed immediately as she put down her bundle and lifted the baby to a more comfortable position.

'There now, pet,' she said. 'We'll be at your grandma's in a minute or two and she'll have a fire to warm you, you'll see.'

'Poor little mite,' the man said. 'Come on, I'll help you into the gig. Going to Blue House, are you? So am I.' He climbed down and helped Eliza into the gig, throwing her bundle on the floor after her.

Chapter Four

'Eliza!'

Mary Anne opened the back door just as her daughter reached it. 'How did you get here? On a stormy night an' with the babby an' all. By, you want something to do bringing the canny bairn out on a night like this. He'll be lucky if he doesn't catch his death an' you an' all!'

'Let me in, Mam,' said Eliza. 'I can't get past you.'

Mary Anne, now she had paused for breath, stood aside and Eliza came into the kitchen where the warmth from the fire in the grate radiated through the bars. Now she had reached Blue House she felt ready to drop. She was shivering and white-faced and her hair had escaped its pins and hung down her face in rat's tails.

'Eeh, lass, take those wet things off. Here, Tommy, take the bairn while I see to the lass.'

Tommy, who had been sitting in the wooden rocking

37

chair by the fire, enjoying his first clay pipe after the back shift down the pit, stood up ready to protest at being asked to do anything after grafting on the coal face, but on looking into Eliza's face he took his grandson and held him in one brawny arm while putting his pipe down on the hearth with his other hand. The three boys, the only survivors of the six born to Mary Anne, sat in a row on the old horsehair sofa. They were still in their black, having come in with their da from the pit. The youngest, seven-year-old Miley, was asleep and leaning against the wall of the inglenook. He had only been a doorkeeper in the pit for a few weeks and hadn't yet got used to the long hours and the dark. Albert and Harry sat and stared at their father holding the baby. He had loosened Thomas's clothes and a small fist waved in the air. Steam was already rising from him and he let out a cry.

'He's a braw babby, he is an' all,' Mary Anne observed. 'Good lungs on him, the Lord be praised.'

'I'd best change him, he's that wet,' said Eliza. 'Only all his spare clothes are wet, the whole bundle.'

'By, I don't know, our Eliza,' snapped Mary Anne. 'Why you brought him out in this weather is beyond me.'

'I had to,' Eliza replied. 'The candymen were in the house and Jack was away out.'

'The candymen? Whatever for?'

'Jack hadn't paid the rent and he is in debt an' all.'

Mary Anne paused only for a minute. She was well used to dealing with crises. 'There's an old shawl in the bottom drawer of the press. You'll have to wrap him in that. Get on with it,' she said. 'I'll get you some dinner.' She took some soused herring out of the oven and added a dollop of mashed potato from the pan on the bar then set the plate on the table for Eliza.

'That's thy dinner, Mary Anne,' Tommy protested.

'Aye well, I'm not hungry now. I'll have a bite later on. Mebbe you can bring me a penny pie from the inn?'

'I'm not going out the night,' Tommy asserted. 'I have nowt.'

'I'll give you tuppence for a pint of porter,' Mary Anne coaxed him. 'Me an' our Eliza have to talk.'

Eliza was already starting to eat but she paused in the act of lifting the fork to her mouth. 'Are you sure, Mam?'

'Get it down, our Eliza. I have to get the bath ready for the lads; young Miley there should be in his bed.'

'Aye, poor bairn, he doesn't like the dark. I found him begging a bit of candle from the night-shift men coming on. Then I had to carry him up the ladders, I was fair done in by the time we got to bank.'

Mary Anne gave her youngest a worried glance. 'Mebbe he's too little for the job. He's still a babby.'

'I was minding the doors, lifting the fire-flaps when I was his age,' said Tommy. 'It never hurt me. He'll have to get used to it, be a man.'

'Tommy, he's just a babby, I telt you.' As she talked, Mary Anne was setting the tin bath down before the fire. She poured hot water in it from the iron kettle on the bar and added cold from the bucket she had brought in earlier from the pump in the street. It was water pumped straight from the pit, for Blue House was a wet pit, but it was clear and fairly pure though smelling a bit of the coal dust.

Miley protested when she woke him and took off his clothes but sat docilely enough in the water. She soaped a piece of flannel and washed him while having the usual argument with Tommy. 'Dinna flannel his back, woman!' Tommy roared. 'You'll weaken it, he has to grow with it strong, the washing'll make it femmer!'

'There's plenty of time for him to get a strong back,' said Mary Anne, not raising her voice at all. 'Any road, don't shout, you'll wake the babby.'

Thomas was warm and dry and fast asleep, wrapped in the old shawl and laid across his grandfather's knees. In spite of the shabby furniture, the scrubbed table bare of a cloth, and the battered press and ancient settee, it was cosy in the kitchen. The fireplace was small and without an oven or water boiler or even a proper hearth, just a stone and an iron fender with a brass rail, but it was home to Eliza and she was slowly relaxing. All she felt for Jack at that moment was a slowly increasing anger. After the boys were washed and tucked into the bed upstairs in the one bedroom, she took the baby from her father and laid him on the settee. He slept on, seemingly none the worse for the soaking.

'Now then, our Eliza,' said Mary Anne as she sat herself down in the chair just vacated by Tommy, who had gone to the inn, 'you'd best tell us what's happened. Have you left your man? If you have, you'll get no sympathy from me. You've made your bed and you'd best lie on it. I know what you said, Jack's got himself in a right bad seam, by the sound of it, but you should stick by him. For better for worse, the minister says. And any road, what are you doing getting a ride from that one, the new owner's son? He has a name for himself, he has, and you want nowt to do with him.'

'The owner's son? Is that who he was? Eeh, Mam, I didn't know. But he was coming this way and I was fairly on me last legs, I was.'

'Aye, likely. Just don't do it again, the neighbours might see. You don't want to get a name for *yourself*, do you?'

'No, Mam,' Eliza said meekly.

'Well then,' said Mary Anne.

'Mam, I had nowhere else to go and Jack wasn't there. He took off, I told you.'

Mary Anne sighed. 'Well, there's nowt to be done the night any road. But you must see we can't keep you. I'm sorry, lass. Did you not manage to save anything?'

'No, I did not. Jack took the necklace out of the drawer. That was all I had. The candymen let me keep a few clothes for me and the bairn, but that's all.'

'Aye well, we'll leave it for the night and work something out come the morn,' said Mary Anne, sighing heavily. 'You'd best sleep down here on the settee with the babby. I cannot have him waking the lads through the night. They have to go on shift first thing.' She shook her head worriedly. 'I don't know about our Miley. He's taken badly to sitting in the dark for twelve hours at a time.'

Eliza went to sleep the minute she laid her head down. She was worn out with the day and her sudden change of fortune. She didn't even hear her father come in and hang his jacket on the hook behind the door before slipping through to the front room where he and Mary Anne slept.

Mary Anne was awake. She was worrying, her mind going round and round her problems and getting nowhere. Tommy lit the stub of a candle and handed her the pie he had brought from the inn.

'I cannot eat it, Tommy,' she said.

'Aye you can,' he replied stolidly. 'Get it down you, woman, we cannot do with you being bad an' all.'

In fact she found she was ravenous as she took a bite and gravy ran down her chin. She caught it with her forefinger and pushed it into her mouth. By, it was grand, she thought. Likely she would feel better after she got it down. Tommy took off his boots and stripped to his undershirt, then climbed into bed. He usually went straight to sleep but after a while she realised he was lying awake.

'Tommy?' she whispered.

'Aye?'

'Our Miley looks badly, Tommy, I wonder if he should have the shift off the morn.'

Tommy moved restlessly. 'He has to get used to it, Mary Anne, you know he has. In a month or so, he'll be fine. The other lads were.'

'I don't know,' she fretted, thinking of the lad she had lost from bad blood. He'd only got a graze when he fell against the pillar of coal that was supporting the roof. In the dark it had been, his stump of a candle had run out. It had turned to the bad though and spread to the rest of his thin little body.

Tommy grunted. 'He'll be fine. Look you, he's close to me, I made sure of that. The other two are with me an' all, they're better off with me.'

'An' what about our Eliza and that canny babby?'

'Aw, man,' Tommy said irritably, 'things'll look better come the morn. Any road, I need me sleep. It'll be five o'clock and the pit hooter going before we know it at this rate. Shut thee gob, woman.' He softened this last remark by turning over and flinging an arm around her. 'Things'll be all right I tell you,' he said, 'settle down.'

Things! Mary Anne told herself. Aye well, mebbe he was right. She turned her thoughts to her daughter and little grandson. Once she had thought that Eliza had made a good marriage, one away from the pits. But Jack had turned out to be a gambler and gambling was the ruination of families. Hadn't Mr Wesley said so? Any road, Eliza and her babby had to be kept somehow, fed and all. Mebbe there was work at the pithead for there surely was none anywhere else in the village, not for a lass like Eliza.

Eliza, for her part, was lying awake too, despite her weariness. She was thinking of Jack. Where was he? Oh, she was so angry with him she was churning up inside when she thought of the happenings of the morning. To have the candymen, the bum bailiffs, throw her out of the house, by, she'd not be able to lift her face in the street again, she was so mortified. Eliza turned over on the lumpy settee and almost fell off its narrow seat. The horsehair prickled her skin even through the old blanket her mam had covered it with. She thought of the comfortable bed she and Jack had shared at his father's house. But then she thought of her mother-in-law's sharp tongue and the way her father-in-law had tried to rule their lives, hers and Jack's. Old John Henry had a nasty tongue, too, and he hadn't failed to use it on her. He'd made scathing remarks about her family, contemptuous ones about pitfolk. By, she was sick of being put down, she was an' all.

Oh, Jack, she cried inside. You didn't have to leave me and the bairn, not again. I would have stood by you, I would. Now here she was back at Blue House and she had to find work of some kind for she had to keep herself. There was no way she would take little Thomas into the workhouse, no, never. Yet her mam and da couldn't keep them, that was for sure. She thought of her brothers with pity. The two older ones were putting, drawing the corves of coal through the low seams not big enough for a man. Bent double over the wagons, one pulling in a harness like an animal and one pushing. They had both had sore spots on their backs and after their mother had washed them she had put vinegar on them. They had whimpered a little when it stung the button-shaped sores from catching their backs on the the roof of the seam. And there was little Miley, a trapper boy, sitting by the fire doors. By, she swore to herself just before she fell asleep with exhaustion in spite of her uncomfortable couch. By, my Thomas will not do that, no indeed he will not. Beside her little Thomas slept on a blanket in a drawer from the press.

Eliza woke from an exhausted sleep when Tommy came downstairs carrying Miley and with the other two lads behind him. Her mother was already up. She had lit the fire and was heating a pan of broily, milk and crusts of bread sweetened with a little sugar. The only light was that from the fire, for Mary Anne was saving the candle end for Miley. She had put it in his bait tin, his food box, so it would be a nice surprise for him. The boys, all three of them, were rubbing their eyes.

'Don't do that,' she said sharply, 'you'll most likely just rub them sore and that'll make them really bad.'

'My eye itches,' said Miley.

'Aye. It's the coal dust,' said Tommy. He was eating a thick slice Mary Anne had cut from the heel of bread, left after putting a slice in each of their bait tins. 'You'll get over it. Howay now, the pit hooter will be blowing again in a minute.' It blew as he swallowed the bit of bread and the lads hurriedly finished their broily and licked the tin bowls clean.

'Ta ra,' said Mary Anne as she handed each of them a bait tin at the door. She bent to kiss little Miley, but he was having none of that, for after all, he was a worker now, wasn't he?

'Be'ave, Mam!' he said, ducking his head and racing after the others. Mary Anne sighed and went back to the fire. She shook the kettle and nodded her head. There was enough water left in it for them to have a drop of tea, she reckoned. Eliza was changing Thomas's sopping wet nappy and the baby was gurgling and waving his legs in the air.

'Howay then,' said Mary Anne. 'Have a bite of break-fast.' The pit hooter had stopped blowing and it was suddenly peaceful in the little room. She cut the heel of bread in two and smeared the two halves with dripping before mashing the tea and pouring out two cups. 'I'll need some more yeast before I can make new bread for them coming off shift,' she said as she sat down with Eliza to the meal.

Chapter Five

'I'll get the messages,' said Eliza. 'I'm going to the offices to see if they'll put me on the screens. Next week. Then I'll make the bread when I get back. You'll watch Thomas for me, won't you?'

It was a couple of days later and yet again there was bread to be baked in the communal baking oven in the pit yard. Mary Anne had to bake three or four times a week to keep her family going. If Eliza kneaded and worked it up ready, that being the main part of the work, Mary Anne would take it to the baking oven, where she would meet the other women for a 'bit of a gossip', as she would say. The working of the dough gave her a pain across her chest and she was glad of Eliza doing it.

Eliza tied her shawl round her shoulders and set off towards the pithead that loomed over the short rows of cottages clustered round. She would go to the office first and she might catch the owner in. The men were paid every other Friday in the Blue Bell and the owner would be there later on but she couldn't go in a public house.

'Get a stone of flour and a quarter of yeast, will you? A bit of butter would be lovely an' mebbe a bit of brawn, if you can get it on the slate,' said Mary Anne, looking hopeful. 'And mebbe a screw of tea?' After all, it being the end of the fortnight, the tally would likely be paid today. The shop was owned by the pit and the money advanced for groceries deducted at source.

Eliza knocked on the office door and a gruff voice told her to come in. The young man sitting in the chair beside the manager was the same one who had given her a lift in his gig two nights before. He looked up and stared at her without a sign of recognition on his face.

'Well, what do you want?' the manager asked. 'It's a busy day for us, we haven't time to waste. So get on with it.' He was recently promoted; Eliza knew him as a shift overman who had often been in dispute with the men such as her father. Robinson was his name and he had a hard reputation in his dealings with the men. It stuck in Eliza's throat to call him sir but she did.

'Please, sir, I wondered if there was work on the screens? I'm a good worker and strong.' She didn't look at the other man but she was very conscious of his gaze.

'Aren't you Tommy Teesdale's lass? I thought you got wed and went off to Northumberland? Where's your man?'

'He's dead,' said Eliza. Well, he was dead to her, she thought bitterly. She would never have him back now, not if he offered her a gold cow.

'You have a baby, haven't you?'

It was the other man who spoke, his voice quiet but authoritative. Eliza looked at him. He had sat back in his chair and crossed his legs, which were clad in good quality broadcloth, one over the other. His knee-high boots, though mired with the mud and black coal dust of the pit yard, were of highly polished leather. He had a superior look about him, she thought. Well, he was no better than she was.

'I have a baby, yes, sir,' she replied. 'My mother will be seeing to him.' She turned back to Jim Robinson. 'Can you give me a start?' she asked.

'Well—' he began but was interrupted by the man sitting by his side.

'For God's sake, man, set her on. I haven't time for this, I have to be somewhere.'

'Aye, Mr Jonathan, sir,' said Robinson hastily, then to Eliza, 'start the morn. Six o'clock sharp. What name do you call yourself now?'

'Elizabeth Mitchell-Howe,' she replied and 'Mr Jonathan' cast her a surprised glance.

'A double-barrelled name,' he said with a hint of sarcasm.

'My married name,' said Eliza stiffly, omitting the 'sir'.

As Eliza walked to the shop just around the corner from the office, she was jubilant. At least her mam and da wouldn't have to keep her. It was hard work on the screens, she was well aware of that, but at least it was work and would put her over for a while. Of course, Jack might come for her, if he got lucky again. But even if he did, she told herself, she wouldn't let him talk her round again. He'd let her down once too often.

Eliza walked into the shop on the corner by the yard gates and went in to do battle with the shopkeeper. Fifteen minutes later she returned to her mother's house in Alice Street, triumphant. Mary Anne put the kettle on to celebrate with cups of fresh tea.

Coming home the next night after ten hours picking stone from the coal as corve after corve came up the shaft, Eliza didn't feel so lucky. She was bone-weary, as weary as the donkey travelling round and round, winding the corves up on the end of the rope. It stood with its head drooping almost to its feet as she walked past it, patiently waiting for the horse keeper to untie it and take it away. Eliza's head drooped too, onto the shawl thick with coal dust that covered her aching breasts.

She had rushed home in the half-hour she was allowed

for her dinner and breast-fed little Thomas while wolfing down a slice of her mother's warm stotty cake spread with a thin layer of melting butter. She had washed it down with warm, sweet tea and then almost ran back to the pit yard.

Now as she went through the door opening directly into the kitchen-cum-living room and heard Thomas wailing hungrily, she knew she had to do something, anything, to earn her living otherwise than sorting waste from the coal.

'There now, here's your mam,' her mother said to the baby. 'Howay, Eliza, give the bairn suck. I've tried cinder water and sugar water but he'll have none of it.'

'I'm fair clemmed meself,' said Eliza as she shed her dirty shawl and picked Thomas up from the drawer where he was lying and waving his fists in the air in temper. She settled him at the breast and adjusted her clothing, pulling a cloth over herself modestly. The boys were seated on the settee and she turned slightly away from them.

It was warm in the kitchen. A pot was bubbling on the fire and giving off delicious smells when Mary Anne lifted the lid and stirred the contents. The sensation of the baby pulling on her nipple was pleasant and Eliza was soothed and sleepy.

'I wonder if that man of yours is coming after you,' said Mary Anne.

'Aw, Mam, I don't care if he does,' said Eliza. 'He can keep away for all I care.'

'Eliza!' said Mary Anne, shocked. 'He's your husband!'

'Aye well, he should act like a husband,' said Eliza, her voice hard. The mention of Jack had brought her out of her trance-like state. 'He's no good to me like he is.'

Mary Anne sighed. 'Aye well, you wed him and you know what the minister says, marriage is for life.'

Eliza didn't reply. She lifted Thomas from her breast and held him over her shoulder for a minute to get rid of any wind, then put him to the other breast. The sound of him suckling made her look down at him. There were tears still drying on his cheeks and she wiped them away with the cloth she was using as a shield. Babies shouldn't have to wait for their suck, she thought bitterly. It was all Jack's fault. The sudden change in her circumstances struck home with renewed force.

'You'll feel better when you've had your supper,' said Mary Anne, noticing she was upset. 'Everything looks better on a full stomach.'

'I will not,' said Eliza forcefully. 'Indeed I will not, full stomach or not. I am going to find a way to live without Jack. He will always be a gambler.'

Mary Anne looked shocked but just then Tommy came in from the inn where he had been to collect his and the lads' wages for the last two weeks. He looked grim.

'What's up with you?' Mary Anne asked, but her heart sank as she began putting the food on the table. She had a fair idea what was wrong. 'That thief Robinson robbed us again, has he?'

'Shaking tubs, man,' said Tommy. 'Six tubs he says weren't full and he won't pay.'

Sometimes the owners and the managers colluded to rob the miners of the wages they were due by employing someone to shake the corves and tubs so that the small coal settled and left room at the top. Consequently they could say the tubs weren't full. The pitmen received nothing for tubs that were not properly full.

'By, I don't know how he sleeps on a night,' said Mary Anne bitterly.

'It's the young gaffer, he was there the day,' said Tommy. He sat down on the chair by the fire and unbuckled his knee protectors and took off his helmet. The firelight glinted on the coal dust on his worn pit jacket and breeches. He bent and removed his clogs and put them by the fire to dry, for the leather uppers were soaked through with working in the wet seam. Eliza watched him as he took off his jacket, taking a few coins from the pocket before dropping it on the flagged floor. Mary Anne would pick up his pit clothes later and dash them against the outside wall of the house to rid them of excess coal dust before drying them by the fire.

'By, that lad's worse than ever his father was,' said Mary Anne. She stared at the money on the table, fourteen shillings and sixpence for a fortnight's work from her man and all three of her sons. Of course the tab from the shop would be already paid and deducted before Tommy saw it. She wished they hadn't bought brown now but it had been a little treat for the boys. Eliza knew what her mother was thinking.

'The bairns enjoyed their tea, Mam,' she said softly. 'Any road, next week I'll be bringing in something extra.'

'Aye, well, we have to live,' said Mary Anne. 'Although sometimes I don't think the gaffer agrees with that. Likely he thinks we should work for nowt like those poor black folk in America.'

'Nay, man, if nowt else they must get their bread,' said Tommy. 'But I think we're likely worse off, nobody has to feed us.'

A minister had been to the chapel to give a talk and he had told them all about the poor black folk in America. The whole congregation had been up in arms about the iniquities of the slaveowners in America. Just about everyone had given a penny towards the fight for justice in the slave states.

'Aye well, they're not free, are they? Stands to reason we're better off than them.'

'Why, man, how are we free? We're bonded to the pit

for a year after we've made our mark, aren't we? The owner can do as he damn well likes with us after that.' Tommy hawked and spat phlegm mixed with coal dust into the fire where it sizzled among the cinders.

'You didn't have to make your mark,' Eliza put in. She was tired and very low in spirits. All she wanted was to put her head down. The baby lay heavy in her arms. She looked down at his sleeping face, the firelight flickering across it. 'Where's your daddy then?' she whispered to him. By, she'd never forgive Jack, never. Not for letting her down like this, never again.

'No, I didn't,' Tommy was saying. 'I could have left and gone looking for other work but I'd likely be no better off in another pit. They stick together, the owners, don't they? An' what else could I do? I'm a pitman; always was an' always will be.'

In the quiet that followed, there were only the noises made by Mary Anne as she prepared the bath for Tommy and the dropping of a cinder in the grate. Eliza was glad when the family went to bed at last and she had the kitchen to herself and her baby. She heated more water and bathed Thomas and then washed the coal dust from her own face and body; something she couldn't do while the boys and her father were there. It was a matter of decency.

Oh, she would better herself, she would an' all, she thought as she laid down on the settee at last. She would think of something, but for now she was bone-weary; her eyes closed as she stretched out her aching limbs.

Eliza woke suddenly, disorientated. Her mother was stirring the fire and adding a few sticks to coax it into a blaze before raking coal down from the shelf at the back of the grate. It was still dark, the only light that given by the flames of the fire. Outside, the pit hooter began to blow its warning that the first shift was due. It must be half-past five then, Eliza thought groggily. Mary Anne went to the bottom of the ladder and called up to where it disappeared into the bedroom.

'Howay, lads, time to be away,' she called. 'I've warmed up a bit porridge for you and I've got a bit sugar to put on it,' she added as an inducement. Thomas began to cry in protest at being woken up.

'Give me a bit porridge, Mam,' said Eliza as she reached for the baby in the drawer beside her. She settled him to the breast first, for sometimes he took a while to take the first feed of the day and she needed to fill his stomach. It was a long time before dinner, when she would be able to feed him again. Once settled, she could hold him in one arm and eat her own breakfast.

The family was still eating when the pit hooter sounded again; a warning that there was only ten minutes for them to get to the pithead. Eliza swallowed the last spoonful of porridge and followed the boys down the yard and up the lane to where lights burned by the pithead, throwing the shape of the buildings into black relief against the sky.

It was a cold, dark morning and she shivered and pulled her shawl tightly round her shoulders. There were a few other women there, some with men's caps over their hair in an attempt to keep out the coal dust, but Eliza had a cotton square she knotted round her head, covering her forehead and her ears. The corves began to come up, dragged by the donkey working the pulley, and the job of sorting the stone from the coal started.

After a while, Eliza found she could work at it without thinking and allowed her thoughts to wander. Where was Jack? By, if she could get hold of him she'd show him what for, she thought savagely. But then, she couldn't get hold of him so thinking like that was going to get her nowhere. No, she had to have a plan. First of all, she had to find other work that didn't make her back feel as though it was about to break in two, but what? Before her marriage she had worked at Brands the butchers in Haswell. She had cooked meat for pies and tripe and onions to sell, but also she had swept the shop and cleaned the shelves and swilled down the yard after the butchering. It had been hard but not as hard as this. But Brand had married a young lass when his first wife died and now she did all that so he didn't have to pay anyone else.

Saturday afternoon she would walk into Haswell and try every shop in the High Street. Or there was Wheatley Hill or Thornley. Surely she would find something? She worked on automatically, her thoughts going over and over the possibilities. She was very quiet and the women working at her side nudged each other and grinned.

'Her man's left her,' one said in a low voice. 'Thought she was something better than a pithead lass, she did.'

'Couldn't even keep her man,' her neighbour observed loudly. She was not above having a set-to with one of the others. Livened the day, it did. But Eliza was oblivious to what they were saying. A strand of dark hair had escaped from her kerchief and she pushed it back absentmindedly, leaving a streak of coal dust across her forehead. She was still trying to think of a way out when the hooter went and the screen stilled for the half-hour allowed for dinner.

'I'm looking for something else to do,' she said to Mary Anne when she was settled once more with Thomas at her breast.

'Aye well, I hope you find something,' said Mary Anne but she didn't sound very optimistic about it. 'There's not much for the lasses round here,' she added as she put a plate of boiled leek pudding and no meat in front of her daughter. 'There's a bit of barley cake you can have if you're still hungry after that.'

'I thought I'd go into Haswell on Saturday after I've finished on the screens,' said Eliza.

'Hmm,' said Mary Anne. She thought about Jack Mitchell-Howe bitterly. He was big nowt, that's what he was. Likely only got that fancy name because his mother or his gran had done something she shouldn't before she was wed. Mitchell was likely her maiden name. He was a true bastard, that's what. What proper man didn't do his best for his wife and bairn?

Chapter Six

Eliza walked with high hopes through the fields to Haswell. It was five o'clock on Saturday afternoon and she had finished work for the week, rushed home to wash and change into her good dress and Sunday shawl and left Thomas with her mother.

'I'm due to my rest an' all,' Mary Anne had observed mildly.

'I won't be long, Mam, I promise,' Eliza had replied.

'Aye, go on then.' Mary Anne took the baby from her daughter and sat down in the rocker beside the kitchen fire. She had a good two hours before Tommy and the lads came in from the pit and there was a pot pie bubbling on the fire so with Thomas asleep it was her chance for a rest. She rocked gently with her arm holding the baby supported by the chair arm.

Eliza was practically running through the fields now as she thought about her mother and Thomas at home waiting for her. Soon she was in the streets of Haswell, a small mining town, and going into every shop to ask for work.

'Well, lass,' one butcher said as he sharpened his knife on a whetstone. 'There's not much work round here, not for lasses, any road.'

Indeed, Eliza could see for herself that trade was bad; there were few shoppers around. Most miners' wives were in debt to the village shops belonging to the pit owners. She stood in the dirt of the road for a while, trying to think of other places to look. Head down, she pondered her chances on the surrounding farms, but folk who worked the land usually had hiring fairs and no one took on extra people in between unless someone had fallen ill or died. She didn't even consider approaching the Parish Guardians; after all, she was able-bodied and in work.

'Hey there, get off the bloody road, you fool!'

The shout made her look up, and there, bearing down on her, was a horse and trap. She jumped back towards the shop and the horse ran past with the driver tugging hard at the reins. It stopped about ten yards further on. The driver secured the reins, climbed down and strode back to where Eliza stood, trembling with shock.

'What the hell do you think you're doing?' he shouted. Dimly she realised that the butcher was peering out of the window and a small crowd had gathered across the road. Red with embarrassment, she looked up at Jonathan Moore. He had his horsewhip in his hand and for one horrified moment she thought he was going to hit her with it, but instead he stood there, waiting for her to speak.

'I'm sorry. I was thinking,' Eliza said.

'Oh, thinking, were you?'

His voice was heavy with sarcasm and her blush deepened. 'You might have ruined a good horse with your daydreaming. You gormless girl!'

Eliza was becoming angry herself. She lifted her chin and stared him in the face. 'Don't call me—' she began furiously, then remembered just who he was. He could get her dismissed and even persecute her father and the lads. Dropping her gaze she bit off her words.

Jonathan knew exactly what she was thinking by the expressions chasing one another across her face. The spirit making her dark eyes sparkle, and the way it was suddenly extinguished, struck him. He suddenly realised who she was, a widow who worked on the coal screens. She certainly looked different, in a decent dress. The dress was a warm brown and her shawl a cherry red like her lips. Now he had got over the shock of the near accident his anger was dying too. There was no doubt she was a fine-looking woman. A widow too, she probably missed her husband in more ways than one. He smiled.

'It's Mrs Mitchell-Howe, isn't it?' he asked. 'I do apologise for shouting at you. It was the shock.'

Eliza was taken aback by the sudden change in his attitude. She looked up at him suspiciously. He was smiling at her for the entire world as though he had not, only a few seconds ago, sworn at her.

He took her hand and held it. Looking at the broken nails with coal dust still embedded around them in spite of her scrubbing earlier, he smiled inwardly. She was bonny but she was just a pithead lass. Still, he was willing to pretend. He had to go to the colliery as it happened.

'You're trembling,' he said. 'Can I take you back to Blue House?'

Eliza thought for a moment. She had been going to go to Thornley but it was a long walk and she was tired after seven hours on the screens. Besides, the situation was probably no different in Thornley. She was really down after her lack of success in Haswell. And she had a longing to get back to her baby. She was barmy looking for work where there was none.

'I would be grateful for a lift, sir,' she murmured.

Jonathan smiled and handed her into the trap for the entire world as though it was a grand carriage and she was a real lady. That was the key to attracting the lasses, he had found. Untying the reins, he clicked his tongue at the horse.

'Gee up there, Polly,' he said.

Eliza glanced sideways at him. By, she thought, she knew what he was after an' all. Well, he wasn't going to get it but it would serve the lecher right if she got everything she could from him. By, owners thought they could do what they liked with the pit folk. Well, she would string him along as far as she could. No doubt he thought widows were desperate for what they were missing but she was not, oh no, she was not a widow nor desperate. Eliza smiled sideways at him.

The trollop, he thought and took a sharp right on to a farm road, which went through a stand of trees.

'Hey, where are we going?' Eliza demanded.

'Don't worry,' he replied. 'It's a short cut.'

Eliza knew the countryside around and she knew the cart track they were on led nowhere but to an old un-inhabited farmhouse. She clutched her shawl close across her breasts and edged to the side of the seat. Jonathan Moore had all his attention on the horse for the moment as he threaded his way through the trees, going slower now. In fact he was stopping, she realised, and she readied herself to jump out and run.

'I could get you indoor work, my mother needs a maid,' he said, turning to her with a slight smile. But Eliza jumped out of the trap before he realised what she was doing. She turned her ankle as she fell heavily on it and a shaft of pain shot up her leg but she hardly noticed. She set off, back up the track towards the road, ran the short way to where the true path to Blue House began, and raced along it.

'Wait!' he shouted after her. 'Wait or you'll be sorry!' But by the time he had turned the horse and trap and got back on to the road there was no sign of Eliza.

'Blast her eyes!' he muttered as he whipped Polly into a trot. 'I'll show her, though.' Next time he would try harder and there would be a next time. Didn't she work for him?

Eliza slowed down; she had to as every step was becoming more painful than the one before. She felt as though there was a black weight pressing on her stomach and it was more unbearable than the pain in her ankle. She had set out with high hopes and here she was coming back no better off than when she started. Worse, she had likely made an enemy of Jonathan Moore. She probably didn't even have a job on the screens any more. She stopped behind an oak tree on the edge of the field. She would sit down for a while and rest her foot. A sob escaped her as she lowered herself to the ground and leaned back against the tree. Though her ankle throbbed, the relief of taking her weight off it was exquisite.

After a few moments she undid the lace of her boot. The swelling was going to be bad; she had a struggle to take off her boot and then immediately wished she hadn't. She would never get it on again.

Eliza sighed and leaned back against the sturdy trunk of the oak. She looked up at the sky; already it was beginning to darken for it was still early spring. She closed her eyes, just for a minute or two, she told herself.

It was the ache in her breasts that woke her. That and the cold breeze playing on the wet patches where milk had leaked through to her dress. Thomas must be crying for her. She jumped to her feet and collapsed immediately back to the ground as pain shot up her ankle. She was sobbing as she pulled herself up and leaned on the trunk of the tree. She had to get back to Alice Street, she thought, even if she had to hop all the way. Limping, she set off, holding on to the fence where she could, stumbling and falling where she could not.

'By heck, our Eliza,' cried Mary Anne, when she finally made it to the door. 'I thought you'd got yourself lost. The bairn's in a right state an' all. I gave him a bit of broily, I got a drop milk from the shop an' he was that hungry he ate it. Poor little sod—' She broke off as she took a good look at Eliza and saw her distress. Her boots were strung round her neck and her dress had great dirty patches on it where she had fallen down on the way home and she was shivering uncontrollably. 'Eeh, Eliza, what happened to you?'

'Good God, Eliza,' said Tommy who had risen from his chair by the fire and rushed to her when he saw how she was. 'Let's give you a hand, lass; have you been set on? I swear I'll swing for whoever did this to my lass, I will!'

'No, Dad, I fell and twisted me ankle,' said Eliza, and collapsed into his arms.

'Get off the settee, lads,' he ordered. 'Your sister needs it more than you do.' The boys scrambled off, gazing wide-eyed at Eliza. Their father carried Eliza to the settee and laid her on it. She sighed with the relief of resting her foot. The blessed warmth from the fire made her stop trembling so much and she began to feel stronger in spite of the continued pain in her foot.

'I can take the babby now, Mam,' she said, for Thomas was still wailing fretfully. Mary Anne handed him over and he nuzzled at her breast. She undid her dress and he grasped at it with both hands and began to suck while looking up at her reproachfully with wet, red eyes. Milk from the other breast began to leak and her mother handed her a cup so she could catch it to save for another time.

'Hadaway out to play for a bit,' said Mary Anne, seeing the interest the lads were showing, though there was little to see, as Eliza was adept at covering herself with her shawl.

'Aw, Mam,' said Miles, 'it's dark and the bladder wants mending any road.'

They had a pig's bladder begged from the butcher, which they used as a football.

'Get some coal then,' she snapped.

'We can't see on the waste heap in the dark!'

'Well, take a candle and scavenge some bits of coal from the road.'

The road along the top of the row was used by the coal wagons and was known as the black road because of the coal that got spilled on it. The pitmen, though working the coal every day, were still fighting the owners for a coal allowance for their own houses.

'Let them be, Mary Anne,' said Tommy. 'They're not hurting nowt.'

'They're all right, Mam,' said Eliza, who had turned towards the wall to shield herself more. 'Have a look at my foot, what will I do with it?'

'Aye, I was going to,' said Mary Anne. She sounded tired and irritable for she had had no rest that day.

Tommy knew the signs and he got to his feet. 'I'm away out any road,' he said. He took his jacket from behind the door and put it on and wound a muffler round his neck. 'See you when I see you.' The nails in his pit boots rang on the stones outside as he walked past the window.

'I'm coming back as a man next time,' said Mary Anne as she frequently did. Eliza took Thomas off her breast and held him against her shoulder. He smelled of milk, fresh and sour, and also urine. He burped gently and she smiled.

'You're all the world to me,' she whispered into his ear. A dribble of sour milk came out of his mouth as he smiled back at her revealing two small teeth in his upper gum.

'Ow!' Eliza jerked as a sharp pain went shooting up her leg. Mary Anne had lifted her foot and was gazing at it critically.

'Mind, our Eliza, it's going to be a bonny size if we don't bind it,' she exclaimed. 'Albert, away and get some cold water from the pump, will you? There's a good lad. I think I've got a rag that will do for a binder.'

'I hope it's not broken,' said Eliza. 'How could I get to work on Monday if it is?'

'Nay, I don't think it is,' said Mary Anne. 'You'd never have got home if it had been. As it is you've made it worse with being on it.' She went to the old press and brought out a bottle of vinegar and doused the injured ankle liberally with it, then she dipped a strip of rag in the cold water brought in by Albert and bound it as tightly as she could.

'There now, that'll have to do,' she remarked. 'You might get your boot back on come Monday. By, our Eliza, you're gormless. You should never have taken your boot off, it would have stopped the swelling.'

'Thanks, Mam,' said Eliza. 'By, it still hurts, though.'

'Aye well, even if I had any laudanum I wouldn't give you it. Not when you're feeding the bairn.'

'No.'

Eliza laid Thomas down on her lap and untied the sopping rag he was wearing as a nappy. The skin beneath it was red up to the band he still wore over his navel. She removed the band too.

'His belly button looks fine, Mam,' she said. 'I think I'll leave the band off now. He's fine.'

Mary Anne pursed her lips. 'He's your babby,' she observed, faintly disapproving

'He's nigh on five months, Mam,' said Eliza.

'Aye. Will I get you a basin of water?' Mary Anne didn't wait for an answer but brought the basin and ladled cold water into it, then hot from the iron kettle. Eliza washed Thomas and put a clean nappy rag and flannel gown on him. It was a fine gown, bought when she lived in Durham and had a bit of money. He looked and smelled sweet, as a babby should, she thought. Already he was dropping asleep and Mary Anne took him and put him in his drawer.

'He's getting a bit big for that,' she observed. 'Mebbe Tommy will get some wood from the colliery joiner and make him a cot. I gave ours to a lass up the row when Miley grew out of it.'

It was cosy in the small kitchen-cum-living room, Eliza thought as she lay back on the settee. Mary Anne had made broth from the liquor she had boiled a ham shank in. It was thick with barley and lentils and also

71

had shreds of cabbage and bits of turnip in it. Now she ladled it out into thick white bowls and the boys clustered round the table in the old shirts they wore for bed. Eliza ate hers on the settee, savouring the bits of meat that had fallen from the shank. There weren't many, for the family had already eaten what meat they could find with fresh, boiled pease pudding when they came in from the pit. Still, there was bread that Mary Anne had baked yesterday in the communal oven.

Eliza was drooping with fatigue but still she was thinking of Jonathan Moore and whether he would take it out on her that she had refused his advances. Had he really thought she would *go* with him? Or had it been her imagination? No, it had not, she decided. Why else would an owner give a pithead lass a ride home?

Eliza finished her broth and her mother took the bowl from her.

'Away to bed, lads,' said Mary Anne, and they climbed the ladder to the attic room, murmuring their good nights. The last sound Eliza heard was the squeak of their iron bedstead as they climbed into bed. She did not hear her father come in from the Blue Bell Inn nor the sound of his hobnailed boots dropping on to the rag mat before the fire. He tiptoed past the settee where she lay and went into the front room to Mary Anne.

Chapter Seven

Come Sunday morning Eliza found she couldn't put her foot to the ground without it throbbing painfully. She lay for a moment or two after her first attempt, gathering her strength. It was barely light outside and only a thin grey light penetrated the small window. It must only be about five or six o'clock she surmised. Thomas was crying and trying to sit up in his drawer on the stone floor beside her. It was cold, for the fire had died to the merest hint of red among the ashes.

She had to get up to see to the baby, she told herself. In any case, she needed to pass water. She sat up and swung her legs over the side of the settee then made herself get to her feet before hobbling to the old bucket that served her for a chamber pot. She went back to the baby, finding it easier to hop than hobble.

Thomas was dripping wet yet again and his legs waved furiously in the air, damp and cold. She removed his nappy rag and cuddled him to her so he could suck.

He was old enough now that she should think of getting him used to taking other food besides milk. Her mother gave him broily but he wasn't keen. But if she herself got a job further away from home he would have to eat something during the long hours she was away.

Eliza sat and pondered on her problems while Thomas fed. She pulled the thin blanket over them both and cuddled him. His limbs were warming up at least. When he had finished she laid him down on the settee and his eyes followed her round the room as she raked out the dead ashes and built a small pyramid of twigs and bits of dried moss over the remaining cinders. A small curl of smoke rose and she blew hard on a cinder until it suddenly glowed red. The moss and thinner bits of twig darkened and smoked, then tiny flames appeared. After that she soon had the fire burning. She put on a few pieces of coal her brothers had brought in the night before and propped the tin blazer on the bar to draw the fire.

Her leg was throbbing mercilessly by the time Eliza had a proper blaze. She filled the kettle from the water bucket standing by the side of the fire and placed it on the flames. Usually, on Sundays, her mother made tea with fresh tea leaves and there was some sweetened condensed milk left in the tin she had bought at the shop a few days ago. Eliza measured out a spoonful of the precious tea leaves and added a little of the condensed milk. By, it was lovely to have something sweet, she reflected. She dipped a finger into the tin and took a tiny amount and put it on Thomas's tongue. His mouth worked and he made a smacking sound with his lips. Eliza smiled at him.

'That's nice, pet, isn't it?' she said. The kitchen was beginning to warm up. Eliza sipped her tea, as the light infiltrating the tiny window grew stronger. She could hear voices coming from the other room so she put the kettle back on the fire, added a little more tea to the pot and, when the kettle boiled, brewed more.

'I've made some tea, Mam,' she called through the door, and Mary Anne came out with a shawl over her nightgown and took two cups through for her and Tommy.

Eliza pulled on her weekday dress and put the kettle on for water to wash her good one. By this time she was getting used to the throbbing pain in her foot. Using the broom with a cloth over the bristles as a crutch she took her slop pail outside and hopped to the midden at the end of the row to empty it, trying at the same time not to breathe the malodorous air around the muckheap.

Mary Anne was just coming through with the empty cups. 'Thanks, lass, that was nice,' she said. 'Shout up to the lads, will you? I'll make some porridge for them.

Before they go to Sunday School.' The boys were learning reading and writing and their numbers at the Wesleyan Methodist Sunday School. Already they could write their names, even Miles, the youngest. Mary Anne was very proud of them. She tried to save a halfpenny each week for them to take for the offering.

The boys went off happily enough after porridge laced with the scrapings from the condensed milk tin. They were followed soon after by their parents who were going to the service in the little chapel at the top of Albert Street. Eliza was left with the baby and strict instructions to rest her leg.

'You'll be good for nowt if you don't,' Mary Anne warned her as she went out of the door with Tommy. He had on his only jacket, the one he wore to go to the pit though not to work in. It was hot in the pit and the men usually worked in pit hoggers, a sort of cotton drawers and a cut-off old shirt. In any case, the jacket had been well dashed against the outside wall to get rid of any coal dust. He also wore a pious expression, being fairly newly converted. In fact he hadn't given up the drink entirely and was still quite easily persuaded to join in a game of 'pitch and toss', behind the pit heap on a Sunday afternoon after chapel.

Eliza was smiling to herself about her dad's relaxed attitude to John Wesley's teaching as she wrung out her good dress and hung it over the string line above the fire.

She dared not go so far as to hang it outside, not on a Sunday. The row was solidly chapel and it would shame her mother for washing to be hung out on a Sunday.

'Ahem!'

Eliza turned in surprise at the sound from the door and in the process put some weight on her injured foot and winced with the pain. She had thought the row deserted with everyone at chapel or Sunday school and she hoped fervently that was true, because Jonathan Moore was standing there and poking his head round the door to look at her. If anyone saw him it would be around the rows like wildfire that she was carrying on with the owner's lad.

'May I come in?' he asked. Not waiting for a reply he stepped through the doorway, having to bend his head to do so.

The barefaced impatience of him, thought Eliza. Coming to the house when he had been the cause of her accident an' all.

'What do you want?' she asked, forgetting for the minute that he was her gaffer and she had to be polite to him.

Jonathan raised his eyebrows. 'Please!' he replied. 'I simply wanted to make sure you were all right. You went off in such a hurry and I'm sure I don't know why. I was, after all, simply taking you home. Along a short cut, it's true, but—'

'That track leads nowhere,' said Eliza.

'No,' he admitted, 'you're right. But you surely don't blame me for doing what any red-blooded man would do if a bonny lass like you got into a trap with him? Not for the first time, either. Now then, admit it, you fancy me. Just playing hard to get, aren't you?' He was walking towards her as he spoke and instinctively she grabbed her broom, which was leaning against the stone fire surround.

Jonathan Moore stayed his approach. 'What are you going to do with that?' he asked softly. 'Defend your honour? The honour of a pithead lass?' He laughed loudly and Thomas whimpered then began to wail.

'Get out,' said Eliza. 'Please go now before I stick this handle where it hurts.' Her heart was beating so loudly she thought he might hear it. He stared at her for a minute or two then looked towards the baby, who was still crying.

'You'd best put that down and see to your child,' he said.

'When you get out,' said Eliza. He took another step towards her and he was directly in front of her. He leaned towards her and she jabbed him hard in the stomach with the broom handle.

'Ah!' The air was expelled from his body and he bent over for a second or two. In that short time she had crossed to the baby and picked him out of the drawer that served him as a cot and hugged him to her. She looked to left and right frantically for a way to get round him to the only door of the pitman's cottage, but there was none, he was directly in the way. He straightened and glared at her and his face was full of anger.

'Don't you touch me,' she warned though she was shaking with fear. Dear God, what was she going to do? By, he picked his time, he did, when he knew the rows would be just about empty.

'Nay, I won't touch you,' he replied. 'I've never yet forced a lass, I haven't felt the need. Mostly they're willing enough.' He chucked Thomas under his chin. 'As you will be when you've thought about it.'

'I will not,' Eliza avowed. Jonathan Moore smiled. 'Oh aye, you will.' He was close enough to lift a hand and she shrank back, but he simply chucked Thomas under his chin again and the baby smiled and gurgled and hid his face in his mother's shawl.

'Shall I do it to your mam?' he asked and laid his finger on Eliza's neck, crooking it under the collar of her dress. She moved sideways quickly and he laughed.

He walked to the door before turning and saying, 'Don't bother to come to work on Monday. I'm afraid your employment is at an end. Unless, of course—' He didn't finish the sentence but left.

Eliza breathed out slowly. She sank on to the settee, feeling nothing but relief at first. Then her ankle began to throb with pain. She had been on it too much, she knew, but what could she do? And what was she going to do now? She had to earn her bread. The Poor Law Guardians would not help her while she was living with her family and not while her husband was alive. She had nothing. She lay back against the head of the settee and closed her eyes. She was still holding the baby and he struggled to sit up on her lap, making unmistakably demanding cries.

'Aye then,' she said. 'All right,' she said and sat up straighter. He smiled at her with satisfaction and her mood lightened. How could she say she had nothing when she had Thomas? He was so precious to her. He was all she had of Jack and just now she ached for Jack. She buried her nose in Thomas's neck and breathed in the baby smell of him.

The sound of someone at the door made her jump, her pulse fluttering wildly. He'd come back and it would be another hour before the family returned. When she saw who it was for a minute she thought she must be hallucinating.

'I reckoned you would be here,' said Jack. It was as if her longing for him had somehow spirited him up. But when he strode over to the settee and took her and his son in his arms he was solid and very real.

'Oh, Jack!' Eliza cried and clung to him. Between them, Thomas wriggled and protested and they moved apart a little. 'Where have you been?' Eliza couldn't bear to let him go yet her joy at the sight of him was turning to anger.

'I—' Jack began but she didn't allow him to finish.

'Do you know what you put me through?' she shouted at him and Thomas began to wail. 'I lost my home! I've had to work at the pithead! Have you any idea what I've been through?' She was on her feet yet again and her foot suddenly gave way so that she fell back on to the settee. She sobbed now, her spurt of anger almost spent. Automatically she rocked Thomas to reassure him.

'I know,' said Jack. 'But I swear to you I never thought for a minute that they would take the house from you, I didn't.' He sat down on her father's chair by the hearth. 'I had to go, pet, they were after me. They would have killed me if they'd caught me.'

'You owed so much? You were gambling when you'd promised me you wouldn't ever gamble again? Jack, man, what about me and the bairn? You never even told me you were running away. Why didn't you take us with you?'

'I couldn't. Anyway it was partly your fault. If you'd given me the necklace when I asked for it I could have sold it and the money would have held them off for a while. Why, there was a big race on at York and I had the winner, it was a certainty, I tell you—'

'For the love of God, stop it, Jack. You never learn, do you? You can't win, you cannot!'

'I won before, I won enough for the house and the business, didn't I?'

'Aw, Jack, don't talk soft; you lost it all again, didn't you? I tell you, you don't win in the end.'

They were quiet for a minute or two; both of them were swamped with emotion. Then Jack said bitterly, 'I knew there would be hell to pay when I came back.'

'Watch your language,' said Eliza, equally bitterly. 'You don't want Thomas to pick up bad language, do you? Any road, you took the necklace after all, didn't you? No thought to how I was going to manage—'

'I said, I didn't think they would take the house! An' I've come back as soon as I could, haven't I? I needed the necklace to start over again.'

'So even that's gone, has it?'

Jack reached into his pocket. 'No, it has not,' he asserted. 'I bought it back. Eeh, Eliza I have so much to tell you, you wouldn't believe.' He brought out the case with the necklace in it and smiled. It flashed through Eliza's mind that he appeared to think that would make everything all right again, for he smiled at her as he handed it over.

'Howay then, Thomas,' he said, taking the baby and holding him up in the air. Thomas crowed and gurgled and slavered down his chin.

'Mind,' said Jack, 'he's grown hasn't he?'

Eliza opened the case and gazed at the necklace. 'When you pawned it why didn't you send me some money? You knew how hard it would be for me.' But she was aware he wouldn't think of her, not when the gambling fever was on him. He wouldn't think of anything else then, of course not. She shut the case with a snap and handed it back to him. 'You might as well keep it, it does me no good,' she said.

'Aw, don't say that,' said Jack. 'If it hadn't been for the necklace I wouldn't have been able to get back on my feet, would I?'

'You are back on your feet, then? Really?'

'I am, my love. I'm going to get you a home to be proud of and everything you and little Thomas want.'

'For how long, though?' Eliza was still bitter. 'Until the next big race, that'll be it, won't it?'

'Nay, Eliza, it won't happen again. I swear it will not.'

'Mind, where've you been all this time, then?'

Absorbed in each other, neither of them had heard the door opening again. Mary Anne came in and shed her shawl and hung it on the hook behind the door before going forward and confronting Jack from only a foot away. Hands on hips, she thrust her face forward and glared at him.

'Leaving your wife and bairn to God and providence, that's what you did. Howay now, what have you to say for yourself?'

'I . . .' Jack spluttered. He was uncharacteristically out of countenance.

'You can say nowt, can you? What sort of a man are you? Our Eliza and the babby would have starved but for me an' Tommy!'

'I knew you wouldn't let that happen,' said Jack quietly.

'Oh aye? Supposing Tommy wasn't in work? Supposing he and the lads had been laid off? They couldn't have gone to another pit, you know that, not when the yearly bond was signed. Bad cess to it!' Neither Mary Anne nor any of the pit folk ever mentioned the hated yearly bond without the curse on it. Now she was working herself into a rage, not just with Jack's behaviour but also with all the frustrations and hardships of her life. And Jack was the only one she could take it out on.

'By, you're a nowt, Jack Mitchell-Howe, in spite of your fancy name, you are an' all. Some fella should give you the hiding of your life! It's a pity your mam didn't—'

'Mam, give over,' said Eliza. 'Jack's back now.'

'Aye, all ready to do it again,' said Mary Anne.

'You've just come from chapel,' Eliza reminded her. 'You're supposed to forgive folk, aren't you?' She was forgetting her own bitterness and anger with Jack and in face of her mother's tirade felt the urge to defend him. Jack himself stood blushing like an errant boy.

Mary Anne glared at her daughter for an instant then shrugged. 'Aye well,' she said 'I speak my mind. Wait until Tommy comes back in and see what he makes of it. Likely he'll want to knock him into the next world.'

'No, he won't,' said Eliza. 'Jack is my man, after all.' And so it proved. When Tommy came in from the 'toss penny' school at the back of the pithead he had had a run of luck and won a couple of shillings, which he had spent on a couple of tots of rum for his marras. He was in too good a mood to fight with anyone and went straight into the front room for a lie-down.

Chapter Eight

'I've rented us a house in Haswell,' said Jack. 'At least it is a short walk from Haswell. I want Thomas to grow up breathing clean fresh air.'

'Haswell? What are you going to do in Haswell? You'll never settle there, Jack.'

'It's just for a short while. When I'm properly on my feet again I'll write to my father. He'll take me back into the business when he realises how well I've done.'

Eliza stared at him in disbelief. 'Oh, Jack, he won't. Don't think he will, man.' He was fooling himself, she thought in despair. John Henry would never take him back, no matter what Jack did. And if he did she would never go back to Alnwick. She had been treated as less than dirt by Jack's parents.

'He might,' Jack asserted. 'I am the eldest son, Eliza.'

'Aye. The one cut off without a penny,' said Eliza and smiled grimly. 'Well, we'll wait and see. Meanwhile we have to live. I asked you, what are you going to do in Haswell?'

'Oh, didn't I say? I'm going in with Mr Benson, the cabinet maker.'

'Going into partnership with him or working for him?' Eliza was surprising herself by how she questioned everything Jack said. It was as though she was at last seeing him as he really was. What choice did she have, though? She had to stay with him. Besides, she still had feelings for him. When her mother had berated him she had been defensive of him.

'Get your bundle together, Eliza,' he said now. 'Then we'll have a mashing of tea and be away.'

'Whose tea will that be?' asked Mary Anne with a hard look.

'Mam!' Eliza was shocked. Her mother was usually hospitable with what she had.

'Aye well,' said Mary Anne. 'It's hard not to be mad with that one.' She shrugged and went on, 'Aw, hadaway then. I'll mash the tea, you go and pack your bundle.'

Jack and Eliza set off towards Haswell along the path through the fields that Eliza had taken the day before. Eliza carried Thomas and Jack the bundle. She thought about the time they had travelled to the house in Durham in very different style and how happy she had been. This time she wasn't so sure that their troubles were over.

She had kissed Mary Anne's cheek awkwardly when they left.

'I can't thank you enough for all you've done for us, Mam,' she said softly. 'Don't be angry, eh? Jack's my man and I have to go with him, you know I do. I wed him, didn't I?'

'I know lass, I know. By, it's hard for a woman in this life,' Mary Anne replied. 'Though mind, it's hard for lads an' all. When I think of Miley in the pit and him so frightened of the dark – eeh, what's the good of talking. But I can't help wondering what God's been thinking about letting it happen. I know it's a sin.'

'I'll be back whenever I can,' said Eliza. There was nothing else to say.

The house Jack had rented was up a muddy lane about a mile the other side of Haswell. It stood next to another exactly the same but ruined, both by fire and the elements. There was a garden, rank with dead weeds, though under the tiny window of the downstairs room there were a few green spikes of spring flowers showing against the dirty sandstone of the cottage wall.

'It's better than it looks from outside,' Jack said quickly when he saw her expression. He pushed open the batten door and led the way in. The downstairs room was as poky as the miner's cottage she had just left but there was a back door, she saw. It had only a rusted iron sneck to the door and daylight could be seen through it.

But Jack must have lit the fire in the grate and the room was reasonably warm. There was a table and two wooden chairs and even a rocker by the hearth. A hanging cupboard on the wall by the fireplace completed the furnishings. There was a rough wooden ladder leading up to the upper room, which must be half inside the roof, Eliza judged. She said nothing but sat down in the rocking chair with Thomas as Jack added a log to the fire from the pile on the hearth. A thick depression was settling on her. Jack was talking quickly as though to cover her silence.

'I got some groceries in,' he said. 'And I can get some eggs from the farmer who owns this place. I've made the bed upstairs. It'll be all right, Eliza, really it will. The bairn can sleep with us until I've made him a cradle. I'll soon make some bits of furniture, you'll see. It's my trade, after all.'

Eliza watched him, the expression on his face, for he was eager to show her how earnest he was to make it up to her. He took the iron kettle that stood on the stone before the fire and took it out of the back door to fill.

'There's a spring, it's lovely sweet water,' he said over his shoulder.

'Hmm,' said Eliza.

'Aw, howay, Eliza,' he said. 'I know it's not as good as Durham but it's better than nowt, isn't it? We'll be together after all. I spent most of my winnings getting the necklace back for you but I've got a job with old Benson. He's getting too old for the work and I'll be able to take over before you know it. It's a grand chance, Eliza.'

'We'll see,' said Eliza. She thought of the necklace, hidden in the pocket she had sewn into her skirt. By, she thought, she would make sure he didn't take it away again, she would an' all.

May came in and Thomas was crawling all over the floor and even beginning to pull himself up to a standing position with the aid of a chair or the table leg. The weather was turning fine after a wet spring and there were primroses in the grass growing along the hedgerows in the lane.

Eliza was hanging out the washing in the strip of garden at the back of the cottage one morning towards the end of the month. Thomas was standing by her side and clinging on to her skirts with tight little fists. When she moved along the line she dragged her foot and he leaned against her and walked with her, concentrating hard on not falling. She smiled down at him, 'Who's a clever lad then?' she asked and he cooed and gurgled back at her.

'He'll be working as a trapper boy before you know it and bringing in good money,' said a voice behind her. She looked back towards the cottage in surprise; there was no way into the garden except through the house.

'How did you get in?' she asked. 'I didn't ask you in!' The front door was open but they were so isolated here on this lane. The only other person who ever used it was the farmer and he had another way in to the farm.

'The door was open,' said Jonathan Moore. 'I must say, Eliza, you look blooming. It suits you living in the country.'

'What do you want?' she asked. She felt very nervous at being on her own; something she hadn't felt before since coming to the cottage. Bending, she picked up Thomas and held him to her. The baby stared at the intruder with his violet-blue eyes, so like his mother's now, unwavering. He put a thumb in his mouth.

'I was just passing on my way to see Farmer Dean,' Jonathan said smoothly. 'I heard you were living here with your husband. He came back then? Is he staying or planning to desert you again?'

'He's not!' Eliza blurted out. 'He didn't desert me before, he was coming back and he did, as soon as he could.' Thomas was becoming upset, she could feel it. 'Go away, Jonathan Moore,' she said. 'Leave us alone. Jack will be in for his dinner in a minute.'

Jonathan laughed. 'No, he won't,' he said. 'He's working on a tallboy up at our house. I left him there. He won't be finished before nightfall. So I said that as I was coming to see Farmer Dean I would call in and let you know he won't be in for his dinner. He can have bread and cheese with the other servants in the kitchen.'

He had planned this, Eliza realised. He was here to finish what he had started in her mother's house. She clutched the baby tightly and Thomas began to cry.

'Put him down, Eliza,' said Jonathan. He closed the space between them and stood very near. He held out a hand and touched the baby and Thomas shrieked louder.

'Shut him up, Eliza,' said Jonathan.

'Ssh, babby,' she said. Then, 'You said you wouldn't force me. Were you lying?' She spoke very softly, trying to reassure the baby.

'I was not,' he replied. His voice was as low as hers. 'Before I'm done, Eliza Mitchell-Howe, you'll be wanting it as much as I do.' He ran a finger down her neck, exposed as it was with the top two buttons of her dress undone on this balmy May morning. He touched the swell of her full breasts and she stepped back automatically.

'Don't touch me,' she said.

'Are you there, Missus?' Jonathan stepped back as Farmer Dean appeared in the doorway of the cottage. 'I couldn't make you hear, so I came through – oh! Good morning, Mr Moore.'

The farmer looked curiously from one to the other of them and Eliza felt the colour rising in her face. She bent forward to hide it and stood Thomas against her leg again. He clutched at her dress, burying his face in the rough serge.

'Good morning, Farmer Dean,' said Jonathan, quite unfazed. 'I was on my way to see you so you've saved me a journey up the lane. I wanted to talk to you about the chances of driving a shaft on your land.'

'You did? But I thought the limestone shelf here was too thick to get at the coal,' said the farmer. 'That's what I was told when it was surveyed before.'

'Well we're not sure—' said Jonathan vaguely. He looked at Eliza. 'Now I've delivered the message from your man, we'll leave you in peace.' He took the farmer's arm and led him back through the cottage. 'Jack is doing a job for us at the house,' he said offhandedly. Within a few moments the two men were gone and Eliza and Thomas were on their own again.

'Why doesn't he leave me alone, Thomas?' Eliza asked the baby.

'Da, da,' he replied and smiled at her, his face grubby with streaks of soil he'd picked up from the garden.

'Aye, you're right,' she said and scooped him up and took him inside. She would have to tell Jack about him.

'Has he touched you?' Jack demanded when she brought up the subject of Jonathan Moore that night. 'I mean, if he has I'll—'

'Nay, he hasn't,' she replied quickly. She could still

feel the touch of his finger in the neck of her dress but she couldn't really call that *touching* her, could she?

'Well,' said Jack, 'that's all right, isn't it? Likely he's like that with all the girls.' He nibbled at the skin beneath her ear. 'Let's away to bed.'

'But, Jack, he threatens to, he says things—'

'Aw, man, Eliza, he's not hurt you, has he? We have to keep on the right side of folk like the Moores. They can put a lot of work in my way. I know you wouldn't let him do anything, would you?' Jack was beginning to sound impatient. Obediently she followed him up the ladder to the bedroom under the eaves. In the light from the candle he carried it looked a lot better than when she had first seen it. Jack had made a dressing table for her and a bed and cot with a wooden hood to keep out the draughts. They were plain and built with offcuts from Mr Benson's workshop but Jack was very good at his job and they made the room look quite luxurious compared to what it had done before.

Their love-making was deeply satisfying and as usual she forgot everything else but him. Afterwards, as she drifted off into sleep, the thought of Jonathan Moore came back to her but somehow it didn't seem to matter so much. He was not important. She had Jack and Jack would look after her and Thomas. He was not going to desert her again; she had his solemn promise.

All the same, for a while Eliza kept the front door of

the cottage closed and took out the sneck so that it couldn't be opened from the outside when Jack was at work. After all, you never knew, there might be gypsies about, or Irish tinkers. There were a lot of those since the famine. But the spring had turned into summer and no one came down the lane except Farmer Dean, and Eliza lapsed into leaving her front door ajar to let in the air, just as her mother had always done. There were no locks on the doors around here.

One afternoon in July she decided to walk into Haswell and maybe go on to Blue House if Thomas wasn't too tired. He was getting big now, too big to carry far, but he could walk fairly well by then. If she let him make his own pace he usually managed to get to where they were going. Jack had gone to Sunderland to deliver a cabinet and the long empty day and light evening stretched ahead of Eliza and she was bored. Anyway, she hadn't been to see her family for more than a month.

She and Thomas ambled down the lane, Thomas stopping to pick daisies, or rather daisy heads, and handing them to her, smiling. 'Dais, dais,' he said, pleased with himself.

'Daisies,' said Eliza. 'Say daisies.'

They came out onto the road into Haswell, which was thick with dried mud, black with the coal dust, and rutted with the passage of coal wagons, so that she had to take

Thomas's hand to help him over the ruts. A bee buzzed busily among the blossoms of the 'black man's baccy' plant and the blossoms filled the air with their perfume. Eliza felt supremely happy, a feeling that only a few months ago she thought she would never have again.

Thomas was stumbling with tiredness now and she picked him up and carried him on her hip.

'Not far now, pet,' she said and turned off on to the path across the fields to Blue House colliery. Soon the colliery buildings came into sight. There were a few men hurrying about in the yard, and corves of coal were being drawn up to the shed where the platform with the coal screens was housed. Through the gaps in the wooden wall she could see the women and girls bending over the moving belt and picking out stones from the coals.

Dear God, it was back-breaking work! She was well out of it, she was indeed. This lovely spring day emphasised the fact. She walked on to the colliery rows. Most of them had their doors open to let in the air, though here it was polluted with the smell of the midden and the coal dust. Some women were standing in the door-ways taking the air and children played in the dust at their feet. There was no proper pavement and the road was hard-packed, rutted mud, so the dust was inevitable.

Even so, lines were strung across the street from iron hooks in the walls of the cottages and washing hung on them under the watchful eyes of the women. Should a cart make its way along the women would rush out to rescue the clothes. Usually the cart drivers called out to let them know they were coming but Eliza knew some drivers did not.

As she drew near the house belonging to her mother in the long, straggly street she realised there was some kind of meeting going on. A group of men were sitting on their hunkers along the wall. This was the position most comfortable to men who spent their working lives in this position, wielding a pick and shovel in small seams of coal. A man was walking up and down in front of them as he talked and by his accent he was from further west in the county.

Eliza was alarmed. He looked like a union man and if he was they were in serious danger. And anyway, what were they doing having a meeting in broad daylight? As she approached her father got to his feet and looked at her.

'Hadaway inside to your mother,' he ordered. 'This has nowt to do with you, nowt at all.' The group of men were all staring at her as though they didn't know her and the man stood waiting for her to go.

'Da, what are you doing?' she cried.

'I telt you, get inside,' he ordered again. Eliza stood by the door to the cottage, trembling. The door opened and her mother's arm came out and grabbed her shoulder and pulled her inside. The door was closed behind her.

Chapter Nine

'What are they doing out there in the middle of the rows?' Eliza asked. 'Are they just looking to be thrown into Durham gaol? For God's sake, Mam!' She was shocked and full of fear, not just for her father but also for them all.

'They have to do something,' said Mary Anne. 'They're laid off and have been for a fortnight. What are we supposed to live on, then?'

'But the pit's working, I saw it,' said Eliza. She sank down on to the settee with trembling knees. The day had started out so fine and she had felt so happy walking over from Hazelrigg Farm. Now everything was changed, even the sun had gone behind a cloud. Danger was everywhere, or so she felt.

'Aye, the pit's not idle but half the men are, your da and the lads among them. It's the fault of the bond,' Mary Anne sounded bitter. 'The shop won't let us have any more on the slate and we don't even know if they can go back to work next week. It depends on orders for coal, that swine Moore says. If they hadn't signed a bond they'd be free to look for work elsewhere. There's that big pit at Murton. There's hundreds of pits in the county but the men can't go because they are bound to Blue House. Him out there reckons it's time the bond was abolished.'

'But what if Mr Moore sees him here? They're not even behind the slag heap or in the clay pit, Mam!'

'No, but why should they hide? Anyway, the lads are on the lookout at the top of the rows.'

'I didn't see them,' Eliza said. 'I hope they haven't wandered away.'

'Nay, they wouldn't,' Mary Anne asserted, though she looked uncertain. 'If they are I'll skelp their behinds, I will an' all.'

The two women were quiet for a while, then Eliza stood Thomas on the floor by the settee so he could hold himself up and went to the table where she had dumped her basket when she came in. 'Put the kettle on, Mam, I've brought a paper of tea and a few bits,' she said. 'We can have a cup of tea, any road.'

'Nay, lass, you don't have to do that. We'll get through, we always do. Tommy caught a rabbit up at the bunny banks early on the morn. We'll have a stew later.'

'An' we'll have some tea now,' said Eliza. 'I'm ready for it.'

'Does your man not mind you bringing us stuff?'

'Even if he did I just have to say how you kept me and the bairn when he deserted us,' Eliza said in a hard tone. 'He's doing fine at Benson's, any road.' She took half a pound of sugar and a pound of barley from her basket. She had been going to make barley water for Thomas but that wasn't important now.

'If you're sure,' said Mary Anne. 'I can make barley porridge for the lads, that will fill their bellies.' She looked brighter, less careworn as she filled the kettle from the bucket of water standing by the hearth and placed it on the fire. 'I wasn't going to put the fire on when there was nowt to cook,' she said. 'But the lads brought some coal in from where a wagon overturned on the black road.'

Outside, there was a rumble of men's angry voices. 'One of the first things we will do is ask for a proper coal allowance,' the stranger was saying. 'It's off the map that we should labour all day getting the coal and not have enough for our own fires.'

'Just what we were thinking,' Mary Anne said to Eliza. 'I tell you what, we do need a union and we won't get it without a fight. But it'll be a hacky mucky fight, I can tell you.'

Oh aye, it would, Eliza thought as she brought the last bag out of the basket. 'Six eggs, two for me da,' she said.

'He'll be glad o' them,' said Mary Anne quietly. 'An' I'll do the bairns some eggy bread. It'll be a treat when they come in.'

She measured out a careful spoonful of tea and poured boiling water on it. They drank it without milk but as a treat they sweetened it with a little of the precious sugar. A few minutes later the door opened and Tommy came in and with him, the stranger. They were quickly followed by the three boys, all panting from the run up the row.

'Up the ladder, now,' said Mary Anne, shepherding them to the corner where the ladder led up to their bedroom. 'Keep quiet an' all.' They nodded and fled upstairs as a peremptory knock on the door made everyone jump. The sneck was lifted and in walked Jonathan Moore.

'I didn't say come in,' Tommy muttered and Jonathan smiled.

'No? Aye well, it's a pit house, isn't it?' He looked at Eliza, who had risen to her feet and taken hold of Thomas. The baby gazed at the interloper and put his thumb in his mouth. Jonathan smiled at the baby for all the world as though he was a welcome visitor.

'He's growing,' he said to Eliza.

'What do you want, gaffer?' Tommy asked. 'Are we back to work the morn?' Jonathan shook his head. His smile had vanished and he stared at the stranger.

'Who's this?' he asked.

'He's my cousin from yon side of Durham,' Tommy replied.

'He doesn't look like you,' said Jonathan Moore.

'Does he have to?'

'There are agitators in the area. I had a message from the Owners' Association.'

'Are there now?'

'If anyone is caught inciting to riot he'll be for a spell in Durham gaol.'

'Are you speaking for your da or are you just a lackey of the Owners' Association, then?' This time it was the stranger who spoke and Jonathan reddened with anger. The stranger turned to Tommy. 'I can speak for meself, don't fash yourself,' he said and turned back to Jonathan. 'I'm Peter Collier,' he said. 'Here to tell my cousin that our granda is dead.'

Eliza looked up in surprise. Her great-grandfather was indeed dead and had been since before she was born. Peter Collier was looking at Jonathan Moore, one eyebrow raised quizzically. Mary Anne licked her lips nervously but Tommy lifted his chin.

'I'm sorry to hear that,' he said. 'A grand old man an' all. When is the funeral?'

'Saturday, four o'clock,' Peter Collier answered before turning back to Jonathan.

'Well, Mr Moore?'

'Get off our property before you are thrown off,' said

Jonathan. 'If I find out you are in any way connected to the rabble-rousers I'll see every last one of you hounded out of the place.'

'Your da made his mark on the bond as well as me,' said Tommy. 'It has three months to run an' all.'

'Father *signed* the bond,' snapped Jonathan. 'He is not an ignorant pitman. But don't think we cannot throw you out, we can and we will. Good day to you, Eliza Mitchell-Howe.' He turned and stalked out. Tommy went to the tiny window and saw him walk up the row.

'He's gone,' he said to the man who called himself Peter Collier, and they all smiled. This time they had bested the owner's son but Eliza doubted he would leave it at that. But she was taken aback when her father turned to her.

'Why does he speak to you like that? Have you been with him? I'll bray the hide off you if you have!'

'No, Da, no, I haven't, he was just trying to make trouble,' said Eliza. 'I'm a married woman, Da, I wouldn't.' Eliza trembled with the need to assure him she hadn't done anything.

'Aye well,' said Tommy grudgingly. 'I expect you haven't.'

'I'll be away then,' said the stranger. 'I have a bit more visiting to do.'

'Won't you have a bite first?' asked Tommy and glanced at his wife who looked alarmed.

103

'Well, there's some eggs,' she began.

'Nay, lass, thanks for the offer,' Peter Collier said swiftly. 'I have bread and a nice bit of Cotherstone cheese, I can eat as I go along.'

He made his goodbyes and chucked little Thomas under the chin before going to the door. 'Remember, Saturday, four o'clock,' he said to Tommy. 'The old quarry, you know where.'

It had been an interesting day, all right, Eliza thought to herself while she was walking back to Hazelrigg Farm cottage by the path across the fields. The weather had changed and rain threatened while a cold wind blew from the north-east. She carried Thomas on her hip inside her shawl and he leaned against her, his eyelids drooping. She bent her head and kissed him on his hair, now turning as dark as her own.

'Mind, you are a bonny lad,' she sang softly to him and his eyes closed properly. A few drops of rain began to fall and she put her head down and hurried into Haswell. She would shelter in Benson's doorway until it passed. It was probably only a shower.

'Come inside, lass.' Mr Benson opened the door behind her and motioned her in. 'The rain won't last long, then you can be in your way.' He was a pleasant enough chap, thought Eliza as she followed him into the warm interior of the shop-cum-workroom. A middle-aged man with grizzled grey hair going thin on top and a kindly smile, he chatted to her as he took up his plane to continue smoothing the piece he was working on.

'Your man's away delivering the day,' he said between strokes. 'I bless the day I set him on, I do that. A good workman is Jack, you should be proud of him.'

'Well, I am,' said Eliza, but in her own mind she thought, with a few reservations.

'Used to work on the Duke of Northumberland's estate, so I understand.' He looked up from his work and stayed his hands for a moment. His eyes were bright and enquiring, as though he wasn't quite believing of that.

'Aye, he did,' said Eliza. 'Him and his da.'

'A good position that. I wonder he would come south to work in a colliery village.'

Eliza didn't know what to say to that so she simply smiled and nodded.

'I suppose you wanted to be near your family,' he went on. 'Women are like that.' He shook his head in disapproval. 'It's a pity, though. I'm glad to have him, you understand, but he was better off up in Alnwick, wasn't he?'

Eliza was angry. What had Jack been saying to him? That everything that had happened to them was her fault? She opened her mouth to tell him the truth but then closed it again. How could she say anything against Jack to his employer? Mr Benson was looking at her kindly. No doubt he thought he had given her a gentle reprimand and she should not have influenced her man. Mr Benson was a pillar of the chapel in Haswell and a lay preacher who sometimes came to Blue House to preach.

He returned to his rhythmic planing of the chest he was working on. Evidently he felt he had done his duty and made his point. She turned and gazed out of the window. The sky was clearing and the rain had stopped. She'd best go before she said something she would regret.

Negotiating the lane to the cottage was difficult. The rain had turned the dried mud into a quagmire and she slipped and slid her way along, clutching Thomas to her. He struggled and cried in protest and she was glad when she got to her front door without actually falling. Her boots and the hem of her dress were thick with mud and streaked with coal dust and she was thoroughly out of humour, in contrast with how she was in the bright beginnings of the day.

Later though, looking pensively out of the window, she noticed that the climbing rose she had planted under the window was starting to bud and she smiled to herself. No one, not even Jack, would think of looking underneath the rose to where she had hidden the necklace wrapped in oiled canvas among its roots. Next time, and she was sure there would be a next time, she would not be left destitute when Jack got the gambling fever.

*

Jack came in very late in the evening after his trip around the countryside. Eliza had not bothered with a candle, for not only did the fire show a good light but moonlight was streaming through the window to where she sat in the rocking chair he had made for her. Thomas had been in bed and asleep long since and there was an appetising smell from the pot of stew simmering on the bar of the fire.

'By, it's good to be home,' Jack said as he came in. 'Don't get up, hinny, you look a picture sitting there in the moonlight.'

Eliza laughed and stood up anyway. 'Who's to give you your supper if I don't get up?' she asked. 'You're fond as a gate.' But she was pleased all the same. For by, he was a grand lad. If only he didn't gamble, she couldn't help thinking. There was always a part of her now that stood aside coldly and watched even in their most intimate moments.

Over supper she told him about Peter Collier and the meeting the men had had in broad daylight outside her parents' house. 'It frightens me, Jack,' she said. 'I don't know what they would do if they were thrown out of the house.'

'Hovel, more like,' said Jack, spooning meat into his mouth before mopping the gravy with a heel of bread. 'Some of the pit houses have ash closets nowadays instead of a stinking midden at the end of the row. Mebbe your da would be better off finding himself a more modern pit. Mind, I don't hold with agitation. The men and the gaffers should be able to come to an agreement about their differences, settle them, like.'

'Sometimes the men have to band together to get their just rights,' Eliza declared, which was a bit strange for she had been against just that earlier in the day.

'Rights? They don't have any rights,' said Jack. He sat back in his chair and took the clay pipe he had taken to smoking lately out of his pocket. 'Any road, get us a light, pet.'

Jack didn't really understand, she thought. But then Jack was not a miner.

Chapter Ten

'I'm going up to Alnwick to see me mam,' said Jack, one Saturday morning in July. He had just walked in the door of the cottage though he had only been gone about two hours. Eliza looked up from scouring the hearthstone in surprise and was even more shaken to see Henry, his brother, behind him.

'What is it? What's happened?' She rose to her feet, still holding the piece of wet sandstone she had been using.

'Da, Da,' chirruped Thomas in delight, and waddled towards him from under the table where he had been playing with a peg dollie. For once, Jack ignored him even though Thomas clung to his gaitered legs. The baby howled and Eliza picked him up automatically. She gazed anxiously at Jack then Henry. Her brother-in-law nodded curtly.

'Me da's dead,' said Jack. 'Henry came to tell me.

He's had a job finding us and the funeral is at four o'clock. We shall have go into Durham for the train.'

'Haven't you got your trap, Henry?' Eliza asked.

'It'll take too long,' said Henry. 'We must get back. Mother wanted Jack there, she's fallen to bits, like.'

Eliza thought of the hard-faced woman she knew. She couldn't imagine Annie falling to bits over anything but still, John Henry was her husband and despite everything that had happened she couldn't help feeling sorry for the woman.

'Do you want me to tell Mr Benson, Jack?' she asked. 'I can go into Haswell if you like.'

'He knows. It was there I met Henry. Make us up a bite to take with us, pet.'

Within ten minutes the two men were on their way, taking Henry's trap to the station and leaving it at the stables there. She watched them drive down the track to the road, their shoulders touching in the small vehicle. She had not seen them so close together since she had known them. Then she went into the cottage, quiet now but for Thomas mumbling to himself as he played with his dollie.

What was going to happen now? she wondered. Would Jack be able to go home to Northumberland for good? Would Annie forgive him and welcome him home? Eliza looked at little Thomas, oh it would be a good thing for the bairn if they all went to live in Northumberland again. He would be a cabinet maker like his father and grandfather and he definitely would not have to go down the pit. Her heart lightened at the thought of it.

Late on Sunday evening Eliza discovered how John Henry's death was going to affect her little family and it was not at all. Jack came staggering in the door, dirty and dishevelled and stinking of ale and the honeyed sweetness of mead. He leaned over the table and hiccupped.

'What? What's happening Jack?' she cried.

'Happening? Nowt's happening,' he replied, his words slurring into each other. 'My gracious mother, my lovely, forgiving mother welcomed me back with open arms, oh aye, she did. Then as soon as the last funeral guest had gone she turfed me out, her and that thieving reiving brother of mine.'

'Jack, you knew you were going to be disinherited,' said Eliza but in truth she herself was bitterly disappointed. She had been weaving daydreams about life in Alnwick for her little family all day. 'Did you get nothing?'

'Oh, aye. Henry said I could have the old pony and the tub trap he left in the stables at the railway station. Only it will cost twelve shillings to pay the stabling charges. Have you got twelve shillings?'

'Jack, you know I haven't. It will have to wait until you've earned the money.'

'Or we could sell something.'

Jack sat down on the settee and Thomas stood at his knee, looking up at him with adoring eyes. 'If we wait till the weekend and I get my dues from Benson it'll have gone up a couple of shillings.' He sniffed and looked up at Eliza. 'I'll sell the necklace.'

'You will not!' Eliza burst out. 'You said you would never take it again, you promised me, you did.'

'Aye, but it's just to get the pony and trap out, it's not for gambling. I'm not going to gamble, I told you I wouldn't.'

'No.'

'I'll pawn it then. I can get it back at the weekend if I pawn it. Where is it, any road?'

'I'm not telling you. Not even if you bray me.'

'I'm not going to hit you,' said Jack in disgust. 'I wouldn't.'

'You've done it before.'

'Shut your mouth, woman!' Jack suddenly lost his temper. He jumped to his feet and went over to a small chest of drawers he had made for her only the week before. It was built of oak and he had put on brass handles, which twinkled in the firelight against the dull sheen of the polished oak. He pulled out the drawers and threw out the cloths and other things he found in them.

'You're not taking them!' Eliza ran over and tried to

pull him away but he shoved her aside roughly and Thomas began to scream in terror. The baby sat down on the clipped rag mat and howled and Eliza couldn't bear to hear it. She went to him and picked him up and hugged him to her. His sobs lessened and he quietened down and buried his head in her shoulder. She heard the door bang behind Jack and when she looked up he was striding away with the chest humped on his shoulder.

After a while Eliza took Thomas up the ladder to bed with her. She lay with the sleeping child cuddled against her breast but she couldn't sleep herself. Every noise from outside the cottage alerted her: the hoot of an owl, the screech of a vixen in the covert over the field at the back.

If she hadn't taken food to help out her mam she would have had enough to pay the stabling bill, she thought as she tossed and turned restlessly. As it was, she had only a few shillings to last the week, 2/5d in fact. Though mebbe she could have got something on the slate in Haswell. She could have given Jack what she had. Now he might get three or four pounds for the chest and have money left to gamble with when he had paid to get the horse and trap out of the stable. He might lose and then borrow again and not come home at all. He might – but what was the good of thinking like this? As the night wore on she became less and less hopeful. By, it had been a flaming rotten day, it had an' all.

In the grey dawn, Eliza was wakened by the sound of someone fumbling at the door downstairs. She was filled with relief; thank God, Jack had come home. Everything would be all right now for she would make it up to him. Carefully she picked up Thomas so as not to wake him and laid him in his own little cot. She waited for Jack to come to her bed, she waited and waited and in the end she got out of bed herself, pulled on her shawl, for it was chilly in the early morning air, and went down to find Jack slumped in the chair by the cold grate. He still stank of drink.

'Did you sell it?' Eliza asked. 'Did you get the pony and trap?'

He looked at her blearily. 'Pony and trap? Eeh, I forgot.'

'Jack, did you sell the chest of drawers?'

He nodded and closed his eyes. 'Let me alone, woman, I'm worn out.'

'Come to bed, Jack, please. Come to bed.' It was a waste of time talking to him, the state he was in, she thought.

He snored loudly and stretched out his legs before him. His head lolled against the back of the chair. There would be no waking him for an hour or two at least. Eliza raked out the grate with some difficulty for she had to step over and round his legs and feet all the time. Eventually, though, she managed it and lit the fire with twigs and bits of rag, blowing carefully on a cinder that was still showing a little red. She added a few lumps of the coal she had garnered from the black road on her return from her mother's house a day or two ago and brought home in the basket she had used to take the food.

The room began to warm up. She looked doubtfully at Jack's boots and gaiters. She should try to take them off, for they must be uncomfortable for him. But when she tried he moved and muttered something unintelligible. Best leave him alone. If he had a couple of hours sleep he might go to work at Mr Benson's. Even if he were late he would be able to make it up at the end of the day.

Eliza went through the day in the way she usually did. She brought in water and searched beneath the trees and hedgerows for kindling to bring in and dry on the hearthstone. She made porridge for Thomas and herself and swept and tidied the room, though working all the time round Jack, spread out before the fire.

He stirred at last and sat up and stretched himself and groaned at how stiff he was. He did not speak to Eliza, though he frowned at her when she offered him porridge and instead took a piece of cheese and bread and wrapped them in a handkerchief. Then he rinsed his mouth with a dipper of water from the pail and went out, she hoped to work.

It was another fine day and Eliza couldn't bear just

waiting to see whether he would return or not. She took
Thomas out and they wandered slowly into Haswell as
they had done the previous day. The little boy toddled
about happily enough, decapitating daisies and bringing
them to her. The breeze in her face was warm and her
natural optimism began to return.

What did it matter that they couldn't go back to live
in Alnwick? John Henry had said he would cut Jack and
his family off without a penny so why should she or
Jack think he might have changed his mind? They were
young and healthy and Jack would get over his disappointment and his ill temper with her. He was a good
carpenter and he would make his own way. Just so long
as he didn't get into bad company and start gambling
again.

Eliza bent down to Thomas, who was holding up a
squashed handful of daisy heads for her, pleased with
himself. 'Thank you, Thomas, they're lovely,' she said.
'We'll put them in a saucer of water and show them to
Daddy when he gets home.'

'Dada,' said Thomas and hurried off to garner more.

Soon they were entering Haswell. Eliza didn't go
near Mr Benson's shop just in case Jack should think
she was checking up on him. But she did go round to
the stables to see if Jack had got the pony and tub trap
out. He had not, at least not yet; she could see the
animal tethered and grazing on a patch of grass bordering

the track outside the building. Well, she thought, it was early yet. She bought a sheep's head at the butcher's and a pound of lentils and a stick of barley sugar for Thomas and set off home again with a halfpenny left in her purse.

Jack did not come home at the usual time and Eliza told herself he must be making up for his late start that morning so she wasn't unduly worried. Around tea time, Farmer Dean came past, herding cows back to the milking parlour. He called, 'Cush! Cush!' softly to them and Eliza took little Thomas out to watch, and he called, 'Cush! Cush!' in imitation of the farmer and his arms waved about in excitement.

Farmer Dean smiled at him. 'If you come up to the farm the wife'll give you a few cracked eggs,' he called to Eliza. 'They'll be good for the lad. We have some to spare this time of the year.' His old dog, Jessie, wagged her tail at Eliza, panting and sticking her tongue out. Thomas pointed and said 'Bow,' and Eliza didn't know whether he was trying to say bow-wow for the dog or moo for the cows.

She got her shawl from behind the door and followed the farmer up the lane. Their progress was necessarily slow for the cows ambled at their own pace, turning curious eyes to the woman and child, their full udders swinging slightly.

'I heard there was trouble over by Blue House.' said Farmer Dean.

'Trouble? I was there a few days ago, it was quiet enough,' said Eliza. But she thought of the stranger and the group of laid-off miners listening to him and she was anxious. Had something happened after she left with Thomas?

'The men are agitating for an end to the yearly bond,' said Farmer Dean. Eliza waited as he guided the cows through the gate into the farmyard and the leader headed for the byre. The herd was hurrying now, lowing gently as they found their stalls. Farmer Dean paused and looked at Eliza. He had known her since she was a child and raiding the clover in his meadow with other children from the miners' rows to suck the sweet nectar from the flower shoots. They were sometimes in trouble for climbing his haystacks and loosening the hay or crawling on hands and knees through the ripe barley, playing hide and seek. Still, he liked to see them for he and Alice had no children of their own.

'I don't hold with men rebelling against their masters,' he said. 'They should be able to talk reasonably without any bother.'

'They should,' agreed Eliza. 'But the gaffers have the power, haven't they?' What, after all, did the farmer know? He'd been his own boss for most of his life.

'Well, where would the men be without them giving the work?'

'Free to look for it elsewhere,' said Eliza. 'If my dad is laid idle he can't even take work elsewhere because of the yearly bond. How are they supposed to live?' She was upset; the farmer saw with some alarm that though her eyes flashed angrily they were bright with tears.

'Nay, lass, I was only saying what I think,' he said. 'Away in the kitchen and ask Alice for those eggs.'

'I won't if it's all the same to you,' said Eliza. 'I'd best get the bairn home.'

She turned and marched back down the lane with Thomas on her hip. Farmer Dean called something conciliatory after her but she didn't turn round. He stood, scratching his head. Alice would be wondering why the lass hadn't gone in to see her for hers was a lonely life and she liked company. But he had only said what he thought.

Jack didn't come home that evening and Eliza spent a restless night tossing and turning. Thomas slept well after his day out. When she did eventually fall asleep she woke early in the morning and was filled with thankfulness to realise that Jack had at last come in and was actually already in bed with her. She lay for a few moments, enjoying the feel of his hands on her, ready to kiss and make up. Only his hands were different, not

like Jack's at all for they were softer with not so many
calluses. What's more he didn't smell the same as Jack.

The hands slipped to her breasts and she tried to jump
up but even then she didn't scream, mindful of the baby.
He put a leg over hers to hold her down and a hand over
her mouth and she stared at him in the gloom of the
early dawn. It was Jonathan Moore. Oh God, what was
she going to do? She began to fight against him with all
her strength.

'Lie still! Do as I say,' he hissed at her. She tried to
shake her head but he held it clamped to the pillow.
Beside the bed, Thomas whimpered then lay still.

'You don't want to wake the lad, do you?' he asked.
Carefully he removed his hand, ready to clamp it back
should she shout.

'Get out of my bed, get out,' she grated at him. She
could hardly breathe for the weight of him and her
breasts hurt with the pressure.

'No, I will not,' he said and smiled, his face so close
to hers she could see hair up his nose. She tried to bring
her knee up between them but he was too strong for her.
She managed to curl her fingers into his hair and tugged
as hard as she could and he slapped her roughly.

'Jack will kill you!' she hissed and he laughed.

'He will not, he knows I am here,' he said.

'You're a liar, a rotten, bloody liar!' Eliza was
sobbing now.

'I tell you he knows I am here,' said Jonathan. 'Now come on, be nice to me or it will be the worse for you and your brat too.' For Thomas had woken and was whimpering again, obviously frightened at the strange voice in the room.

'Let me go to the bairn,' said Eliza.

'You think I'm a fool? Let him scream as loud as he likes, there's no one to hear,' said Jonathan. 'I told you, Jack won't come. I won this night with you at cards. Oh, it was all fair and square. Your precious Jack put you up against the pot.'

'I won't do it, I won't be passed around like a whore!'

Jonathan had hold of her hands as he sat up, still astride her. The dawn was becoming brighter and she could see his face properly now. 'It is, after all, a debt of honour, my dear,' he said. 'You know I don't like to use force but that's not to say I won't.'

'It's not my debt!'

Thomas was sobbing now, no longer screaming but sobbing hopelessly. Oh dear God, she thought, how could Jack do this? She felt utterly betrayed.

'You might like it,' said Jonathan and leaned forward and kissed her hard on the lips. Eliza stopped struggling. She gave in not because of the man and his attempt to make this an act of love rather than sex alone but because of little Thomas, still sobbing in the cot by the bed and because of the terrible shock of Jack's betrayal.

Afterwards, when he fell to the bed beside her, still panting with the effort, she got up and went to the cot and picked up the little lad. 'There, now, hinny, there, my bonny,' she murmured as she hugged him to her. She couldn't bear to give him suck with Jonathan in the same room so she went down the rickety ladder into the cold, grey kitchen. She raked the ashes from the fire and added sticks and coal so that it smoked and then blazed up and sat down in the rocking chair and fed the boy. She was not thinking of anything. She didn't allow herself to. Only of the warmth from the fire and the feel of Thomas at her breast.

Jonathan came down the ladder some time later. He looked quite normal, not ashamed, nothing. After the first quick glance Eliza couldn't look at him. She pulled her shawl further over to cover the boy's head and her breast.

'I'll be off now,' said Jonathan. 'I'll see you later on.'

'You will not,' Eliza replied.

'Look, I know the arrangement with Jack was for only one night, but it is not enough. I want you to leave him, I want you for myself; I will protect you.'

Eliza's head shot up at this astonishing statement. She laughed. 'It's a pity it's not going to happen then, isn't it? I'd kill myself first!'

'Eliza, don't say that. I promise you, I won't let you down, not like that man of yours. I never wanted anyone as I want you. I thought once we'd – well, I thought I'd be over it but I'm not and I never will be. Eliza, I'll give you anything, anything you want, just tell me, please!'

Eliza took the boy off the breast, wincing a little for her nipple was sore, not just from Thomas's vigorous suck now he was bigger but also from the man's attentions. She buttoned up her dress and turned to him. She had made up her mind.

'Come tonight if you like,' she said.

Chapter Eleven

Early one morning, a few days after she had found Jonathan Moore in her bed, Eliza set out from her temporary lodging in the Gilesgate area of Durham city. She had left the cottage and gone to Gilesgate as she thought that neither Jonathan nor Jack would think of looking for her there. Besides, she needed to be near the city so she could get the best possible price for the necklace.

'Dada?' Thomas asked and looked into her face enquiringly. 'Dada?'

'Dada's gone away,' she replied. 'There's no one but Thomas and Mammy now.' He would soon forget about Jack, she told herself.

As she walked along, down the hill and up the other side of the valley towards the great cathedral just looming out of the mist, she was filled with hope for the future. The shock of Jack's betrayal was still like an open wound in her breast but at least it had made her realise she could rely on no one but herself. Her mam might rail against Jack but she believed that a woman leaving her man was beyond forgiveness. It was just not Christian. No, she was on her own now.

She wondered what her mam would have said if she had known about Jack's gambling with her favours. Or Jonathan Moore turning up in her bed. She did not wonder what Jonathan's reaction had been when he turned up at the cottage the night before last and found her gone. Not that she cared at all. She didn't want to think of Jonathan Moore ever again.

Eliza smiled bitterly to herself as she hoisted a still sleepy Thomas higher on her shoulder. By, the lad was heavy now he was almost two years old. The sun broke through the mist and lit up the battlements of the castle and towers of the cathedral and Eliza brightened. Yesterday she had taken the necklace to three pawnshops and got three different estimates as to how much it was worth. Now she had it stitched securely into the pocket of her skirt and was taking it back to the first pawnbroker's, the one who had offered her the most money.

'Stand down, now, pet,' Eliza said to Thomas. She put him on his feet and took hold of his hand. The path was climbing now and she was becoming short of breath. Also, she was hungry; she had had no breakfast though there had been a small piece of bread left from the loaf she had bought yesterday. Thomas had needed that; he was too big now to be dependent on the breast totally. Soon her milk would dry up altogether.

'Howay, hinny,' she encouraged him as she took his hand. 'You're a big lad now, aren't you? Not a babby any more.' They went on up the hill, slower than before because she had to adjust to his pace. Still it would not be long before they reached Silver Street where the shop was located.

As they walked Eliza went over her plans. Some of the money would have to go on keeping her and Thomas until she had learned to read and write properly. That was the first objective. When she could do that she was going to get into a hospital where nurses were trained. For that was what she had decided to do, train as a nurse. There would be enough money to have little Thomas looked after while she trained, she was sure of that. After all, the necklace was worth two hundred and forty pounds. She had had to ask the pawnbroker twice for she could hardly believe it. Mr Timms was a jeweller as well as a pawnbroker and he had been suspicious at first and asked questions as to how she had come by it. Eliza had told him it came from her husband, now deceased, who had worked for the Duke of Northumberland. It wasn't totally a lie, Jack was dead to her, oh yes he was.

They were approaching the market place now and Eliza kept Thomas close to her skirts for there was a good deal of traffic: carts loaded with produce for the market and a couple of carriages turning to go up the cobbled street to the grand houses around the castle and cathedral. Her heart beat fast in anticipation of the moment when she would have the money in her hand and her new adventure would begin.

'Please, sir, are the reading and writing classes still held here?'

Eliza looked at the clergyman in the black robe and white collar who was standing in the entrance to the town hall. He looked up from the papers he had been glancing through and gave her his grave attention. She looked him in the eye, secure in the knowledge that she had forty pounds (forty pounds!) in her pocket beside the bank draft for two hundred stuffed between her breasts. She felt as rich as the queen.

'They are,' he replied. 'A class is just starting, in fact. Go through that door on the right.'

Eliza thanked him and went into the room he indicated. There were perhaps fifteen or twenty people already there, sitting quietly at deal tables and each with a slate and stick of chalk. A lady dressed in a plain black skirt and white shirtwaister stood at the front of the room beside a blackboard and easel. She beckoned to Eliza to come forward.

'Have you come to join the class?' she asked, and Eliza nodded.

'I'm Miss Johnson and I will be your teacher. Is the child well behaved? I'm afraid we can't have any disruption. Can't you get someone to mind him while you are here? You realise that if he makes a noise you will have to take him out?'

'Aye, I do, miss,' Eliza mumbled as Miss Johnson paused for breath. Her elation at actually starting on her plan had disappeared. For two pins she would have gone back out of the door, for everyone in the class was staring at her.

'I'll fill in this form for you, then. You have the two pounds fee?'

'Aye, I do, miss,' Eliza said again. In fact she had two sovereigns clutched in her hand. She watched as Miss Johnson wrote something on the paper. The teacher took her name and age, raising one eyebrow at the double-barrelled surname as though she doubted it could be right.

'To which parish do you belong?'

'Emm—' Eliza paused, unsure.

'Where do you worship?' Miss Johnson demanded. That was easier, Eliza decided.

'Blue House Wesleyan Methodist Chapel,' she replied and hoisted Thomas, who was unsmiling and sucking his thumb, higher onto her shoulder.

Miss Johnson put down her pen. 'I'm sorry,' she said. 'To join this class you have to be a communicant of the

Church of England. I'm sure the Wesleyans run some sort of literacy scheme of their own. Apply to them.'

Eliza found herself back out in the market place among the stalls loaded with fruit and vegetables and fish from Shields. She stood for a few moments, utterly crushed, then she lifted her head and stuck her chin in the air.

'Howay, Thomas,' she said. 'We'll have a penny dip from the butchers down Silver Street then we'll go and see if there is anyone at the Wesleyan's in Elvet. That woman was likely right about them running classes. An' it'll be cheaper an' all.'

They sat beside the Wear, which flowed under Framwellgate Bridge at the bottom of the bank and ate the penny dip. They shared it, for the bread bun was quite large and the butcher had dipped it into the brown gravy in the tin after roasting pork and not just the pork fat. Thomas munched away, totally absorbed in the food for he too was hungry. When they had finished, Eliza dipped her handkerchief in the river and rubbed the grease from Thomas's mouth and chin. Then they climbed the hill to Castle Chare and down the other side to Elvet.

She found the chapel easily enough and there was activity in the schoolroom, she could see. Hoisting Thomas higher on her shoulder once more, she went in.

'You want to join our adult literacy class?' The elderly man who was there looked her over as she nodded and murmured she did. 'They are held in the evening, every weekday evening in fact. Can you manage that?' He looked at Thomas, sleeping on Eliza's shoulder. 'Can you get the lad minded?'

'I can, sir,' she replied, though she had not even thought of how she would do that. Then, more honestly, 'At least will try, sir.' Desperately, she hoped that adult literacy meant reading, writing and arithmetic. But the man had been standing before a group of children, all seated at wooden desks and poring over slates.

'It will be threepence a week, can you pay threepence? You are a widow?'

'I am, but I have a little money.'

'Well then. My name is Mr Wood and I am a retired schoolmaster. We make it a rule that members of the class must come every weekday evening and attend a place of worship every Sunday. You can start tonight. I can enrol you now if you wish.'

In ten minutes she was back outside on the road with a piece of paper clutched in her hand. She was to hand it over to the teacher at seven o'clock that evening. At last, she thought, she was on her way, she had made the first step. The next one was to find lodgings close to the chapel and also someone to mind Thomas for a few hours every night. There would be plenty on offer this near to the gaol, she thought. People didn't like to be too close to such a forbidding place. Jack wouldn't look for her there either. It was as good a hiding place as Gilesgate.

'I'll look in on the bairn while you're at the class,' her new landlady, Mrs Reynolds, conceded. 'It'll cost you threepence a night, mind, and he has to be in bed before you go an' all.'

Eliza considered this. Threepence a night, but really, she had no alternative if she was to start that evening. 'Thank you,' she said eventually. 'Thomas goes to bed at six every night and he's a good sleeper.'

'Aye well, I don't mind helping out a poor widow,' said Mrs Reynolds in a virtuous tone. 'Though I suppose your husband, God rest his soul, left you something to live on?'

She didn't mind robbing a widow, either, Eliza thought savagely. Though she smiled enigmatically and didn't answer the question. The room, in the basement of the old stone house, smelled of damp and the rent was two shillings and sixpence a week plus the one and threepence for the babyminding. But still, it was in the shadow of the prison walls and not five minutes,' walk away from the chapel schoolroom. Jack wouldn't look for her here, she told herself again. Jonathan Moore, she reckoned, would not be looking for her at all for he would have found someone new to chase after.

*

Within a month, Eliza could sign her name and print out the alphabet. She spent her mornings practising and in the afternoons took Thomas out for fresh air and exercise whatever the weather, though luckily that summer was unusually fine and they could take the footpath behind Elvet and play in the fields there. She encouraged him to run about and tire himself out before taking him home to supper and bed.

They lived frugally and the money lasted well so that she had almost two hundred and thirty pounds left by September. Eliza counted it carefully before going to chapel one Sunday morning. She walked holding Thomas's hand as he toddled beside her. He had grown in these last few months since she had weaned him and he was turning into a proper boy rather than a baby. His vocabulary increased by the day and he played imaginary games by himself and chattered and sang snatches of nursery rhymes and songs he had learned at Sunday School.

'We won't be long before we go to London, Thomas,' Eliza said to herself rather than the boy and he looked up at her and smiled.

'Tot come,' he said. It was his name for himself and even though he could say Thomas now he insisted he was Tot. Eliza felt a surge of anticipation. The future stretched out before her and she was ready for it. They were turning in the gate of the chapel when she heard her name called. She froze for a moment, her heart plummeting. Grasping Thomas's hand tightly, she turned slowly round. It was Peter Collier, the union man.

'Mrs Mitchell-Howe, isn't it? It's good to see you. But what are you doing here? Apart from coming to the service, I mean.'

'I-I – live here,' she stammered. Thomas clung to her skirt and stared up at the strange man with large, wary eyes.

'There now, so do I,' he said. 'Is your husband inside?'

'No,' Eliza replied, then in a rush went on, 'Thomas and me, we are on our own now.'

'Dear me! I'm sorry to hear that, lass,' Peter said kindly. 'An accident, was it?'

'No, it—' Just then the organ began to play as the service began. 'I'll have to take the bairn to the Sunday School,' she said. 'I'm sorry.'

'I'll speak to you afterwards?' he called after her as she picked up Thomas and sped round the side of the building. He heard that she said something but her answer was lost as she went inside the schoolroom.

Later, as she crept into the back of the chapel, she saw him sitting only a few pews in front of her. His head with the dark hair speckled a little with grey was bent over his hymn book as he joined in the singing. She watched him, unable to keep her mind on the service for her thoughts were in a whirl. She realised that he thought that she was a widow. Well, she would not tell him otherwise. She thought of slipping away before the end of the service to avoid meeting him again. That was best; he wouldn't find out whereabouts she lived. Besides, he wouldn't be that interested, of course he would not.

Accordingly, Eliza slipped out as the congregation bent heads for the benediction and went to pick up Thomas from the Sunday School. But then, there he was, standing by the side door into the schoolroom, waiting for her.

'I thought we could walk by the river along Elvet fields,' he said. 'If you have no objection, of course.'

Eliza's normally quick mind seemed to have slowed considerably. When she didn't answer immediately he offered his arm and they walked down the bridle path away from the houses of Elvet towards the Wear. On the opposite bank the woods rose to the skyline; some of the leaves were already showing coppery and russet hues. Thomas, released now to run about as he liked, did just that, chasing after starlings and wood pigeons pecking about in the grass, and shouting, 'Shoo! Shoo!' and laughing with delight when they flew up into the air in alarm. Eliza watched him in case he strayed too near the bank-side of the Wear.

'I'm working from Durham now,' said Peter. 'It's fairly central to the county and we'll have the union on its feet soon. The government and the owners must see that even pitmen have their rights.'

'I don't know if they will,' Eliza said doubtfully. She thought of Jonathan Moore and his father. They were small when it came to colliery owners, for some of the iron-masters owned many large mines in the county. But even the Moores were powerful compared with the miners. Those who hewed the coal had no power at all.

Peter looked down at her. 'I'm sorry,' he said gently. 'I should not be burdening you with my problems for you must have enough of your own.' He hesitated for a moment. He had the sense that she did not want to talk about the past. Perhaps it was too painful for her.

'Tell me about your plans,' he went on. 'Are you happy here in the city?'

This Eliza could talk about and with enthusiasm. She told him proudly of how she had learned to read and write and was even now working her way through the first novel she had read in her life. She had borrowed it from a cheap lending library in Saddler Street.

'It's called *Adam Bede*. And it's written by a woman though she has a man's name. George Eliot, she is called. Mr Wood told me it was a woman, though. It must be hard for a woman, even if she is educated,' Eliza added. She looked up into his face and her dark violet eyes sparkled. 'The whole world seems different when you can read,' she said.

Chapter Twelve

Peter Collier walked back to his lodgings in a thoughtful frame of mind. He knew more about what had happened to Eliza than he had revealed. For instance, in his travels around the coalfield he had heard rumours of her husband being a gambler and of the scandalous bet he had had with Jonathan Moore. It was impossible to keep things like that quiet. He thought about these things as he walked over Elvet Bridge. He had enjoyed being with Eliza, he admitted to himself that he liked her; more than that, he was attracted to her.

'She is married,' he said aloud to himself and a clergyman, the only other person in hearing distance, looked at him in surprise then hurried on his way.

Peter knew also that Eliza had not been in touch with her family. Of course, even if she sent a letter, something she could now do, her parents couldn't read. Though perhaps her brothers could by now as they attended the

Sunday School. Peter wondered about her husband. Eliza had not said so but the implication had been that she was a widow. Jack had disappeared from the area, according to gossip, but Peter doubted he was dead and if he was not then he still had rights over Eliza and the lad no matter what he had done.

Well, he decided as he opened the door of the small terraced house under the shadow of the railway arch where he was staying, he would tell no one he knew where Eliza was. Not even her parents. Meanwhile, he needed to find some sort of work that would keep body and soul together yet allow him time for his main purpose in life. That was to improve the condition of the men in the pits and get rid of the iniquitous bond.

It would only come with a strong union, a union with enough power to stand up for the men in the pits and he was determined to achieve it. This time the union would not fail as it had done a few years ago. No, indeed, it would not.

Eliza walked back to her lodging feeling relaxed and happier than she had for a long time. She walked along holding Thomas's hand at first, until he stumbled and she realised he was almost asleep on his feet. She swung him up into her arms and cradled him and his eyelids closed immediately. She kissed his forehead, overcome with love for him. Oh, she thought, she would succeed in making a good life for them both. Thomas would have a good start in life, she swore it.

She turned into the mean street under the shadow of the gaol and suddenly a man stepped out in front of her and barred her way. For a minute she didn't realise it was Jack, for she was looking down at her little son.

'What are you—' she began to ask and then she looked up into his face. 'Jack,' she said. 'Go away, Jack, I'm not coming back to you. Not after what you did.'

He was dressed in a suit of good broadcloth and a white shirt and neck cloth. His hair was combed back from his forehead and he looked like a prosperous gentleman. She took all this in as she took a step back away from him. 'Go away,' she repeated.

'Don't fret, I haven't come for you. You can go to hell for all I care. No, I've come for my son. You're not fit to look after him.'

What was the matter with him? Eliza had never seen Jack like this. He was a gambler and he'd made that terrible deal with Jonathan Moore but he was not a vindictive person. Looking up at him now she saw his face was contorted with fury. He looked at her as though he hated her. She tried reasoning with him but to no good at all.

'Don't be soft, Jack, you cannot take Thomas! A little bairn belongs with his mother.'

'Not when that woman runs away from her man, he

doesn't. And robs him blind an' all! What did you do with the necklace?'

'I sold *my* necklace. What do you think we're living on?'

'You mean to say your fancy man isn't keeping you?'

'Fancy man?' Eliza was genuinely bewildered. 'I haven't got a fancy man!'

'Oh aye? Then I didn't see you all cosy with that Peter Collier down by the racecourse then?'

Eliza gazed at him and clutched Thomas more tightly to her. He stirred and started to protest but he was not properly awake and settled down again.

'I just met him at chapel,' she said. 'And any road, what is it to you? You handed me over to Jonathan Moore on a bet.'

'I was desperate. You should have been glad to do it for me, get me out of a hole! An' if you think for one minute I believe that you just met him in chapel . . . By, Eliza, you're worse than a whore! Just met him in chapel, indeed, and I saw you with your heads together over my lad down there by the Wear.'

'We were only talking!'

'Aye, only talking, I know.'

A few people had gathered nearby and were listening avidly to the row. Someone gave a short laugh and they murmured to each other.

'Give her what for, lad; show her who's boss,' a male

voice shouted. But Eliza hardly heard. Her head was whirling with fear and anger.

'My God, Jack, you think you own me.'

'Aye well, I do own you,' Jack replied. 'And the lad too, he's mine and I'm taking him an' all. I'm not having him brought up by a loose woman. Now give him to me or I'll take him. A bairn belongs to his father, that's the law.'

He grabbed Thomas and wrenched him from her and Thomas woke up with a scream of alarm.

'Give him back! Give him back, Jack! Jack, you can't take him!' Eliza turned to the small knot of people standing round. 'Help me, please help me, he's stealing my bairn!'

'Nay, lass,' a woman said. 'He has the right. You should have thought of that before you went a-whoring.'

'I didn't I – Jack! Where are you going? Come back, come back or I'll get the polis!'

'Aye, do that,' said Jack and laughed. He was heading for the bridge and for the first time Eliza noticed the cab waiting there. She ran after him but the man who had advised Jack to hit her stuck out his foot and she fell to the ground.

'There was no need for that,' a woman said. 'Poor lass has lost her bairn.'

She bent down and helped Eliza to her feet. Eliza rushed after the cab but Jack had Thomas inside by then and the cab man was setting the horse off at a gallop. Eliza ran after it but it was hopeless. Any other day the traffic in the narrow streets of the city would have slowed down the cab's progress, but it was Sunday and there was no other traffic about.

Eliza ran, her breath ragged and with an agonising stitch in her side, but the cab was getting away from her. It turned into the market place and by the time she managed to get there it had disappeared from view. She ran round the market place, looking down every exit but there was no sign of the cab. She sank down on the cobbles to get her breath back. She was sobbing and crying and her dress had dirty streaks down the front from her fall and her dark hair had pulled loose from its hairpins and hung over her face. Somehow she had lost a shoe and there was a hole in her stocking where she had carried on running over the rough cobbles.

'Bloody tinkers, cluttering up our streets and on a Sunday an' all.'

Eliza pushed her hair back from her face and looked up. A couple stood there and it was the man who had spoken. Hastily, she wiped her face with the back of her hand and stood up.

'Hush,' the woman replied. 'There's something the matter with her.'

'Aw, man,' said the man. 'She's just a heathen Irish tinker looking for sympathy. Get off the streets, woman, you're a disgrace. You lot shouldn't be let in the country.'

Eliza lifted her chin. 'Let in the country? I have as

much right here as you, I was born in Durham! Well, in the county any road, my father is a miner.'

'Aye, well, that's as bad. The blight of the county are the bloody pitmen. Give the place a bad name. Shouldn't be allowed in the city.'

Eliza drew herself up. 'You are impittent,' she said as loftily as she could manage and walked away as best she could in one shoe. Once out of sight she took off the shoe and went on in stockinged feet.

The incident had steadied her somehow and as she walked she was planning what she could do to get back her child. First of all she would pack her belongings and pay the landlady. And then she would go in search of Jack and she would find him, even if she had to search the length and breadth of England. Aye, and Scotland an' all, she vowed.

Eliza broke down once when she was back in her room on Elvet. It was when she was packing little Thomas's clothes in the straw luggage basket she had bought to go to London. She had seen the basket one day on a second-hand market stall and realised it would look better than carrying her clothes in a bundle.

Sitting down on the bed she cried. Deep wrenching sobs that came up from her very soul. She allowed herself a few minutes then got to her feet, washed her face in the chipped enamel basin on the washstand and tidied her hair. She forced herself to think of other things; maybe she should have bought a Gladstone bag instead, but the only one she saw was very dilapidated so she had decided on the basket. She had better change her dress, for this one was dirty and torn and she needed to look respectable.

Would Peter Collier help her find Thomas if she could only find him? No, that was no good. She would only waste valuable time looking for him. No, she would catch the train to Alnwick and see if Jack's family had any inkling of where he and Thomas were. Thomas . . . Thomas. The ache deep within her swelled and the pain intensified. Dear God, Thomas! Was he crying for her? Oh, please God, no. He was with his da after all. He loved his da, didn't he? Though he hadn't seen him in a few months surely Thomas remembered his father?

No, she wasn't going to think about Thomas, she reminded herself. She was going to do something about it. She buckled the belt around the straw basket then checked the sovereigns sewn in the skirt of her best serge dress and put it on together with her shawl and straw hat and tied the ribbons of the hat under her chin. There, she was ready. She would walk to the railway station and wait for the next train going north.

'I'm sorry, Missus,' the man said. 'There's no more trains the night. There aren't any on a Sunday night. The next one is the milk train come the morn. Five o'clock, that is.' He tipped his cap to Eliza and turned to go back into his office then turned round. 'Listen, lass,' he said, looking at her woebegone expression. 'I'll open the ladies' waiting room for you if you like. I'll have to lock it after you. But if you don't mind me mentioning it, there's a closet in there, a netty, like. And there's still a bit of life in the fire.'

'Thank you,' said Eliza. 'Oh, thank you. You're a real gentleman.' There were benches in the waiting room and the earth closet was in the corner behind closed doors. She tried lying on a bench, using the straw box as a pillow, and only slept at all because she was exhausted and what sleep she had was but fitful and filled with dreams of Thomas sitting on his own and sobbing for her. He held out his arms to her and she ran to him. 'Mammy's here, pet,' she called but she couldn't reach him, always there was something in the way.

She woke to the porter shaking her shoulder. 'Get up, Missus, you don't want to miss the milk train, do you?' he asked. 'The stationmaster will be here in a minute anyway. I might lose my place if he finds out you've been here all night.'

Eliza struggled to her feet feeling as though a great weight was pressing on her forehead. She thanked him and offered him a threepenny bit but he shook his head.

'Nay, lass,' he said. 'I didn't do it for a tip. You likely could do with it yourself.'

Indeed, he was a gentleman, Eliza said to herself as she climbed aboard the train. She winced as she sat down on the hard wooden seat. She was stiff and sore from her night in the waiting room and in a fog of tiredness. But she was not hungry even though she had eaten nothing since the afternoon before. She felt as though she would never eat again or if she did the food would choke her.

She sat and watched the smoke from the engine float off in front of her for she was sitting with her back to the engine. It swirled rather like her thoughts, she mused. And the chugging and clicking of the wheels on the rails seemed to say over and over, Thomas, Thomas, my little Thomas. Thomas . . .

She began to wonder if she was doing the right thing, flying off to Alnwick. Maybe she should have looked nearer to Durham. Jack must be living somewhere near, else what was he doing in the old city? Was she travelling away from her bairn? Anxiety clutched at her: while she was in Northumberland Jack might go somewhere away, down south, even abroad. He had looked prosperous yesterday; he would have enough money to buy tickets on a steamship. He must have had a big win at the races or something. Eliza stared out of the window as the train slowed.

They were on Stephenson's railway bridge; soon they would be in Newcastle where she would have to change for Alnwick. Once again she had to force the panic down. She couldn't afford panic; she had to get Thomas back.

*

'Mammy? Mammy?'

Jack looked at his little son's tear-stained face. Thomas sat on the bed in the room Jack had taken in a coaching inn in Neville's Cross. Thomas sat very still and gazed beseechingly at his father. The boy had run to the door time and time again and tried to get out; hammering on the wooden panels with his tiny fists. Each time Jack had brought him back and sat him on the bed. The last time he had started to get annoyed with Thomas and had practically thrown him on the bed. He had been rougher than he had intended and Thomas caught his hand on the brass rail and his screams had intensified. The owner of the inn had knocked on the door and asked if Thomas was all right.

'Aye, he's fine,' Jack had replied. 'Only tired and in need of sleep.' The innkeeper had gone away and after a while Thomas calmed down. Still, he wanted his mother, Jack thought. Well, he would soon forget her. Children did, didn't they?

Thinking of Eliza, Jack was filled with a black rage. By, he had never known she was a whore, no, he had not. So he had made that bet with Jonathan Moore but he was desperate, wasn't he? It had been a chance to recoup his losses at that fateful card school. Jack did not normally associate with Jonathan and his friends but the mineowner's son had sought him out and invited him to join them and Jack had been pleased and excited at the chance to make a big win. In the end, he had not enough money for the last big game. The pot was full; his eyes had glistened at the thought of gaining enough to start up again on his own.

'I didn't expect her to go through with it,' he said to Thomas. 'Why did she go through with it? She should have refused. He wouldn't have raped her, of course he wouldn't. And I would be away by then and with the pot an' all.' In fact he had been on the next train for York and the races. With such a stake he was going to win a fortune.

'Tot wants Mammy,' the boy said. He had stopped crying and spoke quietly, gazing up at his father.

'Aye, never mind, pet. I'll get you a sugar bullet,' said Jack.

He thought of how he had come to the city that morning, determined to forgive Eliza. He had found out where she was living after months of searching. After all, he reasoned, it hadn't been all her fault, what had happened. No doubt she would be delighted to see him after trying to live on her own with the bairn. But he had soon found out that she was not. She had been carrying on with that bloody union man. By, the next time he saw Collier he would thrash him to within an inch of his life.

The black rage and jealousy overwhelmed him again.

Chapter Thirteen

'Good day to you, Mr Oxley. Is it all right if I leave my basket with you?' Eliza asked Bill Oxley, the grocer in Alnwick. 'It will be only for a short while.'

'Eeh, it's Mrs Mitchell, isn't it? Mrs Jack Mitchell, that is. By, you do look tired. Aye, of course, leave the basket here, I'll put it in the corner out of the way.'

'Mitchell-Howe,' murmured Eliza automatically. She was about ready to fall down, she was so exhausted. 'And thank you, Mr Oxley, I'm obliged to you.'

'What? Oh aye, but the family has been known in the town as Mitchell a long time. It's more convenient, like,' said the grocer. He looked at Eliza's pale face, the shadows under her eyes. 'I tell you what, why don't you go through to the back? Mrs Oxley will make you a bite to eat and a pot of tea.'

Eliza was about to refuse but she was hungry and tired, she realised. And she had to have her wits about her when she talked to Henry. If Henry consented to talk to her, she thought bleakly.

'It's very kind of you, Mr Oxley,' she said. 'I will be glad to if it's not too much trouble for Mrs Oxley.'

The room behind the grocery store was warm and smelled of new bread. Mrs Oxley was a little woman almost as round as she was tall. She had bright dark eyes and snow-white hair combed back into a bun. Tendrils had escaped from the bun and she was perpetually pushing them back beneath the white cap she had perched on the top of the bun. Her smile was friendly but inquisitive.

'Mrs Mitchell, I am pleased to see you. Sit yourself down and I'll make you a bit of breakfast in a trice. Would you like a bit of bacon and an egg? The bacon is from one of our own pigs and the eggs new laid. There's a fresh stotty cake just out of the oven—'

'Thank you, Mrs Oxley. A slice of stotty cake will be fine,' Eliza interrupted the flow. 'I've just got here and the journey is tiring.'

Mrs Oxley chatted on as she pushed the kettle from the bar on to the fire and got out the bread and a pot of fresh butter. 'The butter's fresh an' all, I made it only yesterday,' she said as she put the plate on the table in front of Eliza. 'By, it was a shame about Mr Mitchell, wasn't it?'

For a moment Eliza thought she was talking about

Jack and she looked at her in surprise. Then she realised that Mrs Oxley meant John Henry.

'Yes, a pity,' she murmured and took a sip of tea. It was strong and sweet and instantly reviving. The flat bread cake was warm and the butter melting into it. It tasted heavenly to her. She was hard put not to wolf it down for she was ravenously hungry.

'You'll be going on up to the house to see the family? I could get Bill to drive you, it's a fair step,' offered Mrs Oxley.

'No, thank you, but no. The walk will do me good.'

Mrs Oxley sat down at the table and watched as Eliza finished off the stotty cake. Eliza ate a second slice but then refused a third.

'I must be getting on,' she said, then realised she was being abrupt. 'I'm grateful to you, you've been kind.' The grocer's wife seemed to accept this.

'Oh aye,' she said. 'I suppose you'll have to get back to your man and the little lad.' She walked with Eliza to the front door of the shop. 'How are they, in good fettle? A lovely bairn he is, I'm sure.'

A stab of pain shot through Eliza at the mention of Thomas. Her face must have changed because both Mr and Mrs Oxley looked at her curiously. She struggled to keep her composure.

'He is,' she murmured. 'Thank you.'

'Living in Durham, aren't you?' Mrs Oxley asked. By

this time they were out of the shop and standing on the step.

'Yes,' said Eliza. Unable to bear any more questions, she thanked her again and headed off up the street, walking at a fast pace with her head down. It took her ten minutes to get her emotions under control and by then she was in sight of the house.

Her heartbeat quickened as she braced herself to open the gate, walk up the path and lift the heavy brass knocker. The house was silent and she began to wonder if she had wasted precious time coming here. She lifted the knocker and banged it as hard as she could against the brass stop. The sound of it was very loud. She waited a few minutes, then was turning away when the door opened and there stood her mother-in-law. She was dressed in black bombazine and wore a white cap on her hair, pulled low on her forehead. She was thinner than Eliza recalled and it made her nose look even sharper than she remembered it.

'What do you want?'

The woman stood with one hand holding the door and the other the doorpost, as though she feared Eliza would force her way in.

'Good morning to you, mother-in-law,' Eliza was stung into replying. 'I want to come in, I need to talk to you.'

'You can say all you want to say where you are,' said

Annie. 'Have you come to plead for that good-for-nothing man you married? I told him to keep away; he's no son of mine. More like a son of Satan. I don't want to see him again. Any road, where's the little lad? By, I expect he doesn't grow up like Jack. I did my best for Jack but he was born a bad 'un.'

'I thought you might know where Jack is. He's took the bairn,' said Eliza. Her heart had plummeted. All the way here she had thought that Annie might know where Jack and Thomas were. Even though she knew Jack and his mother were not so much as speaking to each other she had thought Jack's mother would know where Jack was staying. For goodness sake, she was his *mother*.

'Took the lad? Why would he do that? He cannot keep himself never mind a bairn.' Annie opened the door a little wider. 'He's left you, has he? Well, I'm not surprised. But why has he taken the lad?' She gazed at Eliza with a mixture of disdain and suspicion. 'Howay in if you must. I'm not some pit wife to gossip on the doorstep.'

Eliza's first instinct was to turn and walk away. Why had she come here? Annie was a nasty-tongued, terrible woman, oh, she was. Her own mother was worth two of her.

'I said come in, howay then,' said Annie and opened the door wider. Perhaps if she went in and talked longer with her mother-in-law she would pick up a clue as to where Jack was likely to be. In spite of Annie's talk, surely she had some motherly feelings towards him. Eliza couldn't imagine ever cutting Thomas out of her life altogether and surely, deep down, Annie felt the same? She followed her mother-in-law into the house. Annie led the way into the kitchen; evidently she wasn't good enough for the front of the house. Eliza didn't care.

The kettle was singing on the hob of the black-leaded grate but Annie did not offer Eliza a cup of tea or ask her to sit down, against all the rules of hospitality that Eliza had grown up with. She still didn't care; she stood straight and lifted her chin. There was no sign of Bertha.

'Well, are you going to answer me? After all, the babby is my grandson, I have a right to know what is happening with him.' Annie stood with her back to the fire and her arms folded over the black bombazine bodice. Her thin lips worked together and her chin quivered though her expression was as forbidding as ever.

'And I'm his mother. Though I know you would like it better if just about anybody else was.' Eliza was trying hard to hang on to her temper. 'Do you know where Jack is living now? 'Cause if you don't I'm wasting my time.'

'I haven't heard a word about him since Henry threw him out of the house after his father's funeral. I don't want to neither.'

'What about Henry? Do you reckon he's heard anything?'

Annie shrugged. 'How do I know? Henry tells me nowt. Now tell me, why did he take the lad? What have you been up to? It must have been something bad. Been with another man, have you? You're just the sort—'

'Shut up! Shut your mouth. I've done nowt wrong, I haven't. Except leave Jack. You don't know what he did, neither.'

'No an' I don't want to. But if you left him he has a right to take the lad.'

She wasn't going to find out anything from Annie, Eliza realised. And standing here arguing was just wasting time. Oh, she had been a fool to come. She turned and marched out to the front door and pulled it open, taking great gulps of fresh air. By, she couldn't stand the atmosphere in that house, she thought as she began to walk away, going back towards Alnwick. Behind her she heard Annie shout something after her but she did not turn round. Her head throbbed and her eyes were blurred. Dear God, what could she do now but go back to Durham and start her search all over again? Oh Thomas, she thought, Thomas, where are you?

Eliza went into Oxley's shop to pick up the oblong straw basket. Mr Oxley had put it behind the counter for her. 'Seen to your business then, Mrs Mitchell?' he asked, the curiosity returning to his face. She nodded, too full to speak.

'You look upset, hinny,' he said. His head was on one side as though inviting her confidence.

'I'm just tired,' she managed to say. 'Thank you for everything, Mr Oxley. I must go for the train now. I have to get back.'

'Oh aye, the bairn.' He nodded in understanding. She picked up the basket by the leather belt that held the lid closed and hurried out.

Eliza was almost to the train station when she ran into Bertha, the little maid who worked for Annie. She was carrying a bundle tied up in a grey woollen shawl.

'Mrs Jack.' The girl smiled. She had grown in the last couple of years but she was still small and thin. Her mousy-coloured hair poked out from under her bonnet. As she stood for a moment she transferred the bundle from one hand to another as though it was heavy.

'Bertha, it's lovely to see you,' said Eliza. 'Where are you going with that bundle?'

'I'm off to Newcastle, I've got a place there,' Bertha replied. 'I was turned off at the Mitchells'. Only I've not been on a train before.'

Eliza looked at the girl. She did have a frightened look about her and her normally rosy complexion was pale. Now she came to think about it, she remembered that Bertha had been a workhouse child; she had no family of her own. She would have to find a place and they were hard to come by in Alnwick, especially for young girls, and Bertha could not be more than fifteen now.

'Well then, we can travel together,' she said. 'For I'm going back to Durham. We can be company for each other.'

Bertha looked relieved as they walked together to the ticket office. They had a wait of half an hour before the southbound train puffed into the station, and they sat on a bench outside the waiting room.

'What happened? Why did you have to leave the Mitchells'?' Eliza asked. 'I thought you were happy there, happy and settled.' Not that she had thought much about the girl at all. But then, she had had a lot on her mind at that time just as she had now.

'It was all right but Mrs Mitchell was a bit sharp,' Bertha replied. 'But it wasn't her what sacked me. It was Mr Henry's wife. By, she's a mean one, that.' The girl looked up at Eliza and seemed to have come to a decision. She sighed. 'She reckoned I was up to something with Henry.'

Eliza was astonished. 'With Henry? What do you mean? You're just a bairn.'

'I'm fifteen. But I wouldn't, no matter what.'

Eliza gazed at her. Bertha was small but now she looked more closely she saw that her figure was definitely developing: there was a curve to her bosom and the shapeless brown stuff dress she wore couldn't entirely hide her neat waist.

'I was down on my hands and knees scrubbing the floor in the hall, like. Mr Henry came up behind me and touched my . . . my bottom. I jumped and spilled the pail. There was soapy water all over the floor. I could have mopped it up but Mrs Henry had seen it all and she turned me off.'

'Oh, Bertha,' Eliza said sadly. Bertha's eyes were swimming but she brushed away the tears with the back of her hand.

'She said I'd tempted him but I didn't, I wasn't even thinking of him. Well, I don't care; I've got another place. Only I've not been out of Alnwick afore. Any road, I reckon it was just an excuse. Mrs Henry was going to get rid of me. She thinks the old woman can do my job now she's got nowt else to do. At least she gave me a reference.'

'The old woman?'

'Aye, Mrs John Henry. Mrs Henry is the gaffer now.'

Eliza thought about it all as they climbed on to the train, one of the third-class carriages now. It took her mind off the continuing ache in her heart for Thomas. Was he crying for her or had he got used to being with his father? No, of course not, it was only a couple of days, not that, even. But she hoped he wasn't too upset.

The carriage was open to the elements and a cold wind was blowing. The two women huddled together for warmth on the wooden bench. If only the rain held off they would be all right; if it didn't they would get soaked. Luckily, the rain held off though dirty smoke swirled into the carriage, leaving smuts on their faces and clothes.

'Did the bairn get a fever?' Bertha asked, peeping at Eliza. She had been wondering about the baby since she had met Eliza in the street. It was not usual for a mother to be anywhere without her baby. But if he was dead, she did not want to remind Eliza of it.

'No, he's fine. He's grand, in fact, running about all over the place. He's with his father the day.' Eliza said it as though she was going back to him now. Bertha had enough troubles of her own. Besides, what she had said was true for she was going to find Jack and Thomas. She would find them and then she would get the bairn back, oh yes she would.

They steamed into Newcastle and it was time for Bertha to get off. She clung to Eliza for a few moments and couldn't control her tears, even though they had not been close when they lived in the same house. Yet Eliza was the only link Bertha had with her old life. For her, Newcastle was another world.

'Listen, Bertha,' said Eliza on impulse. 'I live in Durham city. I do at the minute, any road. If your place doesn't work out you can find me through the chapel at Elvet. They know me there.' The train was in the station now and preparing to move off so Bertha had to alight.

Eliza bit her lip as she watched Bertha fading into the distance, wrapped in swirling smoke. Maybe she shouldn't have said Bertha could seek her out. She had given up her room and she didn't know what her plans were except that she had to search for Thomas. The wheels of the train were picking up speed and going clackety-clack and they were saying 'Thomas, Thomas, Thomas . . .' Please God, she prayed. Let me find Thomas.

For want of knowing whom else to ask for help or, indeed, where else to go, Eliza began to look for Peter Collier. At least he was easier to find than Jack. Though the union had not found a proper home as yet, it was more frowned upon by the authorities than actually outlawed. And there were miners living in the city. So it was barely six o'clock when she knocked on the door in Claypath. And she breathed a sigh of thankfulness when Peter answered her knock.

'Eliza?' he said in surprise and gazed at her white face and dark shadowed eyes. 'Are you in trouble?'

'I am. My husband has stolen my little Thomas,' she said and swayed with fatigue. Her purpose had carried her through this endless day but now she was ready to drop. Peter grabbed hold of her arm.

'Come away in,' he said. 'You can sit by the fire and tell me what this is all about.'

'I told you, Thomas has gone,' Eliza cried but he shook his head.

'Wait. You can tell me inside,' he insisted. 'I've just mashed the tea and there's soup. You look as though you could do with sustenance.'

Chapter Fourteen

The room Peter Collier ushered Eliza into was small and sparsely furnished. There was a deal table set with plain white crockery and a glass salt cellar. A chair was drawn up to the table; evidently Peter had been about to eat. A wooden chair with a high back and a patchwork cushion was drawn up by a small grate set in an iron surround and a pot bubbled on the coals, filling the air with the aroma of boiled mutton. Eliza swallowed the saliva the smell had brought instantly to her mouth. She had not eaten since she was in Alnwick.

'Sit down and get warm,' said Peter. 'We can talk later. First of all you look as though you could do with something in your stomach.'

'Thank you.' Eliza sank down on to the chair by the fire. Though it was early summer the evening was cool. The heat from the fire assailed her and she closed her eyes for a moment and leaned back against the wooden slats. Peter busied himself bringing her a mug of tea, strong and sweet and with a tiny amount of real milk. He moved between a shelf in the corner alcove and the table, bringing another bowl and spoon and setting them on the table. Then he brought up another chair.

'Are you sure you have enough?' Eliza asked anxiously. 'You needn't feed me.'

'There is enough,' Peter said firmly. 'Don't worry.'

She sipped the hot tea, feeling it revive her a little and moved aside slightly as he lifted the pan from the fire and took it to the table. He ladled out the soup into the two plates and brought half a stotty cake from a tin on the shelf.

'Now then,' he said. 'Come on, tuck in while it's hot.' He sliced the bread cake thickly and handed her a slice. The soup was more like a stew for it was thick with lentils and barley and slivers of mutton. He ate with all his concentration on the food and she followed his example. The room was silent.

At last he wiped his plate clean with a piece of bread and chewed it thoughtfully. He sat back in his chair and turned to her. 'Well now,' he said. 'Tell me what's to do. I thought you were a widow. You made out your man was gone.'

'I'm sorry. I didn't mean to say he was dead but when you picked it up like that I let it lie. But he did an awful thing and I left him. I should have told you. Then Jack, my husband, came looking for me and he saw us together yesterday afternoon.'

Peter shrugged. 'We weren't doing anything wrong.' He didn't comment on her leaving her husband. She must have had good reason, he reckoned. It took a lot of courage for a woman to run away from a marriage. Nor did he ask what was the terrible thing Jack had done. It was her business and if she wanted to tell him she would.

'No, but he thinks there is something between us. He took Thomas,' she said in a low tone.

Eliza was holding on to her composure but the effort was tremendous. She gazed down at her empty bowl and blinked rapidly.

'You mean for good?' Peter stared at her incredulously. 'You're the lad's mother, I didn't realise you meant that.'

'He did, he took Thomas and now I don't know where they are.'

'Well, he'll have to bring him back, won't he? How can he look after him properly? A bairn needs his mother,' said Peter. He watched Eliza. She started to tidy the table; more for something to do than anything else. Her expression was desolate and he felt a surge of pity for her.

'Leave the pots,' he said and put out a hand to stay hers. 'Let's talk about it. We must see if we can find them. I'll tell him there's nothing between us. He must believe me.'

Eliza gazed at his hand on hers. It was strong from his work at the coal face and there were a few blue marks from the coal. The nails were clean and cut short. It was a capable-looking hand. She lifted her head.

'Even if we do I might not get Thomas back. Jack is his father. He has all the rights. I didn't realise but it's true.'

'I'm sure Jack will come round. You did nothing wrong after all.'

'I don't know where to look. I've been to his family's house in Alnwick to see if his mother knows where he is but she doesn't.'

'Are you sure? It will be a strange thing if she doesn't. She is his mother after all.'

'They don't get on. His father threw Jack out of the house before he died. Jack is a gambler, you see.'

'Is he?' Peter nodded as though the fact that Jack was a gambler explained a lot. He did not tell her he had heard the scandalous rumours about Jack's gambling. He paused for a while as he tried to think of a plan of action. 'Maybe I can find him through his work,' he said after an interval.

'He's a carpenter,' said Eliza. 'When he's not got the gambling fever on him he is.'

'I can try then. You can try the carpenters in the city and I'll ask as I go round the county in my work,' said Peter. He looked thoughtful, as though he was planning his strategy, but Eliza was horrified.

'That'll take ages,' she said, her voice breaking. She had thought that he would be able to find Jack quickly; she had pinned her hopes on it.

'I'm sorry, lass. But I can't think what else I can do. I have to go about union business.' He looked at her with pity. 'Look now,' he went on. 'Why don't you go back to your lodging and get some sleep? You'll be the better able to search come the morn if you do.'

'I haven't a place. I gave it up this morning. I thought – I don't know what I thought but I just went off. Looking for Thomas. Oh, I'm a fool, I am. Where will I find a room at this time of night?'

Peter pursed his lips. He should have realised when she had her basket box with her. Now what was to do? This was a mean little cottage with only one bedroom and that right under the eaves. There was not even a settee in the room they were in; nothing but the chair by the fire with its one cushion. It was almost eleven o'clock according to the wall clock above the fire.

'If you stay here you can have the bed upstairs and I'll manage in the chair. If we're careful, no one will know. You can't wander the streets all night.'

Eliza gazed at him. 'Oh no, I cannot,' she said.

'I won't bother you,' said Peter.

'It's not that, of course it isn't. I mean I cannot take your bed. I'll sleep in the chair.'

Peter started to protest but she was adamant. In the end that was how it was arranged.

In spite of the hard chair, Eliza was so exhausted that she slept immediately Peter had extinguished the lamp. She woke early in the morning and for a few moments couldn't think where she was. She had slid from the chair during the night and she couldn't even remember when and was lying on the old clippie mat with her head on her arm for a pillow.

She had heard something, was it Thomas? The fire was but a pile of grey ash in the grate and a cold draught was blowing in under the ill-fitting door. A child was crying somewhere very close.

'Thomas? Thomas? I'm coming, pet, I'm coming,' she cried and stumbled to her feet. The room was so small that she cannoned into the table, hurting her hip. Awake fully now, she remembered where she was and the circumstances and she leaned over the table as the black despair washed over her yet again.

There were noises from the cottage next door: someone moving about. The baby stopped crying. The wall must be very thin, she thought dimly. She wondered if Thomas was crying; if he had woken up in an unfamiliar room and was crying for her. Tears stung her eyelids and she brushed them away furiously.

'Are you decent, Eliza?'

Peter was on the stairs. He must be wanting to go to

his work. Well, she was decent if you could call it that. She hadn't even taken off her dress to sleep.

'Come in,' she said and crossed to the small window to draw the thin cotton curtains. Not that it let in much more light, for the curtains were so thin it had penetrated them easily.

'I have to be at Seaham this morning,' said Peter. 'I thought I'd make an early start.' He looked slightly embarrassed as he felt the stubble on his chin.

'I'll go now,' said Eliza. 'Thank you for everything. I'll slip away before anyone notices I'm here.'

Peter nodded. He could not afford for anyone to know she had spent the night in the cottage with him. No one would believe it was innocent.

'I will seek out every carpenter's shop in the city,' she said. 'And Sherburn too if I have the time.'

'Come back tonight,' he said. 'Leave your basket box here. Maybe I can get you lodging for a few nights up the street. There's a widow woman, Mrs Hill, she sometimes lets out a room.'

There were men about when Eliza slipped out into the street but they weren't interested in her or anyone else at that time of the morning. They trudged along on their way to work with their heads down and hands in their pockets against the early morning chill. She made her way up to the market place past St Nicholas's church and went first to the carpenter's shop that had once belonged to Jack. Of course it was still shuttered for it wouldn't open until eight. But the name over the door said the proprietor was someone called Jenkins and it was unlikely that Jack, flush as he was now (he must have had a big win), she thought distractedly, well, Jack wouldn't be working for someone else.

Still, she walked around the side when she heard the sound of a saw coming from there. After all, a carpenter might know someone of his own trade was working nearby. This line of reasoning soon proved false.

'I've heard of Jack Mitchell-Howe,' the workman who came to the door said. 'The name sticks in the mind, like, don't it? But he's not working round here, lass, not as I know of.'

He watched as she walked away along the alley, wondering why a good-looking lass like that one was asking after a man. She didn't seem like the sort of woman a man would walk out on. He wouldn't, any road. He took a last breath of fresh air and went back in and picked up his saw.

Eliza started on a systematic search of all the carpenters' shops in the city, pausing only to buy bread and cheese at the market. She ate as she went along. The day brightened and a slight breeze blew as she walked but she hardly noticed. All her attention was on her search for Jack and, more especially, Thomas.

*

Jack was filled with fury and jealousy as he sat in the cab, holding on to Thomas, who was trying to get out even when the cab was rolling over the bridge at a good pace.

'Tot wants Mammy,' the little boy cried piteously to him. 'Tot wants Mammy, please?'

He fought against Jack and Jack held him by his upper arms but the boy still struggled. Eventually his sobs died down and he stopped asking for Eliza. They drove down Silver Street and along to the house where he had brought Eliza and the baby when they came down from Northumberland. For Jack had taken the house again when he had a great stroke of luck on the horses. He told himself it would bring Eliza back to him. He would explain that it was all a mistake: he hadn't intended to lose his bet with Jonathan Moore; he had been on a sure thing. Jonathan had cheated him, oh aye, he had. The man had lechered after Eliza ever since he met her, he knew that an' all. But the other card players were friends of Jonathan, they had backed him up. Blast them to hell, he thought savagely.

Still, Eliza had no right to leave him; they were man and wife, weren't they? It was a sin to break the marriage vows. Jack stared out of the small window of the cab as it pulled up before the house. Thomas had fallen asleep with tears still wet on his cheeks. Aw, Jack told himself, the lad would forget about his mother. He was young enough.

He paid off the cab and went into the house, carrying Thomas, and laid him down on the sofa. Thomas murmured and stuck his thumb in his mouth but did not open his eyes. Jack sat down on a chair and stared at the small form. What was he going to do with him? He thought about the races at Doncaster. He had intended to take the train next week in time for the start of the meeting.

He had a foolproof system for winning now and he was desperate to try it out. It involved the favourite of each race, and as soon as a crony of his had explained the system to him he had known it would work. Oh, it was a sure thing and it would make his fortune and when it did Eliza could go to hell. He wouldn't have her back if she came crawling to him on her hands and knees. What's more she wouldn't see Thomas again, oh no. Jack smiled mirthlessly.

Still, for the moment he had the problem of what to do with the lad while he was at the race meeting. He thought about his mother. The only interest she had shown in him and his family at his father's funeral was when she asked about Thomas. But she was living in the family house at Alnwick with Henry and his sour-faced wife and though they were childless they would not welcome Thomas. Maybe he had acted too hastily in taking the lad; it could have waited until after the meeting. It was too late now, though. Or was it?

Jack was so filled with feverish anticipation of the Doncaster races and the killing he was going to make there that he almost decided to take Thomas back to his mother. He could say he had only done it to frighten Eliza and give her a shock, punish her. But maybe it was worth making a last appeal to his mother. The family owed him something, didn't they?

He rose to his feet and went to fetch one of the wooden writing cases he had made to sell. They were handsome boxes of polished mahogany with fancy brass catches and tooled leather on the writing surface, which was really a sort of inside lid that lifted up to show a cavity holding paper and a few of the newfangled envelopes. He took the pen from its slot and dipped it in the inkpot.

'Dear Mother,' he wrote in his stylish flowing hand, 'I am appealing to you for help with my little Thomas. I had to take him away from his mother for she proved to be a loose woman . . .'

Annie Mitchell-Howe, opening the letter only a few minutes after Eliza had disappeared round the bend in the road leading to Alnwick, read it through twice. She sat down at the table she was laying for the dinner that was eaten in the middle of the day and read it through again.

She had to admit she would like to have a baby to look after again. Thomas was the only grandchild she had and a grandmother had a right to see her grandchildren. She laid the letter down on the tablecloth and tried to think it through.

Oh, she had had enough of being a servant in her own house, she had indeed, she was sick of it. Amelia had turned the little skivvy off and said she and Annie could manage the housework but in truth it was usually Annie who bore the brunt of the work. Annie began to plan what she could do to get her own way. She had sworn she would not take Jack back but there was no reason why she could not let him think she might. Just while she got her hands on the lad. By, she would bring him up to be different from his father, she would an' all.

There was a little house on the edge of Alnwick that would just do her lovely, especially if she had the lad. John Henry had left her a bit of money an' all.

Chapter Fifteen

By late afternoon Eliza was dropping with fatigue. She had trudged round every carpenter's shop in Durham that she knew of and a few that she did not but was told of by workmen. There were the outlying villages, of course, but she was not hopeful of these. She walked up the hill to Neville's Cross. Someone had told her there was a carpenter's shop there; a small factory, in fact, and she supposed Jack could have taken temporary work there. She had a compulsion to try everywhere, however unlikely.

'Nay, lass, we've no one of that name.' A man in shirtsleeves and a brown apron covering his protruding stomach answered her anxious question.

'Thank you anyway,' she said and turned away, her shoulders drooping. As he walked back into his office he wondered about her. A young lass let down by a man, he reckoned. And now she was chasing after him. Aye well, it was a common occurrence.

Halfway along the road back into the city, Eliza sat down on a low wall by an ancient, stone-built water pump put there for the benefit of horses mainly. She cupped her hands and took up water from the basin running round the tap and drank thirstily. The water was cold and delicious on her tongue and throat. She dampened her kerchief and dabbed her cheeks and brow, enjoying the feel of the water evaporating on her skin in the slight breeze. She wasn't thinking straight, she realised. Of course Jack wouldn't be working in a factory. Hadn't she already decided he was not even likely to be working for someone else?

Weariness threatened to overwhelm her but she fought it off. She had to get back to Claypath. First, she thought, she would call in at a butcher's shop and get a pie to eat. She could not expect Peter to feed her again. For a moment or two she closed her eyes and allowed herself to think about Thomas. Then she got to her feet and walked on down the steep bank towards the city.

After a while, she was very close to the little house where she had lived with Jack and Thomas in happier times. It seemed a very long time ago now. On impulse she turned off the main road and walked along the small street. The front door of the house was closed, unlike the doors of most of the rest of the row. There must be no one at home. She peered through the window but couldn't see much because of a net curtain, which she recognised as one she herself had hung when she lived there.

'It's Mrs Mitchell, isn't it?' The voice came from the doorstep of a house a few doors down the street. Eliza turned to see a woman standing there. It was the same woman who had watched with avid curiosity the day the candymen had come to evict them a couple of years ago. 'Mind,' the woman – Dora her name was, Eliza remembered – went on, 'you've just missed your man. He went off in a cab just half an hour ago. Carrying the bairn, he was. By, the little lad's grown, hasn't he? A fine bairn he is, though he looked a bit pale and he was crying an' all. I hope he's not sickening for something.'

Eliza stared at her. 'He had Thomas? Did you say he had Thomas?'

The woman looked surprised. 'Aye, he had. Did you not know? Eeh, I thought—'

'Did he say anything? Jack, did he say anything?' Eliza interrupted her. 'I mean, did he say where they were going?'

'No, he didn't say nowt. He had enough on his hands with the lad. Men haven't got much idea when it comes to bairns, have they?'

'You didn't hear what he said to the driver?'

The woman shook her head. 'No, I didn't. I don't listen to folk when they're talking. None of my business, is it?'

Eliza started to turn away but then she turned back. 'You're sure it was Jack? He's been living here?'

Dora stepped forward eagerly. 'Is something the matter? Have you been away, like? I thought I hadn't seen you about.'

'No, there's nothing. I've just missed them, that's all,' Eliza replied. She hurried off, breathing a sigh of relief when she turned the corner away from the curiosity in Dora's eyes.

She arrived at the house Peter Collier rented at the same time as he himself returned. On the way she had bought two pork pies and a cabbage she had cheap from a stallholder in the market place who was closing up for the night.

'You didn't find them then,' Peter said as he sat down in the chair by the fire and took off his boots. He sighed heavily and lifted his feet onto the fender. Now he was off them they ached sorely.

'I just missed them, Mr Collier. Can you believe it? He was in the house where we used to live. A neighbour told me that he called a cab and went off with Thomas.'

He began to lay the fire while Eliza cleaned the cabbage and laid out the pies. She filled a pan from the bucket of water he brought in and put it on to boil. Not that she felt like eating now but she knew she had to keep up her strength for the search.

'I will go round there again tonight and wait for them.

Jack will come back; I'm sure he will. And I will get Thomas from him. I know Jack cannot be so cruel as to keep him from me for long.'

'I'll come with you,' said Peter. 'There may be trouble.'

'No, it's best if I'm on my own,' said Eliza. 'I'm grateful for the offer, though.'

They sat silent for a while, watching the flames lick round the pan on the fire. She ought to be with her family at a time like this, he thought. And he had the cause to think about. It occupied all of his time. There was talk of the yearly bond being abolished.

Eliza got to her feet and took the pan from the fire and out to the back yard to drain the water from it. Coming back in, she took a pat of the pork dripping she had been given by the butcher and chopped the cabbage and mixed in the fat and salt and pepper. She was still not hungry but she felt she had to force the food down. It was a sin to waste food and she needed to eat to be able continue the search.

Surprisingly, after the first few mouthfuls her appetite returned and she was able to finish what was on her plate. Peter made a pot of tea and there was sugar to go into it. Eliza began to revive a little. A restless energy filled her now she had eaten; Jack might be back home and Thomas with him.

'I should come. I promise I'll keep out of the way. It would be safer,' said Peter and Eliza sighed.

'Perhaps you're right.'

It was almost dark by the time the two of them set off. All the way there Eliza was buoyed up by the thought that she would see Thomas soon; he would be back. But as they approached the house she saw that it was quite dark within, no light shone through the net curtain and she was plunged into disappointment.

'How will you get in?' Peter asked her.

'The back way. The gate to the yard will be open and I can get in the window, it doesn't lock.'

'Are you sure? Only I can't afford to be caught helping you, it could be considered an offence. How the mine owners would love it if I were caught committing a crime! It would discredit the union.'

It was true and Eliza knew it. 'I'll be fine, don't worry,' she replied. 'I'm so grateful to you for what you've done for me already.' They were speaking in low tones just above a whisper. 'Go now,' she went on. 'I can get in. And Jack will come back, I know it. I'll have Thomas back with me, I will.'

'If you don't, think about going to your parents,' he said as he handed her the basket box he had been carrying for her, before turning away. 'Promise me you will think about it.'

Eliza nodded and watched as his tall figure disappeared into the smoky dark that had descended. She slipped down the narrow back street until she came to a gate leading into the tiny back yard of the house, glancing up at the neighbouring windows. The bedroom windows were still dark, though within half an hour the residents would be going to bed, she knew. Then she tried the small sash window by the door.

It wouldn't budge at first but after a moment or two it gave an inch then stuck. She heaved at it to no avail, then looked round for a piece of wood or anything that would provide some leverage. There were some logs in the corner but nothing suitable for what she had in mind and in an agony of frustration she forced her fingers through the gap at the bottom and gave it one last heave. The window flew up with a cracking noise and she paused for a moment in case anyone came to investigate, but no one did. She heaved her basket box inside. Hitching up her skirts, she climbed over the sill and at last she was in.

There was usually a candlestick on the shelf near the door that connected to the living room, she remembered. She felt around the wall with her fingers until she came to it. There was even a box of lucifers beside the candlestick and she struck one and lit the stub of candle.

The room was bare; only a small deal table and a few packets of dried food on the shelf. There was a cold-water tap on the wall at about knee height and a bucket beneath it. Eliza faltered for a moment for it reminded her of how happy she had been when she and Jack were living there, how he had had water piped into the house for her. No good thinking about those days.

She carried the candle through to the main room. The furniture had changed since she had lived in the house but there was a sofa and a comfortable-looking armchair that was actually padded. A table and four dining chairs stood in the middle of the room. They didn't look like Jack's work so he must have had enough money to buy them from a furniture shop. He must have had at least one good win, she thought cynically.

She sat down on the sofa and loosened her shawl. She would wait. Wait until hell froze over if she had to. After a while she blew out the candle and put her feet up on the sofa. She spread her shawl over her hips and legs and closed her eyes.

Jack took the train to Alnwick, changing at Newcastle. He bought a cup of milk for Thomas from a vendor on the station but the little boy refused to drink.

'Please yourself,' said Jack shortly. He was heartily sick of playing nursemaid and couldn't wait to see his mother and get her to take over from him.

Thomas no longer cried. His little face was white and pinched-looking. 'Mammy?' he asked Jack. 'Tot wants Mammy.' But he appeared to have lost hope that his request might be answered.

'Aw, shut your mouth about your bloody mammy, will

you?' Jack said savagely and Thomas whimpered then relapsed back into his silence.

When they finally arrived in Alnwick it was almost midnight and Jack had to walk to the house carrying the child, who was at last asleep. He had sent a post message to his mother so there was still a light at the back of the house. This was what he had been expecting and he walked round the side and in through the door leading to the kitchen. His mother had been sitting at the kitchen table and now she rose to her feet.

'Give me the bairn,' she said and held out her arms. 'And keep your voice down, I don't want Henry to wake up.'

'He's bound to know in the morning, Mother,' said Jack. She had given him no greeting and so he gave her none.

'Aye, but you'll be gone by then and he won't throw the lad out. Any road, I'm taking the cottage down the road for me and Thomas. I'm not going to be a skivvy in this house, indeed no.'

'I'll be coming back for him at the end of next week, Mother,' said Jack.

'Aye, I know. But you can take your time. I can look after a little lad, can't I?' She gazed at her oldest son. By, he had been a disappointment to her and to John Henry. His gambling let him down every time. Well, she reckoned she would be able to turn it to her own advantage.

'You can't sleep here yourself,' she snapped. 'Go in the barn if you like. Or I'll give you a sovereign, you can get lodging in the town.'

'Mother! By, you're a hard one, you are.'

'That may be. But I'm having no more upset than I have to over the bairn. You're best out of the way.'

Jack was so angry he didn't even look at his son as he turned away and opened the door. 'Keep your flaming sovereign,' he hissed. 'I'm not completely destitute.'

'No? That is a change then,' his mother replied. 'Don't forget, *if* you come back it'll be the cottage just down the lane.'

She watched as Jack disappeared into the dark then put out the lamp and carried Thomas upstairs to her room. He would have to sleep in her bed tonight. Tomorrow she would get the old cradle out of the attic. After all, though John Henry had left the house to his second son he had left her the furniture. She would take what she needed to furnish the cottage. Any road, she thought, it didn't look as if Henry and his sour-faced wife would be in need of the cradle.

Eliza woke as the first rays of the sun penetrated the window of the living room. She sat up, disorientated, and looked around before she realised where she was. The sunbeams through the window were hazy for the window was mottled with dirt and the net curtain was grey around the sides. It probably hadn't been washed since Jack came back to the house. Obviously there was no woman coming in to help him, then.

Where was Thomas? Why had Jack taken him away? The familiar desolation filled her. She had to find her boy, she had to. But she couldn't go out and look for him in case Jack came back with him and she missed him again.

Restlessly, Eliza went into the back room. The larder in the corner was about empty but there was a packet of porridge oats on the shelves and a bag of sugar. She lit the fire and cooked some oats in water and sweetened them with a spoonful of sugar. She put the kettle on to boil while she ate the porridge, forcing herself to finish it for she needed the stamina it would give her. The tea caddy was empty but an opened packet of Rington's tea was on the table. She drank a cup without milk for there was none.

There was no clock on the wall; the candymen had taken the one that used to hang there and no doubt the tenants who came afterwards had taken theirs when they went. But the bells of the churches of the city told her it was already nine o' clock. Perhaps Jack would come back soon. She stood looking out of the window. The street was just about empty for the men were already at their work and the women would be cleaning the houses. Only a couple of children bowled a hoop up and down the flagged pavement outside, laughing and shouting.

She would clean the window, she decided. It would pass the time until Jack came home and she would see Thomas. Filled with a new energy fuelled by hope she took down the curtain and washed it and hung it in the back yard to dry. She found a wash-leather and scoured the fly dirt off the windowpanes until they sparkled. She barely heard the bells strike ten o'clock.

She was not aware of what time it was when she heard a key in the lock and Jack walked in. She had washed the furniture with vinegar water and polished it until it shone then washed the floors and tidied up the back kitchen. She turned eagerly to the door for the first sight of her child but when Jack walked in he was quite alone.

'What the hell are you doing here?' Jack demanded.

'Where's Thomas?' Eliza asked almost at the same time.

'Never mind Thomas, I asked you what you were doing here,' Jack snapped. 'How did you find me?'

'I came for the bairn, of course, and you weren't hard to find,' said Eliza. 'Where is he? He must be missing me, he's never been away from me since he was born.'

'He's all right. He's in a safe place; safer than he was with you.'

'Jack, how can you say that? A baby is best off with his mother!'

'Not when his mother is a whore,' Jack replied, his voice dangerously quiet. 'Anyway, how did you get in here? Did you think you could worm your way back into my life?' He shook his head. 'I don't think so.' He was weary from the travelling and lack of sleep and now, seeing Eliza, he was filled with bitterness. Not only bitterness, though. He couldn't help the old feelings rising in himself. Had she come back because she couldn't keep away from him? He took an involuntary step towards her.

'Jack, I did nothing wrong,' said Eliza. 'Please let me have Thomas, please.' She had seen the slight softening in his eyes. Dear God, let him give me my baby back. I'll do anything, she prayed.

'You deserted me, your lawful wedded husband,' Jack reminded her.

'But you staked me on a wager!' The retort sprang to Eliza's lips but she bit it back. She had to if she wanted Thomas returned to her, she had to.

Jack was directly in front of her now and she put out a hand to him. With an oath he took hold of her and brought his mouth to hers so hard that her lips were bruised against her teeth. He held her with one arm while he tore at her dress until he had uncovered a breast and squeezed it ruthlessly.

Eliza gasped and cried out but he was past hearing as he bore her to the floor. He pulled up her skirts and held her while he unbuttoned his flies and entered her with no more ado, heaving himself again and again so that her back was scraping on the floor and pain seared through her.

It was all over in a minute. He lay panting over her then pushed himself away and got to his feet and straightened his clothes. Eliza lay for a few moments, catching her breath. Tears ran down her cheeks but she brushed them away. Wincing as she stood up, she turned to him.

'What about Thomas?' she asked.

Jack laughed. 'Thomas? You thought that would buy you back my son? No, lass, it will not. I told you, Thomas is somewhere safe and he will stay there. You're not going to see him again. Now, get out of this house, I don't want to see you again.'

PART TWO

Chapter Sixteen

1869

'Monday, March 1st,' Eliza wrote in the ward day book. Her writing was copperplate and easy to read as she had been taught in the Methodist literacy class five years ago now. She paused after writing the date as she did every day, for every day it reminded her of how long she had been separated from Thomas. Today was special however, today was Thomas's seventh birthday. Dear God, where was he? She prayed he would be safe and well. He would have forgotten her but that didn't matter so long as he was well.

After a moment or two she continued writing up the history of the last twelve hours of each patient in the ward.

'Bed no. 1: Alice Donavan, age thirty-three,' she wrote. 'The patient slept poorly. Complained of pain in her

189

chest. Tincture of digitalis 5 minims administered at 2am according to doctor's instructions. A little brighter this morning. Took a little light breakfast of coddled egg.'

Alice Donavan was not going to go home to her ten children and miner husband. Alice's heart was close to giving up altogether, worn out as it was with hard work, childbearing and a poor diet. Of course she didn't know that, or didn't admit it. Alice lived for the day she saw her children again but they weren't allowed to visit her in hospital. Her husband had brought them to the window near her bed so that they could wave to her but she had been so upset when they went he was frightened to do it again.

'Bed no. 2,' Eliza wrote. 'Betsy Jane Hopper.' She stayed as she was about to write, 'Prolapse of uterus,' and looked up as there was a knock at the door and Nurse Jones came in. Nurse Jones was the day nurse and her relief. Eliza immediately felt guilty for she was late with the report. There had been an admission during the night, a woman haemorrhaging copiously from a knife wound to the upper arm. Sarah Brown lived only a few streets away from the hospital, a fact that probably saved her life. Her husband was with her and he was deathly pale and trembled almost as much as his wife.

'She did it herself,' he kept repeating to anyone who was willing to listen and to Dr Parsons and Eliza, who were too busy staunching the flow to listen. Dr Parsons ordered him to leave to the ward. Luckily, the blood was flowing from a vein rather than an artery and eventually they had it stopped. Eliza washed the arm with a solution of sublimate and the doctor stitched the wound and Eliza bandaged it. All the while Sarah said not a word but watched everything with large, frightened eyes.

'I'll get on with the breakfasts then,' said Nurse Jones. 'I'll get the report after.' She pinned on her cap and went out to the ward kitchen.

Eliza went back to her writing. It took her another half an hour to finish, and by the time she had read it out to Nurse Jones and reported to Matron's office it was already eight o'clock before she could at last walk across the grounds of the North Durham Infirmary to the nurses' hostel.

Eliza was weary but she took that for granted. She always was after a night on the ward. The women's ward held both medical and surgical cases though not anyone with contagious diseases. The policy now was to keep them in a new block away from the main hospital.

The air was fresh with a cold wind blowing from the north. She huddled into her cloak, pulling it closer around her shoulders. As always, her thoughts turned to Thomas. He was seven years old now. She imagined him on his way to school, carrying his pencil and slate. He would be going to school she was sure, his father would want him to, surely. Did he remember his mother? Please God, he did.

Eliza ate the porridge and bacon and bread provided for her breakfast. She was almost too tired to eat but forced herself to and washed the food down with two cups of tea. The dining room in the nurses' hostel was painted a stark white with only the dark varnished doors for relief. The only decoration was the picture of Florence Nightingale gazing sternly down from one wall. Most of the other night nurses had already finished their meal and gone to their rooms so it was quiet except for the rattle of pots and pans from the kitchen at one end of the hall.

Eliza sat back in her chair and sighed. She would have to summon the energy to climb the stairs and get ready for bed soon but for a few minutes she was enjoying the peace. Oh, she thought, it had been hard work on the coal screens, hard, labouring work. But nursing, she found, was just as hard in its own way. She glanced up at the portrait of Florence Nightingale and stuck out her tongue inelegantly at it. The lady had issued a decree recently when there had been a movement from the grass roots for nurses to have more time off duty and even a holiday.

'If a nurse has a true vocation then she will not wish to be away from the work,' she had said, or words to that effect. So nurses had only one day a month off or, in Eliza's case, one night. It was due on the following Monday, only two days away, and Eliza planned to visit her mother and father and her brothers in Blue House colliery village. At least she would be able to stay overnight. If she didn't go to bed on coming off duty on Monday morning she could stay until Tuesday afternoon.

'Can I clear your pots now, Nurse?'

The voice intruded on Eliza's thoughts and she looked up and smiled. It was Bertha, the diminutive girl who had once worked at her father-in-law's house in Alnwick. She had managed to follow Eliza to the North Durham Infirmary, somehow ferreting out where she was. Now she worked as a maid in the nurses' home.

'Morning, Bertha,' Eliza said. 'I was just thinking of my night off on Monday. I'm going to Blue House. It's a while since I saw my mam and dad.' She rose to her feet and pushed in her chair. 'I'd best get to bed anyway or I might fall asleep walking.'

'You've been busy?' Bertha asked sympathetically. She knew what it could be like on the wards at night and with only one nurse on duty and a helper running between wards. She had started work at the hospital as a helper but for all her upbringing she couldn't stand to see the human misery and pain of the disease-ridden or injured patients. So she had been allowed to transfer to the nurses' home for she was soon recognised as a hard and honest worker.

'When are we not busy?' Eliza asked. 'I don't know what they did before this hospital was built.'

'You do,' said Bertha. 'They got better or they died.'

Eliza sighed. 'Yes. Well, I'm away to my bed. Good morning, Bertha.'

'Sleep well. Mind the bugs don't bite,' Bertha replied.

Once in bed, Eliza found herself almost too tired to sleep. Her thoughts roamed restlessly over the last few years. Years of pulling herself up the ladder of the nursing world. She had started off as a nurse's helper just as Bertha had done but by dint of hard work and determination had managed eventually to be accepted for training. Of course the fact that she had enough money to keep herself for the year's training had clinched it for her. She would never have been able to do it if she were penniless. Even with enough to fund herself she had been obliged to swear she was a widow with no dependants. No dependants, the phrase was like a knife in her heart. Where was Thomas? Where had Jack taken him?

Sometimes she thought of going back to Alnwick, of making sure that her husband had not taken him to his family. After all, Thomas was Annie's grandson, she might have changed her mind. But no, he wouldn't have done that, Annie would not have taken them in. She was too filled with hate for that. Hadn't she made it plain? No, any time she had off duty was better occupied searching elsewhere for her baby. Though he was not a baby now, she reminded herself. He was seven. Please God, let him be all right, she prayed again as she did ten times a day. And there was the nagging worry about Miley, poor Miley.

Peter Collier had written to her on behalf of her parents. There had been an accident at the pit. A coal tub had come off the wooden rails and pinned Miley to the ground. Miley was a putter by now and his job was to push the tubs to where the seam was large enough for the pit pony.

'He has some damage to his spine,' Peter had written. 'But the doctors think he might recover enough to walk a little. Your mother would be very glad to see you if you can manage to come to Blue House.'

Eliza had the letter on the deal table by the bed and she stretched out a hand and picked it up and read it again. It was short but it conveyed a world of information to her. She had seen many boys maimed by the coal tubs coming off the wooden rails leading to the shaft bottom and also some by them 'going amain', out of control on a slight downward incline. She had seen one lad almost sliced in two by such a happening. Even though Miley's accident had not been so bad as some it was unlikely that he would work again in the pit. And what else was there for him? Well, she told herself, she would see the lad when she went to Blue House on Monday.

*

It was two o'clock when Eliza came out of the station at Haswell and took the footpath across the moor to Blue House colliery. The place seemed little changed since her last visit, which had been a disaster. Her mother's hard tones rang in her ears still.

'It's your own fault, my lass, you left your man. He had a right to take the lad. By, I didn't fetch you up to break your marriage vows, I did not!'

Mary Anne would not listen to her daughter's protests. 'Go back to Jack,' she said. 'Don't come here crying because you lost your bairn. Jack didn't whip you, did he? He treated you well. You don't look as though you're starving neither.'

Now her mother wanted her back. Eliza was not bitter, she was just glad to come. Oh God, what was she thinking? How could she be glad to come when the reason for her return was so terrible? Poor little Miley; she remembered him being born. He had been a tiny scrap of a baby and the lying-in woman had shaken her head over his chances of living, but Mary Anne had succeeded in raising him. But for what?

'Good day, Mam,' said Eliza as she opened the door leading straight into the main room of the house. Mary Anne was kneading bread in a brownstone bowl on the scrubbed table. There was flour on her apron and on her chin, matching the white strands in her hair that were new to Eliza. She gazed anxiously at her mother; she was thinner and her face seemed to have aged twenty years since Eliza saw her last.

'Oh, Mam!' she said helplessly and hurried over and put her arms around her. Mary Anne stood stiffly for a moment then returned her embrace.

'I expected you earlier on,' Mary Anne said. 'Mr Collier said you were coming this morning.' She stepped back and dusted the flour from her hands into the bowl then rubbed them on her pinafore. 'I'll put the kettle on.'

'I had to work until eleven,' said Eliza. 'I'm off tonight, though. I don't need to go back until tomorrow afternoon.'

She watched as Mary Anne pushed the kettle onto the fire and spooned tea into the pot. The actions were automatic for tea was made for every visitor when there was tea to be had. The kitchen seemed smaller to her than it had when she was last here and the furnishings meaner. The clippie mat on the flagstones before the fire was just a bit grubby and looked as though it should be taken out into the fresh air and given a good shake. There were ashes overflowing from the box under the grate.

Eliza took off her nurse's cape and cap and hung them behind the door. Her mother had gone back to her bread-making while the kettle came to the boil. Now she shaped the dough into loaves and put them into the greased oven tins, before putting them back on the hearth to rise.

'I'll have to get them to the baking oven,' she said.
'You'll stay with the lad? Mrs Sumptor pops in usually.'

'Of course I will.' Eliza paused. 'Where is our Miley?'
she asked. 'How is he?'

'Fair to middling,' said Mary Anne. She appeared too
exhausted to say much except for the absolute essentials.
After a moment she went on, 'He's in the room.' She
nodded towards the middle door that led into the only
other room downstairs, the room where she and Tommy
normally slept.

'I'll go in to him,' said Eliza.

'Yes.'

Eliza lifted the sneck on the door and went into the
room, pinning a smile on her face as she did so. 'Now
then, our Miley,' she said. 'What have you been up to?'
Then she froze. Miley was sitting on a chair with wheels
rather than legs. It had obviously been adapted from a
wooden chair with a horsehair pad on the seat. The
bottom of the chair had been extended with a piece of
wood and his legs were stretched out on that. He had a
pillow supporting his back. He gazed back at his sister
with pain-glazed eyes. He was fourteen years old though
he looked no more than ten.

'Now then, our Eliza,' he said and closed his eyes. His
lips moved but she couldn't catch what he was saying.

'Mam! Mam!'

Mary Anne appeared beside her as Eliza called for her.

'What?' She looked at Miley and then at her daughter. 'Don't shout, the doctor says we must keep him quiet. He's had a dose of laudanum, he's just a bit tired, that's all. Howay, lass, let him be.'

'But shouldn't he be lying down? All our spinal cases are on their backs.'

'Mebbe so, mebbe so. But Miley gets too agitated on his back. The doctor said this was mebbe the best position for him. The carpenter at the pit did the chair and put the wheels on an' all. By, the manager and the gaffer's lad have been good to him, they have. Mr Moore gave him half a sovereign an' all.'

'Oh, Mam, it's awful,' said Eliza and reverted to the local dialect. 'He's nobbut a bairn.'

'Aye well, he could have been dead,' said Mary Anne stolidly. 'Now there's a chance he will walk again. Only it's hard. He's a bit big for me to manage. But the lads help me. They're on a different shift to Tommy now so that they can help me with the lifting. For the time being, any road. Now then, lass, I know it's a shock but you should know, if anyone does, that it happens all the time in the pits.' She brewed the tea and poured out three cups and spooned sugar into them.

'I'll just drink this then I'll away to the bread oven,' she said.

Chapter Seventeen

'What should I do, Mam?' Eliza asked. It was Monday evening and Tommy and the two older boys had returned from the pit and were in the back street playing quoits with their friends. Tommy had helped Eliza to lift and bathe Miley and make him comfortable for the night. Then he too had disappeared out of the door, mumbling something about 'the lads' and wanting to see them.

Eliza was weary to the point where her brain was barely functioning. She and her mother had been talking about whether she should leave the Infirmary and come home to help with the bairn, as Mary Anne still called him.

'Nay, lass, I don't think we could afford to keep you,' Mary Anne answered. 'Me and your da will manage. Other folk have to do it. Any road, you've done so well, you've got on, I'm real proud of you, I am. But Tommy would be on at you all the time to find Jack and go back to him.' It was true; Tommy had barely spoken to Eliza when he came in, and then only to ask pointedly after 'her man'.

'He didn't tell me to get out, though, did he? He would get used to it,' said Eliza. 'And besides, haven't I spent all the hours God sends looking for Jack and my little Thomas?'

All the hours she wasn't working, she thought, and even then she had scrutinised the face of every little boy who came into the Infirmary, just in case.

Mary Anne sighed. 'By, lass, I thought you were doing well to marry out of the pits but I was wrong. Any man that would take a little lad from his mother has no heart, no heart at all.'

'I have to go to bed, I'm dead on my feet,' said Eliza. 'We'll talk about it the morn.'

'Aye, lass, good night. I've strung a blanket on a line to separate your bed from the lads. Now, up the ladder with you. I'll have a rest by the fire. The lads will be in soon.'

For all her weariness, Eliza lay awake for a while. The twilight still lingered and the room was not completely dark. She lay on her back and gazed up at the rafters. After a while she said her usual prayer for Thomas and turned over onto her side. Perhaps she could spare a few shillings a month to pay for a woman to come in and help her mother with Miley? She tried to work out in her head how much exactly but her brain couldn't. Abruptly, she fell asleep.

In the end, that was the arrangement. Eliza was now a senior night sister and she managed to take three shillings every month to Blue House. Miley's back was proving slow to heal and it meant that she had little time to search for Thomas. One day, when she got the chance, she would go up into Northumberland again if only to satisfy herself that he was not there. One day when Miley was better and her commitments were less. Meanwhile Eliza immersed herself in her work on the ward.

'Can I speak to you for a minute, Nurse?' Bertha asked respectfully one morning when Eliza entered the dining room. Though they had been friends for so many years they were still expected to maintain a distance between them when at work. Nurses were not supposed to treat the domestic staff as equals; they had to be aware of their place and the domestic staff also.

Eliza glanced about the dining room; there was no one near her, the room was almost empty. 'Morning, Bertha,' she said and smiled at the earnest little woman. Bertha was wrapped in a voluminous overall and wore a cap that came down almost to her eyebrows and showed only a few strands of hair at the sides and back. Her plain face was made attractive by her expressive dark eyes and mobile features.

'What is it?'

Bertha did not sit down in case anyone of authority came in. Instead she leaned over the table and lifted Eliza's used plate and cutlery.

'I was up at Alnwick on my day off. Went to see my friend from the workhouse, Maria. I haven't seen her for years but now, since I can write, I sent her a letter.' Bertha blushed and her eyes shone; it was a great achievement for her to do such a thing. Eliza smiled and nodded in understanding.

'She wrote back to you?'

'Aye, she did and asked me to go up and see her. She's got five bairns now; she married the under-gamekeeper on the Castle estate. They're bonny bairns, oh they are an' all. But while I was up there I saw something.' Bertha paused and glanced round before continuing. 'I saw the Missus, you know, Mrs John Henry. She was in the butcher's. By, she's looking her age an' all. Well, she came out of there and climbed into a trap and a little lad with her. A lad about seven, I'd say.'

Eliza's heart began to race. 'Seven? A lad about seven? Are you sure?'

'Oh aye, I'm sure. I went up to them and nodded. "Do you remember me?" I asked the Missus. I got a good look at the lad.'

'What did she say?'

'Nay, she didn't say much, just mumbled and shook

her head like. Then she whipped up the pony and went on her way. Not up to the house, though, another way altogether.'

Eliza's mind raced. As far as she knew Henry had no children and certainly not a seven-year-old lad.

'Mind, it doesn't mean it's Thomas,' she said.

'No, I thought that. But I had a good look at him and he had lovely dark blue eyes and long lashes such as are wasted on a lad. Eyes just like yours.'

'Oh, Bertha do you think it is?'

'Well now, I'd lay a bet on it if I wasn't chapel,' Bertha replied then straightened up hurriedly as Cook called from the kitchen door.

'How long does it take to clear the covers, Bertha?'

'I'm just coming, Cook,' she said and gathered the pots quickly and sped away.

'I'll meet you outside, over in the wood,' said Eliza before she went. 'When?'

'An hour,' Bertha replied. 'I'll be able to get ten minutes.'

Eliza was waiting on the outskirts of the wood within half an hour. She couldn't rest; she was filled with hope and dread alternately and in equal measures. She was beginning to despair of Bertha managing to get away when the sound of the church clock striking ten came across the fields. And then at last she saw Bertha coming along the path. Eliza backed into the cover of the trees and waited anxiously.

'Are you sure, Bertha, are you really sure?' she asked as soon as the girl drew nearer.

'I am,' she said. 'I think the old besom has your lad. I followed the trap, it was easy enough. I kept to the side and the pony wasn't one you'd put in Blaydon Races. It was a Galloway; it took its own sweet pace. Any road, it was there by the last house on the edge of Alnwick. A lad was just leading him round to the back.'

'But the little lad? Where was he?'

'Loitering by the door. He was talking to the stable lad.' Bertha leaned forward and went on. 'He was talking and the lad was laughing and the old woman came to the door and shouted. She said "Come away in, Tot, I told you once! Do you want the belt? That's what you'll get if you don't come this very minute!"'

'She called him Tot? Are you sure?'

Bertha sighed. 'I wish you wouldn't keep asking me if I'm sure. I was there, I heard the woman and that's what she said. The bairn ran in looking a bit scared, I will say. I don't know, a little lad shouldn't be scared of the belt, that's what I think any road. Look you, I'll have to go back or Cook will be spitting feathers.'

'All right, go on. Thanks, Bertha.'

Eliza watched as Bertha sped back through the fields. She hugged her arms around her and tried to think. Would Annie call Thomas Tot? Maybe it wasn't him. Maybe it was another lad altogether. Oh, it was hard to know, it was. She walked up and down, her weariness following the long night's work forgotten, and tried to marshal her thoughts. Whether it was Thomas or not, she had to go and find out. But her next night off duty wasn't for a fortnight and then she had to take the money for Miley to Blue House. No, she had to get time off before that. She would go mad if she worked at the Infirmary for two weeks before she went.

'Please, Matron, I need leave of absence,' she said, and even in her present state of mind she quailed at the unblinking stare directed at her.

'You *need* leave of absence? Explain yourself, Sister.'

Eliza looked at Matron, feeling as intimidated as she did when she first started her training five years before.

'I am afraid so, Matron,' she said.

'And may I ask why, Sister Mitchell-Howe?'

Eliza normally used the name Mitchell except in her hospital life. She had given the double-barrelled name Mitchell-Howe on her application form and she knew it had helped in securing her training. Hadn't Miss Nightingale said that nurses should be of good family? A double-barrelled name usually meant a good family. Together with various other characteristics. These raced through her mind as she tried to think of an answer. Sober, honest truthful, trustworthy, punctual, quiet, orderly, cleanly patient, kindly – a nurse had to be all of these.

'For family reasons, please, Matron,'

'This hospital is your family, Sister.' Matron sat back in her chair and gazed at Eliza. She herself was from Hertfordshire and had trained in the great Florence Nightingale's school in London. She tried to follow her mentor in everything, but it was hard here in the north of England where nurses were different from those in the south. It was hard to put a finger on the reason why or how this was so. Oh, they were hard-working and dedicated, especially the one before her now, but they were different.

'Am I permitted to know why you need the time off?' Matron asked.

Eliza hesitated for just a moment but Matron did not miss it.

'Well, Sister?' she demanded.

'My little brother has injured his back, Matron.' She realised Matron wanted more. 'He was pushing a wagon and it fell on him,' she elaborated. She was not going to mention the pit if she could help it. Matron would not like to think she was a pitman's daughter.

Matron sighed. She looked down at the rota she had been busy drawing up when Eliza requested an interview. It would have to be adjusted.

'How long do you need, Sister?'

'One week, Matron. Please.'

'Very well, Sister. You may go. Report back to me in

seven days' time.' Matron looked down dismissively and picked up her pen. 'I hope your brother is not too badly injured, Sister.'

Eliza went out of the room with a feeling of having been let out of prison. Which was surprising, really, for she loved her work. Yet she soon forgot about Matron and the Infirmary and even her lack of sleep as she packed a bag and set off for the station. She didn't even care about telling a lie about her reasons for needing the time off.

The problem was that as soon as she sat down on the train the lack of sleep caught up with her and she closed her eyes, just for a minute or two, she told herself, and slept immediately. She dreamed of Thomas taking his first steps down the lane leading to Farmer Dean's farm, chuckling and picking daisies and dandelions under the hedge. In her dream there were no shadows and she was happy as she walked with him and caught him up in her arms when he stumbled. In the distance she could hear the roar of a steam engine on the line and the clickety-clack of the wheels on the rails.

It was semi-dark when Eliza woke up. She had a crick in her neck and her left arm had gone to sleep where she had leaned against the wooden ridged side of the wagon. She stretched and groaned to herself as her aching muscles cried out in protest. The train was stopped in a siding and it was semi-dark all around, that particular dark that is midsummer night in the north.

'Now then, Missus,' a gruff voice said. 'What are you doing here? Nobody can sleep the night on the train. It's an offence, that is. You'd best be gone or I'll have the polis on you.'

The voice belonged to a man in a railwayman's cap and coat and he held a lantern high over the half door of the third-class wagon. 'Now then, be off with you.'

'Where are we? I missed my station, I was asleep. Have we passed Alnwick?'

'Passed Alnwick? Why, we're long past. This is the junction. You'll have to wait for the morn to get back to Alnwick.' The man looked at Eliza in the light of his lantern and evidently decided she was not a vagrant. 'If you walk back along the wagonway you will come to the platform. You can wait there. It'll be half-past six mind, afore the train comes.'

Eliza picked her way over the stones and gravel by the side of the track until she reached the platform. She had to scramble up onto it for there were no steps or gradation from the rough track. The morning was beginning to lighten from the east, though it was only half-past three by the station clock by the time she sank down on a bench thoughtfully provided outside the locked waiting room and put her Gladstone bag at her feet. She sat, leaning back against the brickwork of the waiting room for a while and closed her eyes. A small pain throbbed behind her left eye and her mouth was dry and foul-tasting.

After a while she got to her feet and walked to the end of the platform in order to stretch her aching legs. It was very quiet as she gazed out at the surrounding fields and distant woods. Birds were starting to sing. She amused herself trying to make out the different songs. Anything rather than think about Thomas, for when she did that she alternated between soaring hope and deep pessimism. After all, there was so little for her to go on, just Bertha's encounter with her mother-in-law and a small boy. Bertha could be mistaken about the boy, perhaps he was only four or five, perhaps he was Henry's child.

She forced her mind back to the dawn chorus; there was a blackbird's sweet trill and the chattering of sparrows, the harsh call of starlings. And as the sun rose a skylark rose too. She watched the tiny speck in the sky and listened to its song. It made her feel better. She walked back to her seat and without realising it she was humming the old folksong, '*Early one morning just as the sun was rising. I heard a bird singing in the valley below.*'

'It won't be long now, Missus,' the station attendant said. It was five o'clock according to the station clock, the long night was over. Eliza hadn't even noticed he had come on duty as she watched and listened to the birds. He opened the waiting-room door for her and it put her in mind of the last time she had come. It was five years ago now.

The ladies' waiting room was small and with only bench seats round the walls, but there was an ash closet behind a door in the corner and in another corner a tap and a fixed basin beneath it. She was able to wash the smuts from her face and neck, though she had to dry them on the hem of her petticoat. She took off her nurse's cap and smoothed her hair before replacing it. There was no looking glass but she was reasonably sure she was as presentable as she could make herself with such limited facilities.

When the train steamed up to the platform she was waiting to board it, having bought a first-class ticket this time so she could ride the short journey in a proper carriage. Soon she would see her little lad, oh, soon she would. She sat down on a comfortable seat at last and the train started on the journey back to Alnwick.

Chapter Eighteen

Tot walked slowly around the side of the cottage to the kitchen door for he wasn't allowed to go in the front. Granny said there was enough dirt in the place without him bringing it in. At the thought of dirt he looked down anxiously at his boots but they carried no mud, they were just dusty from the road. He rubbed the toes on the back of his stockings. The stockings were a thick grey wool and the dust wouldn't show. He knew that from experience. He didn't want the belt; he could still feel the welt on his legs from the last time he had upset Granny.

He sat down on the step to unlace his boots and pulled them off with the help of a boot scraper embedded into the stone beside the back door. Then he put them neatly side by side just inside the door and went in to face Granny.

'How many times have I told you not to talk to

Barney?' Annie demanded from her place at the stove where she was dishing up the dinner. It was scrag end of mutton and cabbage and boiled potatoes and she put a plateful on the table. 'Now then, eat up,' she said.

Tot looked down at the greasy mutton and felt faintly sick but he knew better than to say anything about it. He picked up his knife and fork and began to eat, going solidly at it and trying not to think of the taste. The last time he had said he didn't like it and refused to eat it the plate had been brought out at every mealtime until at last he managed to push the food down his throat.

Tot had developed a strategy, though he wouldn't have known what was meant by the word. He imagined himself in another world where there was a shadowy figure that cuddled him and kissed him good night. He couldn't see her face but he knew it was his mammy. And she made him nice things to eat and sometimes lemonade to drink just like Alfie's mammy. Alfie's mammy lived a few doors along the street and once when it was hot and he was walking home from school with Alfie she had given them both a drink of dandelion and burdock pop.

'I got it from the shop today,' she had said, 'and saved some especially for you two.' Alfie's mam was lovely and so was his own mam if only he could find her. But he couldn't. When he had asked Granny where she was Granny said his mam had gone off and left him. Once again he wondered what he had done that was so wrong for his mam to go off and leave him. Sometimes he thought he could remember his mammy. She hovered on the edge of his mind and memory but he couldn't see her face. She wouldn't go off and leave him, oh no, she would have protected him from Granny and from Uncle Henry as well. Not that he saw much of Uncle Henry lately. Granny had had a falling-out with him.

All the time Tot ploughed through his food his thoughts were busy far away. He began his favourite game, which was that he was sitting at the table with his mammy and he was eating panackelty. He was sure his mam had made him panackelty. He remembered the funny name but he couldn't really remember the taste of it. But he was sure it tasted lovely.

Annie watched as he ploughed his way through the food. By, she thought, she had brought him up different from the other two, ungrateful varmints that they had been. That Henry never came near her except to pay her the money due her from John Henry's estate. He was waiting for her to die, oh, she was well aware of that. Well, she would live to spite him, she would an' all. And then there was Jack. She had been too easy with him all right. Too easy altogether. Jack had gone and killed himself by jumping off the cliff at Tynemouth. What he was doing there was something she never fathomed but then, she didn't pry too much. Really, she didn't know whether he had thrown himself off or had been pushed for there was talk of someone dunning him for money he owed. Aye well, she told herself, she wouldn't be so easy with this one. It was like having a second chance.

'Can I go now?' Tot asked. She had been staring at his plate without seeing it but now she realised it was wiped clean.

'Hadaway then,' she said. 'Mind, you have to help me in the garden as soon as I've cleared away here. Don't go off and play with that good-for-nothing Alfie, you hear me?'

'Yes, Granny,' said Tot.

She watched him as he sat on the step and struggled with his boots. They came halfway up his calves and took a lot of lacing but in the end he managed it and went out into the garden. Annie supposed he wasn't too bad for a seven-year-old lad. She remembered when she first got charge of him, how he had cried for his mother.

'Me Tot,' he had insisted whenever she called him Thomas and in the end that was what she had called him. It was the only concession she made to him. Oh, it didn't do to let him get away with anything.

Tot walked to the corner of the garden where the hedge was thin and he could see up the road to Alfie's house. There was no sign of his friend but if he waited long enough and his granny didn't come out and set him to work with the trowel digging up dandelion roots, Alfie might come out and talk to him through the hedge. The road was empty, though, everyone was eating at this time of day. No it wasn't, someone had just turned into the street and was walking along it. It was a woman, he saw, a young woman in a funny hat and cape.

'Tot! Get you here, my lad, never mind standing there dreaming.' Granny had come out and she had on the sacking apron she used for gardening and a trug in her hand with the hand tools in it. Tot forgot about the woman in the road and turned to her, taking the trowel she handed him.

Dandelions were a pest in the cottage gardens. Just when you thought you had got rid of them they popped up again. It was the long roots. Granny said he had to make sure he got all the roots and he dug carefully round them. He really liked dandelions, they were a nice sunshiny yellow and so were the pittly-beds that grew on the verges of the road. That wasn't the right name, though. Barney, the stable lad said so. They were called— His thoughts were interrupted by the sound of the garden gate opening.

'Good day, Annie,' a woman's voice said. Tot scrambled to his feet. She was the woman in the cloak and funny hat he had seen coming down the road. She had spoken to his granny but she was staring at him.

'What are you doing here?' Granny sounded strange,

as though she was frightened of something. But she couldn't have been frightened of this woman because she looked nice and kind. He took a step forward and then stopped.

The woman didn't answer Granny but spoke to him. 'Thomas?' she said softly.

'My name is Tot,' he answered automatically. 'I'm just called Thomas in school.'

He regarded her gravely for a few seconds. 'Why do you wear that funny hat?' he asked.

'It's a nurse's cap. I'm a nurse,' Eliza said gently. Oh, the more she looked at him the more she could see the baby Thomas in him.

'Tot! Go inside at once and don't come out until I say you can!' Annie was recovering from the shock of seeing Eliza. She went to him and caught hold of him roughly. 'Do as I say or I'll get the belt,' she warned him.

'You will not belt him,' said Eliza. 'Oh no, my lady, you will not belt him again.' She stepped closer to the boy but was not quick enough for Annie grabbed him and he issued a small cry.

Annie didn't reply; she was dragging the boy towards the front door and even though she was hurting his arm by the way she was gripping him, he had time to wonder at them going in the front door with his boots on and soil from the garden on the boots an' all. Once inside, she slammed the door behind them and dragged him

217

through to the kitchen in order to lock that door too. But Eliza was before them. She had slipped around the side and was standing in the open kitchen doorway and as they appeared she took a step inside.

'Get out,' said Annie. 'He's my lad now. Jack gave him to me. I paid for him.'

'You did what?'

'I paid Jack's debts. I have a right to him.' Her fingers were digging in to Tot's shoulder and he squirmed free suddenly and stepped away from her.

'Come back here this minute!' said Annie. Tot hesitated. He knew he should obey her or she would belt him, but he lifted his chin and stared at her.

'No,' he said. His heart pounded in his chest and his voice quavered but he defied her. Eliza stepped forward and took hold of his hand.

'Tot,' she said. 'I am your mother. It's all right, I won't let her hurt you again. Now go into the garden and wait for me. Will you do that? I have to talk to your granny. I won't be long.'

'My mammy?' Tot looked up at her and his eyes were swimming in tears. 'But Granny said you didn't want me, you went away and left me.'

'Did she now. Well, well. Look, pet, just do as I say, will you?'

Tot nodded and trotted off out of the back door into the garden. This time he didn't go to his favourite place by the hedge at the front of the house but stayed within earshot of the kitchen. He felt funny, all hot and tingly and his eyes were wet and his heart pounded in his chest. He bent down behind the rows of peas so that he was out of sight of the kitchen door and poked the soil around the lettuces with a stick.

'You're not taking the lad and that's that,' Annie said and Tot's heart plummeted.

'I'm not, am I?' Eliza replied. 'You might be wrong about that an' all. Where's Jack, any road? He had no right to give him to you, not when I'm the lad's mam. What's more, you cannot buy a human being, you cannot. That is slavery.'

'Jack's dead. He's been gone these last three years,' Annie said flatly. 'He could do what he liked with his own bairn an' all and he left him with me, I tell you.'

Eliza was shaken. Jack was dead? Somehow she hadn't imagined that. In spite of everything that had happened she felt a surge of grief for the husband she had loved once. In the good times they had been happy and she knew he had loved her. In the beginning at least.

'How? How did he die? Did no one think to let me know?'

'He went over the cliff at Tynemouth. I don't know whether he fell or was pushed but either way he is just as dead. It doesn't matter now.' Annie's expression didn't change. She stared at her daughter-in-law. 'Why would we bother to let you know? You left him, so he had a right to leave the lad with me. And I'm keeping him. I intend to bring him up properly. You have no claim on him.'

'Oh but I have.' Eliza took a bundle of paper out of the reticule she had over her arm. 'I have a certificate here, signed by the doctor and the midwife, and I have a baptismal certificate from the Wesleyan minister in Durham. Both of them say I am Thomas's mother. And if his father is dead, I am his legal guardian.'

'How do you know what they say? You cannot read or write! You're illiterate!' Annie waved the papers away contemptuously.

'No indeed, but I'm not. I am a trained nurse, a hospital sister trained under the Nightingale Fund. I have progressed since you last saw me.'

Eliza could have laughed at Annie's dumbfounded expression. But she was intent on securing Thomas. She could tell Annie was nervous of her so she must really think Eliza had the right on her side. But the old woman was prepared to fight to the end.

'I'll fetch the polis!' she cried. 'You'll not take him.'

'Go ahead, fetch whoever you like. Thomas is coming with me. I might have not been so sure if he was fond of you but anyone can see you have the lad cowed. I won't waste any more time. Give me his things and we'll be away for the next train.'

'His clothes aren't leaving this house. They are bought

220

and paid for by me.' Eliza smiled. Now she was aware that Annie knew she had lost the boy.

'Keep them,' she said and turned for the door. Outside by the rows of peas, Tot stood up straight and for a few seconds mother and son stared at each other. Then both smiled.

'Howay now, Tot,' said Eliza. 'Say goodbye to your grandmother. You might not see her again. You want to come with me, don't you?'

Tot nodded, and held out his hand to her. 'I do,' he said and looked back at Annie. 'Good day to you, Grandmother,' he said, and clasped Eliza's hand.

'You ungrateful little sod,' said Annie. 'After all I've done for you. You've been a viper in my bosom.'

Tot didn't know what a viper was or a bosom either but he hesitated, looked up at his mother and saw her nod. Releasing his hand, he ran back to Annie and hugged her round her thighs, which was as high as he could reach. Then he ran back to his mammy.

'Oh, Tot, I was going to make a good and honourable man of you,' said Annie. His hug had almost broken her down.

'A pity you didn't manage it with your own lads,' said Eliza. She went round the side of the cottage and opened the front gate. Tot trotted by her side as they headed for the railway station.

'Tot, where are you going?' Alfie was playing with a

ball on the street. He picked it up and came over to Tot. 'I wanted you to play with me, look, my da bought me an India rubber ball.'

'I cannot, Alfie,' Tot said gravely. 'I have to go with my mammy now.'

As they were paused for the two boys to talk, Annie must have recovered and gathered her wits, for she came out into the street, running after them.

'Give him back!' she shouted at Eliza and Tot moved closer and half hid behind his mother's skirts. Alfie's mother came out, attracted by the shouting, and so did a number of other neighbours. 'Help me, the bitch is trying to take the lad away!' Annie appealed to them. They looked at each other.

'Are you really Tot's mam?' One burly man with his shirtsleeves rolled up over his elbows and striped braces asked Eliza. Before she could answer Annie butted in.

'She is but she left him!'

'I did not leave him,' said Eliza. 'Your son took him away and I've been looking for him ever since.' She turned to the small crowd that had gathered. 'I have some papers here—' she began but Alfie's mother shook her head.

'Nay, lass,' she said, 'I believe you. The bairn's the dead spit of you. And her,' she pointed her thumb at Annie, 'she's proper hard-faced, aye and hard-fisted too. She brays the lad something shameful. No, I won't help her, I'm glad you're taking him, I am.'

222

'Aye, me an'all,' said the man. 'That woman wants ducking for a witch.'

The crowd surrounded Annie. 'Hadaway while you can,' a woman advised. 'We won't stop you. The lad cannot have a worse life than he has now. Good luck to the both of you.'

'Thank you, oh thank you,' said Eliza and walked quickly away with Tot trotting by her side. She was supremely conscious of his small hand in hers, warm and trusting. She didn't care that there was no luggage with him, she would buy him new clothes in Durham. Except only—

On the station platform before boarding the train she asked, 'Did you have something you wanted to bring, Tot? A toy, a ball or anything?' She would have gone back and braved Annie if there was something he loved. She would do anything for him.

'No,' said Tot. 'I haven't got a ball. Only—'

'Yes?'

'I'd like to bring Alfie,' he said. 'But he has to stop with his mam, hasn't he?'

'Aye, I'm sorry, Tot. When you're older you can write a letter, to him though. Or I'll help you write one when we get home.'

Tot nodded, instantly accepting her words. 'Lads belong with their mams, don't they, Mammy?' he said.

Chapter Nineteen

Thomas was very quiet on the journey south. He sat gravely looking out of the window as the fields and hamlets of Northumberland went past at an almost steady forty miles an hour. Occasionally he peeped at his mother and she smiled encouragingly but wisely said little. Eliza never took her eyes off him for she couldn't believe how easy it had been to get him back. She felt that if she looked away he would disappear and she would find it had all been a dream. They sat opposite each other and every few minutes she leaned forward and touched him for the reassurance it gave her.

At Newcastle they alighted from the carriage and made their way to where the mainline London train stood, smoke and steam billowing as the footplate men steamed up for the journey. Tot watched the great engine in wonder but was apprehensive of the crowds scurrying about and held on tightly to her hand.

'It's not far now, Tot,' said Eliza as they boarded and took their seats. Normally she would have ridden in the third-class wagon but even though she did not have a great deal of money to spare, she had bought first-class tickets. Third class was packed with labourers and there would not have been a seat for the child even if she had secured one for herself. Most passengers frowned upon children sitting while adults stood.

The ride to Durham from Newcastle was fairly short; it took less than an hour. Soon they were coming out onto the streets of the old city and walking to the market place for the horse bus that stopped outside the gates of the Infirmary. Tot was still quiet though he answered when Eliza spoke to him.

'Do you remember this place?' she asked him as they waited for the horse bus.

'I think I do,' he replied gravely. Of course he couldn't really, she told herself, it had been a daft question. If he remembered anything it would be the cottage at Haswell and maybe Blue House.

Eliza hadn't really thought beyond getting him back. Now she had to try to work out a plan for someone to look after him while she was working at the hospital. The horse bus drew in and the driver offered the horse a drink from a bucket and hung a nosebag filled with hay over his nose.

'We'll be going in ten minutes,' he told the waiting

passengers. Eliza came to a sudden decision. She still had a few days; she would take Tot to Blue House to her family while she decided what to do.

'I've changed my mind, pet, we'll go to see your grandma,' she said and the lad looked startled and apprehensive for a moment then went along obediently beside her back to the train station. 'Do you remember your grandma?' Looking down, she realised he thought she was taking him back to Alnwick and she berated herself for her thoughtlessness.

'Not your granny, pet, never. I won't take you back there, no. To your other grandma, my mother. Do you remember her?'

Tot gulped and rubbed tears from his eyes with his free hand. 'I don't know,' he said. 'Is it far?'

It was a very tired little lad who stumbled by her side along Alice Street an hour or so later. It was almost dark for the nights were already beginning to cut in. Only the lights from the pithead relieved the gloom and the dim glow of tallow candles from the tiny cottage windows.

'By, our Eliza, what brings you here at this time of the night?' Mary Anne looked up as the door opened, still with a pan lid in her hand, for she had been checking on a pot pie bubbling in an iron pan on the fire. Tommy would be in from the pit in an hour or so along with Albert. Harry had been on first shift and was sitting on the settee reading a pamphlet and beside him sat Peter Collier, the union man. Peter rose to his feet as Eliza came forward with Tot. All three stared at the boy.

'You found the lad!' said Peter. 'Heaven be praised, you found the lad.'

'I did,' said Eliza. 'He was with his granny in Alnwick. Tot, step forward and say how do to your granny and Uncle Harry. And Mr Collier too.'

'What about Jack?' Mary Anne asked.

Eliza put a hand on Tot's shoulder before answering simply, 'Jack's dead.'

'Well. God rest him whatever he did,' said Mary Anne piously. 'How did he die?'

'He fell off a cliff,' said Eliza. 'I didn't know, his mother just told me today.' Mary Anne stared at her daughter, correctly interpreting her warning look.

'Well, howay in, lass, and have a bite to eat. Then I'll put the lad to bed. He'll have to share with Harry, mind. He looks dead on his feet, poor bairn.'

'I was waiting for Tommy and Albert,' said Peter Collier. 'But I can come back in the morning before the shift starts.'

Eliza turned to him. 'No, stay, Mr Collier. Don't let me upset your plans. How are you? You look well at least.'

'Oh I am, and the union is off the ground an' all. It won't be long before the yearly bond is a thing of the past. But I've come here tonight to see if Tommy will put his name forward for union man here at Blue House.' He paused and looked at Tot. 'I'm right glad you got the bairn back after all this time, Eliza,' he said in an undertone. 'You've done well for yourself an' all. Who'd have thought it that night you came to my house for help these five or six years ago?'

'I'm grateful to you, Peter,' she replied. 'I couldn't have done it without your help.'

'Get away, I did nothing. You would have got on any road. You have the brain for it, just like your father has a good brain. That's why we want him for union man.'

Eliza nodded. 'He has. The pity of it was he didn't have the chance before.'

'What's that you're saying?' demanded Mary Anne. 'Talking about Tommy, are you?'

Before Eliza could answer the door opened and the two pitmen came in, taking off their helmets to show startlingly white patches of skin above the rest, which was black with coal. They were in their pit clothes. They were short of stature but with powerful shoulders and arms from working in narrow seams, some of which were no more than two feet six inches high. Consequently, most of their working shift was spent lying on their backs, wielding a pick.

'Wotcher, Peter,' Tommy said. 'You been waiting for us?'

'I have,' Peter replied. 'I wanted a word before the meeting the morn.'

'You having a bite with us? There'll be enough meat pudding, I think?' Tommy raised an eyebrow at his wife and Mary Anne nodded. She had boiled extra potatoes when her visitors arrived. The meal would go round, she reckoned.

'I'm beholden for the offer,' Peter replied, 'but I have to get back. There's still work to do for the meeting. I'll talk while you eat, though.'

Tommy and Albert sat down at the table still in their black. Neither had eaten anything but a jam sandwich that Mary Anne had packed in their bait tin nor drunk anything but cold tea from the tin bottle she had filled for them twelve hours ago.

So far Tommy had not spoken to Eliza, but before eating his meal he looked at her as she sat on the settee with Tot falling asleep on her lap.

'Now, lass, what brings you here?'

'I've got the bairn back,' said Eliza. 'I'm a widow now, you've no reason to be ashamed of me.'

'I can see you've got the lad,' said Tommy. He took a long swallow from his pint pot of tea and smacked his lips. In truth he was very proud of his daughter, for hadn't she pulled herself up in the world? But once having shown his disapproval of her leaving her husband he didn't know how to get out of it. But it was different

229

now, Jack was gone and Eliza was entitled to go her own way. He hadn't liked Mary Anne taking money from Eliza when she wouldn't go back to her man.

'Well, I reckon I wasn't ashamed of you, I was disappointed, that's all,' he said. 'Take the lad to bed, he's fair tuckered out.' Having declared peace, he turned his attention to Peter. 'Now then, Peter, what's it about?'

Eliza didn't hear the conversation because she went upstairs with Tot and put him to bed. Afterwards she went into the tiny room that had been built on the back of the house to accommodate Miley. It was a wood and stone structure built by Tommy and his marras with whatever materials were to hand. The uprights were old wooden rails from the wagon ways and the stone had been gathered and sometimes quarried from the fields around. Mary Anne had lime-washed the walls but there was no window and the only light was through the door cut in the original back wall of the cottage.

Miley was asleep. He spent a lot of his life asleep now, since the pain in his back had worsened. Laudanum was the thing to bring his relief. He lay, or rather reclined, against the cushions, his face pale in the light of the taper Eliza had brought in with her. Even in his sleep his face was twisted with pain. Pity welled up in her for the little lad; though he was fourteen he seemed no bigger than when he was six. There was absolutely no flesh on his bones and his skin was translucent.

With a shock, Eliza realised he was not long for this world. He had the look she had seen so often in her years on the wards, the look of someone near death. And she admitted to herself that it would be a good thing if he was taken but it would be devastating for her mother. She pulled the covers up over his thin shoulders and went back into the kitchen.

Peter Collier was just leaving. 'Think well about it. Tommy,' he was saying to her father. 'The union is legal, we know, at least it is now. But if you should have to look for another job you will be lucky to get one when you are a union man.'

'Mr Moore cannot sack me for it, though, not now,' Tommy protested.

Peter smiled. 'You know and I know he'll find another pretext.'

'Aye well, the Lord will look after us.'

Eliza forebore to ask why the Lord hadn't been looking after Miley when the corve came off the rails and fell on him in the pit. Just lately in her work on the wards she often wondered why. Especially when the patient was a dying child or a mother leaving a young family. She shook herself mentally; it was not a bit of use getting morbid.

'Good night then, Sister Mitchell,' Peter said. 'I'm glad you have your lad back at last. I'm happy for you, I am.'

'Thank you,' Eliza replied. 'Good night to you.'

Lying on the settee after the family had gone up the ladder to bed and she was alone, she watched the shadows made by the last flickers of firelight on the walls of the room. She was comfortable enough on the settee though the horsehair prickled a little, but she lay with her head on her hand to keep it from her cheek so it didn't bother her too much.

It had been an extraordinary day, indeed. She thought about Jack with some sadness though she found it hard to forgive him for taking her son away from her. But they had been happy at times. Still she was free now, she was a widow. She needed to plan what she was going to do for she had Tot to care for now. She couldn't stay in the nurses' home. Perhaps she couldn't stay at the Infirmary. Perhaps she could earn a living nursing on the outside. That might be the only option.

'A nurse's first duty is to her patients. I am very disappointed in you, Sister Mitchell-Howe. Very disappointed indeed.' Matron sat behind her desk and stared unblinkingly at Eliza. Indeed, she would be very sorry to lose her, she thought. The sister was a very good nurse, she had proved herself over and over in her work. She was intelligent and caring and seemed to anticipate the needs of her patients before they realised them for themselves. But evidently she had been living a lie.

She had been married and had a child. She would never have been accepted for training if she hadn't lied about that. Well, she hadn't exactly lied but she hadn't admitted the facts.

'I'm sorry, Matron,' said Eliza.

She gazed down at the floor. Last night, lying in bed or rather on the settee, she had decided to confess it all to Matron. After all, she needed a letter of good character from her for the future. Now, seeing the older woman's shocked reaction she was not sure if she had done the right thing. Oh well, it was too late now. She would have to look for work as a jobbing nurse and if Matron would not give her a character she would have to work among the poor. That would not pay very much but they would have to manage on whatever they had.

'I don't know what Miss Nightingale would say about this,' said Matron.

'No, Matron.'

Miss Nightingale would have something to say and it would probably be caustic, Eliza thought. Miss Nightingale had something to say about everything. She did not allow that nurses were persons in their own right, she did not. At least that was the impression she had gained from the lists of rules and regulations that Eliza had had to learn by heart during her year of training.

'Your training will be wasted,' said Matron.

Eliza didn't contradict her outright, she didn't dare. 'I intend to work among the sick in their own homes,' said Eliza. 'I will use my training.' She glanced up and caught Matron's eye. 'I must look after my little boy.'

'Hmm,' said Matron. She appeared to have reached a decision. 'Come back tomorrow at nine in the morning,' she said. 'I will write a reference of good character for you. You will not be required to work a month's notice. I do not think you should go back on the wards.' She rose to her feet and nodded dismissively.

'Thank you, Matron.'

Eliza found herself outside the closed door of Matron's office. She leaned against it for a second or two and breathed a sigh of relief. If Matron had held her to the working of her notice she would have had to leave Tot with her mother, and Mary Anne had quite enough to do.

It was still early in the morning for it had been necessary to catch Matron before she set off on her daily rounds of the wards. So Eliza went to the nurses' dining room to try to see Bertha, who would still be serving breakfast to the night staff. She managed to get a few words with her as the meal was almost finished.

'I want to thank you, Bertha, you don't know what you've done for me,' said Eliza. 'I've got Thomas back with me, I'm so happy.'

'It was the lad then,' said Bertha, smiling. She glanced in the direction of the kitchen but there was no sign of the cook. 'Tell me about it.'

So Eliza told her about Jack's death, about finding Thomas with her mother-in-law and all that had happened since.

'I have given notice to Matron this morning,' she said. 'But I had to see you before I went.'

'Went where? Where are you going? Sister?' There was alarm, even panic in Bertha's tone. 'What about me?'

Eliza gazed at her. Indeed, what about Bertha? An idea was forming in her mind. Bertha regarded her if not as a mother then as an older sister, for she had no family of her own and clung to Eliza.

'Would you like to come with me, Bertha? Between us we could look after Thomas, couldn't we? I could work as a visiting nurse and we would rent a little house. What do you say, Bertha?' Eliza was warming to the idea. It would work all right; she knew it would.

Bertha's eyes shone. 'Do you mean it? We can live together and I'll earn some money somehow. I can take in washing, mebbe, or mending, I'm good with mending, I am, aren't I?'

'You are.' Eliza smiled at the little woman in the all-enveloping apron and large cap that was always falling over her eyes.

'Bertha? When you've finished talking to Sister Mitchell-Howe perhaps you will come and start the washing-up,' Cook snapped from the kitchen door. 'Or do you want to be turned off.'

'If you like, Cook. Will I go now or do you want me to wash up first?' said Bertha. 'You're not turning me off, I'm leaving any road.'

Chapter Twenty

1872

Eliza drove briskly along the road out of Gilesgate to Sherburn in her tub trap. It was a lovely fresh morning in spring and Dolly, the pony, trotted along with her head up at a spanking pace considering the rutted road. Puffs of dust came from beneath her hooves, dust sparkling with coal particles. Dolly's pace slowed as she approached the hill and Eliza clucked at her in encouragement. Dolly was a bit too plump on the spring grass, she thought to herself.

Today Eliza was going out to Blue House colliery but she had a few calls to make on the way. Still, she reckoned she would be finished by one o'clock and then she would be free to go to see her mother. Worry niggled at Eliza's mind at the thought of Mary Anne. Her mother was showing symptoms of heart disease though she tried to hide it.

The miners and their wives had to be in dire straits with regard to their health before they could be persuaded to visit a doctor. Most often it was too late when they did. Eliza was determined that Mary Anne should have medical help. She perhaps needed digitalis, the drug made from foxgloves, and Eliza would prefer she had it from a doctor rather than some concoction brewed up by the local wise woman.

Mary Anne had started to fail after the death of Miley a couple of years before. She refused to be comforted by anyone, even Tommy. Instead she had worked harder than ever, not going to bed at all some nights as the lads were on different shifts and needed a hot meal when they came in after twelve hours at the face. And in spite of this she had begun to take in washing and ironing from a number of widowers in the rows.

'If I have to bury another one of my bairns it will not be in a pauper's grave,' she said to Eliza, her voice hard.

'Oh, Mam,' Eliza said helplessly. She felt guilty because she had not been able to pay for the funeral. Her income was reduced severely after she first left the hospital and she had Tot to keep. Now she had acquired a reputation for excellent nursing and her patients were from the middle classes as well as the poor. But then . . .

'Mary Anne, you listen to our Eliza,' said Tommy as he came in the door. 'I'm not having it, not any more.

You have to think of the lads that are with us, never mind when they are gone.'

Now Mary Anne was not capable of doing any extra work. It was a phase that hadn't lasted long.

Well, I'm making a living for us now, Tot and me and a bit to spare. Bertha keeps herself, practically, Eliza mused as she stopped the tub trap in the street before the house where her next patient lived.

'Stay there, be good, Dolly,' she ordered the pony and Dolly turned her head and regarded her with intelligent eyes. Sometimes she could swear that Dolly understood every word she said.

'Good morning, Nurse.' The girl who answered her knock could have been taken for Bertha's sister. She too had been brought up in the workhouse, where she had been taken at the age of three when her mother, a widow, became too ill to work. Now she was thirteen and hired out as a maid of all work. Mrs Green, who was Eliza's patient, was suffering from rheumatic fever so her husband had taken Lottie from the workhouse to look after him and his five sons. And his wife, of course. Mr Green was a nightshift overman at the pit.

'A lovely morning it is, Lottie,' replied Eliza, stepping over the threshold. 'How is Mrs Green today?'

'Tolerable,' said Lottie. 'She had a bad night, she says. I got up to her twice as Mr Green was at the pit.' Indeed, Lottie's small pale face looked pinched and there were dark circles under her eyes. Eliza paused before going into the downstairs sitting room, which had been converted into a bedroom for Mrs Green.

'Why don't you go out into the lane for a few minutes, Lottie? Just while I'm here. The boys are at school, aren't they?'

Lottie nodded. 'They are,' she said and looked longingly at the sunlit day outside. 'I don't know—'

'It'll be fine,' urged Eliza. 'I can call you if I need you, just stay within earshot.'

'I'll just walk to the end of the road and back,' Lottie decided. Her eyes had brightened already at the idea.

'She's still a bairn herself,' Eliza murmured aloud as she went in to Mrs Green. The woman was lying back on the pillows with her eyes closed. Her lips moved and there was a deceptive flush to her cheeks that could have been mistaken for health, but which Eliza knew showed she was running a temperature. Her hair was lank.

'Don't touch me, please,' she begged. 'I can't bear anyone to touch me.'

'It's only me, Mrs Green. I've come to try to make you more comfortable,' Eliza said gently. 'Is the pain bad just now?'

'Aye, oh aye, it is.' Mrs Green opened her eyes and looked at Eliza. 'Can I have some of my drops? I've not had any since last night and the pain is bad.'

Eliza measured out a dose of laudanum and administered

it to her patient, then waited a while for it to take effect before carefully sponging her down, touching as lightly as possible on her poor inflamed joints. Even combing her hair made Mrs Green moan involuntarily, so Eliza brushed it carefully and tied it away from her forehead with a ribbon. Changing the bed was difficult with the patient still in it but Eliza was well practised at it after five years in the Infirmary.

At last she stood away from the bed and regarded her patient. Mrs Green looked very tired but she was obviously more comfortable than when Eliza came in.

'I'll get Lottie to bring you a bowl of beef tea and a little bread and butter,' she said.

'No, I won't be able to eat, I'm not hungry,' said Mrs Green, her voice barely above a whisper. Eliza felt her pulse and it was fast and thready. The slight effort had taken all her strength.

'You must try to eat, at least take a little beef tea,' Eliza urged. She wondered whether she should ask the doctor to call but decided against it. There was nothing he could do. What the woman needed just now was good nursing. And the family couldn't afford a live-in nurse so young Lottie was the only alternative.

'I'll call in this evening on my way back from Haswell,' she promised. Mrs Green didn't answer for her eyes were already closing. At least the drug gave her some blessed relief.

Lottie was in the kitchen at the back of the house, banging away at the pots and pans from breakfast. She turned as Eliza came in, wiping her hands on the sacking apron she had put on over her overall.

'I'm going now, I'll come back this evening,' Eliza said. 'She's very frail. Try to get some beef tea into her at least. When she wakes, that is. Let her sleep for now.'

'I'll try, Nurse,' Lottie replied. She still retained a little colour in her cheeks from her brief outing and looked almost pretty. 'I made some fresh yesterday. It's in the pantry; I'll just heat a cupful for her.'

Eliza went out to the waiting Dolly, who, in spite of the brake on the tub trap, had managed to pull it askew on to the grass verge in order to snatch a few raspberry leaves that were sticking through the Greens' hedge. The pony regarded Eliza thoughtfully as she came out then took a last bite and chewed in appreciation.

'Dolly, you bad girl,' said Eliza. It took her a few minutes to persuade the pony back onto the road and not before Dolly took another bite at the succulent raspberry leaves. But at last they were on their way.

'Hey up, Dolly,' she said and flapped the reins and the pony set off, still chewing. There were two more patients to attend to before she was free to go on to her mother's house. As they trundled along, Eliza's thoughts turned to her son as they usually did. Tot was ten and she had ambitions for him to go further in school. But he needed a scholarship or a sponsorship for that.

On Sunday last she had spoken to Peter Collier about the possibility of the boy getting the union to sponsor him.

'The lad is bright and it would be a shame for him to have to leave school now,' he said. 'I doubt the union would look favourably on him, though. After all, he is the grandson of a miner not a son.'

'But his father is dead, I am a widow, shouldn't that count for something?'

'It does, but not in this case,' Peter explained gently. He looked thoughtfully at the boy, who came up to them as the Sunday School class was released for the afternoon. 'I'll look into the scholarships available for you.'

Eliza forebore to say she could do that for herself. The trouble was that there were no certainties about getting a scholarship, and she didn't want to take a chance on it. She was definitely not a gambler. The thought put her in mind of Jack. He was a gambler and look where it got him. She wanted nothing to do with gambling; it was a vice that had ruined their lives. Oh, but now, after all these years the bad memories were fading and sometimes she couldn't help dwelling on the good memories, the times when she and Jack were in love, gloriously in love.

She was still a young woman, not yet thirty, yet she felt

as though life, real life, was passing her by. Eliza shook herself mentally; she was becoming maudlin. She was lucky, wasn't she? She was making a comfortable living for herself and Tot, she reminded herself again. They were all right, the two of them. Three of them really, for there was Bertha. But Bertha too was doing well: she ran a business of her own now, hiring out girls for domestic help. And she ran the business fairly, charging reasonable prices and giving the girls as fair a wage as the business allowed.

'Mind,' said Mary Anne as Eliza lifted the sneck into the house in Alice Street. 'I thought you weren't coming.'

Anxiety smote Eliza as she regarded her mother. Mary Anne had lost weight and she was sitting in the chair by the fire. This was significant, for Eliza couldn't remember her ever sitting still doing nothing at all. She didn't even have mending on her lap and the ashes had not been taken out.

'Morning, Mam,' she said. 'How are you feeling today?'

'I'm not in very good fettle,' Mary Anne admitted. 'I fainted this morning and it's left me a bit down.'

'You're taking your medicine?'

'I hadn't any left,' Mary Anne replied. 'I was waiting for you to go and get me some from the chemist.'

'Where are the lads? Couldn't one of them have got it?' Eliza spoke sharply. Mary Anne was typical of the miners' wives, she would not ask her menfolk to do anything besides go to the pit every day.

'The lads are on night shift, they have enough on without running about after me. And Tommy, well, he was away to Durham the morn, first thing. There's great things going on at the union. The yearly bond is finished, you must have heard.'

'I did. A good thing that.'

The union was beginning to find its feet. Apart from the bond being abolished, all the men got an allowance of coal, not just those in the big pits. Though of course the owners fought hard against it, saying the next thing they would be bankrupted and then where would the pitmen be? Why, there was talk of them having to put proper fireplaces in the colliery houses with their own ovens, no less. Eliza had heard all about it from Peter Collier. They usually found time for a short talk after chapel. Sometimes they even shared a picnic on the banks of the Wear.

'Well, I still think they should do more for you,' said Eliza.

'I'd have to be in a very bad way to ask them,' Mary Anne retorted with a sudden show of spirit. 'Lads who've put a full shift in at the face.'

'Oh, Mam, I'm sure they would do it. They're just used to you running after them all the time. You've brought them up wrong.'

'They're good lads,' Mary Anne insisted. 'Mind, if you'll give me a hand to clean their boots for tonight

I'd be grateful.' She nodded to where two pairs of pit boots stood at the side of the fireplace, drying out from the wet conditions in the seam they were working this quarter.

'All right. First, though, I'll away into Haswell to get you your medicine.'

'Have a cup of tea and a bite first,' said Mary Anne.

By the time Eliza was driving back from Haswell in her tub trap it was already well into the afternoon and she had to call back to see Mrs Green before she went home. Thank goodness for Bertha, she thought. Bertha could be depended on to see to Tot's tea when he came in from school. She ran her business from a room in the house in Gilesgate so was there most of the time.

Eliza clambered down from the trap and took the medicine in to her mother, measuring out fifteen minims and insisting that Mary Anne took it and rested by the fire until it was time to call up the boys for their shift.

Later, driving west to Gilesgate once again with the sun low in the sky so that both she and Dolly held their heads down against its brightness, Eliza left Sherburn for the city. Dolly's pace quickened as they neared home and she anticipated her stable and sweet hay and a handful of oats to eat. The pony was wise in her ways as Galloways so often are and knew her own way to the top of the street and down the alley to the stable at the back.

'I'll see to her, Mam,' said Tot, catching hold of the pony's reins and holding her as Eliza got down from the trap. He had been watching for her coming, as he usually did. Tot promised to be taller than her brothers and straight-limbed, though not as powerful in the shoulders as they were at his age. For a ten-year-old he handled the pony well. As always, Eliza watched her son with a surge of pride. Those years without him were like a remembered bad dream to her now, no more.

Bertha was inside, just putting fillets of herring on to the large greased griddle. The table was set and there were boiled new potatoes from the long strip of garden behind the house, and fresh green peas.

'I'm in a bit of a hurry the night,' said Bertha. 'I'm off out.'

Eliza looked at her in surpise. 'Out?'

Bertha didn't look at her but turned the fillets over expertly with a knife. 'I'm going to the magic lantern with Charlie,' she said.

'With Charlie?'

Eliza didn't know why she was so surprised. After all, she knew that Charlie had taken to studying Bertha with a certain look in his eye but Bertha – well, Bertha had never shown an interest in the opposite sex that she could recall.

'Aye, Charlie,' Bertha said now. 'I'm meeting him at the end of the street in half an hour.' She slid the fish on to plates and served out potatoes and peas. 'Give Tot a shout, will you? He's in the field playing soldiers.'

Obediently, Eliza went out in search of her son. He was in the open space behind the houses as Bertha had said he was. There was a gang of lads shooting pretend guns made out of anything to hand, such as broomsticks and walking sticks. She watched for a moment or two as they re-enacted the Battle of Balaclava as they understood it, or rather, made it up as they went along. The ferocious yells and fierce expressions were enough to frighten any Russian, she thought, smiling.

Tot abandoned his game and came to her as soon as he saw her. 'What's for tea, Mam?' he asked. 'I'm famished.'

'Herrings,' she replied. By, he was a different lad from the fearful boy she had brought back from Northumberland, away from his grandmother's clutches.

'You should ask Charlie to tea on Sunday,' she said to Bertha when they were sitting round the table eating the meal.

'Nay, I don't know,' said Bertha doubtfully. She had been as surprised as Eliza evidently was when Charlie, in his mid-thirties and a single man, asked her out, albeit only to the magic lantern show at the chapel. He was good-looking with kind eyes and Bertha couldn't believe he was interested in her. She was past the courting age, in her twenties herself, and had never attracted the attentions of a man and didn't expect to. But oh, he was nice and she liked him; more than liked him. But how could she leave Eliza, who had been her friend for so many years? Mind, she told herself, Charlie hadn't asked her to wed. She was getting a bit in front of herself, like.

'Bertha likes Mr Carr,' said Tot. 'She let him kiss her.'

'Tot!' Bertha was blushing, her face bright red.

'You did, I saw you,' said Tot.

'Well, never you mind, Tot,' Eliza put in. 'If you've finished your tea go on out for half an hour; you can play for a while.'

Tot wiped his plate with a piece of bread and stuffed it in his mouth then stood up. 'Well, I did,' he said and fled the room.

'I'm sorry, I'll have to give him a talking to,' Eliza said ruefully.

'No, it's all right. To tell the truth, he did see me and Charlie Carr together. But it doesn't mean anything.'

'Why not? He's not just playing with your affections, is he? No, he's not the sort to do that.'

'No, but—' Bertha stopped as there came a knock on the front door. 'I'll have to go, I'll be back before nine.' She took off her enveloping overall and Eliza saw she had her best dress on beneath it.

'Bertha, wait a minute,' Eliza began.

'No, I have to go.' Bertha rushed out of the room and Eliza heard her open the front door and say something and a man's voice replying. Then they were gone. She realised that Bertha hadn't wanted him to come into the house. Why was that? Oh, they would have to talk, she thought, she and Bertha.

Chapter Twenty-One

It was hard for Eliza to realise that Bertha had a life of her own. She had grown so used to being able to rely on her. Though she was only a few years older she supposed she was almost like a mother to her. But Bertha was a woman and of course she would want to have a family life of her own with a husband and children maybe. Just as any daughter grew away eventually.

It was brought home to her in the following few weeks as Bertha and Charlie settled down to serious courting. Eliza could no longer rely on Bertha being there any time she needed her, she mused ruefully.

'What time will you be back?' Bertha asked just about every time Eliza went out. 'Only Charlie and me plan to go to the magic lantern.' Or sometimes it was the choir practice, or even a walk along the riverbank. Now, they sometimes went to the farm so Charlie could show Bertha around it.

'Charlie says this,' or 'Charlie says we should do things this way,' were phrases that were often on Bertha's lips. Sometimes Eliza, too used by now to doing things her own way and having Bertha follow her example without question, had to clench her teeth to stop herself retorting. But Bertha was happy. She hummed to herself all day and once or twice Eliza caught her standing and just gazing into the distance with a small smile hovering on her lips.

'Charlie says we can get wed in October, maybe. That's after the harvest and before the threshing,' said Bertha early one morning before Eliza set out on her rounds. Eliza paused in packing her bag and stared at her.

'I thought he hadn't asked you to marry him,' she replied.

'Aye. No, I suppose he hasn't.' Bertha looked a little confused. 'Not in so many words, like.' She shook her head, dismissing the thought and got on with placing newly ironed clothes into piles for her girls to take back to the customers. 'But still, we had an understanding.'

'You didn't tell me.' Eliza was a bit put out, something she knew was silly, really.

'I thought you realised.' Bertha paused again then went on, 'Listen, we'll talk about it the night. We have to have a proper talk.'

As Eliza drove off on her rounds, dropping Tot off at

the school gates on her way, she tried to think through the situation. She didn't really think Charlie was the best man for Bertha. He was a farmer, a middling sort of farmer rather like Farmer Dean, whose cottage she and Jack had lived in near Haswell. Comfortable enough, but he would expect Bertha to work hard on the farm. Not that Bertha would mind that, but Eliza suspected the only reason he was thinking of matrimony was that his mother, with whom he lived, was getting too old to do the milking and butter-making and housework, let alone helping in the fields when extra hands were needed.

Bertha and she herself had grown used to thinking for themselves and Charlie was the old-fashioned sort who would expect a wife to do what he told her to do. Obey would be the main vow in *their* wedding ceremony.

Only yesterday Charlie had come in the house with a bare knock on the door, not waiting for anyone to invite him in. He had walked in and stared at Bertha, who was still in the middle of washing up the tea things.

'Aren't you ready?' he had asked her, when she obviously was not.

'I won't be a minute,' she replied, looking a bit flustered, Eliza had thought and was indignant for her.

'We'll be late for choir practice, did you forget the time? Howay, you can finish that when you get back. Or mebbe Sister Mitchell can do it?' He had given such a look at Eliza as made her feel like a veritable slave-driver.

'Yes, I can do it,' she said, however. 'Go on, Bertha, you go.'

'But—'

'Never mind buts,' said Charlie. 'Let's away.'

Bertha had untied her overall obediently and gone with him. It made Eliza feel unreasonably hard done by, even though she had told Bertha to do just that. She had had a hard day, fitting in extra patients when she was approached in the street, something that happened often now that her tub trap was well known in the surrounding area. She rose to her feet and finished the drying up and put the pots and pans away in the dresser and pantry with some fairly unnecessary banging.

Her bad humour didn't last long for she had to smile at herself. She was being silly. She had no rights at all on Bertha's time: the girl wasn't a servant really, nor a slave. And she had a right to enjoy herself and get wed an' all.

Maybe Charlie did love Bertha. And if he did not then he must be fond of her and she was fond of him besides. And most men expected total obedience from their wives. Hadn't Jack? Still, a girl liked to be asked, she thought as she headed for Sherburn Hill.

Eliza's thoughts returned to the present and the cool of the morning as Dolly slowed her pace and stopped outside the Greens' house. The pony was like a milkman's horse now and knew most of the stops on her rounds.

Lottie opened the door before Eliza even knocked. 'By, I'm that glad to see you, Nurse,' she blurted. 'I was going to ask the lad next door to run for the doctor if you didn't come. Only Mr Green doesn't like me to, he reckons doctors cost money and it's a waste when he's paying a nurse.'

'What is it, Lottie?' Eliza asked over her shoulder as she hurried in. 'Is Mrs Green worse?'

'Aye, she is—'

But Eliza was no longer listening as she entered the front room and saw her patient. Mrs Green was lying very still, with her eyes closed. The skin around her mouth was cyanosed and the lips were sunken in a little.

Eliza took hold of her wrist and saw that her fingertips were blue, too. It took her a while to find her pulse, which was thin and thready. Her breathing was so shallow as to be almost undetectable.

'Go for the doctor, Lottie,' Eliza commanded, without even looking round. 'Tell him I think her heart is failing.'

'Oh!' Lottie started to weep, long, noisy sobs. 'What will Mr Green say?'

'Never mind that, just go. Run!'

By the time the doctor came Mrs Green had finally given up the effort to breathe and slipped away. 'At least she died peacefully,' Eliza murmured. She gently closed the woman's eyes and pulled the sheet over her head. She could do no more, for she was well aware that Mr

Green would not pay a trained nurse's rates for laying his wife out. Not when there were women among the miners' wives who would do it for a few pence.

'A blessed release,' said Dr Gray as he lifted the sheet and looked at the patient. 'Poor woman has had a hard time of it, there's no doubt.' He turned to Lottie, who was still crying, though quietly now. She was just a scrap of a girl with bent legs from an attack of rickets when she was small. Her large maid's cap was falling over her eyes. 'Sit down a minute, Lottie,' he said kindly. 'You look worn out.'

'Eeh, I couldn't, not in the front of the house,' she answered. 'Mr Green would go mad.'

'He's not here, though, is he? And I'm telling you to sit down. Nurse will bring you a cup of tea with sugar in it. It will be good for you. In fact, Nurse Mitchell, bring three cups. We could all do with one.'

Dr Gray was a good, kind man, Eliza told herself as she settled the kettle on the fire and set a tray with cups and saucers. He was not much older than she was herself yet he showed an understanding and empathy with his patients and the ordinary mining folk that was not always found in the doctors she had known. He had lovely brown eyes too and dark wavy hair with a lock that often fell over his forehead.

What was she thinking about? She was finished with men, of course she was. They took away a woman's rights and independence, oh they did that! Eliza made the tea and added the sugar bowl and a jug of fresh milk she found in the pantry and took the tray into the front room.

Dr Gray looked up as she came in. 'Thank you, Nurse,' he said. His accent was not local; there was a hint of a border burr a little more pronounced than what Jack had had.

Lottie sat on the edge of her seat as though she were ready to jump up should Mr Green suddenly return. Though that was not likely, for he had gone out to work with the back shift today and wouldn't be home till the evening. She had stopped crying apart from the occasional sob, though she kept her gaze averted from the bed.

The three of them sat there, sipping their tea, Lottie watching the others surreptitiously and trying to do exactly as they did. And it was true, the sweet tea not only tasted good but she felt the better for it as Dr Gray had said she would.

'You won't go until someone comes in, will you, Nurse?' Lottie asked Eliza fearfully, when Dr Gray had left. 'I don't like to be left in the house on my own with – with—'

'It's all right, Lottie, there's no need to be scared,' said Eliza. 'Look, I'll call in at the mine offices and tell the manager. He'll send Mr Green home early, you'll see.'

'Yes but – can I just go next door until he comes?'

'Get your neighbour to come in here,' Eliza advised. 'Mr Green won't like it if the house is left empty, not now.'

Lottie hurried off, looking relieved, and returned with a solemn-looking woman, so Eliza was able to go on her way. She had several patients to see and it was almost two o'clock before she could pull Dolly on to the entrance to a farm road and put on her nosebag. She sat in the trap and ate her own sandwich and drank water from a bottle she had brought with her. While she sat she went over the morning's work and reflected on the two patients she still had to see. One was a small girl who had fallen into the pithead pond. The water was coal black and fairly deep but at least it wasn't infected and a passing miner had managed to drag her out. Still, the little lass now had pneumonia and needed careful nursing. The other was a miner with a 'bett' hand, a hand swollen and suppurating, oozing pus. It was practically impossible to impress on his wife that the best way of dealing with it was absolute cleanliness. She insisted on putting a poultice of filthy cobwebs on the hand rather than a poultice of linseed, which was what Eliza did. But every time she went back to the house he was sitting in agony from a dirty hand, which now showed ominous red lines beginning to run up his arm.

'See,' his wife had said the day before. 'I think that

stuff you put on is giving him blood poisoning. I don't think you should come back here, Nurse.'

'Florence Nightingale said cleanliness was the most important thing to stop it happening,' said Eliza. 'You needn't pay me, I know you must be hard up with Billy being off work. I'll come anyway.'

'There's no need,' Billy's wife said stubbornly. Her eyes were hard as she stared at Eliza. Billy had wanted Eliza, but as far as his wife could see, the nurse was no better than the old woman who lived on the end of the street. 'A but of dirt never did anybody any harm.'

'John Wesley said cleanliness was next to godliness,' said Eliza desperately.

'Aye, well,' the woman replied doubtfully. 'I don't know.' The minister was always quoting the sayings of John Wesley and she thought more of his sayings than any of Florence Nightingale.

It had been Billy's voice from inside that settled the matter. 'You come the morn, Nurse,' he had said, his voice weak from pain and fever. 'Take no notice of her. She doesn't know what she's talking about.'

The freshness of the morning was beginning to dim as Eliza went into the tiny miner's cottage. Inside the one downstairs room little light got in through the small window and there was an unpleasant smell coming from Billy's hand. He was sitting in a chair before the fire and he was shivering even though sweat stood out on his brow. As Eliza approached him his head fell against the back of the chair as though he hadn't the strength to hold it up.

'The lad's badly, Nurse,' said his wife, who was sitting at the table looking very worried indeed. 'It's not my fault,' she went on as Eliza saw that the poultice she had put on his hand was missing and in its place there was a bandage grubby with cobwebs.

'I asked you not to put that stuff on his hand,' said Eliza.

'Aye well, I know, but he was getting no better and I was talking to the lasses and they swear by cobwebs—'

Eliza sighed. 'Well, I think I'll have to get the doctor to him now.'

'The doctor? Don't be soft, we cannot afford the doctor! I only have elevenpence to last the rest of the week.'

Eliza looked at Billy; his skin was shiny with patches of red on white, his breathing rapid. She bit her lip. It was up to her to do something. 'Put the kettle on, woman, I want a bowl of hot water,' she said, coming to a decision. She had a lancet in its case in her bag; she would have to lance the hand and try to get the pus out. Though it was suppurating very little matter was getting out. She got out the lancet. It was clean at least, she had washed it only last night.

'Eeh, what're you going to do?'

'Leave her alone, Betsy, let her get on with it,' Billy said, suddenly showing a small spurt of energy. 'She can cut the bloody thing off for all I care.'

'No, I'm just going to lance it, let the putrid matter out,' Eliza said. She washed the hand to get rid of the cobwebs in the bowl of hot water provided rather sceptically by Betsy, who really couldn't see the point of such newfangled ideas. Then she picked her place with care and sunk the point of the lancet into the heart of the abscess that had swelled beneath the skin. Billy gasped but didn't cry out.

A few minutes later, Eliza had the hand cleaned up and bandaged and had given him instructions to keep it held high. 'I'll call back later today,' she told Betsy. 'Don't touch it.'

'Well. I don't know—'

'Betsy,' Billy warned. He looked thoroughly washed out, thought Eliza. But she could only wait and see if she had done the right thing.

Eliza had two hours free before she called on the couple of cases she had to see later in the day, so she drove home. She could spend some time with Tot when he came in from school, she thought. Sometimes it irked her that he should seem to be as fond of Bertha as he was of his mother. It was unreasonable, she knew. What would she have done without her friend? Well, if Bertha got wed she would have to spend more time with her son. At least they would be able to manage financially now.

Tot was embarrassed when she met him at the school gates. 'You needn't have come, Mam,' he said, glancing sideways at his classmates. 'I walk home by myself now, I'm not a little babby.'

And he wasn't; that was very evident, she realised. At ten years old he was almost as tall as she was herself and looking more like Jack, apart from his eyes, every day. Her heart swelled with pride just to look at him. She couldn't believe she had such a big lad as he was becoming; she was only twenty-eight after all!

'I was passing, that's all, and I thought you and your marras would like a ride home,' she said apologetically.

Four or five of them jumped into the tub trap with alacrity and poor Dolly had to pull them all home, Thankfully the school was only a few streets away from the house in Gilesgate.

It was as they turned into the street that a voice hailed her from a passing cab. 'Eliza!'

She glanced at the cab, which had drawn to a halt, and felt a shock like cold water as she realised it was Jonathan Moore.

Chapter Twenty-Two

'Eliza,' he said. 'It is so nice to see you again.'

'My name is Sister Mitchell-Howe,' said Eliza. 'I can't say I'm happy to see you.' Jonathan Moore had put on a little weight and there was a sagginess about his face though his eyes were the same as ever, even to the same expressionless gaze.

'Well, Sister Mitchell-Howe, you have come up in the world, I see. You're as lovely as ever, though.'

Eliza ignored this remark. The sight of him had brought the events of the night before she left Jack vividly to mind. She could barely look at him let alone speak to him. He had brought the cab he was in to the side of the road and halted in front of her so she began to ease Dolly around it.

'Wait, you're not going?' Jonathan asked.

'I have to take the lads home,' she replied. She was flustered, filled with dislike. 'Why can't you leave us alone?' It was an irrational remark considering the fact that she hadn't seen him for some years. Except for the once, she remembered; he had stood on the edge of the crowd of off-shift miners when Miley was being buried.

'There is no cause to be unpleasant, Eliza,' said Jonathan. 'I simply wished to say how I admire you for the way you have got on in life.'

The boys in the trap were beginning to get a little boisterous, standing up and pushing and shoving each other. 'Are we going?' one asked.

'Aye, we are,' Eliza replied. 'Gee up, Dolly.' She managed to get around the cab and set off along the street and round the corner to where she stabled the pony.

She hurried Tot into the back door of the house despite his protests and closed the door after her.

'Who's that man, Mam?' he asked.

'Just a man I used to know,' she answered. 'I don't want anything to do with him.'

'Why? He seems like a nice man,' said Tot. But he was losing interest. 'Can I go out and play quoits? The lads are playing a match today.'

'When you've had your tea,' said Eliza. By that time Jonathan would have gone away, she thought. She had a feeling he was still somewhere about. She felt jumpy, unsettled.

Bertha came in, her eyes shining and her cheeks rosy. 'Charlie and me have set the date,' she said. 'We are getting wed in October, as we thought. It is a good time for the farm, before the threshing.' She liked the farm and enjoyed working with the animals. Charlie's mother was teaching her the dairy work, expecting Bertha to take over the heavy jobs such as the scrubbing and the butter-churning, but Bertha was not afraid of hard work. She knew little else. But the older woman had spoken sharply to her for giving a mewling kitten a saucer of milk and she mentioned this to Eliza.

'I'm not supposed to feed them, you know. They have to learn to hunt the rats and mice,' she said. 'But the kitten looked so thin and poorly.' Bertha looked sad for a minute but brightened up as she thought of her wedding. 'I've got enough money to buy some decent material to make a dress. You'll help me, won't you?'

'I will, of course I will. I'm so happy for you, Bertha,' Eliza replied, smiling at her friend.

'Will you be able to manage with the lad an' all?' Bertha asked anxiously. 'That's the only thing that bothers me.'

'Well, he's a big lad now,' said Eliza. 'I was going to enter him for a scholarship to Newcastle School. Or I might even be able to afford the fees; I think there are some assisted places. Mr Collier is looking into it for me.'

'By, won't that be grand,' declared Bertha, looking relieved. 'He could do anything, your Tot, I always said he could do anything. He's got a brain on him all right. He's a grand lad, he is an' all.'

'I couldn't have managed without you, Bertha,' Eliza said. 'It was a lucky day for me when I met you. Now it's time for you to have a bit of happiness.' The two women busied themselves with the meal as they chatted to each other about their day.

'How did Lottie take it, then, when the Missus died?' Bertha asked. She always showed an interest in Lottie and how she was getting on, with both of them coming from a workhouse background.

'She wasn't too bad when I left,' said Eliza. 'Though what she'll be like when she's on her own with Mr Green, I don't know. He's a penny-pinching old sour-face, he is.'

'Poor lass,' Bertha said with feeling, and Eliza nodded her agreement.

The evening passed away pleasantly enough. As Bertha was not going out the two women sat beside the fire after the boy had gone to bed and talked about the future. Yet at the back of Eliza's mind there was a shadow hovering, the shadow that was Jonathan Moore. Years ago, he had seemed obsessed with her but then he just seemed to give up the idea he had of getting her to stay with him. She had seen very little of him for years. Today, however, out on the road so close to where she lived, she had the feeling that he had been waiting for her, and was still waiting for her. It made her flesh creep to remember that night when he had claimed her. Oh, she would never forget it.

When she went to bed she dreamed vaguely threatening dreams and he was always there; not that he did anything to her, not specifically, but she felt he might.

Bertha was away to the farm betimes next morning, for she had promised Mrs Carr that she would help with the early morning milking. The women she worked with in her cleaning business already had their duty list for the day. That was something she had learned working in the Infirmary: the importance of everyone knowing exactly what their duties were. So she could afford to take the morning off her own work. After all, milking couldn't be so hard, could it? She would soon get into the way of it. She had to because it would all be her job when she was wed.

'You're late,' her future mother-in-law greeted her as she opened the door of the cowshed. 'It's six o'clock already. I thought I told you to start at five-thirty?'

'I'm sorry, I had some last minute—'

'We don't want excuses.' Charlie's voice came from the back of the shed. 'You have to be reliable in farming, you know. The animals don't like it if you're not.'

'Well, I'll do better in future,' Bertha said meekly. She had already learned that it did not pay to answer back to her future mother-in-law. Charlie wouldn't like it.

By the end of the first hour her back ached, her wrists

ached and her fingers were as stiff as pencils. Mrs Carr disappeared into the farmhouse kitchen, muttering something about cooking breakfast for Charlie and his hind, Barney. Bertha was left with a list of instructions: carry the pails of milk into the dairy, skim it for foreign bodies and have it ready to take out on the streets of Gilesgate to sell.

'I'm not going out selling the milk!' she protested.

'There's no reason why you shouldn't,' said Mrs Carr, pursing her lips. 'I'm sure I've done it myself afore the day.'

Well, I'm not, Bertha said to herself as she watched the older woman go in the kitchen door. She was not, she insisted to herself. She felt as though she had done a fair day's work already and she was ready for her breakfast. Then there was dairy work to do after that.

'How are you managing?'

Charlie came round the corner and, glancing round to make sure no one saw, kissed her on the lips. Bertha immediately felt better, her lips tingled and she felt funny inside.

'Grand, I like it,' she said untruthfully.

'I'll just turn the cows out, then we'll go in for something to eat,' he said.

'Good, I'm starving,' Bertha replied.

'Well, just take that dead kitten out and put it on the muck heap, will you? Can't have it beginning to stink the place out, can we?'

'Dead kitten?'

Bertha hadn't seen the dead kitten, being so busy with learning how to milk the cows properly, but now she went over to the corner of the cowshed where there was a pile of dirty straw and there it was, the stiff, emaciated body of the little animal she had been about to feed the night before.

'It's starved to death, Charlie,' she said sadly and was amazed when he laughed.

'Aye well, it should have learned to be a bit quicker on the hunt, shouldn't it? A kitten's no good if it doesn't learn its job, is it? There's no sentiment in farming, lass.' He caught her downcast expression. 'Give it here, lass, I'll do it,' he said. 'You'll have to harden up, though, when we're wed, I'm telling you.'

By ten o' clock, Bertha was on her way home to see to her little business. The image was firmly fixed in her mind, the image of Charlie picking the kitten up by the tail, striding to the door and throwing it on the muck heap. She did not tell Eliza about it. Eliza wasn't all that fond of Charlie, she could see it, though of course Eliza tried to hide the fact.

Eliza was on her way to see Peter Collier at the temporary offices the union had in the city. She sat in the tub trap and held Dolly's reins, but it was a straight road to the offices and in truth she had little to do. The roads were fairly busy but Dolly knew them well and was wise in the ways of threading through traffic. So Eliza had time to think even though she was at the same time watching out for any sign of Jonathan Moore.

Autumn was on the way and already some of the leaves on the trees were turning colour and there was a sharpness to the air. Though it was still only August it heralded a hard winter.

She thought about the evening before when she had gone back out to see a couple of patients, one of them Billy, the miner with the bett hand and threatened blood poisoning. Billy had been asleep when she went in.

'Oh, he seems better,' said Eliza, laying a hand on his forehead to check his temperature. It was cooler than it had been that morning. She checked his bandages; they didn't appear to have been removed so Betsy must not have touched them.

'Aye well, he wasn't better,' said Betsy, her voice hard. 'The poor lad was nearly weeping with the pain earlier on.'

'Well,' said Eliza, 'it must have eased off.'

'Aye, it would,' replied Betsy. 'I went in to the chemist and got some paregoric for him. That's what's given him a bit ease.'

Eliza could see now that Billy was drugged; she could smell the camphor from the paregoric as well. She looked at his lower arm for the tell-tale red line running up to his armpit. It was still there but fainter.

'I'll leave the dressing until the morn,' she said. 'You won't touch it?'

'Billy wouldn't let me,' Betsy admitted.

'Well, don't try while he's asleep,' Eliza warned. 'I'll come back then.'

If Billy recovered and his hand was saved Betsy would put it down to the paregoric, which was a camphorated derivative of opium that would make Billy sleep but would not have an effect on the infection in his hand.

Eliza smiled as she drove along the narrow lanes of Durham. What did it matter so long as Billy got better and kept his hand? A one-handed miner was not much use to anyone. The family would be thrown on the parish and likely end up in the workhouse.

She arrived at the union offices and dismounted from the tub trap. Though it was still fairly early in the morning she could see through the uncurtained window that Peter was already at his desk, working. But he put down his pen, rose to his feet and smiled at her.

'Now then, bonny lass,' he said in greeting. 'You're a sight for sore eyes on a grey morning. Do you want to see me for something in particular or is this just a friendly visit?'

'Both, really,' replied Eliza. 'I wanted to ask you about a high school for Tot.'

'Ah.' Peter looked thoughtful. 'I tell you what, Eliza, sit down and I'll see about some tea. It's just about my time for a break, any road.' He went to the inner door and called through it. 'Fetch a pot of tea, please, Meg. And two cups.'

Eliza sat down on a hard chair before the desk and Peter sat opposite. He leaned forward with his elbows on the blotting pad and his hands folded under his chin.

'You want him to go to high school? Aye, of course you do, you want the lad to make something of himself. He's got the brains an' all. You mentioned it before, I know, and I have been thinking about it. Only I don't know, I don't think he can go through the union. We are going to sponsor some scholarships but Tot is not a miner's son, that's the trouble. Sugar?'

Eliza nodded. She supposed that she had expected that Peter might be in a position to at least give Tot a chance to try for a scholarship. She sipped her tea and tried not to show her disappointment. Peter was an honourable man; he wouldn't do such a thing. She watched as he rose to his feet and closed the door between his office and the other room. She was completely unprepared for what he said next.

'There is one way it could be done,' he said.

Eliza sat up and gazed at him attentively. 'Yes? I'd do anything, I would, only tell me.'

'If Tot was my stepson he would be entitled to enter for a scholarship to a school.'

Eliza was speechless. She just couldn't believe she

had heard him aright. Peter Collier was almost as old as her father, why, he must have been in his forties. His dark hair was speckled with grey and there were deep lines in his forehead and running down the sides of his mouth. But he had nice eyes, kind eyes and he had been a friend to her when she needed one.

'You – you want to marry me?'

'I think you would be a good wife, Eliza. Oh, I know I'm not as young as I was but we could be good together. We could work for the pitmen and their families, in our different ways.' He looked at her face; she seemed astonished. His own confidence plunged. 'See, Eliza, don't give me your answer yet. Give yourself time. You have Tot to consider.'

After Eliza had gone, Peter sat staring at his work, but he wasn't seeing it. Why hadn't he told her the truth? he asked himself. Why had he found it so impossible to tell her he had feelings for her, that he wanted to marry her for herself, not for practical reasons at all? Because she might reject him out of hand, he thought dismally. He was a middle-aged man with more grey in his hair than black and she was still a young woman. He couldn't bear it if she rejected him. It was better to go on as they were, good friends.

Chapter Twenty-Three

Eliza acknowledged to herself that she was sorely tempted to marry Peter as she drove Dolly home. She couldn't concentrate on her work, so she thought she would take an early dinner time as the morning was almost over. Then she would do the rounds of her patients in the afternoon. It was Saturday, and she usually tried to finish early on Saturdays but she had too much to do today.

If she married Peter, Tot would have a chance to get into the grammar school on a scholarship sponsored by the miners' union. If not he would have to take his chances in the public scholarship and there would be a great deal more competition for that. She didn't think she could enlarge her practice to make more money to pay his school fees. She hadn't enough time in the day to do what she needed to do now. Of one thing she was certain: one way or another he was going to have a higher education than that supplied by the national school, he was indeed.

She and Peter were not in love, not as she and Jack had been, but look where that had got her. But she was fond of him, very fond. He had been there so often when she needed a friend.

By, she thought, she could do with someone to talk it over with. She thought wistfully of Bertha. They hadn't been able to discuss things as they used to do, not lately. Bertha knew she wasn't fond of Charlie and it caused some restraint between them. Besides, Bertha would be busy all day, what with her own work and farm work and later on she would be going to the choir concert at chapel with him.

Eliza dropped in at the butcher's to buy something for dinner. No doubt Tot had been running and playing football all morning and he would come in ravenously hungry.

'Where've you been, Mam?' Tot greeted her as she went into the kitchen with her bag of meat pies and pease pudding. 'I'm famished. I scored a goal, Mam. You should have seen it, it was grand. I'm a good player, Mam, I am. Me and Albert are going to get a proper team together and we'll play proper matches, we have it all planned—'

'Go and wash your hands under the pump,' said Eliza, 'and then come back and sit down. Where's Bertha?'

'Eeh, I don't know where she is. I scored a goal, Mam, did you hear me?'

'I did, that's lovely, pet,' Eliza replied, looking at his face. He was filled with pride and enthusiasm and she had hardly noticed. 'I think it's grand,' she said, to make amends for her seeming lack of interest.

Tot trotted off, satisfied, to the water pump by the back door and washed his hands. He didn't know why his mam was so insistent on him washing all the time, none of the other mothers were bothered. His mam was different. Maybe it had something to do with her being a nurse. It was when he came back and took a mouthful of pie and spoke through it that he dropped his bombshell. She had opened her mouth to tell him not to speak with his mouth full when she realised what he was saying.

'I'm going to leave school and go down the pit, Mam. I'll be making good money, Albert says—'

'What? Leave school? Of course you're not going to leave school.'

'I am, everybody is. Some of the lads left when they were nine. I'm the oldest in the school, Mam. They only go there to learn how to read and write and figure some. I'm old enough to be fetching money in. Then you won't have to be out so often.'

Oh, she should not have let him go to the national school, she should not indeed. She should have tried to get him into a better school. But the national school was only threepence a week. The Methodist school was cheap an' all but it was on the other side of Durham. The thoughts ran round and round in her mind. In building up her nursing practice she had neglected him, oh, she had. She should have been there for him more.

'You're leaving that school all right, Tot,' she said. 'But you are going to a high school and there will be no arguing about it.'

Tot looked mulishly down at his plate. He stirred his pease pudding with his fork and stabbed at the pieces of pie, breaking them up into little bits. But he had been too well trained by his grandmother to argue any more about it, even now after a few years with his mother.

'Are we going to Blue House tomorrow after chapel?'

It sounded as though he had changed the subject and Eliza was glad of it. 'We are,' she replied. 'Do you want to see your grandma and granda?'

'Aye.' Tot started to eat again, finishing off the food on his plate. He drank the dandelion and burdock pop that was always his treat at weekends and looked at Eliza. 'Can I go out now?'

'All right. Mind, I'll be out this afternoon, working, but Bertha won't be long, I shouldn't think.'

She watched as he pulled on his cap and jacket and went out of the back door and down the yard. The yard gate banged to after him. She cleared the table and got ready to go on her rounds. Not that there were many patients she had to see and those she did were mainly convalescent. Of course there was Billy and she had had a message from Dr Gray to visit the pit manager's little girl at Shincliffe's Banktop colliery. It was a way out on the other side of Durham, though. Still, as Dr Gray had asked for her, she would go.

As she travelled in her tub trap, watching Dolly's fat behind swaying from side to side as she plodded along, Eliza was coming to a decision. She would wed Peter Collier and get Tot away from the friends he had made at the school in Gilesgate. Maybe it wasn't the best reason for marrying anybody but Peter had his own reasons for asking her and she didn't think one of them was love. Peter Collier was in love with the union, he lived, ate and slept the union. He was a kind and caring man, though. He would do his best to get the lad into a decent school; most likely the high school. They would grow to love each other. All it took was effort and understanding. She smiled at herself in mockery. It was not as though she had such a great knowledge of marriage.

It did not occur to her to think that the union was the mineworkers' and Peter wouldn't think Tot's ambitions to be a miner were quite so bad as she did. Having made her decision, she put it out of her mind for the moment. She was approaching Shincliffe and the short drive of the manager's house. It was well rutted by wheels but there had been an attempt to fill in the ruts with gravel and small stones. Dolly picked her way delicately up it to the front of the house.

The door was opened by a maid. Not a little workhouse skivvy such as Lottie or Bertha had been, but a woman of indeterminate age in a clean white apron and cap. She looked Eliza up and down, dressed as she was in her nurse's cape and cap with the ribbons tied under her chin, and evidently decided this was an equal or even an inferior rather than a superior being.

'You're the nurse,' she stated. In her experience nurses were widow women or others desperate to earn a living and some of them were no more than slatterns. This one might be dressed decently but she was still only a nurse. 'You should go round to the back door.'

'And you're a servant and supposed to be polite to visitors,' said Eliza pleasantly. 'Dr Gray sent for me. Please take me to him and ask someone to see to my pony and trap.'

The woman's eyes flashed and she began to splutter, but from behind her came a man's voice.

'Is that Nurse Mitchell-Howe, Jane? Let her in, woman, let her in at once!'

'Yes, sir, I was just about to,' the woman replied hastily and stepped aside so Eliza could walk in to the hall. It was a square hall, not large, but the floor was paved with black and white tiles in a chequered pattern and there was a side table flanked by a couple of chairs. Advancing towards the door was a man of about forty with side whiskers and a frock coat of a good tweed material. He too looked Eliza up and down, but his face was expressionless.

'I'll take you to my daughter, Matilda,' he said with no preamble. 'Dr Gray is with her.' He led the way up a flight of stairs with a bend in the middle. There was a carpet running down the middle and the sides were polished. It was as opulent as her father-in-law's staircase up by Alnwick, Eliza thought. Coal was definitely profitable for some, if not for the men who worked it. She pushed the radical thought from her mind. There was a sick little lass here and that was what mattered.

'Sister, I'm glad you could come.' Dr Gray turned to the door of the bedroom. He smiled warmly; still the same as he had been years ago when she had worked with him in the Infirmary, although as she shook his hand she noticed tiny lines around the corners of his eyes and mouth and a few threads of silver in his hair she had somehow not noticed when she worked with him a few times recently. He drew her forward and introduced her to the woman sitting by the bed, a small woman in the full skirt that had succeeded the crinoline.

'This is Sister Mitchell-Howe, Mrs Prentis,' he said gently. 'You couldn't put your child into better hands.'

Mrs Prentis looked up at Eliza. 'Sister,' she said, nodding her head courteously. She had large brown eyes, which were red with crying. Her hair was drawn back into a bun at the nape of her neck and she was wearing a lacy cap in the fashion of married ladies of the day.

'Perhaps you should go and have a short rest and perhaps a cup of tea, Mrs Prentis. Just while Sister and I look at Matilda.'

Mrs Prentis began to shake her head but the doctor was firm as he put a hand under her elbow. 'I think you should, Mrs Prentis,' he said gently. 'We don't want you ill too, do we?' Somehow his will prevailed and she found herself being escorted to the door. 'I will call you if there is any change, dear lady,' he went on, and closed the door firmly behind her.

'It is so difficult sometimes,' he remarked to Eliza. 'Naturally mothers—' He didn't finish the sentence, just shrugged expressively and returned to the bedside.

The room was excessively hot, for heavy curtains were drawn across the windows, leaving only a narrow slit for light to come in, and a large fire burned in the grate. The patient had thrown the bedclothes back and was restlessly moving her head from side to side. Her lips moved as though she was muttering to herself in delirium.

'She is suffering from diarrhoea,' Dr Gray said. 'I suspect typhoid though I hope it is not. At any rate, the little spots are not evident.' He glanced at Eliza, who was by the opposite side of the bed. 'We need to get her temperature down. But I will have to ask the parents' permission for a cold sponge-down. The mother is against it but if I talk to the father I'm sure I will be able to show him the necessity for it. Will you wait a moment while I do that?'

While he was gone, Eliza sponged the child's face. She picked up the bottle of medicine that stood on the bedside table and saw it was an aconite derivative, which was used as an antipyretic. Oh, she hoped it wasn't typhoid or any of the other fevers, which could sweep through a district and take so many with it.

'You can go ahead, Sister,' Dr Gray said as he came into the room. 'I hope you can stay, at least for a few days. Mr Prentis wants you to stay.'

'I'm sorry, Dr Gray, I cannot,' Eliza replied. 'Surely you can get a monthly nurse to do it?'

'Not one like you, Sister. Not trained in the Nightingale methods.'

'Still, I cannot. I have a boy of my own at home to see to.'

Dr Gray nodded. 'I understand, of course, but I promised I would ask you. Perhaps you will stay long enough to explain what to do to the woman we get?'

Eliza was in something of a dilemma. This was a child and she owed it to her to do her best for her. But there was Tot at home. Bertha had always been there for him but things were changing now. Bertha had her own priorities.

'Mr Prentis will send a message to Gilesgate for you,' the doctor said. He waited for her decision.

'You knew I could only take on day cases,' said Eliza.

'Yes, but you were the only one I could think of with the skills little Matilda needs.'

Matilda moaned and moved restlessly almost as though on cue. 'Well, for the moment I must get on and try to make her as comfortable as possible.'

'Of course.'

In the end, Eliza agreed to stay until the following morning. A messenger was dispatched to Gilesgate to let Bertha know and a local widow woman who earned her living usually as a monthly nurse was brought in. She was at least clean and had a pleasant face and didn't appear to mind being told what to do by a newfangled Nightingale nurse who was half her age. Or she didn't say so to Eliza as so many didn't hesitate to do. By the next morning Eliza felt confident enough to leave Mrs Dunne, as she was called, in charge.

Riding home in the tub trap, Eliza reflected on her patient. The girl seemed better this morning. Her temperature was down slightly and she was not delirious.

'I think she stands a good chance of recovery,' Dr Gray had said to Eliza, 'and she owes it to you as much as anyone. Of course she will still need careful nursing. You will call back this evening?'

'It's away across the city, Doctor. And I have other patients. I will have to visit some today even though it is Sunday. No, I will come back tomorrow if that's all right. Mrs Dunne is very good, there's no need for me.'

'Very well, but I may need to send for you. You will come if you're needed?'

Eliza had assented; what else could she do? There were always so many people, so many patients who needed help, and not enough trained nurses or doctors either. What was worse, some of those were steeped in the old ways and dismissed the idea that disease was caused by living organisms. They refused to wash even their hands between patients. But the idea of antisepsis was gradually taking root at last. As Miss Nightingale had said, the main weapon she had for saving soldiers' lives in the Crimea was the scrubbing brush.

The house was empty when Eliza finally arrived home and put Dolly in her own little stable. The pony trotted in happily, as glad to be home as Eliza was herself. Eliza placed some fresh hay in the manger and, closing the half door after herself, went in by the back door.

Of course, Bertha would be at chapel and Tot with his friends in Sunday School. Eliza put on the kettle to make herself a cup of tea and sat down to wait for their return.

'What's this? Sleeping when you should be at your devotions?'

It was Charlie's voice that woke her and she sat up, disorientated. The kettle had boiled dry and not even the noise of the embers collapsing in the grate and taking the kettle with them had awakened her. Eliza jumped up and lifted it on to the bar before turning to face him and Bertha, who had walked through from the front door.

'Oh, Charlie,' she said. 'I'm sorry.' Though why she was apologising to him she couldn't think. 'I must have dropped off. I was with a patient all night and got home too late for morning service. Is Tot all right? He got off to Sunday School?'

She was speaking to Bertha but it was Charlie who answered.

'You should be home to see to the lad yourself, Eliza,' he said. 'On a Sunday an' all. And you missed divine service. The minister gave a very uplifting sermon on Christian duty. You might have found it interesting.'

'Charlie—' Bertha began but he interrupted her.

'No, Bertha, it has to be said. Today is Sunday and you have a right to have time for yourself. Women who have children should look after them and not expect others to do it for them. Any road, it's Sunday as I said and the Lord's command was that Sunday should be kept holy. Six days shalt thou labour—'

'Shut up,' said Eliza. 'Just shut up.'

'What? How dare you speak so to me?' Charlie was becoming very red in the face but Eliza was too tired and too angry to care.

'I have been nursing a sick child, Charlie Carr,' she snapped. 'Do you think the Lord would have wanted me to abandon her and leave her to look after herself because it is Sunday?'

'I am not going to argue on the Sabbath,' Charlie replied loftily if illogically, for that was precisely what he was doing. 'Bertha and I had other things to do last evening. You sent a message round without so much as asking if Bertha minded seeing to the lad. You demanded it, do you hear? You demanded she do it.'

'Charlie, Eliza and me, we have an arrangement,' said Bertha. She looked apologetically at Eliza. 'I don't mind looking after Tot, I don't.'

'Aye well then,' said Charlie, 'that's all right, isn't it? Never you mind if *I'm* put out. What do I matter? I'm just the man you are going to wed.' His voice was heavy with sarcasm.

'Charlie—' said Bertha, but he was not to be pacified.

'I'll go now,' he said. 'Bertha, you must think hard about this. Your first duty is to me as your betrothed, or so I would have thought. When you have thought, perhaps you will realise this.'

He flounced to the door leading to the front of the house, every ounce of him showing his righteous outrage.

His exit was spoiled a little by the entrance of Tot, fresh from Sunday School and whistling cheerfully 'Jesus bids us shine', only slightly off key. Tot had only recently been able to whistle a proper tune and he did so at every opportunity.

'Mam! Mam!' he cried when he saw Eliza. 'Can I go and play quoits with the lads till the dinner's ready? They're all going along to the play field.'

Charlie bristled even more. 'Quoits!' he said grimly. 'And on a Sunday. By, this is a godless household, it is indeed.'

Chapter Twenty-Four

'I'm that sorry, Eliza,' said Bertha. 'Charlie had no right to speak to you like that.' It was later in the day and Charlie had been gone about two hours. At first Bertha had thought he would come back but of course he did not. Men expected their women to be obedient, Eliza thought, as she looked at Bertha's woeful expression. The problem was that most women didn't so much as question the assumption.

'We've lived too long without a man telling us what to do, Bertha,' she said. Bertha didn't reply to that. She was staring out of the sitting-room window at the play field over the road. Tot was playing quoits out there with a crowd of lads. Their calls and shouts could be heard for it was a hot day for the back end of August; a time when autumn was usually beginning to set in. The road was quiet, for people were enjoying their Sunday rest. The trouble was, she knew that in a way Charlie was right, at least looking at things from his point of view. Eliza did rely on Bertha a lot to see to Tot and make meals and do other household chores. But Eliza had given her a home and looked after her too.

'The lad shouldn't be playing out, Eliza, not on a Sunday. The minister says it isn't right.'

'There's no harm in it,' Eliza replied. In reality she knew it was frowned upon by the chapel folk, but she wasn't going to let Charlie Carr tell her what to do, indeed she was not. On the other hand, she didn't like to see Bertha looking so unhappy.

'Bertha, I'm sorry. If you like I'll tell Charlie I won't put on you any more. Only I had no choice; there was little Matilda Prentis bad with a fever and what could I do? But I know I'll have to make other arrangements now. I can't spoil your happiness, Bertha.'

Not that she could see Bertha being too happy with that sour-faced Charlie Carr, she thought to herself. But Bertha wanted him and she was very fond of Bertha.

'Never mind me, Bertha. I'm tired, I need a good night's sleep. Go on up to the farm if you want to.'

Bertha hesitated. 'I don't know. He should not have spoken to you like that, but Charlie's a good man, really. And if I don't take him I might not get another chance.' She bit her lip. 'That's not a good reason for getting wed, I know that an' all, you don't have to say it.'

'I wasn't going to,' Eliza said gently.

Bertha gazed down at the floor. Ever since her days in the workhouse she had understood that the good things in life were not for her. She would always be looking in from the outside. She knew she wasn't a good-looking lass, not like Eliza. She was well aware too that Charlie wanted a wife for a few reasons but one of them was not that he had fallen madly in love with her. How could he? She caught sight of her reflection in the glass front of the press, which stood by the wall, and studied it for a short while. No, she decided, she would be very lucky indeed to get another chance to have children of her own. She had to follow Charlie.

'I think I'll have to go, Eliza. But think on, if you really need me you just have to let me know and I'll come. Whatever Charlie says, I'll come.'

'I know.' Eliza put her arns round the smaller woman and hugged her. 'You've been a good friend, Bertha, a grand lass you are.' The two of them were almost in tears.

'I'd best be away now,' said Bertha shakily. 'I don't want Charlie to get really angry.'

'Go on then, Bertha. You make your peace with Charlie. I'll just have a rest until Tot comes home.' The two women embraced again, something they rarely did. Eliza saw that there were tears in Bertha's eyes ready to spill and her own filled in response After all, they had been together through thick and thin for many years now, she told herself shakily.

When she was on her own, Eliza sat down again by the fire. The afternoon had almost passed and it was becoming cooler in the small, dark kitchen. She laid her head against the wooden headrest of the chair and wiped her eyes with the corner of her apron. Now she had to come to a decision, one way or the other. In the meanwhile she had to cut down on the number of her patients. Tot was old enough to be in the house alone now, of course he was. Many lads of his age were doing a full-time job in the pits or at least on the coal screens. Still, she would be there to give him his meals and during the night, no matter what happened.

'The hand is all right now, Nurse, see for yourself,' said Billy. 'I cannot thank you enough.' He extended a brawny arm and showed his hand. The swelling was completely gone and there was new, pink skin on the palm where there had been a hard, red patch with lines running from it.

'Well, I'm very pleased to see it,' Eliza replied. 'Now you be careful and try to keep it clean. And if it happens again, come to me first, will you?'

'Oh aye, I will,' said Billy. 'But I doubt it will come back. You don't think it will, do you, Nurse?'

'Not if you're careful,' said Eliza.

Eliza's Child

'How much do we owe you, Nurse?' his wife asked. In these pit communities it was the woman who had control of the money, if she managed to get it from the man on the fortnightly pay day before he had drunk it all away. She held a worn leather purse in her hand. It didn't look too fat, Eliza noted, but then it wouldn't, would it? Not with Billy being off work this last week and more.

'It will be two shillings,' she replied. 'But if you're pressed, I'll take a shilling now and the rest when Billy gets his next pay.'

'Nay, I can give you sixpence now, it's all I can spare,' said Betsy, looking worriedly at the few coppers in her purse.

'All right then,' Eliza said. 'I'll call in a fortnight for the rest.' Not that she expected to get any more and she wouldn't press for it. At least there were a few people like the Greens and Prentises or she would be working for next to nothing most of the time.

Jonathan Moore was again waiting for Eliza when she got home that evening. He was sitting in a trap at the end of the street, watching the children playing in the play field opposite. As she turned Dolly into the road he descended from the trap and walked over to the fence and waved, and a moment later Tot came over to speak to him.

Eliza couldn't believe what she saw. Tot was talking

292

and laughing with Jonathan as with an old friend. As she got closer she heard him telling Jonathan how he had scored a goal. 'You should have seen it, Mr Moore,' he was saying excitedly. 'I kicked it right past the goalie, it went whoosh into the corner of the net!'

'What net's that, Tot?' Jonathan asked, laughing. 'I can only see coats marking out the goal posts.'

'Aye, but see, if there *had* been a proper net it would have, wouldn't it?'

'Tot, get your coat and go into the house,' his mother said firmly as she crossed the road.

'Aw, but—' Tot began.

'Now,' said Eliza.

Reluctantly, the boy picked up one of the coats, to groans from his team mates. He climbed over the fence, muttering to himself, and walked slowly down the street. Eliza watched as he disappeared into the house before turning to Jonathan Moore.

'What are you doing here?' she asked him.

'Oh, I often come here and watch the lads playing,' he replied.

'What, make a special journey for that? All the way from Haswell?'

'Sometimes I'm in the city, Eliza,' he said. 'I'm on my way home.'

'Going home round the houses, are you?' Eliza was seething inside though she was trying hard to maintain a calm exterior. 'Are you trying to get at me through my lad?'

'No, of course not.' Jonathan smiled as though the very idea was ludicrous. 'I like the lad, that's all.'

'If you don't leave me and my son alone I'll call the polis,' said Eliza.

'And tell them I did something – what exactly?'

'Please go away, Mr Moore, leave us alone.'

'Oh, Eliza, Eliza, how can I leave you alone? I think of you all the time.' Jonathan had changed from a light bantering tone to a serious one. He looked at her appealingly. 'Call me Jonathan. I would like to hear you say my name.'

Eliza regarded him for a long moment. His usually arrogant expression had disappeared and he seemed suddenly vulnerable. He was a good-looking man, she thought; why did he chase her when he could have his pick of a few women?

'I have to go in,' she said. 'I have things to do.'

'You could invite me in,' he suggested.

'Why should I do that? Bertha will be back soon and I have to get Tot's dinner ready.' She began to walk away but found he was walking with her.

'Grand night, Sister.' The remark came from a woman walking by, one of her neighbours. Her eyes were alive with curiosity as she glanced at Jonathan and back at Eliza.

'It is,' Eliza replied shortly. Dolly was waiting, tossing her head in impatience, for she was so near her stable and home. She whinnied softly as Eliza took hold of her noseband and led her round the houses, loosed her from the trap and let her into the stable.

'You are very quiet,' said Jonathan from where he was watching her by the door.

'I was hoping if I didn't talk to you, you would go away,' Eliza replied tartly. She finished forking hay into the manger and came out and closed the half-door. 'Oh, come in then,' she said. 'Only don't think it means anything, anything at all, because it doesn't.' She led the way in through the back door to the kitchen. Tot was on the mat before the fire, reading. Her heart swelled with pride; by, it was lovely to see him reading even though she knew all children had the chance in these modern days.

'Come on through to the front room,' she said to Jonathan. 'I can spare you a few minutes.'

'That doesn't sound like the usual hospitality of the mining folk,' he remarked as he sat down on a leather granny chair that had seen better days. 'Mind, I'm not complaining,' he added hastily as she glared at him.

'What I want to know, Jonathan Moore, is why you have come back to pester me after leaving me alone for so many years.' Eliza did not sit down herself but stood with her back to the empty grate and folded her arms before her like a defence.

'Did your family not tell you? I got married.'

Eliza's mouth dropped open in surprise. Married? Somehow she had not thought of him as wed. How could he be wed and still chasing her? She wasn't sure how she felt about that. She found her tongue.

'No, they did not. But then, my family have other things to worry about, haven't they? My brother Miley getting killed when he was just a bairn for one thing.'

'Sometimes it happens, it's the nature of the work. All pits are dangerous,' said Jonathan. 'And you know as well as I do that pitmen take chances with their own lives. They can't be bothered to shore up properly, they don't maintain the rails—' He stopped. 'I'm sorry, I should not have said that, even though it's true.'

Eliza was filled with rage. 'It was the wagon, it came off and fell on him. Don't you remember?'

'I do, of course I remember. Poor lad, it was a tragedy.'

Eliza choked back the recriminations that rose to her lips. She turned to the window, unable to look at him. Across the way, the sun was just beginning to sink behind the slag heap and the room grew suddenly cold.

All the coal owners reasoned as he did, she knew that. It was a bone of contention between the pitmen and the bosses. The men earned little enough without taking time from filling coal to spend more than the minimum on propping up the roof. They thought the bosses should pay for time spent on that but the bosses thought the idea was silly. Well, come the union, and it was coming, according to Peter it was, getting stronger all the time. She turned back to Jonathan.

'Well, and what does your wife think of you mooning after other women? I dare wager she is not aware—'

'She died.'

'Oh. I'm sorry.'

He shrugged. 'It was a year or two ago. I didn't love her as I love you, Eliza. I married her to please my father. Her father is an ironmaster on the Tees and it opened a market up for our coal.'

It took Eliza's breath away to hear him talk so cold-bloodedly about his own dead wife.

'I think you'd best go now,' she said. 'I have to get on with the dinner, I told you.'

'Very well.' It surprised her that he didn't argue but rose to his feet and bowed slightly. 'May I come back?'

Eliza was sorry she had let him into the house in the first place. She just wanted him to go but he was standing there, waiting for her answer. What could she say that would put him off?

'I think not, Mr Moore. I am thinking of becoming betrothed to Mr Collier, the union man.'

Jonathan's face darkened. 'That rabble-rouser? You will not wed him, I'll stop you one way or another, I'm telling you!'

'Mr Moore, you can't stop me,' said Eliza.

'You think not? Well, we'll see about that—'

'Mam? When's supper ready?'

The interruption came from Tot, who had come to the door of the front room when he heard Jonathan's raised voice. He stood there, looking from his mother to the man, who was purple in the face with anger.

'Are you all right, Mam?'

'I'm fine, Tot,' replied his mother and she went to him and put an arm around his shoulders and led him away, back to the kitchen. 'I'm coming now,' she went on. 'Mr Moore is going.'

Jonathan had followed them out and he went to the back door. Turning to face her when he got there, he said. 'Mind what I said, Sister Mitchell-Howe. You just mind what I said. I won't let you do it.' He strode off and round the corner and Eliza let out a breath she hardly knew she had been holding.

'What did he mean, Mam?' asked Tot, looking worried. 'That's what the candyman said to Bert's mam last week, I heard him. He said, "Mind what I say!" I don't like it. You don't owe him, do you, Mam?'

'No, I do not,' Eliza replied and smiled at him. 'It was nothing, nothing to bother your head with, any road.' Tot didn't look very convinced but said no more.

Eliza brought out the pan of stew she had made the day before and heated it on the fire. She cut slices from the new loaf she had bought on the way home and put out three plates. Bertha would be coming in from delivering bundles of washed and ironed clothes and she would be wanting her supper early for she was sure to be meeting Charlie. She was meeting Charlie every blessed night nowadays, thought Eliza. Still, it would be nice to have a quiet night in by herself after the lad was abed.

She had a lot to think about.

Chapter Twenty-Five

Jonathan was seething with anger as he drove home to the substantial stone house he had had built on Haswell moor during his short marriage. It was isolated, about a mile and a half away from any of the pit villages that surrounded it. His wife had insisted on it. She had read and taken notice of the works of Pasteur and Lister and she was a firm believer in the need to prevent the spread of noxious diseases. And noxious diseases were rife in the pit villages, with their giant midden heaps. So often the only water supply serving a couple of hundred pitmen was a single standpipe and that situated close to the heaps.

'I will not live close to these people,' she had said, rather grandly or so Jonathan thought. After all, her father may have been an ironmaster but he was definitely not landed gentry. He had begun work as an iron puddler in his youth.

But the money she brought with her built the house and allowed him to buy more land to sink pits, and for a while he had even forgotten about Eliza. Eliza, who had been like a running sore in his mind, he had wanted her so much. Then his wife had died, ironically of childbed fever, and the child, a puny little thing, had died with her. Jonathan had set about finding the whereabouts of Eliza, which he had done through her brother Albert. The lad was an uncomplicated soul and readily gave his sister's address in exchange for a pint of porter.

Eliza was still as bonny as she had always been, Jonathan had realised. He was older now and she was a widow, and with all he had to offer her it would be easy to get her, to have her, to feel her body against his again. The memory of that inflamed him with desire.

As he drove home, Jonathan gradually calmed down and began to plan a strategy. He would have her and it would be through the boy, oh yes, he would have her. But first of all he had to do something about that pesky union leader, Peter Collier, who was an agitator and a threat to the realm if ever there was one. Oh aye, he, Jonathan Moore, would see him in Durham gaol, he would indeed. But first of all he would have a word with him concerning Eliza.

Eliza knew she should go straight to Peter and tell him of her meetings with Jonathan Moore but she had been used to dealing with her own problems for so long and she liked her independence. Still, she regretted telling Jonathan that she and Peter were practically betrothed. She was uneasy as to what he might do.

Bertha came in and they sat round the table and ate their supper and immediately afterwards Bertha went out. There was some constraint between them and it distressed Eliza but she didn't know what she could do about it. She missed the closeness there had been between them. Charlie did not come to the house now and Eliza supposed it was because of her. He thought she had too much influence on his future wife.

'If I can't go down the pit with the other lads then I want to be apprenticed to a cabinet maker,' said Tot, raising the subject of his leaving school yet again as soon as they were on their own. Eliza looked at him with surprise. His father was not mentioned between them and hadn't been for a long time. She wasn't even sure if he knew his father had been a cabinet maker.

'A cabinet maker? Why?'

'I just do. I could make chairs and things.'

'Well, you cannot,' said Eliza. 'You are going to school, a good school and that's all there is to it.'

'I want to leave school. I can read and write and figure, and why can't I leave school?'

'Don't argue with me, Tot, I said no and I meant no,'

said Eliza sharply. 'And you should be studying your books instead of wasting your time. Go on, into the front room with you. Those books cost money and I want you to make full use of them.'

Tot mumbled to himself but he went into the front room with a book listing the kings and queens of England. Though how he would find knowing all about them would be any use to him at all he didn't know, but his mother thought it might. His mother's thinking was a mystery to him. He threw the book down on a chair and stood by the window, gazing out at the hedge across the road and the field rising behind it. He would be a cabinet maker, he told himself. He would run away and go to work for a real man. His mother was just a woman and she shouldn't tell him what he was going to do.

'Are you reading that book?' his mother's voice came to him through the half-open door.

'Yes, yes, I am,' he replied and picked it up and flung himself on the mat face down and opened the book up at random. 'Richard the Lionheart,' he read aloud. Now that was a daft name, wasn't it? How could a man have a heart of a lion?

In the kitchen, his mother sighed and stretched her feet out along the brass rail of the fender. She would go to see Peter tomorrow, she decided. Best get to him before Jonathan Moore did so she could warn him.

She would not be able to go until she had seen to her patients, though. She had three around the door and she had promised Dr Gray that she would go back and check on the nurse who was attending little Matilda Prentis. And at eleven-thirty there was the funeral of Mrs Green. She needed to go to the church at least if not to the tea afterwards. It was a mark of respect.

It was four o'clock before Eliza found herself free to go to see Peter. It wasn't very far away, but she had to be back to see to Tot so she took Dolly. The pony wasn't too keen on going out again and ambled along the road with her head down and Eliza let her. When they arrived, she tied the nosebag on to the pony's muzzle and left her on the roadside contentedly nuzzling at her oats and chopped hay.

'I'll fetch you a drink when I come out,' she whispered in Dolly's ear and she whickered in return.

'I'm sorry, Mr Collier's gone home for the day. He has a meeting tonight at Murton,' said a man in answer to her query. 'Can I give him a message?'

'No, thank you. I'll see him myself,' she answered. Well, she told herself, it wasn't too much further to go, just a few streets away. Only she had to take the nosebag off Dolly and the pony seemed almost human in the look of disapproval she gave.

Eliza walked along, leading her. It was a lovely evening and her thoughts went back over her day. Matilda

Prentis was obviously much better when Eliza saw her earlier. Her temperature was down and she was propped up on pillows, taking a little gruel that Dr Gray had prescribed for her. The nurse had followed Eliza's instructions, either willingly or under the scrutiny of the doctor, Eliza didn't know which.

Mrs Green's funeral had been sad. Her daughter Joan had turned up at the chapel and there had been a blazing row between her and her father, which only ended when the minister intervened.

'Not here,' he had said sternly to them both, and Mr Green glared and looked ready to tell the reverend gentleman to mind his own business but checked himself just in time.

'You don't know what he's like,' Joan had said to the minister. 'He's a devil, I'm telling you.'

'Show some respect for your poor dead mother,' the minister had replied, sounding stern and sharp for someone who was noted for his gentle demeanour.

The neighbours, some of whom were there out of respect and friendship, and some looking forward to a substantial sit-down funeral tea, were agog.

'You watch out, young Lottie,' Joan said to the little maid, who was setting off for home ahead of the rest so that she could get the kettles on for the tea. 'Don't stand for any impittance from him.' She nodded meaningfully. Lottie looked bewildered but didn't reply. The last Eliza saw of her she was leaving the churchyard at a trot.

She was approaching Peter Collier's cottage. She halted the pony outside of the house and attached the nosebag once more.

'Can I hold your Galloway, Missus?' a small boy asked hopefully. 'I'll do it for a penny.'

'A penny?' Eliza asked, smiling.

'A ha'penny then, go on.'

'All right then, I'll pay you when I come out,' she said. She was still smiling when she knocked at the door of the house before opening it and walking in, as was the custom thereabouts.

'Good evening, Peter,' she said and her smile broadened. He was sitting at the table eating, though he didn't seem to have much of an appetite, judging by the way he was pushing the food around with his fork. He looked up at her and for a minute she thought he must have been expecting someone else for his frown was formidable. He did not rise to his feet immediately.

'Eliza,' he said heavily, and put down his knife and fork. Now he got to his feet and turned his back on her as he reached to the high mantelpiece for his pipe and tin of tobacco.

'Is something the matter, Peter?' she asked uncertainly.

'You might say that, aye,' he replied and set about filling his pipe and tamping down the tobacco. He did

306

not look at her as he did so. Oh, he had heard the rumour of the bet all right but Jonathan Moore had shocked him with what else he said. Was it all lies? He wanted to believe Eliza, oh he did.

'Has there been a disaster, then? In one of the mines?'

'Nay, there has not, not that I've heard, any road,' he said.

'Well, then?'

'I had a caller the day,' said Peter. He held the pipe in his hand, still not putting a taper to it.

'Jonathan Moore,' she said. She had an awful feeling in the pit of her stomach. Oh, she should have got here sooner, she should indeed. What had Jonathan said to Peter?

'Is it true?'

'Is what true?' she hedged. 'What did he say?'

'You lay with him when you were wed to Jack Mitchell? Is it?'

'I didn't. It was not like that.'

'Did you?' Peter persisted, for she sounded hesitant.

'Jonathan Moore is chasing after me. He threatened you when I told him we were almost betrothed.'

'Is it true?'

'Aye, it is. Don't look at me like that, Peter. Jack used me as a stake in a bet—' She stopped, for Peter had sat down again and put his head in his hands. She sat too, in the chair opposite him.

'You knew that Jack had treated me badly; you knew he was a gambler, a fanatical gambler,' she said. She stared at the scrubbed wood of the tabletop, finding herself unable to look at him.

'I didn't know about Moore,' he replied. 'He says you are lovers, you've just had a disagreement. He said he would kill me if I didn't leave you alone.'

'He's a cruel man, Peter, cruel and dangerous.'

'Yet you let him into your house yesterday.'

'I had to. I wanted to tell him to leave me alone. There were people about, neighbours. I didn't want them to think we were meeting.'

It sounded lame even in her own ears. The lines of wood grain on the tabletop were in a sort of pattern, broken where there was a small split, no doubt caused by soap and water and a scrubbing brush. She ran her finger along it as she tried to form the right words to tell him of what had happened and why she had invited him in.

'I came here to say I would marry you,' she said at last.

'I thought you wanted to get here before Moore could tell me the truth,' said Peter.

'I did want to speak to you before he did,' Eliza admitted. 'But I've told you the truth.'

'Eliza, Eliza,' Peter replied, looking at her properly for the first time. 'It will not do, it won't. I have to consider the union. This is a critical time for us. We are at last making progress, standing up for ourselves against the owners. Jonathan Moore is an owner. He is our enemy.'

'You're turning me away because a man like that tells lies about me? I thought you had feelings for me, I really did.'

Peter sighed. 'I did. I do. But I can't throw away the chance we have now, the chance to make our mark in the world. We can show people that the miners are not just ignorant ruffians; we are free men and we want our rights as free men. Don't you see?'

Eliza slowly rose to her feet. 'You didn't have feelings for me, not really. Not as a man should have for a wife,' she said sadly.

'I am fond of you, Eliza,' he replied.

'But you love the union more. Goodbye, Peter.' She turned and went out into the street. She took the nose-bag from Dolly and put it back in the tub trap and picked up the reins.

'Hey, Missus, what about me ha'penny?' It was the little lad who had been holding the horse for her. She hadn't even noticed him as she came out of Peter's house. Now she rummaged in her purse and found a penny and lobbed it to him.

'Eeh, ta, Missus,' said the lad, his grin threatening to split his face.

'Gee up,' she snapped at Dolly and the pony started to amble away in a slow walk. 'Gee up, I said,' she snapped again and flapped the reins hard on Dolly's back and the walk turned into a trot.

It wasn't just because of the lost chance for Tot to get a union scholarship to a good school, she realised. Even though she had been unsure about it when Peter had made her an offer, she regretted the loss of it now it was gone. Contrary was what she was, she thought wryly.

'I'll get an apprenticeship with my Uncle Henry. You wouldn't let me be a cabinet maker so I am going to Alnwick. I will write to you soon.'

The note was signed, 'Your son, Thomas.' There was not a mention of love or affection for her but she shouldn't expect it, she knew. Tot had been reserved in such things ever since she brought him back from Alnwick.

Eliza stared at the beautiful copperplate handwriting, which was beaten into all the children at the national school, where a rap across the knuckles was the punishment for untidy handwriting. Her numbed mind couldn't think of anything else for a few minutes before grief flooded her mind. She sat down at the table where the note had been left in the middle propped up against the glass salt cellar, the silver salt spoon sticking out at the side. Thomas, he had signed himself and he never did that. He had always insisted his name was Tot ever since he was old enough to say it.

Tot was only ten, going on eleven. He was too young to face his Uncle Henry and his sour-faced aunt whose name she couldn't think of. Amelia, was it? Yes, Amelia. Well, he wouldn't get much help from those two, indeed, he would not. Her mind was beginning to work again, her thoughts racing.

If he had gone to Northumberland how had he travelled? She doubted he had enough money for the train. And then he would have to change at Newcastle and as she thought of the station in that big city her heart beat anxiously. He was but ten years old, she told herself again. And while he had been telling her of his ambitions and dreams she had been ignoring what he said, planning a future completely different for him.

'By, Eliza, it's not a good night out there,' said Bertha. Eliza lifted her eyes from the written sheet. She hadn't even noticed Bertha opening the door and coming in.

'Tot's gone,' she said, quite unemotionally.

'Gone? Gone where?' Bertha asked. 'Nay, man, he cannot be far. Do you think he's just down at Bert's or someone else's? I'll go and get him if you like.'

'No, he's gone, I'm telling you. He's gone back to Alnwick. He's run away from me,' Eliza replied and found herself weeping quietly, the tears running down her cheeks. She handed the note to Bertha, then realised that Bertha's reading skills were poor to non-existent and read it out loud. Bertha wasted no time in talking about why or how it had happened. She was always totally practical.

'Right then, we must go to Alnwick,' she said. 'I reckon there will be a train tonight. Don't you worry, Eliza, we'll get him back. Howay, dry your eyes.'

'He's only ten, Bertha,' said Eliza but she had control of herself now and she got to her feet and brought water and sloshed her face and hands. Bertha stood waiting. She was already wearing her shawl and bonnet.

'You have money? Good. I reckon we will be able to buy food on the station so we needn't take any. We'd best go as soon as maybe in case the trains stop running.'

It was only when the two women were actually on the train, sitting in the third-class carriage that offered no comfort whatsoever apart from plain wooden seats, that Eliza thought to ask about Charlie.

'Were you meeting Charlie?' she asked. 'He's going to be very angry, Bertha. Maybe you should not have come. I would have managed.'

'Hadaway, man,' Bertha replied robustly. 'He'll have to put up with it.' She paused before going on, 'Any road, I reckon he won't fall out with me altogether, not before we're wed. Where will he find anyone else to take his mother on?'

Eliza looked startled. Perhaps Bertha wasn't so taken in by Charlie as she had assumed. But she thought no more about it in the all-consuming anxiety for Tot.

Chapter Twenty-Six

Tot trudged along by the side of the Great North Road leading to the border with Northumberland. It was an adventure, he told himself. He was going to Alnwick. To ask his uncle for work. It was the only way he could get an apprenticeship. He had asked Mr Jenkins in Durham but the carpenter had told him he had to have money to pay for it.

'Nay, lad,' Mr Jenkins had said and Tot could still hear the man's voice echoing in his head for it had been such a disappointment. 'Nay, you have to pay the premium and your mam and da will have to sign the contract.'

'Thank you, Mr Jenkins,' Tot had said politely. 'I will ask, then.'

A nice, well-mannered lad, Mr Jenkins thought as he watched him go out of the shop and turn down the street. He would take him on, given that everything else was right. A lad couldn't expect to learn a trade for nowt, though, could he?

Tot felt in his pocket and jingled the three shillings and sixpence he had saved up in his money box. Well, he hadn't saved it all in his money box. Fourpence was money that should have gone on to the Sunday School collection plate. But as soon as he was earning money for himself he would pay it back to the chapel. God would understand that he needed it now in order to get to Alnwick.

Tot's stomach rumbled loudly. He was very hungry. He had been walking for hours and hours and his feet hurt an' all. In his pack, besides his spare trousers and shirt and socks, he had a meat and potato pie he had bought at the butcher's in Durham. Only he had promised himself he would not eat it until he was in sight of the Tyne at Gateshead and he was no further than Chester-le-Street. He sighed and stopped walking to sit down on the grass by the roadside. He took off one of his boots and shook out a couple of small stones, which had somehow or other got inside. No wonder his heel had hurt.

Tot sat for a minute, letting the wind blow on his sweaty sock. By, it was grand. He took off his other boot and let the wind play on that foot too. He would just wait a minute or two or else it would get dark and then what would he do? He had planned to get to the railway station at Newcastle before the last train left for Alnwick. He reckoned his three shillings and sixpence should pay for his ticket.

Tot watched as a couple of tramps walked up the road. One of them had a brown bottle in his hands. As Tot watched he took a swig from the neck then handed it over to his friend. The men went, stumbling a little and tripping, though the road was fairly straight and even. They paused as they came up to him and swayed together, gently.

'What you doing, lad?' one asked, slurring the words together so that they sounded like, 'whadudooin lad.'

'I'm visiting my uncle,' said Tot. They stared at him and at his good coat and trousers and the good leather boots in his hand.

'Where?' asked one and the other nodded.

'That farm there, across the road,' said Tot. He had not missed them eyeing up his possessions and was wary.

The tramps looked at him and at each other then began their slow progress along the road again. Tot sighed with relief. What he had to do was find somewhere safe to stay the night. A barn would do, or an outhouse. He tried to put on his boots but his heel hurt so he walked across the road in his stockinged feet.

By, he was famished, starving hungry. He would just have a bite of pie. He took it out of his pack and bit into the thick pastry and gravy ran down his chin. He pushed it up into his mouth with his forefinger. Maybe he would have just one more bite.

'Hey, lad, what you got there?'

The voice came from behind him. Tot spun round to see the two tramps he had seen earlier towering over him. He had been so enjoying the bit of pie that he had forgotten to keep an eye out.

'Pie. It's my supper,' he said.

'Give it here,' said one of the tramps, the one with a dirty face and wet lips. He held out his hand. The smell from his body was rank and his hand was streaked with something brownish on top of the dirt.

'No, it's my supper,' Tot said. He hugged the brown paper bag with the pie closer to his chest.

'Give it here or I'll clout you one,' the man said, his tone menacing.

Tot backed away and his heel caught on a tussock and he fell. In a minute the tramp was on him, the smell choking Tot as he caught hold of the pie and wrenched it from the boy's grasp.

'Give it back!' Tot cried, scrambling to his feet.

'Nay, you wouldn't take a bit of pie off a starving man, would you?' the man grinned. He downed the pie in two bites, shovelling the bits of pastry into his mouth. 'By, it's grand an' all.'

'You might have give us a bit, Steve,' said the other

one, sounding like a peeved toddler. 'I gave you a dram, didn't I?

'Aw, shite, Silas,' snapped Steve, 'behave your whining. The nipper cannot be going to the farm, can he? Not when he was eating a pie for his supper. No, he would have been getting a grand meal off the farmer's wife, wouldn't he? So you just search his pack, I bet he has money in there, enough to buy us a pint of porter.' He put a filthy finger into his mouth and dislodged a piece of meat from his few remaining teeth. 'You got any money, me laddo?' he asked Tot.

'No!'

Tot was on his feet now, and he started to run even as the one Steve called Silas hesitated. He ran up the ditch, close to the hedge, vainly searching for an opening so he could escape into the field behind. If he could only get to the farm someone would help him, wouldn't they?

It was a vain hope. Steve was surprisingly fast on his feet when he got going, and he flung himself after Tot and landed in a sort of rugby tackle on him, knocking the wind out of the boy so that he couldn't move for a few seconds. It was enough for Steve to go through his pockets and find the three shillings and sixpence.

'Give it me back!' Tot cried. 'Get off me, you stink like a midden!'

'A midden, eh? You impittent little—'

Tot thrust his fist as hard as he could into Steve's

318

stomach, not even realising that he was shouting and crying as he did so.

'You little bugger,' said Steve, and slammed his fist into Tot's face. The boy went limp, his face deathly white but for the fast reddening mark on his cheek.

'I think mebbe you shouldn't have done that, Steve,' Silas observed. 'I expect you've not done for him. 'Cos if you have I'm not getting strung up for it, I'm telling you, I'm not.' He began backing away.

'What's all this shouting? I heard a bairn crying. What are you two bits of nowt doing? Where's the bairn?'

A man was looking over the hedge, a man who could have been the farmer. At any rate, it was a man who spoke with some authority and the tramps fled up the road, suddenly as fleet as fell runners.

The farmer leaned further over and saw what looked to be a bundle of clothes in the ditch. Only a bundle of clothes did not moan, not in his experience. He walked along the hedge to where there was a small, almost overgrown gate and let himself out. Just as he had thought, it was a bairn, a little lad of maybe ten or eleven. The lad's eyes were open and he was struck by the beauty of them, a deep violet they were, and ringed with dark lashes that many a woman would have given her right arm for.

'What's this all about, lad?' the farmer asked as he climbed down into the ditch and lifted the boy's head.

There was no answer. Even as he spoke the lad's eyes closed again and the chin flopped on to his chest. The farmer gathered him up as he would have done a sheep or lamb and put him over his shoulders to carry home, the legs dangling on one shoulder and the head on the other. He hefted him up into a more comfortable position and climbed out of the ditch.

'Here, mother,' he said as he pushed open the back door of the farmhouse and trudged into the kitchen. 'I've brought you another orphan lamb.'

'A lamb?' His wife looked at him in surprise. 'You daft beggar, why would you bring in a lamb at this time of year? Oh, it's a bairn. Set him down on the settle and let's have a look at him. Where on earth did you find him? By, look at his poor little face, has he had an accident on the road? Mind, I tell you, that road's getting busier by the day. Something should be done—'

'Aye well, shut up and see what you can do for the lad. No he didn't have an accident, this was done to him on purpose. He was belted by a couple of tramps, I chased them off him.'

'Eeh, setting on a little lad, the swine,' said his wife as she put a cushion under Tot's head. She fetched a dish of water and a cloth and started to sponge his rapidly swelling face. 'I'll put a cold compress on it. Do you think mebbe we should fetch the doctor?'

'Nay, lad'll likely come round. Any road, what could

a doctor do? And he'd cost a mint o' money if we brought him out and who's to pay?'

'Well, I'll just keep him quiet. See what he's like come the morn,' agreed his wife. 'But if he doesn't wake up properly by then we'll have to tell somebody.'

'Aye well, we'll see,' said Farmer Bates and turned for the door. 'I'd best fasten up the hens or the fox'll be in there.'

After he had gone out, his wife watched the boy for a moment or two then got to her feet and began to prepare supper. She felt unsettled and a bit melancholy. If only she had been blessed with a babby, she thought. A lad like this one must be a bonny lad. It would have been someone to work for, someone to pass the farm on to. She didn't wonder why he had been walking up the road on his own. There were often lads about, looking for work, and some of them as young as this one seemed to be.

Eliza and Bertha stood on the platform at Newcastle station, looking around them at the crowds of people there. Men and boys were going in and out, some of them in working clothes, and once or twice Eliza thought she saw a lad looking like Tot only to realise it was a stranger. As the platform emptied the disappointment was like a hard lump in her stomach.

'I don't think he's here,' said Bertha at last. 'We've

looked all over the station. No, I think you should go on to Alnwick, he's likely there. I'll go back to Durham. You never know, he might have thought better of it and gone home and then what will he do if there's no one there?' She bit her lip as she looked up at Eliza. 'I think that's the best plan, don't you?'

'I don't know, we should have left a note,' said Eliza, sounding fretful. 'Why did we come off without thinking like this?'

'We thought we'd find him,' said Bertha. 'Mind, I think he's likely already got to Alnwick. And he knows the place and he'll find his uncle or his grandma. He'll be fine, I'm telling you.'

'He will, won't he?' Eliza wanted to believe it. Surely neither Henry nor Annie would turn the lad away, they wouldn't. And if he had gone back to Durham, well then, he could slip in the back door and he would be fine until Bertha got home. The back door was always open, no one locked their back doors. So Eliza took the train to Alnwick.

'What the hell are you doing here?'

Henry came to the door of the parlour-cum-sitting room as a maid showed Eliza into the hall.

'I'm looking for my son,' said Eliza, holding her chin high. 'Have you got him here?'

'Why should I have him?' Henry demanded. 'I was

glad to see the back of him when he was living with my mother. He looks too much like that good-for-nothing brother of mine. Any road, how did you come to lose him?'

'He ran off when I wouldn't let him leave school. He said he wanted to be a cabinet maker. But I think he just wanted to grow up before his time. Any road, he ran off, like I said, and left a note that he was coming here to get an apprenticeship with you.'

'With me? Why would I give him an apprenticeship? Tell me that. His father nearly ruined the family before he jumped off that cliff, did you know that?'

'You cannot blame that on the lad,' said Eliza. 'Our Tot's a good, obedient lad.'

'Oh aye, a good lad. He's so good he ran off,' said Henry, his voice heavy with sarcasm.

'I'd best go and see if he went to his grandma. Though why he should do that I do not know, I don't.' Eliza turned to the door to go out and back to the town to Annie's cottage.

'Nay, you won't find him there neither,' said Henry. 'The place is closed up.'

'Closed up? Why?'

'The old woman is in her coffin. There's only the laying-out woman there. I gave her a shilling to stay so I could come home.'

'What?'

'Nay, for goodness sake, will you gather your wits if you have any. You sound like you lost them all. My mother is dead and gone. It's the funeral the morn. Is that plain enough for you?'

'Why didn't you let me know? Tot won't know. He might have gone there and not know why he can't get in.' Eliza rushed to the door then turned. 'If he shows up here will you send a message down to the cottage?'

'If it's the only way to get rid of you I will.' Henry turned his back on her and strolled to the window. 'Go on, be off with you,' he said. 'Do you think I've nothing to think about but your whelp? I'll send word if he comes, I'm telling you.'

'I'm indebted to you,' Eliza said evenly.

'Aye,' said Henry.

Tot was not at the cottage. The old woman in charge of the place said she had orders not to open the door to anyone and she wasn't going to, even when Eliza said she was family. The lad wasn't there. If he had been she would kick him out, she said. And if Eliza didn't stop bothering her she would call in the polis; he was due on his rounds just now, any road.

It was too dark for Eliza to look around by now. She walked down the main street and called in the shops to ask if anyone had seen a lad about ten years old but no one had. It began to look as though Tot had not managed to get to Alnwick, not yet.

She was tired and hungry and there was no one left for her to ask so at last she decided to give up the search for the night. She found a bed at an inn on the outskirts and settled in resolving to start searching again in the morning. Annie's funeral was at eight o'clock so that was a good place to start, she told herself, as she lay down wearily on the bed. She had no nightgown with her so she went to bed in her chemise. Not that she expected to sleep; her thoughts were going round and round in her head and all she had managed to get to eat had been a slice of bread and cheese with a mug of ale to wash it down. It lay uneasily on her stomach and she had to prop herself up against the iron and brass bedstead as there was only one pillow. In spite of the hard bedstead, she dropped off to sleep almost inmmediately, however. She awoke to grey daylight and the sound of rain pattering on the small windowpane. A fitting day for a funeral, she thought, as she poured water from a china jug into a china bowl and washed.

Chapter Twenty-Seven

Peter spent a restless night tossing and turning in his bed as he went over the conversation he had had with Jonathan Moore and then the one with Eliza. When he fell asleep just before dawn he dreamed of Eliza. She was watching him, he thought, not saying anything, simply looking at him with a reproachful, sad expression in her lovely eyes. When he awoke he couldn't get her out of his mind. He could not concentrate on anything that was going on in the office.

Now that the hated yearly bond was finally abolished, there were so many other injustices to be fought against, to be set out in a reasonable manner so the owners could not say the miners were becoming too demanding. Oh yes, there was plenty of work. Only today he found himself unable to concentrate on the paper he was working on, a paper asking for an allowance of half an hour's pay for the daily necessity of checking the ribs and stocks of coal left to support the roof of the coal seams where the coal had been extracted. And for the insertion of wooden pit props where needed.

'Peter, get your mind on the job, will you? This is the second time I've had to ask you.' John Woodward, one of his fellow workers, leaned over Peter's desk and raised his voice. 'You dreaming?'

Peter started and looked up at his friend. 'No, I'm sorry, I was just working something out, that's all. What was it, John?'

'I would say you were in love if I didn't know you better,' said John.

'Well, you might be right,' Peter replied but smiling, to show it was only in jest.

'Nay, not you,' said John. 'You're wedded to the job, I know you.'

'I'm only human,' Peter retorted.

They discussed the problem in hand for a few minutes then John said, 'It's almost bait time; we might as well talk while we eat.'

'No, I won't if you don't mind, John,' said Peter. 'I have to be away to Brancepeth this afternoon and I want to call in somewhere first. So I'll go now. I'll be back afore six. I'll see you then.'

John looked surprised but nodded his agreement. Mebbe Peter did have something other than the union on his mind. He did not usually move from his desk when he took a break but ate as he worked.

Peter often walked when journeying from one place to another for he didn't own a horse. There was a horse bus went out by Brancepeth way, however, and he reckoned that if he visited Eliza he could make up the time by taking it to the village. He set off for Gilesgate and Eliza's house.

He had been hard on her, he knew it. When he had listened to Jonathan Moore talking about her, saying the most outrageous things, it had aroused jealousy and anger he hadn't known was in him. Jonathan Moore was a man he had always disliked, apart from the fact that he was a mine owner, a member of the enemy class. His sort thought they were doing the ignorant pitmen a favour by allowing them to work in the pits. They thought the risks they took with their precious capital was more important than the risks the men took with their lives every day, fighting against gases such as choke damp and fire damp and the terrible stythe that ruined their lungs and made them old men at forty.

Peter's thoughts returned to Eliza. She had admitted that what Moore had said was true or at least that there was some truth in it. He remembered the half-smile on Moore's face as he had talked about her.

'Ask her,' Moore had said. 'You don't have to take my word for it.'

Unbidden, the tune of the old ballad, 'The Mine Owner and the Pitman's Wife' ran through his thoughts. He shook his head as though to clear it. When he had proposed to Eliza he had told himself that it was because she would be an asset as a wife for any union official. She came from a mining family; she knew what he was fighting for. Oh, he was fond of her, he was indeed; he remembered the night he had taken her in when her little lad was taken by that blackguard, Jack Mitchell. She had been past herself, poor lass, she was so distraught. Aye, she had had a struggle all her life, he reckoned.

He had been too hasty, he thought. And he had hidden behind his work as though it was a protective wall, using it as an excuse not to show how he really felt. Now he had to put things right, ask her to marry him and tell her the real reason he wanted her to.

'Mr Collier! Come in, come in,' Bertha exclaimed as she opened the door to him. 'Are you wanting to see Eliza? She's not here, she went up to Alnwick yesterday.'

Peter raised his eyebrows. 'Alnwick?' he said. 'Whatever for?'

'It's the bairn, the lad, Tot, he's run off, Mr Collier. He said he was going to ask his uncle to take him on as an apprentice. Eliza's gone after him.' She told him about the note and how they had both gone to Newcastle to try to intercept Tot.

'I thought mebbe it was a message from her when the knock came to the door,' she went on. 'I thought I'd best come home in case the lad changed his mind. They often do when they run away, don't they?'

'They do,' said Peter. He bit his lip. The silly lad, he thought. Newcastle was a dangerous place for a lad and if he had got there and hadn't enough money to buy a ticket for Alnwick goodness knows what might have happened to him. Someone might have taken him from the station. He himself had heard of lads being enticed aboard boats bound for foreign parts when they strayed by the quayside. But surely Tot had more sense than let it happen to him? Peter berated himself for imagining the worst like an hysterical woman.

'I'll come back the night,' he said aloud. 'I'm sure Eliza will find the lad. Any road, nothing will happen to him, I'm sure. He's not a bad lad, he's only in a hurry to grow up and be a man.'

'Aye,' said Bertha. But she sounded dubious. Still, best not to meet trouble afore it came, she said to herself. Going into the kitchen, she got the flat irons out of the cupboard and put them on the bar to heat by the fire. She took the old blanket she used as an ironing cloth and spread it on the table, and brought out the basket full of ironing that should by rights have been on its way back to the owner that morning. She spread a shirt on the blanket and took an iron from the bar with an old cloth to protect her hand. She spat on it and it sizzled satisfactorily and she started to press the under-manager's Sunday shirt, sleeves first then tails and back, and finally the double front. There were two collars but they were separate. The lad might have run off but still money had to be earned to pay the rent and buy a crust.

Peter took the horse bus to Brancepeth and, remembering he hadn't eaten his bait, took the bait tin out of his pocket and the sandwich from the tin. He ate it as the bus jogged along, looking out all the while just in case Eliza's lad had changed his mind about where he was running away to and was about somewhere close.

He had been hesitant about asking Eliza to wed him, fearing she would refuse. He was a fool really, he thought, trying to rationalise how he felt about her, saying it would help her get the lad into a school. He had talked about how they could help people, their own people, together. He had not talked about love. He wasn't sure if he did love her, the idea was so new to him. And of course she had said she didn't know, she would have to think about it.

It was only when he felt such rage when Jonathan Moore had boasted about enjoying her favours that he began to analyse his own feelings. His thoughts were interrupted as the bus stopped in Brancepeth and people began to get off. He put the bait tin back in his pocket and climbed down on to the dusty road. There was work to do; he couldn't let the men down, they had to come first.

Eliza stood in the churchyard watching as the small procession wound its way towards the newly dug hole prepared for Annie Mitchell-Howe. Though she had been in the church for the main service she had slipped out early to take her place under a tree out of the line of vision of anyone standing at the graveside. She was no longer a member of the family; she had left Annie's son even before he had died. She was a scarlet woman. She half-expected the old woman to sit up in her coffin and point a finger at her for having the temerity to be there. Now she was being silly, she said to herself. The vicar went through the words of the committal part of the service and the coffin was laid in the ground. There were very few mourners and of those only her son Henry and his wife Amelia availed themselves of the soil offered them to throw in. It was only a few minutes after that before the churchyard was empty but for the sexton who was shovelling in soil.

Now it was safe to come out with no one to see her, Eliza swiftly left and walked up the road towards the Hall. A grandiose name for a house built by a tradesman for himself, she thought, but then John Henry had been like that.

She came to the low wall surrounding the house but did not go in. She was looking for any signs that Tot had been there. You never knew, he might have come during the funeral service after all. But though she walked all round the property, looking in the windows and ducking out of sight if anyone looked out, she didn't see the slightest sign of Tot. She saw Henry and Amelia and a strange man in a black suit with a stand-up collar and the maid who had let her in the evening before, but there was no sign of a child.

She would look around the cottage where Annie had lived for the years of her widowhood, some of them with Tot. He might, just might, go there. But when she got there, there was no one; even the woman she had spoken to was gone.

The day was slipping away and she was no nearer to knowing what had happened to Tot or if anything had happened to him indeed. Her heart missed a beat at the thought that anything might have happened to him. Dear God, she prayed, do not let anything bad happen to him, please God.

Eliza climbed on to the train going back to Newcastle with despair in her heart. Where was he? Oh, she would agree to him leaving school and training to be a cabinet maker; she would do anything he wanted, she really would, if only he was home and safe.

*

'What are we going to do now?' Mrs Bates asked her husband, her voice despairing. 'We should have called the doctor last night and the polis an' all.'

Farmer Bates bit his lip. He felt guilty, for hadn't he put the cost of the doctor against the lad's life? He gazed at the boy, his face swollen and discoloured grotesquely and his eyes still closed. He had no experience with bairns, he thought, but he knew what he would do with a young animal he found in this state. Only you couldn't put a bairn to sleep like you could an injured calf or lamb. He transferred his gaze to his wife. She was sponging the lad's face again and as she did so his eyelids fluttered.

'He's coming round!' said Farmer Bates. 'Look, he's coming round.'

'Nay, he is not,' replied his wife. 'He's done that a few times during the night; I've kept a watch on the lad. No, I reckon you'd best fetch the doctor and if you don't want to pay I will out of the egg money.'

Mrs Bates looked after the hens and the agreement was that the money from selling eggs was hers to spend. She looked at her husband, waiting for him to protest, but he did not.

'I'll send the lad as soon as he comes,' he said. In this case the lad he meant was a thirteen-year-old he had taken on straight from school. He lived in Chester-le-Street but his day on the farm started at dawn when he mucked out the horses. 'I'll get him now,' said the farmer.

Dr Jones was a young man who had recently bought a practice from Dr Ridley, who had had a stroke. He was in his eighties and still working, but at last he was forced to retire. Still, the young man was living in his house for a while and Dr Ridley liked to hear everything that went on during the day so that it was late when the younger man got to his bed. So Dr Jones was feeling tired to say the least when he had to turn out with Amos, the farmer's lad, to attend a young lad who seemed to be a vagrant or a runaway. He'd be lucky to get his fee, he reckoned, and he needed all he could get after spending the whole of the capital left by his mother on buying the practice in Chester-le-Street. Consequently he was not feeling his usual sunny self as he carried his shiny new Gladstone bag into the farmhouse.

Mrs Bates looked at him suspiciously. 'Where's Dr Ridley?' she asked.

'Dr Ridley has retired. I'm Dr Jones, I've taken over his practice.' As the woman was still crouching protectively over a young lad who was lying prostrate on the settle, he asked her to move away, which she did so reluctantly. The doctor sighed.

'How long has he been like this?' he asked.

'My man brought him in from the roadside last night. He'd been attacked by a couple of drunken tramps,' Mrs

Bates replied. Then, having decided to trust the young doctor after all, went on, 'He's fluttered his eyelids a bit once or twice but he hasn't come to.'

'Have you called the police? We don't want ruffians roaming around attacking children.' Dr Jones was feeling gently round the bruise on Tot's face and now he felt around the back of the boy's head. 'Ah yes,' he said as though to himself, 'there's a lump there as well. I think he must have bumped it on a stone when he fell. That's probably caused the concussion.'

'Knocked him out, do you mean?'

'I do. I think it's best to leave him here, lying flat on his back. Don't try to wake him up.' The doctor got to his feet, still looking down at Tot. 'He's fairly well dressed for lads round here. And in pretty good condition physically. Someone is probably looking for him.' He snapped his bag closed. 'That will be three and sixpence for the call out,' he said.

'Three and sixpence? By, that's seven dozen eggs, man! Do you think I'm made of money?' Mrs Bates sounded remarkably like her husband suddenly.

'It is early in the morning. But if I have to make a return visit it will only be two shillings,' said Dr Jones evenly. He was determined not to go without his money. The farm looked prosperous enough.

Mrs Bates gave him an expressive glare but she went to a drawer in the dresser and took out a bag, which clinked satisfactorily. She counted three shillings and sixpence out carefully and handed it to him.

'I'll come back tonight if you think he needs me,' said Dr Jones. 'Just send the lad.'

'I don't think you will,' said Mrs Bates to the unconscious boy. 'By, he never even left a drop of medicine. I don't know where he gets his prices from.'

The farmer came in for his breakfast and they discussed the situation over home-cured ham, eggs and black pudding.

'Well, the doctor must have thought it wasn't serious,' said Farmer Bates. He cut a piece of ham and held it on his fork for a moment while he thought. 'I reckon we should call in the polis,' he said at last and put the ham into his mouth and chewed. 'I'll send the lad.'

'You'll not get much work out of him if you are forever sending him on messages,' observed his wife.

'Aye, that's a fact,' he replied. 'Still, we'd best do it.'

It was about two hours before the policeman turned up on the doorstep. 'I understand you've got an injured lad here,' he said as he followed the farmer into the kitchen.

'Aye, we have,' said Farmer Bates. 'An' you've taken your time getting here. I've had to hang about near the house this morning when I should have been up in the far field, seeing to the tups.'

'I had a busy morning an' all,' the policeman said

imperturbably. 'There's a lot of lawlessness about these days.' He took out his notebook and pencil. 'Is this the lad?' He indicated the boy, still lying on the settle. 'What do you reckon happened to him?'

'He was set on by a couple of tramps,' said Farmer Bates. 'Mind, they should be run out of the county, ruffians like them lot.'

'Aye. It would save me a bit of bother,' said the policeman. 'Now, tell me what happened.'

Chapter Twenty-Eight

Jonathan Moore sat by the manager's desk in the office at Blue House colliery. He eyed the three men standing, cap in hand, before the desk. One of them was Tommy Teesdale, Eliza's father. He was black from the pit and stooped over like Jonathan had imagined an underground hobgoblin would be in the stories he had listened to as a child. The only resemblance he had to Eliza was his dark eyes, shining out of the blackness. This was a miners' deputation. Now that the union had some clout the men thought they could make demands. Well, he would show them who was in charge now his father was gone. He was. And he would close this pathetic little pit down before he would give in to the union. It was the least productive of his mines.

'What we want, Mr Robinson, is a proper allowance of coal for every pitman's house. It's only fair like, nearly all the other companies have agreed to it,' said Tommy, addressing the manager. Jonathan looked up at the ceiling, yellowed with the smoke from clay pipes, and pursed his lips. The other two miners watched him covertly. He was dressed in smart fawn trousers and riding boots in the style of a military man. He had on a white shirt with a high, soft collar and a black coat over it. He had crossed one leg over the other and he tapped at the sole of the boot with a riding whip, betraying impatience.

'Well, lads,' said Robinson, glancing sideways at the mine owner, 'we will have to discuss the matter. I will let you know what we decide.'

'And we need half an hour of the shift for seeing to the safety,' Tommy went on doggedly. He did not look at Jonathan but he was aware that the owner was glaring balefully at him.

'I—' the manager began, but he was interrupted by the mine owner, who suddenly sat forward in his chair and put both feet on the ground.

'Enough!' he roared. 'You think because we had to recognise the union you can ask for anything! Well, I tell you, Tommy Teesdale, you cannot, no indeed.'

'We need to clean up the coal dust afore we set the black powder,' said Tommy stubbornly. 'We cannot afford—'

'Get out! Get out and don't come back. Look at you, call yourself a hewer? You don't look as though you could swing a bloody pick, you do not indeed. No wonder the pit's doing so badly if it's men like you we're using. Get off the premises before I call the constable, do you hear me?'

'What?' Tommy was startled, confused; this was something he hadn't bargained for. No one had ever suggested he wasn't up to the job before and he couldn't believe it was happening now. And by the looks on the men's faces, neither could any of the others. Even the manager was open-mouthed. Tommy was a champion hewer and he still had a couple of years left in him before he would have to go on datal work and be paid by the shift, not by how much coal he shifted. He might be small and bent but he was a man of iron.

'You heard me,' said Jonathan grimly. 'And the rest of you be off too unless you want to go too.'

'We'll stop the pit,' said the miner beside Tommy. He stepped forward. 'You have no right, Mr Moore,' he said.

'Go on strike and I'll have you all out of your houses,' Jonathan warned. 'I'm not having you men telling me what to do, not in my own pit. Haven't we provided you with the work, kept your families fed? Do your bloody worst, that's what I say!'

'Now then, lads, consider—' the manager, Mr Robinson, began, alarmed at the way the confrontation had blown up. How had it come to talk of striking? It had been a routine meeting and if Moore had not been there it would have been sorted amicably somehow.

'Right then, Mr Moore,' said Tommy, drawing himself up to his full five feet two inches. 'I'm going. Don't think I won't get taken on at some other pit, I will. I'm well known as a hewer to reckon with, I am. Howay, lads, I don't need you to stop the pit for me. I'll get along, you just see if I don't.'

'Aye, and take your family with you, I want you out of that colliery house by the end of the week. Or I will bring in the candymen.'

'Mr Moore, it's Thursday today,' the manager put in. He didn't like the way things were going here, he did not indeed. There would be strife; he could feel it coming in his bones.

'So it's bloody Thursday, is it? Aye and it's Friday tomorrow and I want them out, the lads too. Three of them, aren't there? Pay them off.'

Tommy's back stiffened with outrage. 'Do you think my lads would stay after I've gone? Nay, they will not. An', think on, they can go now, they can an' all. Now they're not bound to the pit, thanks to the union.' He stalked to the door before turning and putting in his final shot. 'Three, did you say? Aye, there was three, Albert, Harry and Miley, and good lads they are. At least Albert and Harry are good lads and they look fair to making fine hewers. Miley now, he will not be doing any hewing, no, on account of he's dead and in his grave. Killed in the pit, he was, or as good as.'

The three men walked out and for a few minutes there was silence in the office; the manager didn't speak because he was shaken into silence after the way the meeting had gone. Jonathan didn't say anything for a few minutes either. Then he got to his feet.

'I'll go over the accounts with you tomorrow, Robinson,' he said in his normal tone of voice. 'Just now I have things I must do.'

'Will I pay Tommy Teesdale what he's owed the morn?' asked Mr Robinson. 'He'll be up for it, it being the fortnightly pay day.'

'You will not. He's forfeited it, the insolent rabble-rouser.'

Mr Robinson stared after his departing figure. By, he was a hard man, Jonathan Moore, he thought. Harder even than the usual run of mine owner. He might have remembered how young Miley Teesdale had died. But then, there was no sentiment in business.

The coal was showing signs of petering out any road, in the seams of Blue House. No doubt Jonathan Moore would use this little episode to get rid of the pitmen. Mr Robinson sighed. He himself was getting on in years and he had a bit put by for his old age. But he had thought the owner might find places for the men in his other pits. It didn't look as though that was going to

happen. Tommy Teesdale was likely only the first to be
turned off.

Jonathan mounted his horse and rode away from Blue
House. He should have been feeling better for having
vented his spleen on Eliza's father but in fact he did
not. All he felt was a deep frustration and a longing
for the woman. She was in his blood and he couldn't
get her out. Even now he felt a longing to turn away
from his road home and go to Durham to at least catch
a glimpse of her. He resisted it but he knew it would
turn into a compulsion. He was beginning to hate her
for it.

He wondered what Collier had said to her when she
saw him. He grinned as he thought of it. Oh, he had
really enjoyed describing the details of the night he
had spent with Eliza to him. The fact that it had been
in her man's bed too, that had added to the spice of it.
He thought of Collier's face as he said the words. The
union man would not be able to look at Eliza again, he,
Jonathan Moore, had made sure of that. And yet that
hadn't lightened his black mood either; he was still filled
with fury and frustration.

'Why on earth have you brought your tools home with
you?' asked Mary Anne anxiously. Surely they hadn't
closed the pit, she wondered anxiously, and felt a familiar

tightening in her chest. She tried to breathe calmly, deeply as Eliza had taught her to do.

'I've been turned off, Mary Anne,' said Tommy, shamefaced. He had not been turned off in his working life before, for he was a champion hewer. Besides that, he had always worked under the bond system and was unable to leave a pit once he had put his mark on the bond paper. He had celebrated the end of the yearly bond and the fact that he was free to seek work elsewhere should he want to. But the possibility had not crossed his mind that he might be turned off.

Mary Anne sat down heavily on the cracket stool by the fire. The cracket had been made in the pit by her father for use in a low seam where he had to sit down or squat to swing his pick. Tommy had one almost the same and now he was carrying it by the hole in the middle of the seat, which was there for the purpose, and his pick, broad miner's shovel and black powder tin. He laid them all down in a heap just inside the door.

'Why?' was the only word Mary Anne could manage to get out.

'It was Moore, the young one,' said Tommy. He took his clay pipe from the mantelpiece and poked at it with his index finger. There was a little unburned baccy in it so he lit a taper at the fire and lit it before he went on.

'We went in to ask for the proper coal allowance like the union said. And half an hour datal to see to the safety.

Moore was there. He went wild and turned me off.'
Tommy looked at his wife. 'We have to get out of the
house by the morn. But it'll be all right, it will, I'll get
on at another pit.'

'Will you? What makes you think Moore won't
blacken your name to the other owners? Don't they all
stick together? You know they do!' Mary Anne's voice
was rising; her eyes were suspiciously bright in her now
flushed face. She thought of something else. 'What about
the lads?'

'The lads an' all. They'll be bringing their picks and
shovels.'

Mary Anne suddenly found it even harder to breathe.
She held her mouth open and gulped air.

'Don't, Mary Anne, don't take on,' urged Tommy. He
was thoroughly frightened now. 'It'll be all right, I said,
haven't we got our Eliza? She'll take us in, man, she will!'

'Why did he do it, Da?'

Tommy hadn't noticed the two boys had come in and
were piling picks and shovels on to the pile made by their
father.

'Nay, lad, he just went mad.'

'Bloody gaffers!' said Harry bitterly. He was a tall,
thin lad, taller than his father and gangly, though he had
the shoulders of a pitman.

'Harry, don't you swear,' said Tommy. 'Where did
you learn language like that?'

The lad could have said from his father, for Tommy, unless he was in chapel, was not above the odd obscenity, but he did not. 'Sorry, Da,' he replied meekly. 'Are you badly, Mam?' He had just realised that his mother was breathing badly and had turned a funny colour. He went over to her and put a hand on her arm.

'I'm fine, son,' said Mary Anne and indeed she was getting over the first shock and her breathing had steadied. 'We'd best get packed up then. We'll go to our Eliza's till we get somewhere.'

'You sit still, me an' Albert will do it. When we've had our dinners.'

'Eeh, what am I thinking of?' said Mary Anne. 'There's stew and dumplings on the bar waiting for you. It won't take a minute to dish it out.'

'I'll dish it out,' said Tommy. 'You sit down, you have to look after yourself.' He busied himself putting out plates and spoons and brought the heavy iron pan to the table and sat it in the middle. 'After this we'll pack up,' he said. 'I'll get the carrier; I have a bob or two to pay him. We'll be out the night. I'm not waiting for the candymen to come the morn. I'd not give that young Moore the satisfaction.'

'Aw, Da, I don't want to move to Durham,' said Albert as he ate his stew. He quartered a dumpling carefully and stuck his fork into one quarter. 'Mebbe I can get on at Thornley.'

'He doesn't want to leave his lass,' said Harry, his teeth gleaming from his coal-blackened face as he grinned.

'You get on and finish your dinner,' his father advised. 'You can get your wash and help your mother, do you hear me?'

'Yes, Da,' said Harry and bent over his meal.

'We'll have to leave the chapel,' Mary Anne said sadly.

'Aye well, there's other chapels,' said Tommy. 'Go on, Albert, if you've finished, fetch the water in for your mother.' It was always the woman's job to bring in the water for washing and every other purpose but the lads had got used to doing it as Mary Anne wasn't up to it now.

Usually the men went straight to bed after a shift but there was no time for that now. After all, they did not have to go back to the pit in time for fore shift that night.

It was eight o'clock on the Friday evening when Eliza arrived back at the house in Gilesgate after seeing at least a few of her patients. She hadn't got back from Alnwick until late in the afternoon and Bertha had left her a note telling her of two people who wanted her to call in.

'I am cleening the chaple,' Bertha had written. 'Then quire practice. Mr Collier was heer.'

Then Tot had not come home. Eliza felt a rush of disappointment that was like a great weight on her chest. Automatically she washed her hands, picked up her bag and went off see some of her patients. She was tired, tired and anxious, but still, if she was needed then she had to go. Besides, she had to make a living.

It was already dark by the time she turned Dolly into the back street. As she came to a halt by the stable she glanced across at the back of the house and her heart leaped as she saw there was a lamp burning in the kitchen. Someone was there; it had to be Tot. Oh, thank God, thank God indeed. Not even waiting to uncouple the pony she ran up the yard and into the house, stopping dead as she saw, not Tot, but her mother and father and her two brothers.

'What are you doing here?' she blurted.

'Eliza, is that the only welcome we're going to get?' asked Mary Anne. 'Where's the lad, any road? Mind, we had a carry on finding the place but we found someone who could tell us where the nurse lived. And when we got here the house was empty. If our Albert hadn't read that note Bertha left—'

'Mam, what is it? What's wrong?'

Mary Anne fell silent and looked down at her hands, which were twisting on her lap.

'I've been turned off, lass,' said Tommy. 'Me and the lads an' all. We had a day to get out of the house an' all. I thought we would be out by night-shift time yesterday but it was your mam. We couldn't hurry her.'

'Turned off?' repeated Eliza blankly.

'Turned off and turned out of the house,' Albert put in to make the situation plain. 'Me mam's badly, Eliza, she's worn out, I reckon.'

'Oh, Mam,' said his sister. 'Howay now, sit in the front room. There's a nice comfortable armchair in there. In fact you'd best all go in there and I'll see to the supper. I'll fetch the fire in, it'll soon be cosy. Albert, go and see to Dolly and the trap. Put her in her stable and give her some hay.'

Looking at her mother's pasty face and bright, feverish eyes, the way she was gulping air into her lungs, her nurse's training took over. In no time she had the lads organised to help her. While Albert saw to the pony Harry took a shovel full of live coals from the grate and took them into the front room fire grate. He piled small lumps on top and soon the room was warming up against the chill of the autumnal evening. Mary Anne was propped up in a cushioned chair such as she had never sat in her life, for most of the miners' cottages contained only a settle, a wooden rocker for the man of the house and crackets and backless forms for the children.

Meanwhile, Eliza had prepared a large pan of panacklty with onion and scraps of bacon and potatoes and beef tea poured over the lot, for she had no gravy, and put it into the oven by the side of the grate. And all the time she worried about Tot.

Where was he? Was he all right? It was the not knowing that was killing her, she thought wretchedly. When the meal was ready she shared it out on to plates and called the men through to eat it. Then she put two plates on a tray and took it through to the front room.

Chapter Twenty-Nine

'Charlie wants me to go to live at the farm,' said Bertha. 'He says his mother will be chaperone until we get wed.'

'Oh, Bertha,' said Eliza. 'I had thought you would be here at least until the wedding in October. I'll miss you.' She felt as though her life was changing so fast she wanted to take a hold of it to steady it down.

'You have your family here, though. I was going to tell Charlie I couldn't, not before we were wed. If I'm at the farm I know I won't have the time to help you look for Tot. But as I say, you have the family here and there just isn't any room for me, any road.'

'I'll find Tot, I know I will,' said Eliza, though in truth she was becoming more worried about him as each day passed. She had posted bills in Durham and Newcastle and also in Alnwick, with copies of a grainy black and white photograph of Tot looking stiff and unnatural in his Sunday best suit, which had cost her a fortune at the newly opened photographic studio in Durham. No one had come forward as yet but it was only a week since he had run away. She didn't trust Henry or his wife to let her know if he turned up but tradesmen in the town had promised they would, for a consideration, that is.

'The family won't be here for long,' Eliza said now to Bertha. 'The lads have got taken on at Stanley and Da is hopeful he might be an' all.' In fact, Tommy and the two boys had found themselves blacklisted by the owners around Haswell and east Durham. They had had to travel further afield to look for work. Tommy, being older, was not so lucky as the boys. The manager at Stanley was happy to set him on datal work but he could not earn as much as he had done as a hewer. Datal work was paid by the shift, as the name implies. It was a great blow to Tommy's pride.

'Stanley is a fair bit away, though, isn't it? Your mam won't be near for you to look after her.'

Eliza sat down suddenly and began to cry. The problems besetting her with the family and her anxiety for Tot had finally made her break down.

'Now then, Eliza, don't take on,' said Bertha. 'I'll stay if you want me to, I will, never mind Charlie.' But the storm inside Eliza had found some release and she pulled herself together and dried her eyes on her apron. Her mother was in the front room still and she could not let her see she was upset.

'No, Bertha, you must do what you have to do. Like you say, I'll be all right.' Before Bertha could reply there was a knock on the door and she went to answer it. Most folk round the doors tended to knock and walk in so it had to be something important or a stranger. It was Peter Collier.

'Eeh, Mr Collier,' she exclaimed, 'I was wondering where you had got to and so was Eliza. What are you standing out there for? Howay in, do, Eliza will be pleased as anything to see you.'

'I got held up with a disaster over by Cockfield,' said Peter, following her into the kitchen, where Eliza had risen to her feet at the sound of his voice. He looked closely at her. Her eyes were red and swollen and she had an air of tension about her. 'Do you mean to say the lad hasn't come back?' he said. 'I thought for sure he would have done by now. I'm sorry, Eliza, I couldn't get here before but I've kept an eye out for Tot wherever I've been in the coalfield and asked everyone if they've seen him.' He felt guilty and inadequate as though he had been neglecting his duty. But there had been an accident over in the west of the county and men and boys trapped in the gallery they had been working. The rescue men had not got them out until the day before.

'Why should you hurry to get here?' Eliza asked stiffly. 'We're not betrothed, you and me, are we? You made it plain you didn't want a woman with a tarnished reputation.'

Peter flushed. 'Eliza, Eliza,' he said. 'Listen to me, I didn't mean it. Only I was upset by the way he talked about you. I didn't know what to think at first.'

'And the union has to come first, hasn't it?'

'Well, I asked for that,' Peter admitted. Before he could say more, Mary Anne called from the front room.

'Is that Peter Collier, Eliza? Tell him to come in here, I'd like to see him.'

'I will, Mam,' said Eliza. She led the way to the front of the house and Peter had no option but to follow.

'I'll speak to you later,' he whispered to Eliza, before entering the room where her mother sat, ensconced in the armchair she liked so much she was loath to leave it. Eliza turned and went back to the kitchen where Bertha was just putting on her bonnet and shawl, ready to go out.

'I think it will be best for me to go, Eliza,' she said. 'I'm sorry. But I will call in regular like and ask around for Tot an' all.'

'If that's what you want, Bertha,' said Eliza. She watched as Bertha walked down the yard and turned the corner, but her thoughts were on the two in the other room. She could hear the voices from there for she had left the door ajar.

'Did you hear Tommy and the lads were turned off?' Mary Anne asked Peter. 'After all these years at the same pit, Tommy was turned off. It's off the map, man, isn't it?'

'I hadn't heard, no, not till I got back to Durham,' Peter replied. 'Where's Tommy now? I'd like to hear what happened exactly.'

'The lads have been taken on at Stanley. Tommy can get work there an' all but only datal. He takes it badly, Mr Collier.'

'Aye, he would.'

He was silent for a moment or two, thinking about it. Hewers reaching Tommy's age were unusual; they often started on datal work. It meant that they had to take a fall in wages but usually they could stay on at the pit they had been working. Experienced men such as Tommy were sometimes promoted to deputy overman, but sometimes they were turned off; it was a fact of life.

'It was that young Moore who did it, not the manager,' said Mary Anne. 'Tommy says he was one of the deputation there to see about their rights, but Moore took offence. He threw us out of the house, we had to be gone the next day, Tommy said.'

Jonathan Moore, thought Peter. He hadn't expected him to be so vindictive. To throw a whole family out because a daughter spurned his advances was vindictive indeed.

Peter's thoughts were racing. The problem was that Tommy's life as a hewer was coming to an end, there was no denying it. He looked at Mary Anne's face. She was obviously having trouble getting her breath and her skin had a very unhealthy hue.

'I don't know as I can manage another flit,' said Mary Anne. 'Say nowt to our Eliza, but it's very hard, very hard. To lose my neighbours an' all, they were always willing to give me a hand when I needed it. I miss Blue House.'

'Mining folk are like that, they always help each other,' said Peter gently. 'But you know, you've got Eliza and the lads and Tommy and I'll do everything to help I can think of. You'll manage, you'll see. Rest as much as you can while you have the chance and you'll get your strength up.'

As he left the room to go back to Eliza in the kitchen he doubted she ever would. Eliza was dressed, ready to go out on her rounds. She was very quiet for she had heard what her mother had said and her training told her that in this, Mary Anne was right. She had not up to this minute faced the fact that Mary Anne was not likely to live for much longer.

'If you are going into the city I'll ride along with you,' said Peter. 'We can call in at the police station and see if there is any news of Tot.'

'Do you think there might be?' asked Eliza.

'Maybe,' he replied. He helped her harness Dolly and they drove out along the road to the city. Eliza glanced at him as they went along, and he sensed it and turned to her and smiled. It was a comfort, she realised, having his support. The bad feeling there had been between them meant nothing now; it was unimportant compared with her other worries.

The policeman behind the desk in the police station looked up from a paper he had been studying and gazed at them. Naturally, it was Peter, the man, he spoke to.

'Oh, it's the union man,' he said. 'What do you want?'

'We have come to report a missing young lad,' said Peter. It was unfortunate that the man was one of those who had broken up a meeting being held in the market place at the behest of the owner, who was a magistrate, some time before. Peter had spent a night in the cells before being discharged with a caution. But that had been before the union was properly recognised.

'A missing lad, eh?' The policeman licked his pencil and prepared to take down details. 'Name?'

'Thomas Mitchell-Howe,' said Eliza. 'I'm his mother, Sister Mitchell-Howe.' The policeman shot her an unbelieving glance.

'Mitchell-Howe, eh. A fancy name that,' he remarked.

'Dr Gray of this city can verify it. I am a professional nurse.' The policeman did not seem greatly impressed. In his experience nurses were often drunken and dirty. He had to admit that this one was dressed decently and was clean.

'How old is the lad? How did he go missing?' Best

to fill the form in, he thought. The union man might cause trouble if he did not.

'Ten, going on eleven,' said Eliza. 'He ran away to find work.'

The constable looked impatient. 'Going on eleven?' he said. 'Most lads are working at that age. It's not as though he's a little bairn.'

'Constable, do your duty and look in the book and see if a lad that age has been found hurt or reported taken up from the streets, will you?'

The constable bridled. 'I expect you're not saying I don't know my duty, *sir*,' he said, putting extra stress on the last word. He turned to Eliza. 'How long has he been gone, er, Sister?'

'Almost a week,' Eliza replied.

'A week? Well, that's not long, is it? He'll likely be turning up when he realises it's none so easy to make a living out in the world,' he said easily. He opened a large black ledger and glanced through it. 'No, no lad of that description down here,' he said and closed the book with a snap. 'Now, I'm busy, like. There's criminals and vagabonds about in the city, or hadn't you heard?'

Peter uttered an angry exclamation but the policeman was imperturbable so he took Eliza's arm and led her outside. 'It's no good making a fuss about his attitude, not now,' he said. 'But I will report him, never fear.'

'And what good will that do? It won't get Tot back,' said Eliza despairingly. 'This is the second time I've lost him, remember. I can't bear it.'

'You haven't lost him. We'll get him back, you'll see. I'll search for him. Everywhere I go, I'll ask about him.'

When Eliza got home here was a letter waiting for her; it had come by the midday post. Her mother was sitting in the front room with the letter propped on the small table by her side and she was turned in her chair staring at it. Letters were very rare in Mary Anne's experience as neither she nor Tommy could read or write. Usually they meant trouble and she reckoned they had enough trouble to be going on with, oh yes, she did.

'What do you think it is, Eliza?' she asked fearfully. 'Is it about Tot, do you think?'

Hope leaped in Eliza's breast. Oh, if it was from someone answering one of the posters she had pasted around the area! She picked up the envelope and stared at the writing.

'To the parents or guardian of Thomas Mitchell-Howe,' it said. His full name, Thomas Mitchell-Howe; it must be from someone who had spoken to him, someone who knew his name. And he must have given them his mother's address too. Oh, thank God, thank you, God, she thought and ripped open the seal. She read the contents and sat down abruptly,

'Well? What does it say?' asked Mary Anne. 'Howay, man, Eliza, tell me? Is the bairn all right?'

'It's – it's from a lawyer, Mam. It says Annie left our Tot five hundred and fifty pounds in her will.'

'What? *Five hundred pounds*? It's a fortune!' Mary Anne looked a bit dazed; she couldn't conceive of five hundred pounds. The amount had barely registered with Eliza. What did money matter?

'It doesn't tell us where he is, does it?' she asked bitterly.

'No, that's true.' Mary Anne bit her lip. 'Look, Eliza, pull yourself together, lass, and stop looking on the dark side all the time. He'll come back, man; you've not lost him, not like I lost our Miley.'

Eliza stared at her mother. She had not, it was true; surely she would feel it if Tot was dead? She felt restless; it was already twilight outside but she wanted to go out again and search for him. She picked up her bonnet and tied it back on. She had a new batch of posters fresh from the printers; she would hand them out.

'You're not going out again, our Eliza!' said Mary Anne. 'You've not had your tea, never mind supper. If you go on like this it'll be you that'll be badly.'

'I'll take bread and cheese with me,' said Eliza. 'I'll be fine. Don't take on, Mam.'

Once again she harnessed Dolly to the tub trap and

led her out and up the back street. As she turned the corner she noticed that Tot's friends were having a game of quoits in the play field despite the fading light. When he saw her, Bert, his particular friend, the one who had begun the trouble by encouraging Tot to leave school and go down the pit with him, came over and spoke.

'Did you hear from Tot, Mrs Mitchell?' he asked. 'Only I thought he would have sent me a letter by now. He promised he would when he got to Alnwick.'

Eliza stopped the pony. 'You knew he was going to Alnwick? You didn't say when I asked you if you knew about his plans.'

Bert hung his head. 'I wasn't supposed to tell. Only he did say he would write. Mebbe he couldn't afford the penny post. But he was going to walk up the Great North Road to Newcastle and get the train from there. That would save him a bit of money.'

Eliza closed her eyes for a moment then opened them and said, 'You didn't say that either, Bert. By, I'll have to have a word with your mother, I will indeed. What else did he tell you that you haven't told me?'

'Nothing, Mrs Mitchell, honest,' the boy replied. He gazed at her earnestly. His eyes were rimmed with coal dust for he had already started in the mine, and it gave him a look like one of the actresses she had once seen at the fair.

'You'll be in trouble if he did and you're not telling

me,' she said and flicked the reins over Dolly's broad back and set off for the Great North Road. She should be able to get so far of the way up and put out a few posters on trees and milestones on the way. She felt as though she was actually doing something constructive, something that might help. Thank goodness she had checked the oil lamps on the trap before she set off, she would need them on the way home. She thought of Tot as she pushed Dolly on. No wonder she had missed him. He would hardly have got to Newcastle station by the time she and Bertha had arrived there on the train that evening when he went missing. It must be all of eighteen to twenty miles; it would have taken him a few hours. What a fool she had been, not finding out what Bert knew about his plans before she set off after him.

Chapter Thirty

'Look here, Bates, the lad's coming round,' said Mrs Bates as the farmer came into the house for his breakfast. She did not look up from the boy; she was wrapped up in him. He looked sourly at the boy lying on the settle. Aye, he thought, his eyelids were fluttering and thank the Lord for that an' all. He was fed up with coming in famished for his meals and finding neither sight nor smell of any food on the table nor yet being prepared. It wasn't good enough. Aye, an' he would be telling the woman making such a fuss over the bit lad on the settle, he would indeed.

'Never mind him, where's me bacon and black pudding? I've been looking forward to it this last hour. What's a man supposed to live on, eh?'

'I'll not be a minute with it, I didn't like to leave him. He's moving, man, he might fall off the settle,' said Mrs Bates. 'But look now, you watch him, I'll not be long getting the food on the table.'

He'd been there nearly three days now, though he had turned over on the couch yesterday. Farmer Bates felt thoroughly neglected.

Farmer Bates took off his boots and walked in his stockinged feet over the flagged floor of the kitchen to where the boy lay. 'Hurry up then, I'm fair clemmed,' he said. 'Any road, didn't we say last night we would send him to the workhouse? He'd be all right there, they'd put him in the hospital. He'd get a doctor looking at him for free an' all.' It still rankled with him that his wife was paying that Dr Jones from the egg money. Well, he'd told her straight, he wouldn't make it up for her; last night he'd said so.

He pulled a chair from the table and sat down beside the lad. 'Get on with it,' he instructed Mrs Bates. She had barely brought the bacon from the larder and cut a couple of thick slices before Tot's eyelids opened wide, disclosing the deepest blue eyes he had ever seen. By, they were wasted on a lad, they were, he reckoned.

'Now then,' he said as the lad stared at him. 'Who the heck are you, any road?'

Mrs Bates forgot about the bacon and flew to his side. 'Oh, poor lad,' she said with fervour. 'I'm that glad to see you come to yourself.'

Tot transferred his gaze to her. He didn't know who she was but her voice was familiar. It seemed to him he had heard it a lot and not long ago.

'Who are you?' he asked. 'You're not my Aunt Amelia.' Hadn't he been going to Alnwick?

'Nay, lad, I'm not,' Mrs Bates replied. She smiled widely. 'My name is Mrs Bates and this is Farmer Bates, my man. We've been looking after you since you were set on by tramps, on the road by the farm. You've been here nigh on three days. I've had the doctor to you.'

Tot struggled to sit up properly before wincing and putting a hand to the back of his head. 'Thank you,' he said politely, 'I have to go to Alnwick.' He had no memory of being attacked by anyone, but if the lady said it had happened it must have done so.

'Alnwick? By, that's a long way to be walking, isn't it?'

'I was going to get the train from Newcastle,' said Tot. It felt very odd to be sitting in this farm kitchen with a strange woman fussing over him and a man glowering at him. A man who was obviously a ruddy-faced farmer with his gaiters still on though he was in his stockinged feet. The woman was very nice but his head ached and he really wanted his mam. Maybe he wouldn't go to Alnwick until next week, he decided. He stood up but the room whirled about him and he sat back down abruptly.

'Nay, lad, take it slowly,' Mrs Bates exclaimed. 'I tell you what, I'll do you a pot of porridge with some nice cream from the dairy. You'd like that, wouldn't you?'

'Aye, I bet he would,' said the farmer sourly. 'But before you see to the little prince, mebbe you'll do my breakfast? I have someone coming to hire the boar in half an hour and I'd like to be fed afore that.'

'Eeh, I'm sorry, I'll do it now,' his wife replied. 'Now, lad, what do folk call you?'

'Tot. Tot Mitchell-Howe,' he replied.

'Well then, Tot, just stay still there for a minute. You had a bad blow to the head, you know.' As she fried fat bacon and broke eggs into the pan she got him to tell her where he lived and how he had a mam but no father and why he was going to Alnwick.

'But I think I'll just go back to Durham now,' he went on. 'I'll go to Northumberland next week.'

Farmer Bates grunted and tucked into the food his wife put before him. At least it looked as though they would be rid of the lad in a few days and he would once more be the focus of his wife's world. By, at times like these he was glad they didn't have any bairns. He finished his meal in silence and pulled on his boots and went out of the back door only a few minutes before a trap turned into the gates of the farm, pulling a pig cart behind it. He cheered up as he usually did at the prospect of making a few bob.

'Wot cheor,' said Farmer Dean as he jumped down from the trap and twined the reins around the rail. 'I've come for the boar; ready is he?'

Though Chester-le-Street was only a few miles north of Durham the accent was slightly different and it reminded Farmer Bates of the lad, Tot. Not one for jumping in quickly, he thought about it as he and Dean and Dean's dog, Jess, herded the boar into the pig cart and afterwards when the other man put his hand into his pocket.

'Twelve shillings, you said? For a week? It's a bit dear like, it's gone up, hasn't it?'

'Look, seeing as you've used him afore, I'll knock sixpence off.'

'A deal,' said Farmer Dean and the two men spat on their hands and shook on it.

'By the way,' said Bates, 'I picked up a young lad that was set on by a couple of tramps the other day. I have him in the house, he had a nasty blow to the head. I think he might be from round your way. Durham, he says; will you have a look at him?'

'I don't know, where did you say he's from? Durham? Haswell is a way off Durham, like.'

'Well, howay in and have a mug of tea. You can have a look at him any road.'

'Stay, Jess,' said Farmer Dean and followed the other man into the house. 'I cannot be but a minute, I don't want the animals to get restless,' he warned.

'This is the lad.' Farmer Bates indicated Tot, who was sitting up and eating a bowl of porridge thick with cream from the dairy, he noted sourly.

'Wot cheor, lad,' said Farmer Dean. 'Where did you say you hail from?'

'Durham, sir,' said Tot respectfully. 'Gilesgate, it is.'

The farmer studied him; there was a familiar look about him, especially about the eyes. 'What's your name?' he asked.

'Tot. Thomas really, Thomas Mitchell-Howe,' said Tot, sitting back and rubbing cream from his lips with the back of his hand. He felt pleasantly full and he gave the farmer all of his attention.

'Mitchell-Howe, did you say? I knew some folk of that name once, a few years ago,' the farmer exclaimed. 'I come from Haswell, do you know it?'

'My grandma lives at Blue House,' said Tot.

'I knew it,' said Farmer Dean, grinning at Farmer Bates. 'I can take him back to his grandma's if you like.'

'What now?' asked Mrs Bates in dismay. 'I don't know if he's fit—'

'He's fit, of course he is,' snapped her husband. 'I dare say he can't wait to get home, can you, lad?'

'I'd like to see me mam,' admitted Tot, then remembered his manners. 'Though I'm grateful, Mrs Bates, for all you've done for me. Mam will be an' all.'

'We'd best be off then,' Farmer Dean said as there were sounds from the yard outside. The boar was grunting loudly and Jess gave a small yelp. Even the pony snickered nervously though she was well used to hauling farm animals.

Mrs Bates gathered Tot's bundle together and kissed him on the forehead. 'I'll miss having you,' she whispered, then glanced at her husband, who was looking inordinately pleased with himself. Selfish pig, she thought, startling herself, for she had not thought so before.

'Mind, watch what you're doing, lad,' she said as he climbed on to the cart alongside Farmer Dean. Jess jumped up too and squeezed between the two and sat watching the road with intelligent eyes. She had patches of grey around her muzzle for she was coming up fourteen years old now, but she still seemed as sprightly as she had always been.

'I'll put off the boar at the farm first,' said Farmer Dean as they approached Haswell. 'You can have a rest then I'll take you on to Blue House. Which row is it your grandma lives in?'

'Alice Street,' said Tot. His head was hurting now and every uneven piece of road made it throb. He was desperately tired and sore.

'Where do you reckon the Teesdales went, then?' asked Farmer Dean of the man sitting on his haunches outside the house in Alice Street. The man had told him the reason for the family's flit and he didn't know what to make of it. Surely it was a bit hard to take it out on a whole family. Tommy Teesdale must have done something really bad.

He was in a bit of a quandary now, he reckoned. Here was the lad, and the circles under his eyes were almost as dark as the eyes. He looked right poorly, he did indeed. Now how was he going to hand him over to his grandmother when she'd moved away? He couldn't just leave him here.

The man got to his feet and pulled out a clay pipe from his pocket. 'I did hear they'd gone over to Durham, to their daughter's place,' he said. He glanced curiously at the boy sitting in the farmer's trap. 'He looks like he should be in bed by rights,' he remarked.

'Aye, well, I'll get him there as soon as I can,' Farmer Dean replied and flicked the reins. 'Giddy up, lass,' he said and the horse trundled back the way they had came. 'You'd best stay with us the night,' he said to Tot as they passed the colliery gates. But Tot suddenly sat up straight in his seat.

'There's Mr Moore,' he cried. 'Mr Moore!' The colliery owner was just emerging from the office and he turned to see who was calling his name. He grinned with amusement when he saw Tot. He walked over towards the trap and Farmer Dean slowed to a halt, though impatiently.

Thomas paused for a moment, remembering how his

mother had reacted when he talked to Mr Moore before. But it was the first familiar face he had seen since he ran away to go to his Uncle Henry's. He had to speak to him.

'I was going to my grandma's but she doesn't live here any more,' he informed Jonathan. 'Now I'll have to go home with Mr Dean and go to me mam's tomorrow.'

'I have the farm to see to, the animals, I can't take any more time off,' explained the farmer. 'The lad was set on by a couple of ruffians, bad cess to them for treating a lad like that an' all.'

Jonathan's thoughts were racing as he considered which was the best way to take advantage of this heaven-sent opportunity. He could keep the lad away and get back at his mother that way. He could even put him on a collier boat bound for London; he would probably get lost in the great metropolis. No, he thought, coming to a swift decision, he would take the lad home himself. Eliza would be so grateful for Tot's return she would fall into his arms. Then when he'd had his fill of her he could get rid of her like he had got rid of her family.

'I want to go home,' said Tot, sounding unintentionally pathetic.

'Well, I'll take you,' Jonathan told him. 'I'll take him off your hands, Mr Dean,' he said. 'I have my gig here, I am a friend of his mother's and it will not take me long. Climb down, lad, and come with me.'

Tot got down from the trap, staggering a little as he still felt somewhat dizzy. He stood beside Jonathan and thanked the farmer for all his help.

'I'll away then,' the farmer said with relief. 'There's work to be done. Thank you too, Mr Moore.' He turned to the boy. 'An' you think twice afore you run away again, you hear me? You won't always meet with folk kind enough to look after you.'

'I won't do it again,' Tot said and hung his head before walking away with the mine owner.

It was not until Farmer Dean was home and stabling the pony that it occurred to him to wonder why Moore should go out of his way to help a member of the family he had thrown out of their home at a day's notice. At least, according to the miner who had taken over their house, that was what he had done. Jonathan Moore did not have a name for kindness of heart, so why had he done it? But then, Tot was only a lad and a hurt one at that. Anyone would have done it.

Chapter Thirty-One

'I'm sorry, I'm afraid I cannot give as much time to the work as I should,' Eliza said to Dr Gray. 'So I'm asking you if there is anyone from the Infirmary who will take over my practice temporarily? I know there are more nurses coming out now who have been through the Nightingale course.'

Dr Gray bit his lip. She was the best nurse he had had dealings with in all his professional life and she would be missed in the district, even if it were only for a short while. He got to his feet and walked to the window of his office, staring unseeingly at the busy streets of the city and the towering cathedral on the headland above.

'I'm sorry for your trouble, Sister,' he said. 'I can see how you are held, though. Look, why don't you take a couple of weeks, at least provisionally, and see if you can find your son. There is a nurse who has just returned from Bart's in London. She has not yet been assigned to a ward. I will ask her if she is willing to take over from you for a short while. You would be there for some of the time to watch over her? I think that would be the best we could do. Nurse Henderson is her name.'

As Tommy went along he brooded on the things that had happened to him and his family in the last few weeks. He was like Job, the man who had one misfortune after another piled on him, he thought bitterly. The minister had told the story once again at the service only a couple of weeks before. Well, he wasn't going to cry to God about it, he would do something himself. The lads were all right, they were working and they lodged with a kindly widow woman in Stanley. He himself had not been taken on and he knew it was but a matter of time before he had to accept work and his soul rebelled against it.

The train was slowing down as it approached the station at Chester-le-Street and Tommy raised his head above the side of the waggon and peered cautiously over. No one was looking his way so he clambered over the side, hung there by his fingertips for a moment and dropped on to the line in a sort of crouch. By, his knees were not what they used to be, he reckoned as they creaked in protest. He ran down the embankment and into a stand of trees as there was a shout behind him.

'Hey, you!'

But whoever it was was too late: Tommy was out of sight and already heading for the Great North Road, southbound. Today he would walk back to Durham to see Mary Anne. But on the way he would keep a sharp lookout for any sign that young Tot had come this way. If he had time he would branch out east to see if they needed any hewers around Seaham. Though he didn't fancy working in that Lord Londonderry's pits, bad cess to him an' all. Wasn't he the one who had said his men didn't mind working eighteen hours at the face? At least that was what he had been famous for in Durham. Still, mebbe it wasn't him, mebbe it was his da.

As the sun rose higher in the sky, Tommy began to feel pangs of hunger. He had left Stanley early in the morning to catch the minerals train and he had had only a crust of bread and a heel of cheese for his breakfast. He was approaching the village of Pity Me so he decided to stop at the first butcher's he came to and buy himself a pie. He fingered the tuppence for a while, considering. If he bought a penny dip he would have an extra penny and his money was dwindling fast. In the end he decided a pork pie would last him until he got back to Durham. Eliza was a kindly lass, she would likely feed him a good dinner.

He carried the pie out of the village until he found a low wall by the side of the road where he sat down and took it out of its brown paper bag. By, the smell was grand. When he bit into it the gravy from the pork ran down his chin and he had to mop it hastily with his forefinger and push it into his mouth.

'Wot cheor,' said a voice close to his left ear. Tommy had been so enjoying his pie that he didn't even notice the rank smell of the tramp who had come and sat beside him at first. But now it began to overlay the aroma of his pie and Tommy took strong objection to it.

'Can you not sit somewhere else?' he demanded. 'I'm having my dinner here.'

'Very nice it smells an' all,' said the tramp. 'Doesn't it, Silas?' Another tramp had sat down on the other side of Tommy. If anything he smelled worse than the first.

'Aye, it does that, Steve,' said Silas. 'Are you going to give us a bit?' He grinned at Tommy, showing a couple of blackened teeth punctuating the gums.

'I might,' said Tommy, and took another bite of the pie.

'There'll be nowt left, Steve,' said Silas, edging closer.

Tommy pushed even more of the pie into his mouth and munched away. Steve nudged him. 'Give us it,' he said menacingly. Tommy put the last bit of pie into his pocket and suddenly flung out both arms and knocked the tramps backward off their perches on the wall. There was a small ditch on the other side and they found themselves winded, their heads in the water and their feet in the air. Before they could move, Tommy was on them, one horny finger and thumb round each of their throats and an elbow in one belly and knee in the other. Silas gurgled while Steve's face turned slowly purple.

'Now then, lads,' said Tommy pleasantly. 'Are you going to behave or will I call the polis?' He nodded his head in the direction of Pity Me. 'We're not a kick in the arse from the station, so what is it to be?' The men nodded, they were unable to speak.

'Right then,' said Tommy, 'I'll let you up. Best watch it, though, I'm not a violent man but I can look after meself.'

This was so obviously true that both men clambered to their feet in silence. Tommy took out the remains of the pie, sadly broken now and with crumbs mixed up in the meat and gravy. Never mind, he could still eat it, he thought, and munched it anyway. The men were moving away, watching Tommy warily over their shoulders when he thought of something.

'You lads haven't seen a young lad, lately, have you? A lad about ten? Only he's me grandson and I'm trying to find him.' His tone was perfectly amiable and as though nothing had happened. They stopped and looked at each other.

'About a week ago?' prompted Tommy.

'Well,' Silas began when he was interrupted by Steve.

'Shut your gob!' Steve cried. 'Do you want to go to Durham gaol?'

At this Tommy started after them. 'Durham gaol?' he roared. 'What did you do to him? You've seen him, haven't you?'

The men started to run but they were in no condition for it and one stumbled and fell. Tommy caught up and dragged him to his feet.

'We did nowt!' he shouted, in terror. 'Don't hit me, I'll tell you. He's with a farmer along the road by Chester-le-Street. Bates his name is, he took him in. He'd hurt himself.'

Tommy had loosened his grip on the man and he took to his heels across the fields in the opposite direction to Pity Me. This time, Tommy let him go. He had to go back the way he had come, so he'd best set off as soon as may be. If he was any judge he would say the tramp had been telling the truth. It might not be young Tot that the farmer had taken in but he'd do well to find out. At least Mary Anne and Eliza wouldn't think him such a failure if he came home with the lad. He set off on the long walk back up the road. Luck was with him this time, though. He hadn't gone a quarter of a mile before a carrier's cart caught up with him and offered him a ride.

'It'll cost you a penny, mind,' said the carrier. 'I can't afford to carry folk for nowt. I'm in business, you see.'

'Aye well,' said Tommy philosophically. 'I can manage that.' Now he had to get back to Durham for his supper or he'd be on short commons for sure.

'I want to go home, Mr Moore,' said Tot. He was sitting on a comfortable enough chair in the drawing room of Jonathan Moore's house yet he didn't feel comfortable. First Mr Moore had said he would take him straight home and then he had said they had better go to his house. Mr Moore had been good to him; he had given him supper of cold ham and pickles and a glass of milk but Tot hadn't been hungry and could only pick at the food, though he drank the milk thirstily.

'Well, lad,' said Jonathan. 'So you will go home when I've the time to take you. But it's too dark now to ride into Durham. You're all right here, aren't you?' He gazed at the boy, who reminded him so much of Eliza. He'd changed his mind yet again on what to do with him. Instead of taking him back immediately he would wait a few days, make her even more distraught so that she would be all the more grateful when he delivered him to her.

'How about a game of cards?' he said now.

'I'm not allowed to play cards,' said Tot. 'It's sinful.'

'Oh rubbish. Who said that? The minister, was it? He's an old woman. A game of cards never hurt anyone.' Jonathan walked over to a cupboard and took out a pack of cards. He drew a small table up beside Tot's chair and sat down by him and shuffled the cards.

'We'll play 21s,' he said. 'I'll show you how.' Skilfully he dealt out two hands. 'I tell you what, we need something to play for.'

'I haven't any money,' said Tot. He was tired and his eyelids were drooping.

'We'll play for buttons,' Jonathan decided. 'My wife left a box of buttons in the drawer of her sewing table.' The table, an octagonal one of polished beech with elaborately carved legs and a row of drawers around the top, stood in an alcove and he walked over to it, brought back the box and divided the buttons equally between them.

'Pay attention, now,' he said sharply as he saw the boy's sleepy expression. Tot's eyes snapped open and he sat up straight. There was something about Mr Moore that made him nervous. He would never disobey the man for he realised now that he did not trust him as he had trusted the two bluff farmers.

Tot was quick to learn and as the game went on he became quite skilled at it. Perhaps Jonathan was not giving it all the attention he could but the pile of buttons beside Tot began to grow.

'This game, we'll play double your money,' said Jonathan. He wasn't going to let an urchin like this one beat him even if the stake was only buttons really.

'I know,' said Tot ingeniously, 'why don't we play for

you'll take me home tonight even if it is dark and I'll stay until tomorrow if you win?' Tot was beginning to enjoy himself. He felt a thrill of triumph when he won the next hand.

'Beginner's luck!' muttered Jonathan. 'Best out of three, eh?'

But Tot was on a lucky streak and he was looking better, less tired, his face was flushed and his eyes sparkled. He won the next game too.

'I tell you, it was different when I played against your father!' snarled Jonathan. He had brought a decanter of port over from the sideboard and he was well into it. He poured a glass now for Tot and insisted he drink it.

'Come on, all men drink port, it's what they do! Do you not want to be a man? You don't want to be tied to your mother's apron strings for the rest of your life, do you?'

'You played cards with my father?' asked Tot, changing the subject so he could move the glass out of sight by the side of his chair.

Jonathan laughed. 'I did indeed, and for sweeter stakes than these by far, I can tell you.'

'What do you mean?'

The mouthful of port he had drunk was having an effect on Tot; his head swam. But he heard and understood what Jonathan was saying though the man's voice was changing alarmingly.

'Why, we played for a place in your mother's bed and I won!' cried Jonathan. He was grinning at the boy now, grinning widely so that Tot could see that some of his back teeth were black and rotten.

'You're a liar!' Tot shouted. 'My father wouldn't do that!'

'And very sweet and willing she was, my young friend,' said Jonathan gloatingly.

'Don't speak about my mother like that!' shouted Tot. He rose to his feet and swept his arm across the table, scattering cards and buttons all over the floor.

'Oh, a firebrand, are we? Well, I'll speak about her however I like, you young hellion,' said Jonathan. He leaned across and caught hold of the boy and dragged him into the air, holding him by the scruff of his neck. 'You come with me, Thomas Mitchell-Howe, I'll show you what I do with ungrateful wretches such as you.' He tucked Tot under his arm, ignoring the occasional kick that connected and went over to the door, flung it open and made for the stairs. 'I'll lock you up until you beg my pardon for calling me a liar.'

'I'll never do that,' Tot asserted, though he was having a hard job holding back the tears he was fighting to get his hands free so he could do as much damage to his tormentor as he could. The pain in his head was raging and he was suddenly and violently sick, all over Jonathan and the expensive stair carpet.

'You'll pay for that too,' snarled Jonathan. 'And you can shout as much as you like; there's no one to hear you. The servants only come during the day. I can't abide folk about at night.'

'Let me go,' gasped Tot. 'Let me go!'

'Let you go? No, I'm afraid I cannot do that,' Jonathan replied.

He flung the boy over his shoulder and went on up the stairs. At the top he turned to the left and was about to open the door of a linen cupboard to throw the boy in when there was a sudden thunderous banging on the front door.

'Are you in there, Jonathan Moore?' a hated voice shouted. 'Jonathan Moore, do you hear me? I want the bairn, the little lad, you'd best give him up.'

Jonathan flung the boy in and closed the heavy door of the linen cupboard. Thinking fast, he ran down the stairs and drew the bolts of the front door.

Chapter Thirty-Two

'You're the second man to come asking after the lad,' said Mrs Bates. 'So I'll tell you what I told him. He's gone; he went this morning with the chap who came for the boar.'

Peter stared at her with disappointment. He had been so sure he had at last caught up with Tot. He had asked in every place around Chester-le-Street until one man had suggested he ask the local doctor. 'The polis won't be interested,' the man had said. 'Lads are always running away and he's old enough to work, isn't he? Now if he's been hurt, well then, the doctor is the man to ask, I'd think. Or mebbe the workhouse.'

So Peter had made his way to Dr Jones's office and Dr Jones had pointed him in the direction of the farm. He had hired a trap in Chester-le-Street; he was so sure he would find Tot and take him home to his mother. Now he thanked Mr Bates and asked him how much he was owed for the boy's keep and doctor's fees and they had come to a sum acceptable to them both. Peter was desperate to get on his way to Haswell and Farmer Dean's place. And it was Farmer Dean who had told him he had gone with Jonathan Moore.

'Mr Moore said he would take him home,' said the farmer. 'That was all right, wasn't it?' He had noticed Peter's expression and now had doubts himself. He remembered rumours about Moore and some sort of feud with the Teesdale family.

'You weren't to know,' said Peter, but he was already turning the trap around and hadn't time to say more. A quick check with Jim Robinson at the colliery office had confirmed that the mine owner had taken the boy home with him.

'What do you want, damn you?' Jonathan demanded as he opened the door. He was dishevelled; there was a stink about him like vomit and stains on his shirt and trousers. 'I'm busy, how dare you come here at this time of night. Don't you pester me enough at the pits?' He held on to the door with one hand, barring Peter from entering.

'I want the lad,' said Peter grimly. 'And don't you tell me he's not here because I know he is. I've followed his trail all day.' He shoved at the door but Jonathan held on tight.

'What lad? I haven't got any lad. I'm on my own here, but don't think I won't call the man in from the stables to throw you out. The union has no jurisdiction here; this is my private house. Go on, be off with you.'

'Farmer Dean said you took the lad; said you would deliver him to his mother. Don't deny it, Jim Robinson backs him up. Now let me in and tell me where he is.' This time when Peter flung himself at the door it was pulled from Jonathan's grip and Peter pushed him out of his way as he went in.

'I'll report you to the union. The Association of Mine Owners will have something to say about this!' shouted Jonathan as he stumbled after Peter, who was going from room to room looking for Tot.

'Why did you take him?' Peter countered as he searched, not even looking back at Jonathan. 'Why? Were you getting at the mother through the son?' He had checked every room downstairs and now he started up the stairs.

'How dare you go up there! This is my private house!' howled the mine owner. 'By God, I'll get you and when I do I'll break your bloody neck.' He had picked up a cricket bat from somewhere and he followed Peter, waving it in the air. But his progress was erratic. He was feeling the effects of the bottle of port he had drunk and the smell of the vomit on his person didn't help at all.

Peter went from room to room but found nothing, while Jonathan stood at the top of the stairs, in front of the door to the linen cupboard. He gasped for breath for a minute before turning and lifting the bat in the air again, ready to strike. And just then, there was a muffled cry from behind him.

'What's that?' asked Peter, whirling round and facing Jonathan. In a second the two men were fighting over the cricket bat but the drink told on Jonathan and Peter easily disarmed him and shoved him away. Jonathan fell and tumbled down the stairs but Peter hardly noticed, for he was opening the door to the linen cupboard and lifting Tot up and bringing him out. Tot was sobbing and clinging to him and Peter held him tight and sat down on a chair with him.

'I thought he was going to kill me, Mr Collier,' Tot said shakily. 'I'm all right now, though, I am.' He loosened his grip on Peter and stood up on his own. 'I'm not really frightened,' he asserted. 'Just my head hurts, that's what it is.'

The two of them didn't see but Jonathan had picked himself up and was starting up the stairs again with the cricket bat raised once more like a weapon. It was the muffled cry he gave next that alerted them. Tommy had arrived, having followed almost the same trail as Peter but on foot. As he came in the open front door he took in what was happening, came up behind Jonathan and took him in a bear grip around his arms so that the bat fell with a clatter on to the stairs and then down, all the way to the hall floor.

'I wouldn't be using that if I was you,' Tommy observed. 'I've had a hard day, the day, and I'm just in the mood for a fight.'

'Granda!' cried Tot.

'Now then, young shaver,' said Tommy, his arms still around Jonathan like a steel band. 'Where the heck have you been? Do you know your mam has been looking all over for you? I reckon you're in for a bit of bother when you get back to Durham.' He looked to Peter. 'Can you find something to tie the gaffer up? I can't hold him like this till the polis comes, can I?'

'By, I tell you, I'm that glad of a ride home,' said Tommy. 'Me poor old legs is just about worn out.' He and Peter were sitting on the narrow driving seat of the trap with Tot squeezed between them. Tot leaned heavily against his grandfather, his head supported by Tommy's arm. He was fast asleep.

At this time of night the road was quiet. Clouds chased each other across the sky, allowing only occasional glimpses of moonlight to show through to illuminate the way ahead and the fields on either side. Now and then they skirted round a colliery with its lighted pit yard and belching smoke emerging from a tall chimney. A pit hooter sounded once and men came streaming from houses and into the pit yard to start the fore shift. But it was the swinging paraffin lamps hanging from the front of the trap, one on either side, which lighted their way in the main.

Peter nodded in agreement. It had been a long day for him too and he was glad to be nearly home. In the distance they could see the shape of the castle with its battlement on the ridge above the Wear and beside it the great mass of the cathedral, all against a sky briefly lit by the moon before it once more hid behind a cloud.

Peter had simply told the policeman that the boy was in danger. The constable was sceptical, though; Jonathan Moore was a figure of some standing in the town. Still, it wasn't far to go and there was nothing else on. Tommy had stood guard over Jonathan, who alternately uttered threats about how he would haul them up before the magistrates for grievous bodily harm and how the Mine Owners' Association would back him up.

'You can do that,' Tommy agreed. 'If you are fit to after my marras find out you took a lad like Tot and kept him a prisoner. Any road, we'll see what the polis has to say.'

In fact, Tommy did not have any faith in the police to back him and a union man up against a mine owner but Peter had insisted they do it legally. 'It'll be all over the village and Haswell an' all by the morn,' Tommy went on. Jonathan was sitting in a chair with his hands and feet tied. He had given up struggling to free himself.

Tommy heard the clip-clop of hooves in the yard as Peter returned with the trap. It was safe enough now, he reckoned.

'Now then, gaffer, I'll untie you now,' he said and started on the knots in the rope around Jonathan's legs. 'I think it will likely be all over the coal field any road,' he went on, speaking quietly, for Tot had fallen asleep in the big padded armchair and he didn't want to wake him. He leaned forward and said in Jonathan's ear, 'The lads are not going to like it, no indeed. I should think you won't have a pit working come a couple of days' time. We look after our own, don't we like?'

'Don't you threaten me,' warned Jonathan. 'Who do you think you are?'

'Well,' Tommy replied. 'I'm just a poor coal hewer or I was till you turned me off for nowt. I reckon the lads already know about that. What is it they call it? Perse – perse—'

'Persecution,' said Peter, who had come in quietly along with the policeman who happened to be on night-duty at Haswell station.

'Now then, what's this all about?' asked the policeman, taking out his notebook and pencil. 'I heard something about a lad, the lad I did hear had disappeared. Mr Moore?'

'It was a mistake, constable,' said Jonathan, rubbing his wrists. He was raging inside but he was aware that Tommy was right. The men would stand so much but they wouldn't stand for what he had done this night. Any more unrest in the coalfield could ruin his business, he knew that too, though it went against the grain to admit it. He had been a fool, he ought to have taken the lad home. At least he might have stood a chance with Eliza if he had done so.

'A mistake? How could that happen then?'

'I was just seeing to Thomas,' said Jonathan. 'I gave him some supper. He wasn't feeling so well. That was another mistake as you can see, or rather smell. Poor lad was sick all over me.'

'What does the lad say happened?' asked the constable of Peter. He was beginning to realise he had been brought out here on a wild goose chase.

'We won't wake him if you don't mind,' said Tommy. 'He's not well, poor lad. I'm sure what the gaffer says is true. He'll have the rights of it.'

Peter was bewildered. He had been working out in his mind how he would fight the mine owner when he brought a case against them. He knew he was taking a

392

risk bringing in the police but he had thought they had no other choice. Yet here was Tommy evidently having the man eating out of his hand.

'So long as no one is making a complaint,' said the constable. 'I'll have to mention it to the inspector, though, see what he has to say.'

'We'll take you back if you like, constable,' said Peter. Tot was beginning to stir and he moaned gently. 'Now we must get the lad home. We'll meet again, Mr Moore,' he said over his shoulder as he picked Tot up in his arms and carried him out.

The trap descended slowly down the hill into the city. The cathedral bells rang out one o'clock and Tot stirred in his sleep and sat up. 'Mam?' he asked.

'In a minute, Tot, in a minute,' said Tommy. 'You're home now.' It was but a few minutes' drive to the street. Peter stopped the horse outside the front of the house.

'You take him in, Tommy,' he said. 'I'll take the Galloway round the back. If there's no room for him in the stable I'll put him in the yard with some hay. It's a warm enough night.'

'Aye, fine,' Tommy answered; he got down from the trap and Peter handed him the boy into his arms, but Tot insisted on standing on his own feet. The house had been dark but light showed suddenly in the front room. Tommy and Tot went to the door, their two shadows almost the same in the moonlight for Tot was as tall as his bent grandfather.

They did not have to knock for the door was opened at once and Eliza stood there in her nightgown and with a shawl flung over her shoulders.

'Tot! Oh Tot!' she cried and stepped out into the street and took hold of him and hugged him to her. In the process her shawl fell off her shoulders and Tommy picked it up from the ground.

'Here, lass, wrap up or you'll catch a chill or something,' he said mildly. 'Any road, it's not decent.'

Eliza laughed shakily. She took the shawl and stepped inside the house, drawing her son with her. 'You bad lad,' she said, as anger and reaction took hold of her. 'Why did you run away like that? Do you know you had me half out of my mind? How could you do that to me?'

'Mam—' Tot began but was interrupted by Tommy.

'By, our Eliza, leave the lad alone. He's been through enough, I reckon. Any road, remember the prodigal son? His father welcomed him back and showered him with gifts, so Jesus said. Behave yourself.'

Eliza struggled to control her feelings. She held on to Tot and took him into the kitchen, for Mary Anne was in the front room and she had had a bad day and Eliza had given her a sleeping draught. She sat Tot on the settle in the inglenook and stirred the fire and put on the kettle, for surely none of them would sleep tonight with the excitement of having Tot home again.

'Oh, Da,' she said, 'I'll never forget you getting him back for me. I'll always be indebted to you, I will. I can't thank you enough.'

'Nay, lass, it was Peter Collier who found him. I just came in at the tail end, like. And any road, he's my grandson, isn't he?'

'Peter? Where is he?'

'Oh heck, he's out the back. He took the pony and trap round. He hired one to bring the lad home. We'd best let him in.'

They slipped the bolt on the back door and lifted the sneck, and as the light from the lamp shone out they saw Peter just bringing a forkful of hay into the corner of the yard where he had tethered the Galloway.

'Howay in, lad,' said Tommy with a touch of impatience. 'What's taking you so long? I'm ready for my tea and a bite to eat. I expect that smell is something keeping hot in the oven, our Eliza. Hotpot, is it? That's grand! We could do with some good red meat after this night's work.'

'Come in, Peter,' said Eliza. 'There is plenty for you too. The pony will be all right there until the morn.'

She was so happy at that moment she could hardly believe her ordeal was over; she had her son back. She kept looking from Tot to Peter and back to Tot as they

ate. Tot fell asleep in his chair after only a few bites and
Peter lifted him up and he and Eliza went upstairs with
him and laid him on his bed. Eliza took off his boots
and trousers and pulled a cover over him in his combin-
ations.

'I'll never forget what you've done for me,' she whispered
across the sleeping boy.

'I'm only sorry I didn't find him sooner,' Peter whispered back. 'He would have been home anyway without
my help but for Jonathan Moore. But *he* won't be bothering you again, I shouldn't think. If he does I will want
to know the reason why.' He hesitated for only a moment
before leaning over the narrow bed and kissing her gently
on the lips. 'I love you, Eliza. I realise now that I always
will.'

Eliza too leaned over the bed and kissed him back.
But they must have disturbed Tot for he rolled over and
opened his eyes.

'I love you too,' he said and smiled at his mother.
'I'm not going away again, not ever.' His eyes closed
again and he slept.

Peter and Eliza tiptoed out of the bedroom and went
downstairs. Tommy was asleep in his chair by this time,
but as they entered the kitchen he woke up and yawned
hugely.

'I'm away to my bed,' he said and stood up before
looking hard at Peter and Eliza. 'You two behave yourselves,

mind, it's time you were in your beds an'all. Separate ones,' he added warningly. He had not missed the doting way they were looking at each other and he said so to Mary Anne when she woke in the early morning.

'Aw, man,' Mary Anne said comfortably. 'They're grown-ups, aren't they. It's no business of ours what they get up to.'

Chapter Thirty-Three

'By, I'm that glad you got the lad back,' said Bertha fervently. It was seven-thirty the next morning and she had left the dairy work to Charlie's mother as she had done since she had gone to stay at the farm. 'My friend is in trouble,' she had said firmly to her betrothed. 'I cannot leave her until she finds Tot.'

Charlie had agreed, much to Bertha's surprise. Already she could see she would have to stand up for herself in this marriage, though she would not admit such a thing to Eliza. Standing up for herself had shown Charlie in something of a new light. He was not so unreasonable as she had feared he might be.

Eliza sat with her mother and Bertha in the front room, having an early morning cup of tea. She felt so lighthearted it was almost what she imagined being intoxicated must feel like and if it was then there might be something to say for it after all. Even Mary Anne seemed better this morning. She had a little colour in her cheeks and she was breathing easier. Of course this could have had something to do with the fact that Dr Gray had only just left, having called in before starting his rounds on the wards at the Infirmary. While he was there he had examined Mary Anne and prescribed a new routine of care and medication for her. The very fact that a doctor had bothered with her was something new for Mary Anne and she had brightened. He had looked in on Tot before he went.

'It's not serious,' he had pronounced as he felt the bump on the back of his head. 'He seems to have got over the worst. He'll need to take it easy for a few days, that's all. It's a good job for you, young man, that you were taken in by a good, kind couple. You *could* have been press-ganged on to a boat bound for China, do you know that?'

'Could I?' Tot had asked, an interested gleam in his eyes. 'Wouldn't it be grand, going to sea? And as far as China! I would see elephants and maybe even tigers!'

'Don't even think of it,' warned Eliza.

'I was only saying,' said Tot. 'I don't want to leave you now, Mam.'

'I should think not,' the doctor said.

'I'm afraid Nurse Henderson has changed her mind,' he told Eliza. 'After yesterday she thought she could not manage an outside practice, not yet. Not until she has a little more experience.'

Eliza thought of yesterday, when she had taken the nurse on her rounds. She had been so obviously shocked at some of the conditions in the colliery villages around the city, the lack of even clean water in some. Perhaps she was better working in the Infirmary.

It didn't matter now. She would carry on with her work. Peter would want her to, she thought happily. Peter was different from most men. He understood her as Jack had never done. She smiled, a secret little smile, thinking of his love-making of the night before. She hadn't known a man could be so gentle and considerate and yet passionate at the same time.

'What is it?' asked Bertha. 'Did I say something funny?'

'No,' Eliza replied. 'By the way, Peter and I are getting wed.'

'When?' asked Bertha. She didn't sound in the least surprised.

'As soon as we can arrange it with the minister.'

'Mind, not before time,' remarked Mary Anne. 'I could tell it was in the wind.' Bertha nodded agreement. 'What about Tot?' she asked now as she collected the teacups ready to take into the kitchen. 'Will he be going on at school?'

'I hope so,' Eliza replied. 'But I don't mind so long as he is happy. He can be anything he wants to be and if he wants to be a cabinet maker then he can. Though

I'd like him to go on at school. And now with his inheritance, he can. There is more than enough. The rest I will put in a trust fund for him. How can he really know what he wants if he doesn't know about other things?'

'Aye,' said Bertha over her shoulder as she went through to the kitchen. 'I suppose you are right.'

As she sorted the washing she had collected the day before and put it into piles to give to her washerwomen when they came in during the morning at different times according to what shift their men were on, she found herself thinking of the farm and quite looking forward to getting back there. It wouldn't be a bad life, she reckoned, so long as she stood up for herself and didn't let anyone shout her down. Even her future mother-in-law wasn't going to be allowed to do that, she decided.

She was bending over a bundle of washing, which she was tying in a sheet, when Tot came up behind her and flung his arms around her waist.

'What—' she began. 'Eeh, it's you, Tot, should you be out of bed? What about your poor head?'

'It's not so bad,' Tot declared. 'I've missed you, Bertha.'

'What are you going to do when I wed?' she asked him.

'I can come up to the farm and see you, can't I?'

'Course you can,' Bertha replied. 'Come on, now,

you'll have to go back to bed. Didn't Dr Gray say you should stay there for a few days?'

Tot nodded. In truth he was feeling a little bit shaky still. He climbed the stairs to his room and got back into bed. Maybe he would go to the grammar school, he thought, as he drifted off to sleep. Maybe he would learn Latin and stuff and be a doctor like Dr Gray. He was fast asleep when there was a knocking at the front door, just a timid knock, so it did not wake him.

Eliza happened to be in the hall at the time and she wasn't even sure it had been a knock but she opened the door anyway. Outside a young girl was huddled on the doorstep. It took her a few minutes to realise it was Lottie. Lottie, who had looked after Mrs Green before she had died: Lottie, the girl from the workhouse. She was sobbing her heart out. Eliza took one look and drew her inside.

'Come into the kitchen, pet,' she said. 'I'll put the kettle on and you can tell me what has happened.' As she filled the kettle and settled it on the glowing coals, Eliza studied the girl. She had a rip in the bodice of her dress and she held it together with one hand. Her face was bruised, with one eye beginning to swell and close.

'Has someone attacked you, Lottie?' Eliza asked. 'Has someone stolen your purse?' There were stories of a pickpocket going round the city, there always were, but surely it didn't happen at this time of day. These people usually worked in the dark. Lottie shook her head.

'Mr Green did it,' she whispered. 'I wouldn't let him do what he wanted so he hit me and put me out of the house.' She hung her head, unable to look at Eliza. 'I just walked around all night and then I sat down in the market place, I was that tired. I didn't know what to do. I didn't have any money nor nothing. I thought mebbe I'd best go back to the workhouse. Only I know the matron will be mad at me. She'll say I should have stayed with Mr Green, I know she will. She won't believe me when I tell her what he did.'

'Oh, Lottie! Let me look at you. I'll bathe your poor face, shall I? I'll get some clean water and put a drop of white vinegar in it, that will help it feel better.' Eliza gave her a cup of tea with sweetened condensed milk in it. 'Drink that first, it'll do you good. When did this happen?'

'Last night, about eleven, I think. The church clock had just chimed eleven and he came into the kitchen. I was just banking the fire before I went to bed, Sister. I hope you don't mind me coming here but Bertha found me in the market place and she told me it would be all right.'

'So it is, pet, so it is,' said Eliza, though in truth she didn't know where she was going to put her. The house was bursting at the seams as it was. Still, she tended the girl's bruises and made her some toast and took her in to sit with Mary Anne in the front room.

Mary Anne was all sympathy. 'Poor lass,' she said to Eliza. 'The fella wants stringing up. I'd do it meself if I was fit. Sit down, pet, and tell me all about it. You go on, Eliza, I know you have your rounds to do. Me and Lottie can shift for ourselves for the minute.'

Eliza hesitated, but only for a minute. She knew that the two of them would manage together, for Mary Anne would mother Lottie and Lottie would help her mother. In any case, her father was within call upstairs in bed should he be needed. She had patients she should see, for she had not been able to visit them all the day before.

Tommy was not upstairs in bed. He was only a mile or two from Stanley, for he had decided to go back and accept datal work there. He had seen the way things were going with Eliza and Peter Collier and he reckoned he and Mary Anne had to shift for themselves. Together with the two boys he could get a colliery house at Stanley and they would be a family again, taking 'nowt from no one' as they had always done. One thing he knew, they might have stopped Jonathan Moore from putting the law on them but the mine owner would prevent him, Tommy Teesdale, from ever working in the pits around east Durham again.

*

'We'll get wed as soon as we're able,' said Peter. 'I cannot wait.' He put his arms around Eliza and kissed her lingeringly.

'Peter!' she exclaimed. 'Someone might come in.'

'They might,' he agreed. 'Does it matter?'

'No, I suppose it doesn't,' she said and kissed him again before going on, 'We'd best get home, there are things to see to. There's Tot and my mother and now there's Lottie. What will I do with Lottie? I can't let her go back to that house nor can I let her go back to the workhouse.'

'She can stay with us when we're wed,' said Peter, still holding Eliza to him and stroking her back, thereby sending shivers down her spine so that she could hardly think straight. Eliza sighed. The problems which seemed insurmountable only yesterday were somehow only minor difficulties today. Now there was Peter to share the burden, and life was looking rosy.

'I must get back to Tot,' she murmured and he immediately dropped his arms and turned businesslike.

'Right, I'll shut the place up and we'll go,' said Peter.

'You're coming home with me?' asked Eliza.

'Where else would I go?' Peter replied. They went outside to where Dolly was contentedly chewing inside her nosebag. 'Just get in, I'll see to the Galloway.'

Eliza did so and soon they were sitting in the tub trap, close together, so that she could feel the warmth of his side against her arm as he took the reins and flicked them over the pony's back.

'Gee up,' he said. 'Home, Dolly.' Dolly lifted her head and pricked her ears at the sound of his authoritative, masculine tone. She set off at what was a spanking pace for her at this end of a busy day.

There were things to be done, problems to be sorted, Eliza thought dreamily as they drove along the short distance to Gilesgate. But the future was going to be as bright as the sunset that lit the sky over the city. Tomorrow would be a lovely day.

Also available from Ebury Press:

EMMA'S WAR

By Rosie Clarke

All she wanted was her husband to come home . . .

Newly married to the caring RAF pilot Jonathan
Reece, Emma thinks that life couldn't be better. But
her happiness is short-lived: within months, Jon's
plane is shot down over France and he is declared
missing, presumed dead.

Alone and with two children to care for, Emma's first
thought is how to support her family. But when she
makes a new friend in the American businessman Jack
Harvey, she is faced with a difficult decision. Should
she take a last chance at happiness?

EBURY
PRESS

Also available from Ebury Press:

THE FACTORY GIRL

By Maggie Ford

From rags to riches . . .

With the Armistice only a few months passed, times
are hard for eighteen-year-old Geraldine Glover. A
machinist at Rubins clothing factory in the East End,
she dreams of a more glamorous life.

When she meets Tony Hanford, the young and handsome proprietor of a small jeweller's shop in Bond
Street, Geraldine is propelled into a new world – but
it comes at a heavy price . . .

EBURY
PRESS